DEMCO

Tyndale House Publishers, Inc.
WHEATON, ILLINOIS

Designed by Beth Sparkman
Edited by Rick Blanchette

Library of Congress Cataloging-in-Publication Data

Stokes, Penelope J.
  Home fires burning / Penelope J. Stokes.
    p. cm —(Faith on the home front ; 1)
  ISBN 0-8423-0851-2 (alk. paper)
    1. Man-woman relationships—Mississippi—Fiction.   2. World War, 1939-1945—Mississippi—
Fiction. I. Title   II. Series: Stokes, Penelope J.   Faith on the home front ; 1.
PS3569.T6219H66   1996
813'.54—dc20   96-16300

Printed in the United States of America

04 03 02 01 00 99 98 97 96
9   8   7   6   5   4   3   2   1

To my mother and father,
whose love has endured for fifty years,
and whose story
will live forever . . .

ACKNOWLEDGMENTS

A work of fiction is never a one-person show. Many people made this novel possible—friends and loved ones who supported me, encouraged me, and put up with me during the writing of this book. Special thanks are due to:

Ken Petersen, who believed in me

Judith Markham, my editor, who encouraged my strengths and kept my weaknesses from showing too much

Jim Hoff, who graciously supplied me with invaluable material

Finbar and Alannah, who guarded the manuscript and provided comic relief,

Cindy Maddox, who survived my fits of insanity, listened patiently to each chapter, and gave crucial editorial response on the entire project

and especially to

My parents, Jim and Betty Stokes, who first lived the story and then generously allowed me the creative license to build a novel out of it.

CONTENTS

PART THREE
PS, I Love You / APRIL 1944

PART FOUR
You'll Never Know / JUNE 1944

PART FIVE
I'll Get By / SEPTEMBER 1944

PREFACE

In 1943, when the United States was embroiled in the largest and most complex military offensive in history, a young soldier arrived at an army base in rural Mississippi on the last leg of preparation before being sent to the front. There, amid the uncertainty of life in wartime, he met a southern girl and fell in love.

They were both young and innocent, and perhaps a little naive. When he was shipped out to France, they pledged their love to one another and waited, certain that he would return and that they would live happily ever after. But he didn't return—not for a long time. And when he did come home, he bore wounds that would stay with him for the rest of his life.

This book is a work of fiction—the product of a writer's imagination, with characters and events that arise out of the universal joys and struggles of human existence. But this young soldier and his girl were real.

They were my parents.

The heart of this novel is their story—and the story of thousands of other young couples who fell in love at a time when love was thoroughly inconvenient.

It is a tale of hope, of faith, of love that endures against all odds.

It is their story, and mine. Perhaps it is your story, too.

ONE

I'll Be
Seeing You

NOVEMBER 1943

1

⋆ ⋆ ⋆

Welcome to Paradise

Eden, Mississippi
November 1943

Private James Lincoln Winsom rubbed his eyes as the lumbering bus lurched to a halt.

"Your stop, soldier. Eden, Mississippi."

Link squinted out the streaked window. All he could see was a tin-roofed overhang and a blur of gaudy color against a dark clapboard building.

"Where are we?" he asked. He shifted his aching body and saw the driver slouched sideways with his arm flung over the back of his seat.

"Like I said, son—Eden. Garden spot of the Delta." The driver dropped the chewed remains of a wooden toothpick onto the floor of the bus and gave a snorting donkey-bray of a laugh. "Ain't really the Delta, though. More like the jumping-off spot. Thirty miles west of here—that's the real Delta. Fella can see forever out there, cross a hundert acres of cotton fields, all the way to the Big Muddy herself."

The driver opened the door and motioned to Link. "You a Yankee boy, ain'tcha?"

Link rose, grabbed his duffel bag, and headed for the front of the bus. "I guess so. From Missouri—St. Joe."

"I been there. Lots of rolling hills and bluffs along the river." The man grinned, his big teeth reflecting the garish neon colors from the bus stop cafe. "Well, good luck." The tone of his voice indicated that Link was going to need some. "Ask Thelma to call the base for you. They'll send someone out."

With that, the driver shut the door and pulled out in a cloud of fumes, leaving Link in front of a small square building.

It took a minute for Link's sleep-clouded eyes to focus on the tremulous neon sign in the window. *PARADISE GARDEN CAFE.*

With a shrug, he hefted his bag and pushed the door open. If this was Paradise, his father had been wrong about God's ability to create a perfect world.

The air was musty, permeated by the smell of old grease and stale cigarette smoke. Along the back wall of the cafe ran a long counter, fronted by revolving stools. On the side walls stood rows of high-backed booths, and in the center of the room a few tables wobbled precariously on the cracked linoleum floor.

The place seemed deserted, and yet music was coming from . . . from where? Link scanned the room. The jukebox next to the door was dark. Maybe there was a radio playing somewhere.

"Hello?" Link's tentative voice echoed in the stillness. "Is anybody here?"

A high cackle, so sudden that it made him jump, answered his question. He whirled around and caught a glimpse of movement—a withered, clawlike hand poking around the edge of a high upright piano. "We're here, sonny—where are you?"

A face appeared, just for a moment—a weather-beaten, stubbled face, sunken at the cheeks.

Just my luck, Link thought. *Alone with a madman in the middle of nowhere.* He snatched up his bag and turned to make his escape, when another sound caught him and rooted him in place. A sweet, haunting ballad, played with feeling in spite of the occasional flat note: *I'll be seeing you in all the old familiar places. . . .*

The song tugged at Link's heart, and almost against his will he followed the compelling music to its source. There, in the corner of the dismal cafe, the old man sat, his gnarled fingers caressing the keys, wringing a sound from the battered instrument that nearly brought tears to Link's eyes. It sounded like . . . like home.

Link settled on one of the stools, propped his elbows on the counter, and listened.

"He's pretty good, isn't he?" The low voice pierced Link's consciousness, and he raised his head to see a tall, buxom woman with bright red hair leaning against the other side of the counter.

She extended a hand toward him. "My name's Thelma Breckinridge," she said. "I own the place."

"Link Winsom. Private James Lincoln Winsom. I'm—"

"You're the new boy, stationed at Camp McCrane. I know who you are, darlin'." She set a cup of coffee in front of him. "Welcome to Paradise."

Link stared at her. Her round face bore the signs of a difficult life, covered up with a bit too much rouge, and her hair color was obviously applied from a henna bottle. But her eyes, brown and warm, crinkled around the edges when she smiled. He decided he liked her and smiled back.

"How do you know—?"

She winked at him. "Old Thelma knows everything, honey." Then she straightened her apron and wiped at the corner of her lipstick with her little finger. "Naw, I'm just kidding. The major's assistant called. Said you'd be coming on the bus from Tennessee. Told me to give you a good breakfast and let you know that somebody would be along for you around seven."

"Breakfast? It's the middle of the night!"

She turned and looked at the clock behind the counter. "It's nearly six. You've been on the bus all night, honey. Now, just make yourself comfortable. My biscuits are almost done, and I'll have eggs and grits for you in a minute. How do you like 'em?"

"Over easy," Link responded automatically, and Thelma disappeared through the swinging door into the kitchen.

Grits, Link thought miserably. *I'm in grit-land.* He debated calling her back to ask for potatoes but gave up the idea when the grizzled old piano-man stumbled out from behind the upright and planted himself on the next stool.

Link studied his uninvited companion out of the corner of his eye. The old man had on rumpled khaki pants and a stained white shirt, and he smelled as if he hadn't had a bath since last Christmas. The skewed black bow tie around his ropy neck reminded Link of a performing chicken he had seen at the state fair when he was nine. A piano-playing chicken, in fact, with a starched tuxedo shirtfront and tiny spats on its little rooster feet.

The memory—and the appropriateness of the image—made Link smile.

Chicken Man evidently saw the smile, for he reached out a yellowed claw and began to stroke at the patches on the sleeve of Link's dress uniform. "I been in the war," he whispered, his voice cracked with age and disuse. "In the Big War. I was a hero. Shot me a officer, right in the head."

Leaning away from the old man, Link focused his eyes on his coffee cup. Maybe the old guy *was* crazy, even though he played the piano like a virtuoso.

The claw dug into Link's upper arm and shook him hard. "I was a hero! I was! Got me a medal to prove it!"

Link turned and looked at the Chicken Man. His eyes were bright and beady, full of memories of the bygone war. "I got me a medal," he repeated. "Wanta see it?"

"The soldier doesn't want to see your medal, Ivory," Thelma's calm voice interrupted. "He wants to hear you play your songs."

The bright eyes gleamed. "You want to hear me play? I play real good."

"Yes, I would like to hear you play," Link answered, casting a grateful glance toward Thelma. The old man jumped up and lunged back toward the piano. Before he had even settled on the bench, he was into a Beethoven sonata and completely lost in the music.

"He plays classical, too?" Link asked as Thelma set a plate of eggs, biscuits, and grits in front of him. "Who is he, anyway?"

"His name is Harlan Brownlee. Folks around here call him Crazy Ivory, mostly—because of his piano playing, I guess. He's not really crazy, just a bit addled."

"Does he live here? I mean, what's he doing here this time of the morning?"

Thelma shook her head and chuckled. "He was born on a cotton spread just west of here. Came back from the war pretty confused, I guess. His folks died while he was off fighting." She paused. "That was before my time, of course, but Ivory has been a fixture around Eden since before the Armistice. He's not as old as he looks—fifty, fifty-five, I guess. Shell shock."

Link nodded, and Thelma went on. "Ivory's granddaddy was a big man around these parts—the Brownlees had the biggest cotton plantation in the county. After the Late Unpleasantness—" She winked and cocked a questioning eyebrow at Link.

"The Civil War, you mean?"

Thelma grinned. "Folks generally prefer to call it the War Between the States. You'll find out that civility is pretty important down here, and most people don't recollect the war as being any too civil."

Link smiled. "I stand corrected." She was an odd one, this brash-looking, forthright Thelma Breckinridge. Yet she had a softness about her that belied the hard shell of her features.

"So," Thelma picked up the story, "by the time Harlan was grown and off to the war, the Brownlees were like most other high-class Delta families— all name and no money. His daddy sold off some of the land and let the rest go to rack and ruin, including the house. It's not much more than a relic now—although it's a big enough relic, I can tell you."

Thelma looked over at Ivory, who had moved into a medley of Irving Berlin songs. "Technically, he lives in one of the cabins on the old place, but he's here most of the time. I open at five-thirty, and he's usually waiting at the door." She lowered her voice and leaned across the counter toward Link. "I swap him meals for music. He doesn't bother anybody, and folks like his playing pretty well."

She reached over and patted Link's hand. "Eat up, now, darlin'. I'll be back with a warm-up for that coffee."

Link took his plate over to a table by the window, ate his breakfast, and listened halfheartedly to the piano. It was a strange place, this Eden, where bums played Beethoven, waitresses offered historical commentary, and Paradise was a greasy-spoon restaurant in the middle of grit-land.

He gazed out at the dismal November day. Dawn had sneaked up on him; it was morning, and he was in Mississippi, waiting for a ride to a new base, a new assignment, and an unknown future. He had never felt so isolated, so alone.

Link's father would tell him that he was never alone, that God was always there, waiting, ready to answer his prayers. But Link hadn't prayed in a long time. He wasn't even sure he remembered how. And even if he did, would God answer him in this desolate backwater town? Did God even know where he was?

The Chicken Man's music washed over him, soothing him like a touch. He felt a hand on his shoulder and thought he had imagined it. Then he looked up to see Thelma Breckinridge beaming her crinkly smile down upon him.

"Brought you some fresh coffee." She poured his cup full and set the pot on the table. "Mind if I sit down for a minute?"

He gestured toward the empty chair to his right. "Help yourself. The breakfast, by the way, was really good. Even the grits."

Thelma's face plumped up in a grin. "You feeling a bit out of place, Yankee boy?"

Link flushed. "It shows?"

"Just a little. But don't you worry. Folks around here are pretty friendly. You being on the base and all, well—you'll see. You won't be alone for long."

Link felt his jaw drop, and he snapped it shut. "Are you reading my mind? I was just sitting here thinking—"

"Thinking how dreary this day is and how you feel like not even God himself could locate Eden, Mississippi, on the map?"

"You *are* reading my mind!"

Thelma laughed. "Naw, hon. Just reading your face. It'll get better." She rose to her feet and picked up the coffeepot. "Don't worry, darlin'. God knows where you are. I guarantee it. And you've already got at least one friend in Eden."

He frowned up at her, then realized what she meant and forced a smile. "Thanks, Thelma. I may need a friend."

"Don't mention it." She pointed out the window, where a green truck had pulled up and was idling its motor. "There's your ride. Come back anytime now, you hear? If you ever need to talk, there'll be a hot meal and a willing ear waiting for you. I'll keep the home fires burning."

"Thanks," Link repeated. He fished in his pocket. "How much do I owe you?"

She waved his money aside. "First meal's on the house. Just don't be a stranger."

Link hoisted his duffel bag onto his shoulder and headed for the truck. In the doorway, he turned and looked back. In the dim light of a rainy daybreak, the Paradise Garden Cafe still looked shabby and worn, but there was something else. Warmth. A welcome. A place to come in out of the rain if he needed it.

He smiled and gave Thelma a salute, then walked out into the dripping autumn morning.

Eden. It wasn't exactly what he had hoped for. But maybe God was in Eden after all.

2

★ ☆ ★

Mississloppy

Link leaned out the open window of the truck and squinted at the gray clouds overhead. The heavens had opened up again, and instinctively he hunched his shoulders against the downpour. *What a mudhole,* he thought. *Camp McRain, Mississloppy.*

"Move it, soldier," the truck driver barked. "This ain't no picnic."

Link slanted a glance over his shoulder and opened the door. His boots sank into three inches of slick red clay. A snatch of a song ran briefly through his mind, something about people beating their feet on the Mississippi mud. The words conjured up an image of smiling, happy darkies dancing on a riverbank. It must have been a different kind of mud.

With a shrug, he adjusted his bag and began slogging toward the nearest building—obviously a barracks, constructed of cheap wood with tar paper tacked to the outside. The cold rain soaked the shoulders of his wool dress uniform and made him itch and shiver.

When he reached the barracks, he stomped his boots on the step, jerked open the door, and ducked inside.

It was a miserable-looking place. One large bare room with forty-eight bunks lining the walls . . . sleeping quarters for a whole platoon. A small coal stove stood in the center. It was clean enough, he supposed—except for where he stood, dripping muddy water onto the wood floor.

"Private!"

Link wheeled around to face a short, stocky man in khaki fatigues. The man was a good head shorter than Link, but what he lacked in stature he made up in intimidation . . . and in sergeant's stripes. The name over the breast pocket read *Slaughter.* How appropriate.

The blazing blue eyes met Link's in a challenge, then traveled down the length of his soggy uniform to rest for a moment on the puddle of reddish mud around his feet.

"Are you aware that this is the army, Private?"

"Uh—yes, sir," Link stammered, coming to attention.

"And are you aware that the army keeps its quarters clean, Private?"

Link nodded. "Yes, sir."

"Where is your toothbrush, Private?"

"My toothbrush, sir?"

"Your TOOTHBRUSH!" the sergeant repeated, glaring up at him.

"Uh, in my kit, sir."

The sergeant pointed to the floor. "Clean it up!"

"With my toothbrush, sir?" Link repeated.

The sergeant folded his arms across his barrel chest. "With your toothbrush. NOW!"

Link squatted to the floor, opened his duffel bag, and began fumbling for his kit. The sergeant loomed over him, watching. When Link stood up again, toothbrush in hand, the noncom was staring at his shoulder patches.

"What's your name, Private?"

"Winsom, sir. Private James Lincoln Winsom."

A glimmer of recognition flashed across the sergeant's face. "You're new here."

Link nodded. "Just in today from six weeks of maneuvers in Tennessee."

A half-smile tweaked the corner of the sergeant's mouth, as if he had suddenly remembered something that amused him. "The CO wants to see you immediately."

Link's heart sank. His record had obviously made it to Mississippi ahead of him.

★ ★ ★

Major Roland Mansfield, the commanding officer of Camp McCrane, flipped through the file on his desk while Link stood at rigid attention in the center of the office. After what seemed like an eternity, the officer slapped the folder shut and fixed Link with a baleful glare.

"AWOL?" he said incredulously, shaking his head. "After three months in the service of the United States Army, you went AWOL?"

Link nodded, trying to look meek. "Yes, sir."

The CO leaned back in his chair and put his arms behind his head. "Tell me about it, Private."

Link didn't know if he had been given permission to stand at ease or not, so he maintained his attention and swallowed hard. "Well, sir—"

"At ease, Private," the CO interrupted. "I've got a feeling that this story is going to be a long one."

With a sigh of relief, Link relaxed his stance and placed his hands behind his back. His knees shook slightly, but he forced himself to meet the CO's icy gaze, took a deep breath, and began.

"You see, sir, we had been on maneuvers for several weeks, and we got a week's leave, beginning the third week in October. My buddy Stork and I—"

"Stork?" the major interrupted.

"Yes, sir. It's kind of a nickname. His real name is Michael, but everybody calls him Stork. He's very tall and thin, see, and . . . well, he and his wife are . . . you know, expecting. We went through basic together, and he's from a little place not too far from St. Joe, my hometown in Missouri."

"Go on," the CO prompted.

"Well, sir, we hitchhiked home to Missouri from Tennessee. Took a couple of days. And then our leave was supposed to be up, and we—"

"You just decided to give yourself a few extra days at home."

"No, sir. I mean, yes, sir. It was kind of an early Thanksgiving, if you know what I mean, sir. I didn't know when I'd get a chance to see my family again . . . if ever. Some of my buddies from basic had already shipped out, and—"

"Spare me the violins, Private. I'm afraid the 'mom and apple pie' routine doesn't hold much water with the army."

Link nodded and stared at the floor.

Major Mansfield leaned forward in his chair and waited until Link raised his eyes again. "Do you know," he said deliberately, "how serious it is for a soldier to go AWOL?"

Link forced a smile. "I do now, sir," he answered.

"How late were you?"

"Twenty-nine hours, sir."

The CO winced. "And what about your buddy, Stork?"

"About eighteen hours, I think, sir. He got back before I did."

"And when you finally did amble on back to your division?"

Link shifted his feet nervously. "They were gone, sir. Shipped out."

"And they sent you here."

"Yes, sir."

"How do you feel about a few more months of basic training?"

Please, God, not basic, Link pleaded inwardly. *Anything but basic.* "Not very good, sir," he replied.

"Well, that's too bad, soldier, because that's exactly what you're going to get. At Camp McCrane, we're in the business of basic training. We've got a bunch of college boys who don't know the butt end of a rifle from the business end. You're going to make soldiers out of them. And you're going to go through every step of training with them, you understand?"

"Yes, sir." Link let out a sigh. Basic training was bad; on the other hand, it was better than a court-martial. Better, as his grandfather would have said, than being hit in the head with a two-by-four.

The CO flipped open the file and once again scanned the records in front of him.

"You had three years of ROTC before basic training?"

"Yes, sir."

"Then why did they assign you to desk duty in ordnance?"

"I could type."

"Did you request such duty?"

Link shook his head vehemently. "No, sir. I wanted infantry duty. I told them that, but they wouldn't listen."

Major Mansfield closed his eyes and shook his head. "Idiot administrators," he muttered. "We got a war going here, and they take a soldier and make a secretary out of him."

"Sir?"

"Never mind. You're off the hook, Private. For now. But you listen, and listen good. You keep your nose clean. You stay out of trouble. And if you ever even *think* about going AWOL again, I'll have your tail in a sling so fast you won't know what hit you."

"Yes, sir. Thank you, sir."

"Report to Company B, 376th Division. Sergeant Slaughter will show you to your quarters."

The rain had stopped. Link Winsom slogged along in the mud behind the sergeant, swinging his arms and whistling under his breath.

Charm, he thought. *All it takes is charm. And when you've got it, you've got it.*

3

✫ ✫ ✫

Daddy's Girl

Libba Coltrain leaned back on the bed and stared at her reflection in the dressing-table mirror across the room. The fingers of one hand absently twisted an auburn curl at the nape of her neck.

She wished she were prettier. Her hair and figure were nice enough, she guessed, but her skin bore the faint scars of adolescent acne, her eyes were too pale a green to be striking, and her mouth was too big. Still, Freddy liked her. He said she had a ravishing smile—that was his word, *ravishing*—and he constantly reprimanded her for covering her mouth when she laughed.

It was a nervous habit, like picking at her cuticles, but she couldn't seem to break it. Someone—an old boyfriend from high school days, whose name she no longer remembered—had made fun of her, said she laughed like a horse. She forgot him, but she never forgot the criticism. And to this day, she always covered her mouth self-consciously.

Libba sighed and twisted the curl tighter, thinking about Freddy.

She probably should just go ahead and agree to marry him. He had asked her twice now, and at least marrying him would get her out from under Daddy's thumb. She had been on her own for nearly four months now, and Daddy still tried to control her every move. On the weekends when she went home, he would interrogate her like the Spanish Inquisition, wanting to know where she had been and what she had been doing, and with whom. What he really wanted to know was whether she had been with Freddy.

Daddy didn't like Freddy. *The understatement of the decade,* Libba thought. The one time she had taken him home for dinner, her father hadn't let up, quizzing the boy unmercifully about his prospects in the army and his plans for after the war was over. *Nobody* made plans for after the war, for heaven's sake. They just wanted to get over there, get it over with, and get back to the business of living.

But Daddy acted like it was a matter of life and death to have your whole future planned out by the time you were twenty. A practical job, a skill—something to fall back on, he said. That was the ticket to success.

Daddy nearly had a stroke when Freddy admitted that he wanted to be an artist. *An artist!* God forbid! A house painter, maybe. But an artist? A limp-wristed pansy who drew cartoons for the newspaper? He'd better be shipped out tomorrow, Daddy declared. A few months in the trenches taking target practice at the Krauts might make a man out of him. But Daddy doubted it.

Libba furrowed her brow into a frown and scowled at her reflection. Why did Daddy have to be so impossible? The man was absolutely insufferable. And Mama wasn't any help at all. She never stood up to him or tried to calm his fits of anger. She just smiled sweetly and said, "That's just the way your father is, dear."

Well, Libba was tired of the way her father was. She would never, *never* take Freddy—or anyone else, for that matter—home again. And if she did marry Freddy, she would insist that they elope. Once they were married, Daddy wouldn't be able to do a thing about it, no matter how mad he might be.

The problem was, Libba wouldn't be old enough to get married without her father's written consent for another two years. *Two years!* It seemed like an eternity. She was old enough to teach in the Eden Public School on a temporary certificate signed by the Mississippi Board of Education. She was old enough to live on her own in this apartment with her cousins Mabel Rae and Willie. And she was certainly old enough to have some soldier's baby—now, *that* was an idea that would give Mama a fit of the vapors! But she wasn't old enough to get married without permission from Daddy, who still thought of her as a child who needed permission for absolutely everything.

Libba jumped up from the bed and banged a hairbrush against the radiator. Didn't that landlady know it was *November?*

Willie appeared at the bedroom door, white up to the elbows with flour. "What on earth are you doing, Libba? Trying to wake the dead?"

Libba turned around and grinned sheepishly. "Trying to get some heat," she said. "I was thinking about Freddy . . . and Daddy . . . and I guess I took it out on the radiator."

Willie cocked an eyebrow and rubbed at her nose, leaving a swipe of white across her ruddy face. "That explains it," she said. "Well, you can't get even with your daddy by tearing down the house. Why don't you come help me and Mabel with dinner? We're having the last of the eggplant and fried okra. And I'm making biscuits."

"So I see," Libba said, wrinkling her nose. "You've got flour all over your face." She paused. "You know I hate to cook, Willie."

"You mean you never *learned* to cook." Willie slanted her eyes at Libba and smiled indulgently. "You're the only woman in Mississippi who makes biscuits that could anchor a riverboat."

"*Southern ladies* don't cook," Libba answered with a lift of her head. "Iris does the cooking in our house; you know that."

"I know you're spoiled rotten," Willie countered. "And you'd better get off your *southern lady* high horse before this Freddy of yours finds out how miserable you are in the kitchen. The way to a man's heart, you know, is—"

"Through his stomach," Libba finished in a mimicking singsong. "Don't you believe it, Willie. Look at you!" She waved a hand in the air. "You'll be an old drudge before you're thirty."

Willie's face fell. "I may be big and homely," she responded candidly, "but there are plenty of men who think there are more important qualities in a woman than being able to jitterbug. Men date a certain kind of girl," she said firmly, "but they marry another kind."

"You mean the kind who will cook and wash and fetch and nurse babies, like a house slave?"

"Maybe," Willie answered. "And just what kind of man do you think you're going to marry?"

Libba considered the question for a moment. "The kind who can cook," she said triumphantly. "The kind who'll treat me like a queen."

Willie regarded Libba evenly. "Good luck, Your Highness," she said. "And now, if I may be dismissed from the royal presence, my okra is burning."

★ ★ ★

Willie slanted a look at Mabel Rae as their cousin made her entrance into the kitchen precisely at the stroke of six. As usual, Libba waited until the last minute to honor her cousins with her presence. She never helped with the cooking, and unless Willie and Mabel Rae physically restrained her, she almost always found an excuse to escape right after dinner and leave them with the dishes. But not tonight, Willie vowed. She had just about had enough of Miss High-and-Mighty.

The look in Mabel's eyes admonished Willie not to start anything, and with a grimace, Willie forced a smile at Libba. "Have a seat, Cousin." She made a move as if to pull out a chair for Her Highness, but once more her sister warned her off with a look. Mabel was right; there was no point in making matters worse.

When they were all settled, Mabel Rae said pointedly, "Willie, I believe it's your turn to say grace."

Willie shifted in her seat and snapped her eyes shut. She didn't feel very gracious at the moment. She cleared her throat and said, "Bless this food, O Lord, and *the hands that have worked so hard to prepare it*. Grant that we may always be *grateful* for what you have given us, and make us ever mindful of the *needs of others*. Amen."

Willie opened her eyes to see her sister glaring at her. Mabel had caught the emphasis of her prayer, but it had evidently gone right over their cousin's head. Libba was buttering one of Willie's flaky biscuits. She raised her head and gazed at them, completely unaware of her transgressions. "That was a nice prayer, Willie," she said sweetly.

"Thank you." Willie snatched up the bowl of fried okra and dumped three spoonfuls of the golden nuggets onto her plate. Just as she reached for a slice of eggplant, she caught a glimpse of Libba looking forlornly around the table.

Mabel Rae began to rise from her chair. "Do you need something, Libba?"

"Sit down, Mabel," Willie muttered. "If she needs something, she can get it herself. She's not a houseguest."

For a moment Libba looked genuinely shocked. Then she murmured, "No . . . I guess not. Isn't there any meat?"

Willie exhaled heavily. "We already used our meat rations—for the roast beef you just had to have last Sunday, remember?"

Libba's expression changed from surprise to hurt. "Oh, I forgot. But it's traditional to have roast beef on Sunday. At home Iris always made a roast, with potatoes and carrots and those little pearl onions—"

Willie raised an eyebrow. "And it's also traditional," she said, forcing a calmness into her voice that she didn't feel, "to have vegetable dinners in the South. A *southern lady* like you should know that—"

Mabel kicked Willie under the table.

"I suppose so," Libba sighed. "But isn't this war just awful? You can't get a decent pair of stockings anymore, and chocolate is so dear that it might as well be gold."

Mabel Rae reached across the table and patted her cousin's hand. "It's for a good cause, Libba—we have to keep that in mind. We're doing our part while the boys overseas are doing theirs."

"I suppose. But—"

"Oh!" Mabel jumped up from the table, nearly upsetting her iced tea. "I almost forgot!" She ran to the pantry and retrieved an envelope from her coat pocket. "A letter came today—from Charlie!"

Willie straightened up and smiled. At last, a diversion from Libba's constant whining and complaining. They hadn't heard from their brother, Charlie, in several weeks, although both she and Mabel wrote to him regularly.

"Open it, Mabel," Willie said. "No, wait—let me see it first." She took the letter from her sister's hand and scrutinized the envelope. "It's not in Charlie's handwriting," she murmured.

"Well, he was wounded in his right arm," Mabel said. "Maybe he can't use it yet."

Willie lifted the flap on the envelope and removed the letter. "Maybe not. I guess I shouldn't be glad he got wounded, but at least we know he's out of the fighting and safe, for the time being."

"I hope he's doing all right," Mabel murmured. A worried frown crept over her face. "Charlie's such a sensitive boy; all this must be very hard on him."

Libba tossed her head. "For heaven's sake, Mabel, you make him sound like he's ten years old. Charlie is older than any of us, remember. He's a man, not a boy. He'll be fine." She turned to Willie. "Go on, read it," she commanded.

Willie unfolded the tissue-thin pages. "It's dated October." She scanned the first page and began to read:

> Dear Sisters,
>
> I can't tell you how much I've appreciated your letters. They really keep my spirits up. I didn't get them for a long time, we were moving around so much, but since I've been in the hospital, they've caught up with me. I'm the envy of every guy here, I get so much mail. I've read some of them to the other fellows, but sometimes I let them think I'm getting letters from a sweetheart back home. Hope you don't mind.
>
> This would be a beautiful country if it wasn't for the war. When we got here in July, it was awful hot—worse than Mississippi in August. Now it's cold and rainy, and the hospital stays chilly all the time. If you could send some warm socks, I'd really appreciate it.
>
> As you can tell from the writing, I still can't use my arm, but I'm better off than a lot of the guys here—especially Boz, the fellow next to me. He got his leg shot up real bad and will

probably lose it. He's only nineteen, and he will be a cripple because of the war. I guess I'm the lucky one.

I hope Mom and Pop are doing all right. I've written to them and received letters from them, too, but they don't say much about themselves. They just try to be real positive about me coming home soon. I feel bad that I got wounded when I did—maybe I'll get a chance to go back to the front and do some more damage to the Germans before my stint is over. If it makes the world safe for democracy, it's worth losing an arm or a leg for.

Pray for me. I hope I'll be home before long.

Love, Charlie

Willie folded the letter and put it back into the envelope. She fought against the tears that rose to her eyes, and when she looked at Mabel Rae, she saw an expression that reflected her own feelings.

"He's so brave," Mabel whispered. "Imagine, after all he's been through, still wanting to go back to the front to fight."

"He's stupid," Libba snorted. "It's all stupid—the fighting, the rations, the boys getting shot up. I hate this war."

"We all hate this war," Willie snapped. "But it's not stupid. It's necessary. And Charlie is a hero."

"Your dear, sweet brother, Charlie, isn't telling everything he knows," Libba countered. "Can't you see he's hiding something? His letters are all so vague, so—"

"Of course he's hiding something!" Willie said. "He can't tell what's going on over there—it's a matter of security." She rose to her feet and fixed Libba with a withering glare. "He *is* brave," she said between clenched teeth. "He's our brother."

Libba softened a little. "I hope you're right, Willie," she said. "I hope you're both right."

4

⭐ ⭐ ⭐

Charlie's Company

**Allied Field Hospital
near Messina, Sicily**

Charlie Coltrain lay on his cot in the field hospital and gazed vacantly at the other men around him. The second wave of old mail had just been delivered. For two months, letters and packages from home had followed them halfway around the Italian countryside. Charlie wished it had never caught up with them. Letters from home only meant that he had to answer, and he didn't know what to say.

In the bed next to him, a gawky, redheaded teenager with the unlikely name of Bosworth Hamilton tore into a package from his mother, only to find stale cookies, crumbled to powder. Boz grinned at him and wolfed down a handful of crumbs. "Want some?" He extended the box in Charlie's direction.

"No thanks," Charlie mumbled.

"Come on, Charlie," Boz pleaded. "My mother made them herself—and here's a note telling me to make sure to share them with my buddies." The boy blushed and ran a hand through his hair. "Mother is the best cook in Boston, and you're the closest thing I've got to a buddy in here."

Reluctantly Charlie took the battered box and fished through the crumbs to find half a cookie still intact. He lifted it in salute, smiled, and put it into his mouth. As he chewed, he watched Hamilton's obvious excitement over receiving mail from home, and a wave of envy rose up to engulf him.

Boz Hamilton could afford to be excited about correspondence from home. He had taken fire on the road to Messina, and his right leg was shattered beyond repair. But before he went down, he had sent six Krauts to their justice and had been hailed a hero in the operation to free Sicily.

Nineteen-year-old Bosworth Hamilton might go home without his leg, but he would still have his chest full of medals and his Purple Heart—not to mention his dignity. His Boston mother and her society friends would give teas and dinners in his honor. Some debutante would overlook his gawky manner and count herself lucky to be escorted to the opera by a war hero. He had nothing to hide, nothing to be ashamed of. His shattered leg might be the best thing that ever happened to him.

Boz Hamilton's wounds were visible.

Charlie closed his eyes and fingered the unopened letter in his lap. Another rambling, cheerful missive from his sister Willie, no doubt. He had gotten three in the past four days—the mail had piled up like cordwood during his days of isolation at the front. He wasn't sure he could stand another barrage of sunshine about how proud they were of him and how he was doing his part to save the world for democracy. And he was positive he didn't know how to respond.

His parents and sisters, of course, couldn't possibly understand how it was out here—the isolation, the frustration, the tension, the . . . did he dare think it? The *fear.*

Fear. That was the one thing Charlie Coltrain was most afraid of. Roosevelt's now-famous line about having "nothing to fear but fear itself" didn't help at all, except perhaps to make him more ashamed of himself. For the fear haunted him even now, when he was safely behind the lines and out of danger. He could taste it every time he tried to choke down the terrible rations, could smell it emanating from his own pores the way he could still smell the stifling dust on the road from Palermo to Messina. When he closed his eyes, he could still see it all . . . and he was afraid.

★ ★ ★

It was supposed to be a glorious liberation, this march into Italy. Spirits were high; the men of the Seventh Army laughed and joked about kicking the Krauts all the way to the gates of hell. But when they landed on the beaches of Sicily and began the long march inland, things began to get ugly—and not because of the battles they encountered along the way.

There were no battles. The Germans had, for the most part, pulled out, and in every village along the road the GIs met only token resistance from the Italian forces, who readily surrendered. Word came down that General Patton, unhappy with a position secondary to Montgomery's, had taken matters into his own hands. He had bullied General Alexander into changing the orders for the Seventh Army, and Alexander had caved in. Patton would lead his troops northwest, to Palermo.

Through stifling July heat and unbearable dust, Charlie staggered along beside the other men in his company. The euphoria had disappeared, replaced by anger and resentment against General Patton, whose ego drove them a hundred miles in four days. At last they reached Palermo, only to discover that there were no Germans there, either. The streets were deserted, except for Italian soldiers waiting to surrender. With almost no resistance, the Allied forces had captured one of Sicily's most significant ports.

Charlie was relieved. Patton was furious.

Charlie saw Patton up close only once, and that was enough. Pacing restlessly back and forth and waving his swagger stick, the general declared that they were moving on toward Messina. Obviously enraged that there had been no combat, no glory, he bellowed, "This is a horse race in which the prestige of the U.S. Army is at stake . . . we must take Messina before the British."

Charlie could hardly believe what he was hearing. The British were Allies, for heaven's sake! This was a war, not a personal vendetta, yet Patton was talking as if his own reputation depended upon beating Montgomery's troops to the Strait.

Charlie wasn't the only one disheartened by this turn of events. Most of the men, including Charlie Coltrain, had started out feeling pretty good about what they were doing—noble, even. Hitler had to be stopped. Everyone knew it. And they were doing their part.

Now the noble effort had degenerated into a footrace to keep General Patton's reputation intact. Some of the men grumbled and cursed and muttered about the egomaniac who was leading them, but most were fiercely loyal to Patton. And it didn't matter how they felt, anyway. The order had been given, and they marched on, toward the northwest, toward Messina Strait—toward Patton's coveted victory.

Then the unthinkable happened.

Just a few miles outside Messina, almost within sight of their goal, a young recruit twenty yards ahead of Charlie tripped a booby-trap wire. Charlie watched, horrified, as the kid's broken body flew through the air like a rag doll in slow motion. Shots came from nowhere. Blindly, Charlie fired back, then went down as something heavy fell on top of him.

When the smoke had cleared, Charlie came to his senses in a ditch, his knees against his chest, trembling and weeping uncontrollably. He felt something wet and sticky oozing from his upper arm, and when he turned his head he saw a piece of shrapnel protruding just above his right elbow.

Charlie tried to move, but something held him fast. Then he looked down. There, in the ditch with him, was a German soldier—or what was left of one. Half the man's head was blown away, and the other half held a fixed look of inexpressible pain and terror. The Kraut's hand, stretched out, had grasped hold of Charlie's sleeve.

Frantically Charlie began to pull at the German soldier's rigid fingers. The touch of the dead man's hand chilled him, but even worse was the look in the glazed and lifeless eye. Cursing him, accusing him, pleading with him.

Charlie began to shake violently. He had killed this man, shot his face off without a second thought. And the eye—that one hideous blue eye—stared at him, unrelenting.

Charlie tried to take a deep breath, but his lungs filled with smoke and dust. He couldn't breathe, couldn't move. He had to close that eye, to stop that accusing look. Gingerly he reached out his hand, but bile rose in his throat, and everything went black.

When he regained consciousness, he was on a stretcher, being carried to a battalion aid station. "Don't worry, pal," one of the litter bearers assured him. "It's a flesh wound—went right through. You'll be good as new and back at the front in no time. And you got yourself a Kraut before you went down."

As predicted, Charlie's wound healed cleanly and without complications. But he didn't go back to the front.

Messina had been taken by Patton's Seventh Army two hours before Montgomery arrived. Patton had won his "horse race" but only in the headlines. As in Palermo, the Germans had already escaped, taking their troops and most of their equipment across the Strait of Messina to the mainland.

Patton had his victory over Montgomery. He got his glory—but at what cost? A young boy was dead, blown to bits right before Charlie's eyes. Boz Hamilton, who took down six of the ambushers before he went down himself, would probably lose his leg. And all for the self-centeredness of a pompous, swaggering general who couldn't stand coming in second to his British counterpart.

Charlie Coltrain was only one of many scarred for life by Patton's arrogance. But Charlie's scars didn't end with the jagged cut in the flesh of his right arm. The worst of his wounds were invisible.

Not a single night went by that Charlie didn't relive the horror of that moment. In his dreams he saw the bloodied body of a young soldier flung into the air. He felt the heat of the road and smelled the acrid scent of dust and gunpowder in his nostrils. He couldn't free himself from the grip of the German soldier's hand and the look in his one blue eye. Even after his shrapnel wound healed, Charlie's hands shook uncontrollably, and chills and sweats assaulted him.

His doctor called it "shell shock."

Patton called it cowardice.

Another soldier like Charlie had made the mistake of admitting to the general's face that his nerves had failed him. Everyone, it seemed, had heard of the incident. It froze Charlie to the bone every time he thought about it.

When the poor infantryman had acknowledged his condition as severe shell shock, Patton had slapped him across the face, drawn his pistol, and pointed it at the soldier's head.

"You're just a lily-livered coward!" Patton had yelled, punctuating his sentence with his infamous curses. "You ought to be shot! I ought to shoot you myself, right now!"

According to the reports, the man's doctor had intervened and ushered the general out of the field hospital, and Patton had almost lost his commission over the incident. Charlie wished the general had been canned, but of course the army protected its own. A general could do almost anything to a private and get away with it—especially a general who had Patton's reputation for battle strategy.

Still, despite his loathing for Patton, Charlie accepted the general's evaluation of his condition. He was a coward. He didn't deserve the Purple Heart that had been pinned to his pillow.

Shell shock was just another name for *yellow.*

★ ★ ★

With trembling hands, Charlie tore the end off the envelope and opened his sister's letter. He glanced at the date—it was written long before she could have received his last letter . . . not that it would make any difference. He hadn't told his family what had happened to him, and he wouldn't. How could he tell them, when he could barely admit it to himself?

> Dear Charlie,
> I hope you're doing all right and that you're getting these letters regularly now. We haven't heard anything from you in a long time, not since that first letter telling us you had been

wounded. But I know it's hard, especially since you have to have someone else write your letters for you.

We hope you are healing well and will soon be returned to us safe and sound. We hate to think of you being wounded, of course, but from the reports we hear it could have been a lot worse. At least you're out of danger and away from the fighting.

We read about General Patton's victory in Messina, and we've told everyone we know that you were there, fighting alongside the great general and being wounded for the cause of freedom. It must be quite an honor to go into battle with someone like that, someone who is such a credit to his country and to democracy. Did you get to meet Patton personally when you got your Purple Heart? I suppose not, since he is so busy with the war, but it would have been a great thrill, I know.

Mama and Daddy and Mabel Rae send their love. The folks are not much for letter-writing, as you know, but Mabel is working on one of her own, and you should receive it soon. Mama is knitting you some warm socks.

Everything is fine here. Libba is constantly in trouble with Uncle Robinson for sneaking around with her soldier boy, but that's not news, is it? I'm surprised he doesn't chain her to the bedpost to keep her under control.

Take good care of yourself and let us hear from you whenever you're able. We know you're in good company there with all the others who have courageously sacrificed themselves for the good of the free world. We are so proud of you—your star is hanging in the front window where everyone can see. We can't wait for our hero to come home.

Much love,
Your sister Willie

Charlie's hand started to shake, and the letter slipped to the floor beside his cot. With a muffled sob he drew the blanket up to his chin, turned his face to the wall, and began to cry.

5

⋆ ⋆ ⋆

I'll Be Seeing You

In the broad light of day, with a weak November sun shining down over the compound, Camp McCrane looked slightly less dismal than it had that first day in the rain. Link Winsom stepped awkwardly over ruts that had dried into red clay ridges. Walking through camp was a little like negotiating a newly plowed field.

He heard an engine behind him and moved to get out of the way.

"Want a ride, soldier?"

Link turned. Sergeant Slaughter sat behind the wheel of a mud-spattered jeep, grinning. "Get in. Where you going?"

"To the USO building. I heard a rumor that a guy could get a Coke on this base."

"We got it all," the sergeant said with a laugh. "Coke, ice cream, beer, cigarettes—whatever you want." He swept his arm in a wide arc to indicate the layout of the base. "Fifteen miles across. It's a big camp."

"So my feet have told me," Link said, pointing ruefully at his battered, muddy boots.

"Aw, don't worry, Winsom," Slaughter chuckled. "Most of the time I can get my hands on one of these—" He patted the steering wheel of the jeep. "Just stick with this old sarge . . . I know just about everybody, and most of them owe me favors."

Link stared for a full minute at the disarming smile on Sergeant Slaughter's face. Could this possibly be the same man who was so intimidating that first day in camp? He seemed so . . . human.

"I heard your little AWOL stunt came out all right," Slaughter was saying.

"Major Minefield could have kicked your rear end all the way back to Tennessee, you know."

"I know," Link said. He paused. "Sarge, let me ask you something. That first day, when you caught me dripping mud on the barracks floor, you were really rough on me. Would you actually have made me clean it up with my toothbrush?"

Slaughter threw back his head and laughed. "Naw. But it pays to put on a tough front with the new boys. Keeps people in line. Lets 'em know who's in charge. I'm really a pretty nice guy once you get to know me."

Link grinned sheepishly. "You could have fooled me."

Slaughter slammed the jeep into gear, lurched forward, and laughed again. "That was the point." He careened the jeep around a corner and jerked to a stop in front of the sprawling USO building. He swiveled in his seat to face Winsom.

"The major says you've got more experience than any private he's ever seen."

"I guess so," Link said. "I had three years of ROTC training. When I came to basic I could break down a rifle faster than most noncoms. But they found out I could type and that I was good with numbers. I worked at a bank before I enlisted . . . so I guess it kind of made sense for them to stick me at a desk in ordnance."

"It doesn't make sense," Slaughter said bluntly. "It's just plain stupid." He shook his head. "But it won't happen here. The CO has plans for you—big plans."

Link's head jerked up. "Like what?"

"I don't know. OCS, maybe."

Link laughed tightly. "No chance. I took the test for Officers' Candidate School. My scores weren't high enough."

"We'll see."

"What do you mean?"

Slaughter narrowed his eyes. "The CO likes you, Winsom. Who knows why—your record isn't exactly flawless."

Link shook his head. "Not exactly. AWOL after three months."

"But there's something about you—something that intrigues the old man. He sees potential in you, boy. Don't mess it up."

"I'll do my best, Sarge."

"Do better than that, Winsom. So far your best nearly got you canned."

Link grinned. Slaughter would be a good friend to have . . . if they ever got on equal ground. But Link Winsom knew his chances of being promoted were nil, no matter what the sarge might say. The army didn't promote green privates who went AWOL on their first leave. And OCS was absolutely out of the question. Charm might get him out of hot water with the CO, but he doubted that it could promote him very far in the army's chain of command.

He shrugged. Maybe it didn't matter. Maybe it was enough that he was here, being given a second chance to do something right. Maybe he could just mark time, do his part to get this war over with, and get back home in one piece.

Link jumped out of the jeep and shook Slaughter's hand. "Thanks for the ride, Sarge. And the advice."

Slaughter gripped his hand and held on for a minute. "I'm in A Company. Let me know if you need anything."

Link nodded. "Sure, Sarge. But right now, what I need most is a Coke."

★ ★ ★

The USO building, next door to the PX, was a rambling wooden structure only a little less shabby than the tar-paper barracks that surrounded Camp McCrane. Link wandered through the PX, bought a pack of gum, and headed into the USO.

In the center of the huge room was a large dance floor, and on the far side stood a raised platform big enough to hold a sizable band. Around the perimeter of the floor, tables and chairs were arranged in a semicircle. Link could imagine crowds gathered here for weekend dances, but at this hour of the afternoon only a few dozen soldiers sat scattered around at the tables.

A beefy, baby-faced private grinned at him across the bar. "Whatcha gonna have, soldier?" he asked, drawing *gonna* into at least three syllables. Link shot a covert glance at the boy's neck to see if it was really red.

"Uh—Coke, I guess."

"What kind?"

Link frowned. "Coke, I said."

"Uh-huh." The boy smiled vacantly. "What kind? We got root beer, orange, ginger ale, and Coca-Cola." He paused and narrowed his eyes suspiciously. "You a Yankee, ain'tcha? Down here everything's 'coke.' Now, what kind? We got—"

"Coca-Cola," Link snapped. "The brown stuff."

The grinning private drew a fountain Coke and handed it over. As Link turned to leave, the boy raised his voice. "Root beer's brown, too," he sneered. "Dumb Yankee."

Link took his drink to an empty table at the left side of the dance floor. He sat back and ran a finger around the rim of his glass, wondering absently what on earth he could do to make his weeks at this forsaken camp bearable. Only Slaughter had shown any interest in getting to know him, and he was, after all, a sergeant.

Briefly Link recalled his meeting with the woman at the cafe . . . what was her name? Thelma. She seemed to understand his loneliness, and for a few minutes she'd made him believe that he had not been forsaken here after all. But the reassurance hadn't lasted very long. He was on his own.

The cold drink helped a little. Link stretched his legs out, trying to relax, but the tune playing on the jukebox grated on his nerves. The Andrews Sisters: *"Ac-cen-tuate the positive; e-lim-inate the negative. . . ."* He sighed heavily. So far he hadn't found anything positive to *ac-cen-tuate* out here in the Mississippi boondocks.

He glared at the jukebox, as if a vicious look might be sufficient to make the Happy Sisters shut up. Then he sat up straighter and squinted through the haze of smoke. A tall, gangly soldier stood leaning over the box, reading the titles intently.

Link watched as the soldier ran a hand through his blondish hair, pushing it up on end. Then he turned just a little, and Link caught a glimpse of the profile—deep-set eyes, a hawkish nose. He must be imagining things. This soldier could have been a twin brother to . . .

Could it be?

Link jerked to his feet, grabbed his drink, and made a dash across the dance floor to the jukebox.

★ ★ ★

Glenn Miller. Tommy Dorsey. Irving Berlin. Stork Simpson read the names with interest. All the latest stuff—big bands, swing, the love songs, even some hot jitterbug numbers. "White Christmas" was there, and some of the tunes from the popular musical *Oklahoma!* "Praise the Lord and Pass the Ammunition," and "Mairzy Doats"—a really stupid song, but the girls seemed to love it. And his favorite, "I'll Be Seeing You."

That one always made him cry, when no one was around to see it. It was "their song," his and Madge's. She wrote the lyrics to it in almost every letter: *"I'll be looking at the moon, but I'll be seeing you. . . ."*

He punched the number in and stood leaning on the glass. She was his wife now, not just his girl. He was a husband, soon to be a father. And he wouldn't be there with her when the baby was born.

Stork twisted his wedding ring around on his finger—a habit that seemed to calm him a little when he got worried about Madge and the baby. What had he been thinking of to get married? He loved her, of course. But there was a war on. He was six hundred miles from home in a boot camp on the outskirts of nowhere. And his girl—his *wife*—was living in one room of his parents' house, trying to keep her spirits up and deal with his self-centered, spiteful mother.

Mother hadn't even tried to hide her disappointment that her "little boy" had been taken captive by a "conniving creature" who got pregnant to trap him. Madge was devastated by this attack, but there wasn't much either of them could do about it. She had no family, nowhere else to go.

Everybody was getting married these days. Or at least engaged. War did that to a guy—made him think about permanence and the future, compelled him to grab for some stability in a world that seemed to be falling apart. But he was too young. Madge was too young. They were all too young—too young to get married and have babies. Too young to die.

What if he came back maimed? Or worse . . . what if he didn't come back at all? What if he was blown to bits in a muddy foxhole somewhere and Madge didn't even have a body to mourn over?

He shouldn't have gone back after Thanksgiving. She'd begged him not to go. She didn't talk about how hard it was with his mother, of course—she wouldn't put him through that. But he could see it in her eyes. She was miserable. Pregnant and miserable. And he left her crying in the rain while he walked out to the highway to thumb a ride back to Tennessee.

He should have just stayed AWOL.

But he had a job to do. Madge knew that. Everybody knew it. The real men didn't stay behind. Even the poor 4F-ers, who couldn't make the cut because of bad eyes or a deaf ear or bum knees, envied guys like him—guys in uniform who were putting their lives on the line for freedom.

It was a noble sentiment, all right. And, as far as it went, a true one. He did have a duty to his country. But what about his duty to his wife and child?

Stork stared into the jukebox. There were no answers for him, he knew. But he wished at least that he could find some hope.

Then the next record dropped, and their song began to play: *"I'll be seeing you in all the old familiar places that this heart of mine embraces. . . ."*

Suddenly he felt a hand on his shoulder and heard, "Hey, buddy."

Stork wheeled around as if preparing for a fight. But as he saw Link Winsom's face, the fire of antagonism turned to relief and pure joy. He lunged forward, enveloping his friend in a bony hug.

"Link Winsom!" he said over and over again. "I can't believe it. I just can't believe it."

"Yeah," Winsom agreed. "Maybe this mudhole has possibilities after all."

6

★ ★ ★

Old Fights
and Longtime Struggles

Libba flopped onto the bed she had slept in since she was four and fixed her eyes on the gray floral rug. "Mama, it's just not fair!" she bawled. *"He's not fair!"*

Olivia Coltrain sank down beside her daughter and began to stroke the girl's hair. Such beautiful hair it was—long and worked into thick curls, and that dark, rich auburn color that used to be her own, before age and the struggle of living as a wife and mother had faded it to a dull reddish neutral shade. *Be glad you got your coloring from the Irish side of the family,* her own mother used to tell her. *Redheads never gray.*

Olivia's mother hadn't known—or hadn't told her, if she knew—that hair wasn't the only thing in a woman's life that could go gray and lifeless. Twenty-five years of living with an impossible man, a man dead set on being right one hundred percent of the time, could take the sheen off the most idealistic southern lady.

Her daughter was right. It wasn't fair. Robinson Coltrain had been accused of a lot of things in his life, but being fair wasn't one of them. He dominated everyone—his wife, his daughter, his customers at the hardware store . . . even his dogs. Robinson wouldn't have a cat in the house—or even out in the yard to keep the mice out of the shed. "Cats are too blessed independent," he'd say. What he meant was, you couldn't make a cat cower and obey, no matter what you did to it. And Robinson Coltrain had built his life around making other people cower.

Olivia knew these things about her husband, of course, but she couldn't—wouldn't—admit them to her daughter. She barely admitted them to herself. Most of the time she managed to avoid the truth by spouting maxims to herself about honoring her marriage vows, respecting and supporting her husband, and living according to the principles of Christian charity.

Sometimes, however, such as today, when Robinson was being absolutely immovable about some molehill he had made into a mountain, Olivia was sorely tempted to stand up to him. Today he had put his foot down—again—and declared that no daughter of his was going to go out flaunting herself in front of a bunch of leering soldiers.

He was wrong, and Olivia knew it. These USO dances were perfectly innocent, well chaperoned, and completely acceptable to everyone in polite society. But Robinson was adamant. Libba was *not* going.

And Olivia didn't have the backbone to stand up to him.

Now, faced with her daughter's tears of disappointment, Olivia's own lack of gumption shamed and saddened her. With a flash of memory that hit her like a summer storm, she recalled how bitterly hurt she had been all her life because of her own father's domineering nature. Her mother hadn't stood up for her, either. She had been made to feel small and worthless and stupid. She had been taught that proper southern ladies—especially proper southern *Christian* ladies—submitted to their husbands in all things. And she had learned her lessons well. She had married a man just like Daddy, and now he was doing the same things to their daughter that her own father had done to her.

But there was a difference. Libba was strong where she was weak. Libba would stand up for herself. She would be the one to break the cycle.

In the meantime, the poor girl suffered terribly. And Olivia had the horrible sinking feeling that once Libba was old enough, she might leave home forever.

Olivia went on stroking the auburn curls until Libba's sobbing subsided. Then she lifted the girl up by her shoulders, wiped her tear-streaked face with a lace-edged handkerchief, and looked her in the eye. "Sweetheart," she said gently, "I'm really sorry about this. I know you were counting on going to the dance with Willie and Mabel Rae. But your daddy's got his mind made up. And we both know there's no changing him when he's set against something. That's just the way your father is."

Libba nodded fiercely and glared at Olivia. Her expression told her mother that they *both* knew all too well the way her father was.

"All right," Olivia said at last. "Now, let's have a smile."

Libba twisted her mouth into a grimace.

"No, now—a *real* smile," Olivia prompted. "A smile always makes things better." She paused and looked intently at her daughter. "Do you think you could *try* not to get into another argument with your father this weekend—for me? You know how it upsets everything. Iris has made a real nice dinner, and if we all try hard, we might be able to have a pleasant time together."

Libba shook her head in frustration. "Mama, *he's* the one who always starts the arguments. If he wasn't so . . . so . . ."

Olivia put a finger to her daughter's lips. "I know, honey, I know. But he is your father. And that's—"

"That's just the way he is," Libba finished.

Olivia smiled sadly. "He's a good man, Libba. Really he is. He only wants what's best for you. He only wants to protect you—"

"Protect me?" Libba countered. "He only wants to run my life, you mean."

Olivia busied herself for a moment, tucking a few strands of hair into her chignon. "He is your father," she repeated finally. "Do try to be nice."

Libba groaned. "Mama, if he has his way, I'll be an old maid living at home for the rest of my life."

"I doubt it," Olivia answered. The girl had spunk, she had to give her that much credit. She rose and patted her daughter's hand. "I'm going to go check on how Iris's dinner is coming along," she said. "Wash your face, dear; you look a sight."

She turned as she reached the doorway and looked back at Libba, still sitting on the rumpled bedspread. "Straighten the bed when you get up, will you?" she asked. "And try not to pout. You know your father hates pouting."

"I know, Mama," Libba said with a tone of resignation. "Daddy hates pouting. He hates whining. He despises it when anyone gets mad . . . except him, of course."

"Libba—" Olivia hated the reproachful tone in her voice, but she couldn't seem to help it. "The least you can do is try . . . for me."

"I'll try, Mama," the girl responded. "For you."

★ ★ ★

Dinner was an excruciatingly tense affair. Daddy sat rigid at the head of the formal dining table with a pained expression on his face, saying nothing but making it perfectly clear that he was displeased with her behavior and attitudes. When Libba came to the table, he raked her up and down with an icy gaze as if to say, *You're wearing that? No wonder the soldiers at that camp think you're playing fast and loose.* He uttered not a single syllable, but with Daddy words were not necessary to convey disgust or disapproval. He simply let fly with one of his looks, and the message was clear.

Mama made up for their silence and uneasy truce by scurrying about and trying desperately to make the "nice dinner" into the "pleasant evening" she had promised her daughter. It didn't work, of course. Even when the silence gave way to small talk, tension hung in the air like toxic gas, waiting to descend and smother them all.

Libba picked at her food and avoided her father's eyes. The clock on the mantel in the living room ticked loudly, and as each minute passed, she grew more restless and agitated.

Finally her father threw his fork onto his plate with a clatter that made Libba jump. "I've had just about enough of this!" he declared. Then he waited.

"Enough of what, Daddy?" Libba knew the question was expected; you were *always* expected to respond when Daddy spoke. She had played this scene a hundred times, but experience didn't help much in handling it when it came.

"Enough of your moping and pouting around," Daddy said, his voice rising. "Iris has fixed a nice dinner for us, and your mama has worked hard to make a pleasant evening. Now you have to go and spoil it with your childish behavior!"

The attack was unwarranted, as most of Daddy's tirades were. Libba *hadn't* been pouting, and she wasn't acting childish. But Daddy had spoken.

She caught her mother's eye for just a second and saw the warning lights flashing.

"Daddy, I wasn't—," she began.

"Don't sass me, girl!" he interrupted. "This is my house, and you are my daughter, and I won't stand for any back talk!"

"I wasn't talking back," Libba protested. "I was just—"

"Are you contradicting me, Tater?" he challenged.

She flinched. He knew she hated for him to call her by that name . . . her childhood nickname. It made her feel small and stupid. When she was a baby with a fine fuzz of red hair, her father had taken to calling her his little sweet potato. The nickname had long ago been shortened to Tater, and he used it incessantly, but no longer as an endearment. Always Tater, or girl, spitting out the words as if they polluted his tongue. Never *Elizabeth* or *Libba*. Once—just once—she had asked him to stop using the name. He responded as she had expected, declaring that she was *his* daughter and he would call her whatever he pleased.

"No, sir, I—"

"I know back talk when I hear it," he said. "You're in a snit because I won't let you go over to that army base and flaunt your wares like all the other cheap girls in this town. Well, no daughter of mine is going to put herself on display. I am a deacon in the Presbyterian church, and I raised you better than that, girl. I raised you to have class and dignity. I didn't raise you to shame your mother and me by acting like a common hussy!"

"Daddy, it's not like that," Libba interjected when he took a breath. "It's not cheap, or crass, or any of those things. It's—" She groped for some reasoning that might penetrate his wall of resistance. "It's part of the war effort. To keep up morale, you know." She shot a pleading glance at her mother for some sign of support, but the woman sat mutely, her head down, twisting a linen napkin in her fingers.

Her father narrowed his eyes. "Morale? I know what kind of *morale* those boys are interested in. And my daughter is not going to be the one supplying it."

Libba sank back into her chair, tears rising in her eyes. How could he make something cheap and tawdry out of an innocent USO dance?

She looked again at Mama. Her mother's eyes were wide as saucers, staring at Daddy with shock. She, too, was obviously appalled by his innuendo.

"Robinson Coltrain!" Mama said, finding her voice at last. "How dare you say such a thing in front of our daughter?"

"Our *daughter,*" he said, leveling an acid gaze at Mama, "thinks she's grown up enough to handle herself. Well, she might as well get a taste of reality. I saw the way that—that so-called *artist* looked at her when she brought him here—"

"Freddy?" Libba choked out. "What does Freddy have to do with all this?"

Her father swiveled in his seat and pointed a bony finger at her. "I know what young men have on their minds, Tater. One thing. Only one thing. And they'll do whatever they have to do to get it . . . even propose marriage."

Libba's stomach tightened into a knot. How could he possibly know about her plans with Freddy? "My letters," she said in a fierce whisper. "You read my letters!"

"I did," he said. "And I don't intend to apologize for it. I have a duty to protect what's mine against evil-minded men who would prey on the innocence of—"

Libba thought she was going to be sick, right there on the linen table-cloth, on the remains of her father's half-eaten dinner. She lurched to her feet, tipping over the chair in her haste.

"You're the one who's evil-minded, Daddy!" she shouted. "I hate you, Daddy—do you hear? *I hate you!* And if I ever get half a chance, I'm going to wipe the dirt of this snobby little town off my feet and never come back again. Never!"

She ran for the hall and grasped the door frame for support, pausing just long enough to hear Mama saying in a consoling voice, "She's just upset, dear. She didn't mean it . . . now, finish your dinner. Iris worked so hard to make it."

★ ★ ★

It was dark when Libba awoke. The house was still and quiet. She pushed herself up on her elbows and rubbed at her face, marked with little indentations from the chenille bedspread. The spread was still damp from her tears.

Mama was wrong. She *had* meant it . . . every word. She hated Daddy— hated his controlling ways, his declarations of self-righteousness. She hated Mama for giving in to him all the time. She hated herself for crying.

Libba always cried when she was mad. She couldn't seem to help it. When she was sad or hurt, she could usually control her tears well enough. But when she was angry—really angry, like she had been tonight at dinner— she always broke down. Then she couldn't talk, couldn't reason. Even worse, Daddy always interpreted her "bawling" as a sign of weakness and childishness. It just proved she wasn't as grown-up as she liked to pretend, he'd say. And it proved that he was stronger, that he had won.

Daddy couldn't stand not winning.

But he wouldn't win this time. She'd show him.

The clock chimed nine; there was still time. Libba slipped out of her shoes, tiptoed to the bathroom down the hall, and fixed her face. She could hear faint sounds of the radio playing at the back of the house, in the enclosed room they still called "the porch."

"Who knows what evil lurks in the hearts of men? The Shadow knows. . . ."

Libba smiled grimly. For a brief moment she wondered how Daddy knew what evil lurked in the hearts of men. How could he imply such a thing . . . that Freddy had proposed to her just so he could have his way with her? It was utterly ridiculous. Why, Freddy had always been the perfect gentleman! Still, Daddy had seemed so certain.

She shook the thought away. Daddy was always certain. Always right.

But not about this.

Freddy understood how Daddy was. He would be waiting, hoping she'd come. He always waited.

With her shoes in hand, Libba padded quietly to the front door, retrieved her coat from the hall tree, and stepped out into the chilly November night.

7

Who Knows What Evil
Lurks in the Heart . . . ?

Olivia Coltrain looked up from the petit point in her lap, and an involuntary shudder ran through her as she studied her husband's expression. Engrossed in *The Shadow,* Robinson didn't even glance her way.

She watched him as if surveying the face of a stranger. He had hard, cold eyes . . . dangerous eyes. A fixed set to his jaw. A permanent scowl etched into his forehead between his eyebrows.

Olivia didn't know him anymore. On her better days, she remembered the early years, when they struggled together to get the business going. They lived on next to nothing, but they were happy. Or she thought they were.

Now she wasn't so sure. These days, when she looked at him, she felt afraid, the way she did when she looked at her own reflection in the mirror too long. Sometimes when she stared at herself, she didn't even recognize the familiar features that stared back at her. She felt as if someone else were inside there, struggling to get out.

And she had the same eerie sensation when she looked at her husband. Especially tonight at dinner, when he had made such a crude and unfair declaration to their daughter about the ulterior motives of men. *Men will do anything to get what they want,* he had said. *Even propose marriage.*

Olivia wasn't certain that was true of all men. But it hit her in a blinding flash of insight that it *was* true of her husband. He had done just that . . . and it had worked. Then, having gotten what he wanted, he had been ready to walk away.

Until he found out about the baby.

When she told him she was pregnant, he had married her, and for a while they seemed to be happy. A new business, a new addition to the family, a new life together . . .

A life founded on lies.

There had been no child. Olivia had deceived him about the pregnancy, just as she deceived him three months later when she pretended to have the miscarriage. But by then it was too late for him to back out. They were already married.

Robinson had gotten what he wanted. And though he had paid dearly for it, so had she. Robinson Coltrain had taken her away from her father. She had bought her freedom with another kind of bondage.

"Who knows what evil lurks in the hearts of men?" the deep-chested baritone on the radio intoned.

The Shadow knew.

Robinson Coltrain knew.

And Olivia knew as well. It was a secret she would carry to her grave. And she would pray every day of her life that her daughter would never make the same mistake.

8

⭐ ⭐ ⭐

Divine Intervention

Link Winsom sat in the mess hall and toyed glumly with what the army called mashed potatoes. For three weeks now he had suffered through the rigors of basic training with his little outfit of college boys: rifle drills, target practice, forced marches, the whole routine. He was exhausted . . . and frustrated.

If these boys ever did get to the front, the entire war effort was going to be in big trouble. They tried, certainly. And they were deadly serious about it. In their own eyes they were the Chosen Few who were destined for greatness. They would be the heroes of this noble war.

If they ever learned how to avoid shooting themselves in the foot, that is.

He sighed and ran a hand through his hair. Maybe a court-martial would have been preferable after all.

Link jumped when he felt a light tap on his shoulder. He looked up to see an apple-cheeked Ole Miss freshman beaming down at him. What was his name—Joke, Smoke, something like that. He peered at the young soldier's name patch. *Coker.* Oh, yeah. Randy Coker. The guys called him "Coke."

"Excuse me, sir—," Coker began.

"Don't call me sir," Link interrupted. "I'm not an officer. I'm a private, just like you." He winced inwardly at the thought. Once a week, at chow, promotions were announced—names called, stripes distributed. So far he and Stork, for all their experience, had been passed over. Their little AWOL trick had become legend. They'd probably be privates forever.

Coker's pink cheeks flushed. "Yes, sir," he said. "I'm sorry, sir."

Winsom's patience was running thin, and he had to work at remaining civil. "What can I do for you, Coker?"

The boy produced a rifle from behind his back. "I just cleaned my gun," he said proudly. "I think I've finally got the hang of it. Want to check it?"

Link pushed his chair back and stood nose to nose with the fresh-faced private. "Where did you learn that word, boy?"

Coker looked confused. "Gun, sir?" At Link's nod, he brightened. "Why, I've been handling guns all my life, sir. My daddy and I used to go rabbit hunting—"

"Rabbits?" Link roared. "You mean little pink-nosed bunnies with furry white hind ends?"

Coker's cheeks flamed, and a roar of laughter rose up in the mess hall. "Uh, yes, sir. I guess, sir."

Link frowned and leaned forward until Coker took a step back. "And do you think this weapon was issued to you as a bunny-hunting gun so you could blow the stuffing out of Peter Cottontail?"

"Uh, no, sir."

"This weapon, boy, is a *rifle*. An instrument of war. If I ever hear you referring to it as a *gun* again, I'll blow *your* tail feathers off with it, and you won't be able to sit down on *your* little hind end for a week."

Coker trembled, but he managed to hold himself at attention.

"Got it?" Link fought to keep a straight face.

"Uh . . . yes, sir," the boy stammered.

Winsom ran a practiced eye over the rifle. It wasn't a bad cleaning job for a second-week draftee. This boy had the potential of becoming a real soldier, with the right kind of training.

"Take it back to the barracks," Link barked. "Break it down again. I want this weapon so clean your grandmother could use it for a fork."

Coker's face fell. "Yes, sir," he said.

"Dismissed."

The boy took the rifle and turned to go.

"Private?" Winsom called as the boy reached the door of the mess hall.

Coker turned. "Yes, sir?"

"What's that weapon called?

Coker grinned sheepishly. "My *rifle,* sir."

"Good boy. Don't forget it."

"Yes, sir."

"And Coker?"

"Yes, sir?"

"Don't call me 'sir'!"

"Yes, sir," Coker responded automatically, then disappeared through the mess hall door.

★ ★ ★

"You were kind of rough on the poor kid, don't you think?" Stork said quietly, looking up from the Memphis newspaper.

Link shook his head. "Maybe. But it pays to be a little tough on the new guys at first. Keeps them in line." He smiled ruefully, recognizing the echo of Slaughter's words in his own. Still, the principle was a sound one. You could always ease up later, after you had worked a little grit and gumption into them. But you couldn't get tougher once they had seen your soft spots.

"You embarrassed him," Stork persisted.

"Well, I'm *sorry!*" Link responded, rolling his eyes melodramatically. "I had no idea you were so sensitive!"

Stork frowned. "What's eating you, Link? You've been on edge for a week."

Link shrugged, then looked his friend square in the eye. "Do you believe in God, Stork?"

Stork sat back in his chair, the expression on his face clearly communicating that this was not at all what he had expected. "I guess so," he said at last. "Doesn't everybody?"

"Yeah, well, I mean in a different way—more *personally.* Do you believe that God actually *does* things in people's lives . . . you know, to help them or protect them?"

Stork narrowed his eyes suspiciously. "What's this all about, Link?"

Link flattened his hand over Stork's newspaper and slid it across the table. He picked it up and flipped through the pages, then folded a page back and tapped his forefinger on the casualty list.

"Have you read this?"

Stork stared at him blankly. "The list of dead and wounded? Sure. I always read it. Nobody we know—at least not yet."

"Haven't you noticed anything . . . unusual . . . about it?" Link prodded.

"In case you haven't noticed, we're in a war, pal. There's nothing unusual about casualties."

Link arched his eyebrows in exasperation. "I *mean,*" he said slowly, as if explaining to a rather stupid child, "that the highest percentage of casualties is among officers, not enlisted men."

Stork's blank expression remained. "Yeah. So?"

"So," Link continued in that same deliberate tone, "maybe it's no accident that we washed out of OCS on the entrance test."

"Let me get this straight," Stork said, shifting in his seat. "You believe that *God* kept us from getting into OCS because most of the present casualties on the front lines are *officers?*"

"It's possible."

"It's preposterous," Stork countered. "If that's true—and I don't believe for a minute that it is—then God must not be doing a very good job protecting those officers. Be logical, Link. If God cares at all, he'd have to care about them, too, wouldn't he?" Stork stared hard at Winsom. "Where did all this come from?"

"Nowhere," Link said evasively. "I've just been . . . thinking."

"Well, there's the problem," Stork said triumphantly. "Thinking—it'll get you into trouble every time."

"Be serious, Stork."

"No, Link. You *stop* being serious. If you go maudlin on me, this is going to be a very long tour." He paused. "I'm the one with a wife at home and a baby on the way. If anything, *I* should be the one with morbid thoughts about dying and questions about what God is doing about it."

"Well, haven't you even *thought* about it?"

Stork shifted his eyes to his empty plate. "No."

Link knew Stork was lying, but he didn't press the issue. Better to just let it drop and do his thinking in private from now on. Stork was his best friend, and if he couldn't talk to him about such things, he couldn't talk to anybody. Still, the question haunted him. Was God—and he did, in a generic sort of way, believe in God—interested in or able to help a guy like him? Could God have kept him out of OCS for his own good? It might not be logical, but he couldn't help wondering.

Link sighed. Suddenly he felt alone again, and rather sad. But he flashed a forced smile at Stork. "Sorry, buddy," he said lightly. "I guess dealing with these college boys has just got the best of me."

"It's OK."

Stork looked past him. "Slaughter wants you," he said, nodding toward the doorway of the mess hall.

Link got up and walked to the door. The sergeant stood there grinning at him, his hands stuck in his pockets. "Old Man Minefield requests the honor of your presence in his office," he said with a chuckle. "You and your buddy. On the double."

★ ★ ★

Winsom and Stork stood at attention in front of the major's desk.

"At ease, men," Major Mansfield said. "I understand you two have been doing a remarkable job with the training in your outfit." His mood seemed unusually jovial today. Link wondered briefly when the other shoe would drop.

It didn't take long. "I agreed to transfer Simpson here to B Company because you two had worked together before. But—"

Link braced himself. What kind of trouble were they in now? Had the major gotten wind of the "rifle and gun" incident already? If so, news traveled faster in the army than it did in Babs Moran's beauty shop back in St. Joe.

"I've reviewed your records," the major was saying. "Apart from that one AWOL incident—and I'm sure you learned your lesson about that—you both have proved yourselves capable soldiers and excellent leaders."

Link slanted a glance at Stork, who stood beside him with his eyes fixed forward. A ghost of a smile flitted across the thin, hawkish face, and Stork's lips twitched slightly.

"You're probably wondering why you haven't received any of the standard promotions," Major Mansfield went on. "Well, I've decided to recommend you for Officers' Candidate School."

"Begging your pardon, Major," Link interrupted, "but we both took the OCS test, and our scores weren't high enough to qualify."

Mansfield silenced him with an upraised hand. "I know, I know. But your scores *were* on the borderline. I've pulled a few strings and managed to get you admitted."

★ ★ ★

Stork felt his heart beginning to race. OCS! This was an opportunity he had never expected—never in a million years, considering the idiot stunt he had pulled going AWOL.

He could sure use the extra money. And Madge would be so proud of him in his officer's uniform. He could imagine her telling their son . . . or daughter . . . how Daddy had been promoted because the CO believed in him, how against all odds he became an important man in the United States Army.

And the best part of all, he and Link would do it *together.* They had promised each other that they would stick together, no matter what. Friends. Best buddies.

Stork could see himself leading men into battle, fighting the Germans or the Japanese, side by side with enlisted men who thought he was the bravest, most competent officer they'd ever known. He would inspire loyalty; he would lead courageously. He might even win the Medal of Honor. . . .

★ ★ ★

Link watched a flood of emotions wash over Stork's face, and he felt his gut grip in a moment of sheer panic. This couldn't be happening. Maybe God *had* protected them by keeping them out of OCS, maybe not. But if there was the slightest chance, he had to trust his instincts. There was no time to lose.

"Sir?" Link began. "May I speak freely?"

"By all means." The major paced across the office and waved his hand in a gesture of permission.

"Well, sir, we . . . uh, that is, if it's all right with you, we'd rather not."

Major Mansfield turned on his heel and fixed Winsom with a disbelieving stare. "You *what?*"

"We'd . . . we'd prefer not to go into OCS. We'd rather stay with our company."

The major looked puzzled. "You're *turning down* a chance at OCS?"

Link took a deep breath. "Yes, sir. If you have no objections, sir."

Out of the corner of his eye, Link saw Stork's head jerk around. Slack-jawed, Stork was staring at him as if he'd completely lost his mind.

"Simpson?"

At the sound of the major's voice, Stork snapped back to attention, his eyes riveted to the window behind Mansfield's desk.

"Do you concur with Private Winsom's rather unorthodox evaluation of this OCS matter?"

Stork swallowed hard and, without moving his head, cut his eyes in Link's direction and shot a series of daggers toward his friend. He said nothing. The moments ticked by, and Link began to fidget.

At last the major cleared his throat. "Simpson? I asked you a question. Do you intend to stick with your insane friend here, or are you going to be smart and accept my offer for OCS?"

"Yes, sir," Stork said after a long and uncomfortable silence.

"Yes *what?*" the major roared.

"Yes, sir . . . that is, I appreciate it, sir, but Link and I, we . . ."

"I see." Major Mansfield shrugged. "Just for the record, I think you're *both* crazy." He moved behind his desk, picked up a sheaf of papers, and tore them in half. "You just lost your last chance for OCS," he said curtly. "And since you'll be staying with us, I have a new assignment for both of you."

Link closed his eyes. "And what is that, sir?" he asked tentatively.

"Gas school." The major grabbed a pen and scratched his signature on the bottom of a single sheet of paper. "Your orders are to report tomorrow morning to Building 6 on the east side of the base. You boys are going to learn everything known to the army about chemical weapons."

Stork looked at Link with a despairing gaze, and Link raised his eyebrows as if to say, *I have no idea.*

Mansfield handed the assignment order to Winsom and returned to his desk. "Dismissed, Sergeant," he said.

Link took the paper and saluted, then turned on his heel. He had his hand on the doorknob when the word sank in: *Sergeant.*

"Sergeant, sir?" Link repeated.

"Yes, sergeant. Both of you. You'll get your stripes at dinner tonight."

Link beamed. "Yes, sir. Thank you, sir!" Grabbing Stork by the arm, he headed out the door.

★ ★ ★

Stork strode through the camp without looking back. He could hear Link running to keep up with him, but he didn't turn around.

"Stork! Wait!" Link gasped. "What's wrong?"

Stork wheeled to face him. "What's *wrong?* You just blew our last chance to get out of this mudhole, that's what's wrong!"

His buddy looked at him without comprehension, a crestfallen expression on his face. He really *didn't* understand, the idiot. They could have had it all—leadership, prestige, more money. . . .

But, no. This crazy man, his best friend, had to turn it down, all because of some insane notion that God was protecting them from being killed by keeping them from a commission as officers.

Stork glared at Winsom. His friend's dark eyes registered confusion. Link was handsome, in a rakish sort of way, with that lean Frank Sinatra build that women these days found irresistible. And he had charm. He could talk his way into—or out of—anything. He could have gone far as an officer, and Stork could have gone with him.

Instead, Stork was going with him to gas school.

"Stork?" Link repeated. "What's the matter?"

Stork turned on him fiercely. "Gas school!" He spat the words out vengefully. "You turned down OCS for gas school!"

Link dropped his gaze and lifted his shoulders. "I couldn't help it, Stork. I just couldn't see us—"

"You couldn't see *us?*" Stork repeated. "Just when did I give you permission to run my life for me? To make decisions for *us* . . . and in front of the major, no less, without a word of discussion?"

Link turned his schoolboy grin on Stork—the expression he always used when he was trying to get his own way. "You agreed to it."

"I *agreed*," Stork said acidly, "because we're *friends*. Buddies. Friends stick together. It's called *loyalty.*"

Link nodded eagerly. "And I appreciate it, buddy. This will turn out all right; you'll see. Gas school will be a breeze. And it will get us out of training with those imbecile college kids. Besides," he went on in a rush, "you heard the major. We've been promoted to sergeant. More freedom, more money—"

"Not as much as if we were *officers*," Stork responded sullenly.

Link threw an arm around Stork's shoulders and gripped his neck, hard. "Ah, come on, we didn't want to be officers, did we?"

"Oh, of course not." Stork drew the words out sarcastically. "Why would we possibly want to do that? Shoot, we might get a little *respect* . . . and we couldn't stand that, now could we?"

Link looked at him intently. "What good is respect," he said solemnly, "if you're dead?"

Stork heaved a long sigh and gave up. There was no point in fighting it; it was done now, anyway. He might as well make the best of it.

Link must have sensed his resignation. "Let's go, *Sergeant* Simpson," he said lightly. "I'll buy you a steak."

9

✯ ✯ ✯

The Doughboy
and the Debutante

When the doors to the Paradise Garden Cafe swung open, Thelma Breckinridge leaned over the counter to get a better look. She couldn't believe what she was seeing.

But her eyes hadn't deceived her. It was Libba Coltrain—that sweet young daughter of Olivia and Robinson Coltrain, now all grown-up and teaching at the Eden Public School—hanging on the arm of some puppy-faced soldier. The boy couldn't take his eyes off her, and Thelma thought he might melt into a puddle at any second. She was about to go into the kitchen for a mop and pail when Libba stopped her with a high-pitched screech.

"Thelma! Thelma, come over here—I want you to meet somebody."

Libba dragged the boy in by the arm and pushed him into a chair. Before he could say a word, Libba relieved him of the packages he was carrying, dumped them on the table, and plopped down across from him.

By the time they were settled, Thelma had made her way over to the table and stood there with a pad and pencil. "Evenin', Libba. Who's your friend?"

Libba giggled loudly and patted the boy's arm. "This is Freddy Sturgis. He's a soldier at the base."

Thelma nodded. "So I see." She smiled at the boy and extended a hand. She saw, all right. The fellow had the pasty look of unbaked bread dough, and no doubt Libba intended to knead him into a shape that would suit her. "Hello, Freddy. Welcome to the Paradise Garden."

Freddy jumped and looked around as if he expected to find a serpent in the midst of Paradise. "Hello," he murmured, not looking at her.

Libba pointed at the packages. "We've been Christmas shopping," she said, then dropped her voice to a whisper. "In *Memphis.*"

Thelma cocked an eyebrow at Libba. "You've been to Memphis? Libba, you should know better. Your father would kill you if he caught you slipping around with a soldier."

Libba waved a hand in the air. "Aw, Thelma, how's he going to know—unless you tell him, and I know you won't. Daddy never comes into town at this time of night."

"Maybe not," Thelma warned, "but Charity Grevis certainly does, and—"

"Mrs. Grevis . . . your landlady?" Freddy said nervously. "Maybe we'd better go." He reached for the packages on the table, but Libba stopped him with a look.

"Not just yet, Freddy." She glared up at Thelma. "So what if she sees me? I'm not breaking any law of the land, am I?"

"Depends on whose law you're talking about," Thelma said. "Don't forget that your landlady is also the postmistress of this town. She sees your mama every morning, and you know how she loves to talk."

"Mama won't tell Daddy," Libba said, twisting a curl at the nape of her neck. "Besides, what if she did?"

"Your daddy would have your hide, that's what. You know how he feels about soldiers—everybody knows."

At the mention of Libba's father, the doughboy grew even paler. Obviously, Freddy had met Robinson Coltrain—or at least had heard enough about him to be scared out of his wits at the prospect of being face-to-face with the man. Thelma couldn't blame him. For all Robinson Coltrain's "good deeds"—serving as a deacon in the church, calling on the sick with food and prayer, doing his "Christian duty" in the community—the man was a force to be reckoned with. He kept his wife Olivia on a tight leash and, until recently, his daughter as well. Now it appeared that Libba was dead set on rebelling against him, and only the Good Lord knew what the outcome of that rebellion might be. Thelma didn't want to be within miles of the explosion when Robinson found out that Libba was seeing this soldier boy behind his back.

"Libba," Thelma said carefully, "I know you're a big girl and can make your own decisions. But you're asking for trouble. You know how people in this town gossip. There's not two of them can get together without meddling in other people's business. It might be smart for you to go on home before word gets out that you've been flitting across the state line with this boy."

"Who I go out with is nobody's business but my own," Libba protested.

"Maybe not. But your daddy will make it his business if he finds out."

"M-maybe we'd better go," Freddy stammered. "I-I've got to get back to the base soon, anyway."

Libba sighed. "All right, Freddy, we'll go." She stood and began loading the packages into his outstretched arms. With a flourish, she ushered him out the door, then turned to Thelma again. "I may be going home," she said with a conspiratorial wink, "but I'm not going alone."

★ ★ ★

Thelma had just settled down at the counter with the evening edition of the *Commercial Appeal,* out of Memphis, when the bell over the door alerted her to the presence of customers. She dabbed on a bit of lipstick, dropped the tube into her apron pocket, and turned around to see two soldiers standing in the doorway. The taller one, a lean fellow with sandy hair, she had never seen before. The other, with dark eyes and olive skin, seemed vaguely familiar to her.

"Hey, fellas," she called. "Have a seat wherever you like. I'll be with you in a minute."

"Thanks, Thelma," the darker one said. "Take your time."

Thelma. How did he know her name? Where had she seen him before?

Then it came to her—the Yankee-boy soldier on the bus. Of course! He had looked so lonely, so abandoned. Ivory had played for him. And she had told him that he would make friends soon enough.

Well, it seemed that she had been right. The two men acted like they had known each other forever—laughing and talking, punching each other on the shoulder. Thelma watched them for a moment, then went over to their table.

"What can I get for you boys this evening?"

The dark one narrowed his eyes and looked her over. "You can get me the name of the girl who just went out of here on the arm of some puny-looking private."

"Excuse me?"

"The girl, Thelma—auburn hair, kind of curly. High heels. Wonderful laugh."

Thelma stared at him for a minute, then realized he was talking about Libba Coltrain, who had just left with her soldier boy. But she didn't dare give this man Libba's name. Robinson Coltrain would have her neck if she was responsible for Libba taking up with the likes of this soldier. The doughboy was bad enough. This handsome rake would keep Robinson awake nights—and keep Libba in hot water until she was thirty.

When she didn't answer, the dark-eyed soldier laughed. "You don't remember me, do you, Thelma?"

She pretended to be puzzled for a minute, then grinned down at him. "Of course I do, hon. You're the Yankee boy who seemed so lost when you came in here on your way to the base. Link, your name is—like President Lincoln." She chewed on her pencil and whispered, "Only in this part of the country, you'd be better off not pointing out that comparison to just anybody."

Link leaned back in his chair. "So you *do* remember me!"

"I never forget a pretty face," Thelma chuckled. "And I told you you'd always have a friend here at the Paradise Garden. What took you so long coming back?"

"I've been kind of busy," Link said. "You know, getting settled—"

"And making friends," she added. "As I recall, you were feeling pretty low that first morning. Thought God had lost track of you. But he hadn't, you know. It appears he's already sent you a buddy."

Link's brow furrowed as he thought about it. "I guess so," he said at last. "But not a new friend—an old one." He waved a hand at his companion. "This is Stork Simpson. We went through basic together, and then got separated by . . . uh, by circumstances. Strangely enough, he got assigned here, too. I didn't even know it until I ran into him in the USO one day. Quite a coincidence, huh?"

Thelma turned to Stork and shook his hand. "I'm pleased to meet you," she said. "And you're no coincidence, Private Simpson. You're an answer to prayer."

Stork gaped at her. "What do you mean, an answer to prayer?"

Thelma squeezed his shoulder. "It's simple, darlin'—your friend Link here was awful lonely when I first met him. I prayed that God would send him a friend. And I expect he prayed for it too, even if he didn't know he was praying. God answered . . . and you're the answer."

A red flush crept up Stork's neck and into his earlobes. "I've never been an answer to prayer before," he said. "Are you sure?"

"Sure as you're sitting here!" Thelma winked at him and pointed to the wedding ring he was twisting nervously around his finger. "And I bet it's not the first time. You've probably been somebody's answer before—just didn't know it."

Link grinned at Stork, obviously enjoying his embarrassment. "Well, Answer Man!" he said. "Let's get this celebration started!" He turned to Thelma. "We want two of your biggest, juiciest steaks, with all the trimmings."

"What's the occasion?"

"A promotion for the two of us." Link laughed. "And, of course, the answer to your prayer."

★ ★ ★

While Stork went outside to get the jeep, Link went to the register to pay the bill. He had left a generous tip for Thelma, hidden under a steak platter on the table. He still couldn't quite figure the woman out. She didn't look the part, yet she seemed to be a combination of mother love and spiritual guide.

"Did you really pray for me?" Link asked as she counted out his change. He couldn't get over the idea that someone he barely knew had cared enough to speak to God on his behalf.

"'Course I did, darlin'. And I'll keep right on praying, unless you've got some objection."

He shook his head. "No objection. I'd be stupid to object, when your prayers are obviously so well connected."

"All prayers are well connected, hon." She looked him in the eye with an expression that unsettled him. "Long as your heart is right, God hears."

"That's what my father used to tell me," Link said. "But how do you know if your heart is right? I mean, how can you know what God's will is, so that you're not praying for something that's out of line?"

Thelma patted his arm. "You don't have to know everything," she said simply. "That's God's job. Your job is to listen and to learn. God knows what you need, even if you don't."

For a minute Link considered telling her about his conviction that God had kept him and Stork out of Officers' Candidate School to save their lives. But it sounded stupid, and besides, he wasn't sure he hadn't fouled up God's will by turning down their second chance at OCS. Maybe God *wanted* them to be officers, and he had messed things up by refusing the opportunity. He still thought they would be better off as noncoms, but it was all so confusing. She was right about one thing—he didn't know what he needed. But he sure hoped God did.

The jeep pulled up to the front door, and Stork sounded the horn. "I've got to go," Link said. "Thanks for the dinner—and everything."

"Anytime." Thelma closed the cash register drawer and smiled at him. "And remember, if you need a friend—"

"I know—I've always got one here. Thanks, Thelma."

She pointed toward the ceiling. "You've always got one there, too."

Instinctively Link turned his eyes heavenward. He wasn't sure quite what to say, so he turned abruptly and headed toward the door. "Good night, Thelma." In the doorway he wheeled around and grinned at her. "You're not off the hook yet," he said. "I'll get you to give me that girl's name if it takes forever."

Link got into the jeep, and as they pulled out of the parking lot, he looked back through the window. Thelma Breckinridge stood behind the counter, waving, her henna-dyed hair like a bright halo around her face.

10

✯ ✯ ✯

Forbidden Fruit

Willie Coltrain settled the Christmas tree into its base, wiped her hands on her apron, and then stepped back to survey her handiwork.

"Not bad," Mabel Rae commented from the kitchen door. "A little lopsided, but if you turn this side toward the wall . . ."

Willie glared at her sister. Mabel was the ultimate critic. She had a suggestion for everything. She actually told other people how to drive, even though she'd never been behind the wheel of a car in her entire life. It didn't matter if Mabel had *done* a thing or not; she was sure she knew *how* to do it better than anyone else.

Willie stretched her aching back and sighed. Mabel was . . . well, just Mabel. She had been like this since they were children, and she didn't really mean any harm. She just honestly thought that her opinion would automatically be welcomed.

Besides, Willie wasn't really mad at Mabel Rae. It was *Libba* she was irritated with. That girl had no more sense than God gave a goat. The Christmas party they were giving for the older students—*Libba's* students, in point of fact—was tomorrow night, and Libba hadn't lifted a finger to help in the preparations. She didn't cook. She hated doing laundry. She wouldn't be caught dead stomping around in the woods with Willie and Mabel to cut down a tree . . . she might break a nail or scuff up the precious new shoes her soldier boy, Freddy, had given her as an early Christmas present.

Now she had disappeared altogether. They still had to finish the baking, get the chickens plucked for the dinner, and decorate the tree. And Libba was nowhere to be found.

"Where *is* that girl?" Willie muttered for the fifth time.

Mabel shrugged her shoulders as if the question actually called for a response. "Who knows? Off with Freddy somewhere, probably. If her daddy ever finds out she's been sneaking off to see that soldier, he will—"

"He'll kill her, that's what he'll do," Willie snapped. "Strangle her with his own bare hands. Unless I kill her first."

"No, you won't," Mabel said in a consoling tone. "You'll try to get her to help, like you always do. She'll find some way around it, like she always does, and the two of us will end up putting on a wonderful party, only to have her take all the credit."

"You're right, I'm afraid," Willie sighed. "Still, she needs a nice long trip out behind the woodshed."

Mabel grinned broadly. "Can't you just see it?" she giggled. "The two of us, razor strap in hand, dragging her out by her hair to give her a whipping?" She raised her voice an octave, mimicking what they called Libba's whiny-voice: "She'd be yelling, 'Not the woodpile . . . you'll run my new stockings!'" Mabel held on to the kitchen doorpost, laughing until her face turned red.

"But she'd have to wear a hat and gloves for the trip!" Willie added, tears of mirth streaming down her face as she joined in her sister's game.

"And a matching handbag!" Mabel spluttered out, then dissolved into squeals of laughter.

"Mabel," Willie chuckled when she had regained control of herself, "how did we ever get in the same family as Her Royal Highness?"

Mabel wiped her flushed face with a dish towel and shook her head. "This is the South," she said with mocking formality. "Nobody's bloodline is completely pure."

"What's this about bloodlines?"

Libba's voice shocked them into silence. She stood in the open doorway, letting in a gust of raw December wind. Behind her, a short, wavy-haired blond boy in an army uniform waited patiently, his arms filled with packages.

"Hello, Cousins," Libba said breezily as she walked into the apartment. "Say hi to Freddy Sturgis."

★　★　★

So this is the mysterious Freddy, Willie thought as the soldier stumbled past her and dumped his burden onto the living room sofa.

They had heard all about him, of course, had seen his picture prominently displayed on Libba's dressing table. They had even caught a glimpse of him in person once, from a distance, at a USO dance. But Libba had been keeping him under close wraps. She had never even brought him to the apartment—an uncharacteristically prudent move on Libba's part, Willie had to admit. From the beginning, their landlady had been adamant: the crime of entertaining soldiers on the premises carried an immediate sentence of eviction.

Now Freddy stood in their very own living room. Libba had just committed the unpardonable sin, and they might all end up paying for her transgression.

Willie studied Freddy's boyish features. According to Libba's glowing accounts, Freddy was young and strong and ever so handsome in his uniform. He had swept her off her feet immediately and had been trying to convince her to marry him for over a month now. He had a wonderful sense of humor and good potential for becoming an officer. And Libba had been sneaking around behind her father's back to see him ever since that notorious weekend when Freddy had met her parents and made such a questionable first impression.

When Willie heard about the Horrible Dinner, she had sympathized with Libba. Everybody knew how unreasonable and controlling Uncle Robinson could be, how nobody ever pleased him. And she was pretty sure she could imagine her uncle's response when his daughter's beau had confessed that he wanted to be an artist.

Now, looking at Freddy Sturgis in the flesh, Willie wondered if Robinson Coltrain might have been right. For once.

Freddy stood there in the center of the room, shifting nervously from one foot to the other. His eyes darted everywhere, resting only for an instant on the rug under his feet. When Libba made the formal introductions, Freddy didn't look *at* Willie so much as *behind* her, offering a limp, clammy, fishlike hand and forcing a wan smile that never reached his eyes.

At least Libba had gotten one thing right about Freddy. He *was* young— twenty at the most, but a very young twenty. He looked far less sure of himself than some of Libba's seventeen-year-old students at Eden Public School. But Libba's reports of his other qualities—his strength, his sense of humor, his handsome countenance—had obviously been greatly exaggerated.

With his wavy blond hair, Freddy reminded Willie of a cocker spaniel one of her fifth-graders had brought to school one day. And, come to think of it, the puppy image didn't stop there. Freddy had big brown eyes, an overly eager expression, and hands and feet that seemed entirely too big for his small, thin frame. When he moved, he seemed to be walking *around* his feet rather than *on* them, and he kept stuffing his hands into his pockets as if he were afraid they might go off on their own and break something.

Willie had to do something to put this poor boy at ease. "Sit down, make yourself at home," she said. She threw a glance at Libba as if to say, *This is your guest, not mine.* But Libba had already settled herself on the sofa and was sorting through her packages. She didn't even see the look, much less respond to it.

Willie turned to Freddy, who had lighted on the edge of a chair and was twisting his cap in his hands. "Would you like some coffee?" she offered.

He jumped slightly and looked up at her. "Milk, please, if you have it."

★ ★ ★

When Willie rounded the door to the kitchen, Mabel Rae grabbed her by the arm, nearly scaring the wits out of her.

"What do you think you're doing?" Willie whispered fiercely. "Trying to give me heart failure?"

Mabel ignored the question. "What is this?" she whispered back. "Libba knows we can get evicted for entertaining soldiers in this house. Mrs. Grevis watches every move we make, and if she finds out—"

Willie clapped a firm hand over her sister's mouth. "Hush!" she said. "He'll hear you."

Mabel ran her tongue over Willie's palm, a move so completely disgusting that it never failed to make Willie let go.

"Well, I don't care if he *does* hear me!" Mabel continued, her voice rising. "Libba's got no business bringing him here."

"I agree," Willie said, patting her sister's shoulder in an effort to calm her down. "But he's here, and unless you want to shoot him and drag him out by his heels, he's probably going to stay awhile."

She peered around the door frame, shrugged, and turned back to Mabel Rae. "Is this what you expected?"

"Freddy the Wonderful, you mean?" Mabel made a spitting noise with her lips. "Heavens, no. Libba had the audacity to imply that he was much stronger, much braver, than Charlie ever thought about being—and here Charlie's at the front, wounded for his country! I can't believe it—she made him sound like a blond Tyrone Power."

Willie poked Mabel in the ribs. "Did you say 'blond' or 'bland'?"

Mabel began to giggle, and Willie felt laughter rising up in her and threatening to take over—the kind of laughter that comes out in snorts if you try to stifle it. She put one hand over her mouth, and her whole body shook.

"What's so funny out there?" Libba's voice drifted in from the living room.

Willie and Mabel Rae straightened up suddenly. "Nothing," Willie called. Her eyes darted around the kitchen and lighted on Mabel's bowl of spiced apple rings. With a flick of one hand she sent the bowl clattering to the floor. Apples and cinnamon sauce went everywhere. "Mabel just made a mess," Willie said. "That's all."

Mabel tried to glare at her, but it just didn't work. Both of them gave in to fits of hysterical giggling. Still wiping her tears, Willie reached into the icebox for the milk bottle. She poured a glass full, slopping it on the counter, then wiped off the bottom of the glass and headed for the living room.

At the door she heaved a sigh, trying to calm herself, but her hand was still shaking when she handed Freddy his milk. Her lips twitched, and she avoided his eyes.

"What's the matter with you, Willie?" Libba demanded, glancing up from her inventory of Christmas presents.

Willie smiled broadly. "Not a thing, Libba," she answered. "Mabel and I were just discussing how nice it was to finally meet Freddy."

She turned to the soldier. "We've heard so much about you, Freddy," she began. Then he turned his innocent gaze up to her. A narrow mustache of milk graced his upper lip. Without another word, Willie dashed back into the kitchen.

★ ★ ★

Later that evening, when Libba returned from saying good-night to Freddy, Willie and Mabel Rae were waiting for her.

Libba waltzed into the apartment, dropped her coat in the center of the living-room floor, and did a little pirouette around the coffee table. "Isn't he just the most wonderful?" she breathed.

Willie and Mabel Rae exchanged a significant glance. *To the woodshed,* Mabel mouthed. Willie grinned in her sister's direction, then turned back to Libba.

"How could you?" she said.

The rapturous expression on Libba's face never wavered. "How could I what?" she asked languidly.

"You know perfectly well what," Mabel put in. "Mrs. Grevis would have our necks if she caught us entertaining a soldier in her apartment."

"Don't be so stuffy," Libba said. "We're having men in for our Christmas party tomorrow, and Old Lady Graveyard approved that. Besides, we didn't get caught."

"Getting caught is beside the point," Willie snapped. "Mrs. Grevis agreed to let us have *students* here for the party. She's been very nice to us, and—"

"Nice to us?" Libba rolled her eyes in exasperation. "We pay her enough to be twice as nice . . . and enough that she should give us some heat!" She walked over to the radiator and raised her handbag to pound on the pipes.

Willie took two steps across the room and grabbed Libba's hand in midair. "It's ten o'clock!" she hissed. "Have a little consideration. You're just cold because you've been out in the dark for an hour smooching with Freddy."

Libba smiled sweetly and fluttered her eyelids. "Ya'll are just jealous," she murmured, "because I've got a fella."

Mabel uttered a snort of contempt. "Is that what you call him?"

Libba jerked around and fixed Mabel with a withering glare. "What kind of comment is that?"

Willie shot a warning glance at her sister, but Mabel ignored it. "He's a mouse, Cousin, not a man! He's a weak-livered jellyfish of a boy who fawns over you like some moonstruck adolescent. For heaven's sake, Libba, you made him out to be some kind of Clark Gable . . . Rhett Butler in a soldier suit—"

Libba silenced Mabel Rae with a poisonous look that reminded Willie— just for a moment—of Uncle Robinson. Did Libba have any idea that she was in danger of turning out to be just like her daddy?

Evidently not. For Libba's next words shocked both Willie and Mabel Rae into disbelieving silence.

"I'm going to marry him," she said fiercely. "As soon as we can make the arrangements."

When she finally recovered her voice, Willie asked the only question she could think of. "Do you love this boy, Libba?"

Libba's eyes flitted around the room, and for just a moment, her face went pale. Then she straightened her shoulders and looked her cousin directly in the eye. Willie saw a kind of desperation there, the look of a wild thing caught in a snare.

"Love has nothing to do with it," Libba said finally. "I can love any man who is willing to take me out of Daddy's clutches."

She stood there for a moment, biting her lip, her hands fumbling in front of her as she picked at her cuticles. "Freddy's a nice boy," she added lamely. "It'll be all right; you'll see."

Then she snatched up her coat, ran into her bedroom, and slammed the door behind her.

Willie shook her head and looked miserably at Mabel Rae. "Come on, Sister," she said. "We've got a party to prepare for." Without another word, she turned and headed for the kitchen.

11

☆ ☆ ☆

A Gift for Charlie

Charlie Coltrain watched as Boz Hamilton lifted himself from his cot and swung onto his crutches. The boy's ruddy face bore the unmistakable signs of exertion and pain, but the wide smile never wavered. With a flourish, Boz catapulted himself across the ward, wheeled around, and came back to stand, panting and grinning, over Charlie's bed.

"How about that, Charlie?" he wheezed. "I did good, huh?"

"Yeah, Boz," Charlie answered absently. "Real good."

Boz sank to the bed, still gripping his crutches, and pointed to the empty space where his right leg should have been. Gangrene had set in, and the doctors had finally decided to amputate at the hip. "I still wish they could have saved it," he murmured, half to himself. "Sometimes at night I still feel it throbbing—ghost pains, Doc calls it."

"Ghost pains?" Charlie repeated. "Don't you mean *phantom* pains?"

"Oh, yeah, I guess so." A frown passed over Boz's boyish features. "Phantom pains. Right." Then the irrepressible smile returned.

Of late, Charlie had begun to wonder whether any human being in its natural state could be that positive or if Bosworth Hamilton was just a shade too slow to understand the gravity of his situation. Whatever the case, the boy's enthusiasm and cheerfulness rarely flagged. Maybe he wasn't playing with a full set of marbles, but he sure seemed happier and more content than Charlie was. Perhaps his way—the way of blissful ignorance—was better.

"You remind me of the Riddle of the Sphinx," Charlie commented.

"Huh?"

"The Sphinx," Charlie repeated. "In Greek mythology. My sister Mabel Rae told me about it. Some hero—I forget who—was supposed to solve a riddle: *What goes on four legs in the morning, two legs at noon, and three legs in the evening?*"

Boz gave Charlie a blank look.

"The answer," Charlie explained, "is man. In the morning, when he's an infant, he crawls; at noon, as an adult, he walks upright; in the evening, when he is old, he goes with a cane—three legs. With your crutches, you go on three legs, only you do it at noon."

Boz frowned. "I don't get it," he said. "What difference does the time of day make?"

Charlie shook his head. Trying to carry on a conversation with this boy was like talking to a fence post. "Never mind," he muttered. "It's not important."

Shrugging, Boz heaved himself onto his crutches and headed for the door.

When he was alone again in his little corner of the ward, Charlie lay down and turned his face to the wall. His fingers sought out the scar on his upper arm, and he stroked the ropy tissue absently. The wound had long since healed; it didn't hurt anymore, except for an occasional twinge when the weather was about to change. Yet here he was, still in the hospital, still unable to return to his unit. Still afraid.

Would it ever end—the nightmares, the memories, the shakes and sweats? How could he call himself a soldier, much less a man, when he couldn't get over this? He should have been back at the front by now, slogging it out in the mud with his buddies. But he could barely make it through the days, and sometimes he wasn't sure he could endure another night without going completely insane.

The doctor, an even-tempered young physician from Minnesota named Leland Carter, assured him that he wasn't the only victim of shell shock in this terrible war. The VA hospitals in the States were setting up whole wards for people like him, with doctors trained to help soldiers overcome what Carter called "the unseen ravages of battle."

As nice and understanding as Dr. Carter had been, Charlie couldn't imagine being confined to one of those wards, being awakened in the middle of the night by screams other than his own. If he wasn't crazy now, he soon would be if he had to be put in one of those loony bins.

And what would his family think—and his friends back home? Nobody there understood shell shock any better than Charlie himself did. They would think he was nuts, that he was just a coward who couldn't take it. He'd rather die than shame himself and his family that way.

Then a thought struck him: *Maybe that was his answer.*

For weeks Charlie had been praying for a way out. He wasn't as good a Christian as his mother and his sister Willie, but he knew enough about God to believe that God listened to his prayers. Chaplain Faderman had encouraged him to talk to God, to seek strength and guidance. The Lord would lead him, the chaplain said, and help him know what to do. Maybe God would even heal him miraculously, like Jesus healed the leper in the New Testament.

The image stung Charlie far more deeply than the chaplain could have known. For in his own mind, Charlie *was* a leper—an outcast, an untouchable. He was a coward, and cowards didn't deserve acceptance in society.

Yet despite his shame and his sense of unworthiness, Charlie had prayed for God to help him. God knew he didn't want to be this way, afraid and unable to perform his duty as a soldier. But Charlie also didn't think he could kill again—not haunted as he was by the look of terror and accusation in the dead German's eye.

He needed a way out.

Maybe death was the only way. Maybe this was his answer from God.

A nagging voice in the back of Charlie's mind made him hesitate. He vaguely remembered something about God being the "Lord of life," and he knew instinctively that his mother and sisters wouldn't accept this as God's answer to his prayers. But if God was a God of love, he wouldn't want Charlie to live the rest of his life like this, would he?

Charlie took a deep breath and closed his eyes. He felt a sense of tranquility sweep over him like a warm breeze—a peace like nothing he had ever known. God was leading him, he just knew it. This had to be his answer, his way of escape.

But Charlie couldn't just get his hands on a weapon and shoot himself. There was no honor in that; it would shame his family even more than his present dilemma. No, it had to be death on the field of battle. If he could just get back to the front, he wouldn't have to kill anyone. All he would have to do was stand there and die. Everyone back home thought he was a hero, and he had perpetuated the deception because he didn't know what else to do. Well, if they wanted a hero, he would give them a hero. He might not be able to live with dignity, but he could die with dignity.

He just had to figure out how.

How could he manage to get back to the front lines and into battle, where he had a good chance of being killed, when he could barely get up in the morning? How could he convince a medical team that he was fit for service when he couldn't hold a cup of coffee, much less an M-1, without shaking uncontrollably? And most importantly, how could he pull it off without endangering the lives of others in his company?

The main problem, he finally decided, was Dr. Carter. The man knew him too well—knew the limitations of his condition. He would never allow Charlie to go back to the front in his present mental state. It would be too dangerous, both for Charlie and for those around him. The army couldn't afford the risk.

No, Charlie knew that Carter would never buy the "miraculous recovery" angle. But he was determined not to give up. This was the answer God had given him--to die with honor rather than live in dishonor. God had led him this far. He would keep on praying until God showed him how it could be accomplished.

★   ★   ★

A gentle hand shook Charlie awake. He blinked, trying to focus his eyes, and at last the familiar face of Dr. Leland Carter came into view.

"Oh, hey, Doc," Charlie said, raking a hand through his hair. "I must have dozed off." He swung his legs over the side of the cot and sat up.

"It's OK." The doctor sat down beside him and scribbled a few notes on the clipboard in his lap. "Sleep will do you good—unless you start sleeping too much."

"What time is it?"

"Almost eighteen hundred."

"Six o'clock," Charlie mumbled. "Did I miss chow?"

Carter laughed and shook his head. "No. Although when you see it, you might wish you had."

"Mystery meat again?" Charlie shook his head. "I guess it's better than C rations."

"Even in the States, hospital food leaves a lot to be desired," the doctor said. "But you may just get the chance to find out."

Charlie straightened up. "What are you talking about?"

Dr. Carter grinned. "I've got a surprise for you, Charlie. A big surprise. You might call it the best Christmas present you've ever had. You're going home, soldier."

"Home? What do you mean, home?"

"I mean home. To the States. Specifically, to Memphis, Tennessee—that is the closest VA hospital to your family, isn't it?"

"Yes, but—"

"But nothing. The army is setting up a shell-shock treatment center at Kennedy General in Memphis. You'll be close to your family, and—"

"No!" Charlie stammered. "I won't . . . I mean, I can't. Doc, don't force me to do this!"

Obviously, Charlie's reaction wasn't quite what the doctor had expected. A disappointed look shadowed Carter's face. He set his clipboard down on the cot and turned to face Charlie squarely. "Look, Charlie, I've done a lot of legwork on this thing. They can treat you there, give you help that I can't. You've been here for months, and, frankly, you haven't made much measurable progress." Dr. Carter shook his head. "This is a field hospital, Charlie. Our job is to fix soldiers up and get them back to the front—or if they can't be fixed, to send them on somewhere else. Look at your buddy Hamilton. He's about to be shipped back to the States, too, and you don't see him resisting."

Charlie raised his chin resolutely. "Boz lost his leg, Doc, not his mind. He's got no reason to resist."

"And you do?"

"You bet I do. What makes you think I want to go home, where people will talk about me behind my back and try to be nice to my face?"

"You were wounded in the line of duty, Charlie, just like Hamilton was."

"It's not the same, and you know it. What will people think when they find out I've been sent home, only to be confined to some crazy ward at the VA?"

"They'll think you've had a difficult time over here—and you have."

"No, they won't. They'll think I'm a coward who couldn't cut it. They'll think I'm nuts. The people who can't avoid me will pity me. What kind of life is that?"

"It's life, Charlie. It's home. It's a chance to get better."

"Not for me. My family is proud of me. They think I'm a—" Charlie stopped. He had said too much, and he knew it. His goose was cooked.

"They think you're a hero." Dr. Carter paused. "You haven't told them, have you, Charlie?"

"No." Charlie could barely get the word out, and he couldn't look Carter in the eye.

"Look at me, Charlie."

Charlie shook his head.

"Look at me!"

Charlie raised his eyes and saw in the doctor's face an expression, not of contempt, but of compassion.

"I think I understand," Carter said softly.

"No, I don't think you do," Charlie responded. "But I sure hope you're trying."

The doctor picked up his clipboard and flipped through Charlie's chart. For a minute or two he said nothing. Then he scratched his head. "Maybe there's another way."

"What other way?"

"You can't stay here any longer," Carter said. "But I might be able to get you transferred to Birmingham—"

"Alabama?"

"England. There's a hospital there, a good one. They don't have a shell-shock ward as such, but I know a doctor on the staff who has had good results with treatments. You might be able to stay there a few months and maybe get back on your feet again."

"And then what?" Charlie felt a surge of hope. This might be his answer.

Carter shrugged. "It all depends on you, I guess. Some of the men have actually gone back to their units—or been transferred to units behind the lines, where they're less likely to see action and end up with a relapse. A lot of the commanders are skeptical about taking on a soldier who's been hospitalized for shell shock, for obvious reasons. But if a soldier is determined enough, he just might make it work." The doctor paused. "To be honest, Charlie, I can't see you getting back to the front lines. But then I doubt that's what you'd be aiming for anyway."

"What I'd be aiming for," Charlie said, "is to get out of this war with some honor." It was not the complete truth, of course, not the way Dr. Carter would interpret it. But Carter didn't need to know what Charlie really meant.

The doctor stood and held out his hand to Charlie. "OK, pal, I'll see what I can do. You keep a good thought. By January or early February, we may have you on your way to merry old England."

★ ★ ★

Charlie leaned back on his bed and sighed. It was almost a miracle, he thought. He had prayed for a way out, and God—or somebody—had opened a door for him.

Once he was at the hospital in England, away from Dr. Carter, he could get his plan in motion. Carter had said *If a soldier is determined enough, he just might make it work.* . . . Well, he was determined, all right—determined to convince this new doctor in Birmingham that he was OK. He had a purpose, a direction.

It didn't matter that his ultimate purpose was to die. Death didn't scare

Charlie, not in the way life scared him. He could face dying; he just couldn't face living like this for the rest of his life.

If he could get to Birmingham, he'd have a chance. A chance at the front lines. An opportunity to give his life for a noble cause—in this case, not the world's freedom, but his own.

Charlie held out his hand in front of him: steady as a rock. A smile crept across his face; it felt foreign and strange, but he liked it. He could do this. He could fake it . . . not forever, but long enough.

For the first time in nearly five months, Charlie Coltrain caught a glimpse of light—just a sliver—at the end of his long, dark tunnel. God had answered his prayers. He had a path to walk, a destiny to meet. And his journey would begin in Birmingham.

12

★ ★ ★

Christmas Blues

Stork Simpson sat alone at a table in the USO, nursing his root beer and waiting for Winsom to show up. Where could the scoundrel be? They had parted company after another dull morning at gas school, bored to distraction by the incessant dronings of Lieutenant Farnam. Farnam had been a high school chemistry teacher before the war. He had obviously found his niche in the army hierarchy—unimaginatively teaching the incomprehensible to the unwilling.

The twelve-week gas school training program could have been summarized in one sentence, needlepointed, framed, and hung over the door: PUT YOUR GAS MASKS ON. But, no, the army could never do anything in a reasonable, logical manner. Instead, he and Winsom were wasting half of every day staring blankly at charts of poisonous molecules, as if they would need a microscope to determine that the Germans had blasted mustard gas into the foxhole.

The other half of every day they wasted in a more enjoyable manner. Shortly after their reassignment, Link had discovered that Major Minefield really knew nothing about what was going on in Chemical Weapons Training. He thought, poor deluded man, that they were actually learning something practical, something that could save lives and significantly contribute to the ongoing freedom of the Western world. He had no idea that they were much more likely to be bored to death than to be gassed into oblivion. And so he had relieved Stork and Link of all their other duties so that they could concentrate on the important task of learning how to prepare for impending chemical disaster.

They spent the first three hours of every day with two dozen other bored noncoms and junior officers, doodling on pads of cheap army paper while Farnam explained in his coma-inducing monotone about the chemical properties of gases and their potentially lethal combinations. At noon, they were dismissed with assignments that no one ever completed and Farnam never mentioned again.

But because of the reassignment, they were permitted to take their meals in the Officers' Mess and use the Officers' Club whenever they liked. All they had to do was flash their gas school ID cards, and the whole east side of the base was at their command.

Link made the most of the privilege, and Stork went along for the ride.

Daily they dined on chicken and fish and huge broiled T-bones, while their comrades in B Company ate mystery meat and powdered mashed potatoes that were alternately runny as grits or stiff as biscuit dough. They lounged in plush leather chairs and hobnobbed with the Big Brass, while the enlisted men who served their dinners shot envious glances at them from across the room.

Several times a week Link would charm his way into the good graces of the ordnance clerk and, on the pretense of running errands for Farnam, commandeer a jeep to drive into Grenada and take in the nightlife at a little club just off the square. Mississippi was a dry state, but the lack of alcohol didn't matter to Link. He didn't drink; he was only interested in the bevy of girls in flashy dresses who hovered around him like flies around a honey pot.

Link figured they had it made . . . at least for the next nine weeks.

Stork had to agree. This was certainly better than running training maneuvers with the new draftees on the steep wooded slopes of Duckback Hill or taking full-pack marches for miles up and down the dusty red gravel roads of Tullahoma County.

Still, Stork had a nagging fear that the Day of Judgment was just around the corner . . . that Major Minefield would discover the truth about their "important assignment" and pull the plug on their good times—perhaps on their careers as well.

He looked at his watch and took another swig of his root beer. Link was supposed to meet him here an hour ago. He was probably off with one of the girls from the nightclub, spending every dime of the back pay that had finally caught up with them, getting in a little pre-Christmas celebrating.

Well, Stork could use the time to himself. He was tired of sneaking around, tired of the late nights and wild life. Tired of everything. It was almost Christmas, and he desperately wanted to go home.

He pushed his glass aside and slid his clipboard in front of him. He might as well finish his letter to Madge, the one he had started today during class. Every day since gas school started, he had spent his three hours with Farnam writing long, passionate letters to his wife. Farnam never noticed; in fact, he probably thought Stork was his most diligent student, taking notes incessantly from the moment he walked into class.

Stork looked down at the half-finished letter and sighed. Link's waitress friend, Thelma, had called him an "answer to prayer," implying that his wife had found God's answer in him. But the idea didn't comfort him; in fact, it made him all the more aware of his shortcomings, the ways he had betrayed Madge and let her down. He scanned the words halfheartedly:

> Dearest Madge,
>
> I'm sorry to hear that you're having so much trouble with Mother. She doesn't mean to be difficult, I'm sure, but she is probably having a tough time, worrying about what might happen to me. And since she was never able to have any more children after I was born, she is no doubt jealous of our good fortune in expecting a child so soon.

Good fortune? How much of a liar could he be to his own wife? The baby was anything *but* good fortune! An extra mouth to feed, no money to speak of, and him stuck in this backwater camp, no doubt on his way to Europe or the Pacific Rim shortly after the delivery. Besides, his mother probably *was* intentionally difficult. She had never approved of Madge, even before the wedding; she thought no woman would ever be good enough for her little boy . . . least of all a "cheap tramp" who "trapped" him into a commitment.

Madge's letters had deliberately downplayed the misery of living with his parents, Stork was certain. She tried to make the best of it, but he knew his mother was not easily pleased, especially when she got her mind set against someone. She didn't forgive readily, and her "martyr act," as Stork called it, was well refined, capable of loading guilt onto the most resistant victim.

Madge, he knew, wasn't strong enough to stand up to her. She probably spent her nights crying herself to sleep. And it was all his fault.

> I've sent presents for you and the baby, although he (or she) won't have arrived by Christmas. I'll try to get to a phone and call you on Christmas Eve.
>
> I miss you, darling Madge. I think of you every day and pray that you are well and happy. Even though we can't be together,

> I am with you in my heart . . . always. I trust God to take care of
> you, and

Stork stared at the last line, where he had broken off the letter when Farnam had dismissed class. Another lie. Did he really *trust God* for Madge? Did he really pray?

Madge believed in God—the personal, involved kind of God Link had referred to when he had pulled the unbelievable stunt of turning down OCS. Madge had standards, based on deeply held moral principles. She loved him desperately, but she had insisted that they postpone sexual intimacy until after they were married. Their love, she said, was strong enough to wait.

But Stork wasn't strong enough.

He had pressured her, using all the tired old arguments designed to break down her resistance. He might go off to the front and never see her again. If she really loved him, she would give him what he wanted. And the worst betrayal of all: Because he loved her so much, they were already married in the sight of God.

In the end, it had worked. On a steamy Saturday night, amid the blazing fireworks of a Fourth of July celebration, his insistent passion had finally overwhelmed all of Madge's good intentions. They made love that night in the backseat of his best friend's DeSoto, a cramped and frantic coupling fueled by the fear of discovery. In the heat of his own desire, Stork hadn't given a thought to how it might affect Madge.

Afterward, as they drove home in a blinding rainstorm, Madge clung to the passenger door and sobbed, trembling with shame and despair. For a long time they sat in the car outside the tiny house she shared with a girlfriend. He tried to comfort her, but she shrank away from his embrace. Over and over again he pleaded with her, telling her that everything was all right, that they hadn't done anything wrong. But she wouldn't hear a word of it. She just kept saying that she had lost everything—her virginity, her dignity, even her faith.

The discussion had degenerated rapidly into a fight, ending with Madge slamming the car door and running into the house. Five days later, Stork entered basic training. The next time he heard from her was in a tear-stained letter when she told him she was pregnant.

They got married as soon as he was able to wangle a three-day pass, defying the strident objections of his mother. But the marriage hadn't solved much. Madge was calmer, more resigned to her role as wife and soon-to-be mother. She tried to put on a cheerful front for his sake, but in her unguarded moments she let her sadness show. He could hear it in her letters and in her voice on the telephone.

Stork truly loved Madge. But he couldn't get away from the nagging feeling that he had spoiled something infinitely precious for her. Maybe that was why he kept mentioning God and prayer in his daily letters. If he believed in God, or convinced her that he did, maybe it would make her happy.

And maybe, after all, it wasn't a lie. Maybe he *was* coming to believe for himself. At the very least, even if he didn't know how to pray, he *hoped* God would give his wife some measure of comfort and joy. Especially now. Especially at Christmas, with a baby on the way.

Stork picked up his government-issue pen and tried to resume the letter. But words wouldn't come. What could he say to this lovely, fragile girl? How could he compensate her for the high price she had paid for loving him?

★ ★ ★

Stork jumped when he felt a hand shaking his shoulder. He raised his head groggily and peered at the face that swam in a haze above him. He must have fallen asleep. The watery remains of his root beer still sat at his elbow; the pages of his letter were scattered over the table.

Link was looking down at him, a mischievous expression on his face. "Come on, Stork!" he said. "We've got to go!"

Stork straightened up and ran a hand through his hair. "Go where?" he muttered stupidly. "What time is it?"

"Time for a surprise," Link said, narrowing his eyes in what must have been intended as a mysterious look.

"Ah, leave me alone," Stork snapped. Couldn't the man see he was in no mood for games? "I've got things to do."

"Nothing so important as this," Link said. "Get on your feet, man—I've got a Christmas present for you."

Link grabbed his arm and pulled him up. Muttering under his breath, Stork gathered up his clipboard and letter and followed Link to the door.

★ ★ ★

By the time they got to Grenada, Stork was really mad. Link would tell him nothing; he just kept repeating, "Don't ask any questions; it's a surprise."

Stork half expected them to pull up in front of the little nightclub Link was so fond of. He grew angrier by the minute. When they rounded the square in Grenada, Stork was just about to say, "Let me out, Winsom; I'm not in the mood for a party." But before the words could reach his tongue, Link drove right past the nightclub and jerked to a stop in front of the Jefferson House, a six-columned antebellum wonder which, according to all reports, boasted a parlor decorated in period antiques and the best restaurant east of the Mississippi.

Stork stared at Link. "What are we doing here?"

"You'll see."

"I can't afford this place," Stork protested.

"You can tonight. Tonight's special." Link waved one hand in the air like an orchestra director. "You've got to ac-cen-tuate the positive. . . ."

Stork groaned. Another of Winsom's crazy schemes, no doubt. "What's so special about tonight?"

"It's Christmas Eve eve, man. Peace on earth, goodwill to men . . . stuff like that."

Link hustled him out of the jeep and up the front steps. Once inside, Stork turned to register another protest, but found himself unable to speak. The opulence of the place left him breathless—crystal chandeliers, ornately carved walnut furniture, carpets so deep he could almost feel the softness through his boots.

"Ah," Stork said at last. "This is beautiful."

Link grinned at him. "Merry Christmas, buddy."

Stork gaped at him. "What do you mean, Merry Christmas?"

Link fished in his pocket and came up with several folded papers. While Stork looked on in wonder, his friend unfolded them one by one and presented them with a flourish. "A three-day pass," Link said, bowing grandly, "signed by Major Minefield himself. And—" He handed Stork a gilt-edged card. "A voucher for three nights in the finest room the Jefferson House has to offer . . . meals included."

"What—?" Stork began.

"Don't interrupt," Link commanded. He took Stork's arm and guided him into the parlor to the left—a softly lit room filled with plush chairs arranged in intimate conversation areas.

"And the grand finale," Link announced. "A suitable companion for your stay."

Link pointed. There, on the other side of the parlor, stood a frail-looking girl with dark hair and a gray cloth coat, a coat that didn't quite reach around her bulging middle.

Stork's heart leaped into his throat and began to pound. Tears rose up in his eyes until he could barely see. In three strides he crossed the room, grabbed Madge in his arms, and lifted her off the floor. He could hardly believe it! His Madge, here, for an entire weekend—for Christmas!

His arms tightened around her, and Stork thought his heart would burst. If he died tonight, heaven could not be more wonderful than this moment with the woman he loved.

At last Stork turned and looked over his shoulder at his friend. Link stood there, grinning, his arms full of packages—the Christmas presents he was supposed to have mailed to Madge two weeks ago. Without a word, Link set the gifts down in a chair, saluted smartly, and disappeared into the night.

TWO

Green Eyes

MARCH 1944

13

$$\star \quad \star \quad \star$$

The Birmingham Connection

Army General Hospital
Birmingham, England
March 1944

All eyes followed Charlie Coltrain as he slowly made his way down the corridor to Ward 6-B of the Birmingham hospital. He could feel their gazes, sense their questions and their hostility: *What's the Yank doing here? Doesn't look wounded to me.*

Charlie took a deep breath. He would ignore them. He would have to if his plan was going to work. He would have to be stronger than he had ever been before, particularly since Messina. He would have to prove to the new doctor that he was well enough to go back to the front.

Then a thought occurred to him, and Charlie smiled to himself. God had done his part in getting him out of Italy even though it had taken nearly a month longer than he expected. God had led him here, answered his prayers. Unorthodox prayers, to be sure, but Willie always said that God had purposes far beyond the ones mankind understood. God had given him one more chance—a chance to make things right—and Charlie was determined not to let God—or his family—down. They deserved a hero, not a coward.

Charlie had just finished unpacking his duffel bag when a squint-eyed orderly sidled up to his bed. The man had a long nose, a narrow forehead, and a definite overbite. He opened his mouth to speak, revealing yellow buck teeth. In a flash, Charlie caught a mental image of himself when he was eight years old, nose to nose with a huge rat in the corner of the barn loft. A shudder ran through him.

"Doc wants to see you in his office, guv'nor."

Charlie stared and said nothing.

"Guv'nor?" The man reached out a claw and shook Charlie's arm. "I say, Yank, you heard me, right?"

Charlie nodded. "Yeah, OK."

"Righto. Follow me, if you will."

The rat scuttled through the ward and down the hall with Charlie on his heels. He led Charlie into a small office where a distinguished and very British-looking man with salt-and-pepper hair sat behind a desk reading from a clipboard.

Without knocking, the orderly entered the office and leaned on the edge of the desk. "Here's your patient, Doc," he said. "He's an odd one, if you ask me."

The doctor looked up with an expression that clearly indicated that he had not, in fact, asked. "Thank you, Dillingham. That will be all."

The orderly slunk from the room, muttering under his breath, and closed the door behind him.

The doctor stood and extended his hand. "Dr. Alexander Worthington," he said with a smile. "You must be Charles Coltrain."

"Charlie."

"All right, then, Charlie it is. Welcome to Birmingham." Worthington settled himself behind the desk. "Do sit down." He motioned to a threadbare armchair and began flipping through the pages of the chart in front of him.

"I see you've met Dillingham," Worthington began.

Charlie suppressed a shiver. "He reminds me of a rat."

The doctor gave a throaty chuckle. "Very perceptive. And, like most Americans, very blunt and to the point."

"Sorry, Doc. I didn't mean to be rude." Charlie felt himself redden. "I—"

"Don't give it a second thought. As a matter of fact, I tend to find American directness rather appealing. We British are characteristically reserved, as you may have noticed."

Charlie nodded.

"But it's ever so much better to be honest with one's feelings, don't you agree? Keeps things on the up-and-up, in a manner of speaking."

Charlie averted his eyes. *Better to be honest.* Something in him hated the thought of deceiving this likable man. And yet his entire mission, the determination that drove him to be here in the first place, demanded that he put on a false face and that he play the role as if his life depended on it.

He took a deep breath and met the doctor's placid gaze. "I couldn't agree more, Dr. Worthington. Honest and up-front. After all, I won't make much progress if I don't face the truth."

The doctor smiled into Charlie's eyes.

Hold on, Charlie told himself. *Don't look away. Show him how strong you are.* His heart pounded and his palms began to sweat, but he forced himself to remain calm.

Just as Charlie was beginning to waver, Worthington looked down at his chart and said, "Now, let's take a look at what we have here, shall we?"

Charlie heaved an inward sigh of relief and gripped the arms of his chair.

"Dr. Carter, your physician at the field hospital in Italy, has provided me with a detailed account of your . . . ah, experiences. You were wounded at Messina?"

Charlie nodded. "Shrapnel through the upper right arm."

"The wound healed cleanly, but you exhibited signs of—" Worthington paused.

"It's OK, Doc, you can say it." Charlie forced a smile. "Severe shell shock."

The doctor raised his head and adjusted his glasses. "You seem remarkably well adjusted for a man who has a history of—"

"Nightmares, sweats and chills, shakes?" Charlie finished. He folded his hands in his lap and looked directly into Worthington's eyes. "When I first came to the hospital from the battalion aid station, everything was very fresh in my mind. It was an ambush, Doc—totally unexpected. I saw a kid blown to bits before my eyes. Then I came to in a ditch next to a German soldier with half his face blown off. And yeah, I had a hard time dealing with it at first. But I'm better now . . . you can see that for yourself."

"According to Dr. Carter's records, you were making very little progress before you were sent here."

Charlie fought for breath. "Dr. Carter was a very nice man," he said at last. "Tried to help people, you know?" He lowered his voice. "I think he wanted to send me home, and the only way he could justify it was to say I was . . . well, not getting better."

Dr. Worthington leaned forward. "Didn't you want to go home, Charlie?"

"Of course I want to go home." Charlie's mind spun, searching for words. He had to do this right—had to make this British doctor believe him. "But not like that. There's a war on, Doc, and I've got a job to do. I want to go home, but not until I've finished what I came for."

The doctor sat back in his chair. "Am I correct in assuming, then, that you wish to be returned to duty?"

"As soon as I'm able," Charlie said. He didn't want Worthington to think he was too eager. He might get suspicious, and that would ruin everything. "I don't want to put anyone else in danger, of course, and I know how the guys—especially the brass—feel about shell shock. They don't trust fellows like me, and that's understandable. But once you feel that I'm ready, yes, I'd like to go back. I owe that much to my country—and to myself."

Dr. Worthington peered intently into Charlie's face, as if searching for a sign—a clue to what was really going on inside him. Charlie kept his expression calm, although his pulse was pounding and his mind was swimming.

"Charlie," the doctor said at last, "I'd like to observe you for a while before I make such a decision. I need to be sure that you are telling the truth—both to me and to yourself—about your feelings." He paused. "I am a psychiatrist, Charlie, and my discipline is not an exact science. I regret that I'm not able simply to take your temperature and declare you well. The mind is much more complex than that, and it often hides anxieties that come back to do damage later on."

Charlie leaned forward. "So, what does that mean, Doc?"

"It means that I want to meet with you every day, in this office, where we will talk about your experiences, your emotions, your reactions. If you have nightmares, we will analyze them and try to understand them; if you experience other symptoms, those will also be subjects for discussion. We can talk about anything, Charlie—your childhood, your family, your fears and hopes and dreams. Anything. But there is one ground rule—"

"What's that?"

"You must be thoroughly honest with me. If you hold something back, you will be the one who is hurt."

Charlie nodded. "It's a deal, Doc. But for how long?"

"A minimum of six weeks. After that, we can reevaluate your situation."

Six weeks! The thought terrified Charlie. He could manage to keep up the act for an hour at a time—keep his hands from shaking, remain calm and rational. Although he couldn't control the nightmares or the predawn sweats, he could cover up their effects. But how on earth did he think he could fool this intelligent, insightful psychiatrist for a month and a half?

Six weeks. The very idea exhausted him. Still, if he could take it one day at a time, one hour at a time, he might be able to pull it off. He had to—this was his one chance at freedom. He *would* do it, even if it killed him.

The irony of the thought struck Charlie like a slap in the face, and he smiled inwardly. That was, after all, his final goal. To be killed in the line of duty. But he hoped that it would happen on the battlefield, not in a cramped and dismal office in a British hospital.

Fortified by his sense of purpose, Charlie stood and shook the doctor's hand. "Thank you, Dr. Worthington," he said. "I'll see you tomorrow."

14

☆ ☆ ☆

Dance Duty

Camp McCrane, Mississippi

Link Winsom wheeled into the gravel parking lot in front of the Officers' Club and slammed on the brakes, sliding to a stop in front of a hand-lettered sign that read, *Reserved: Major Mansfield.*

"You can't park in the major's spot," Stork protested. "He'll have your head if he finds out you took his space."

"Take it easy, pal," Link said breezily. "Old Minefield's never over on this side of the base this time of the afternoon. And besides, how is he going to know? The jeep's signed out to Farnam."

Stork frowned. "If you ask me, Link, you've taken entirely too many chances signing out vehicles under Lieutenant Farnam's name. What if he finds out that he has supposedly approved use of a jeep for 'research purposes' every day for the last two weeks?"

Link clapped his buddy on the shoulder and looked at him intently. A web of fine lines around Stork's deep-set eyes betrayed his fatigue and anxiety. He was probably just worried about Madge. The baby was due in less than a month now, and impending fatherhood had taken the edge off Stork's sense of humor.

"Well, I didn't ask you," Link said at last, keeping his tone light. "You're getting downright paranoid, Stork. We've been on this assignment for twelve weeks, and today we say good-bye to gas school forever. It's spring— the flowers are blooming, the birds are singing . . . what could possibly go wrong?"

Stork looked past Winsom and pointed toward the entrance of the Officers' Club.

Link twisted around in his seat. There, framed in the shadows of the doorway, stood Major Roland Mansfield, his arms clamped across his chest.

"In my office!" he roared. "Now!"

★ ★ ★

"But, Major!" Link protested. "You don't understand! We just—"

"I understand perfectly, Sergeant Winsom," the major said. "I understand that you forged Lieutenant Farnam's name on an ordnance request so that you could take a jeep into Grenada. And I understand that you did this, not once, but repeatedly. And I understand that you used your gas-school privileges to eat aged T-bones in the Officers' Club and to waste the army's time goofing off instead of doing what you were assigned to do."

Link tried in vain to suppress a smile. Obviously the T-bone violation was high on Major Minefield's personal list of offenses.

"Do you find humor in all this, Sergeant?" the major roared.

"No, sir," Link said, infusing his voice with every shred of humility he could muster.

"What do you have to say for yourselves?" The major turned from Link to Stork. "Sergeant Simpson? You seem to have more sense than your friend here."

"Yes, sir," Stork muttered. "I mean, no, sir . . . I guess not. I mean, I went with him. We were wrong, Major."

Link held his breath, hoping that Stork would come to his senses and shut his mouth. The major was mad, but he would be even madder if Stork kept acting like a fawning, groveling coward.

"We shouldn't have done it," Stork continued. "We should—"

"Shut up, Simpson," the major barked. "You sound like a whining baby."

Stork shot to attention. "Yes, sir."

"Now, listen, and listen good," Major Mansfield went on. "You boys have spent the last twelve weeks goofing off, riding around in the army's jeep like some kind of royalty. You like our jeeps so much, I'm going to give you a real good view of the rear end of one."

He pressed the intercom on his desk and yelled, "Send Slaughter in here!"

The office door opened and Sergeant Slaughter appeared. "Yes, sir?"

"Sergeant," the major said, pacing from his desk to the window and back again, "I'd like you to escort these boys on a little excursion around the countryside. Sixteen miles, forced march, full pack."

Link watched Owen Slaughter out of the corner of his eye. Slaughter didn't crack the first sign of a smile, but his eyes twinkled with delight. "Yes, sir," he said.

"When they're done, bring them back here. I've got another assignment for them."

Link heaved a sigh. He didn't dare look at Stork, but he could imagine the scowl on his friend's face, the set of his jaw, the blaze in his pale hazel eyes.

Poor Stork. Link didn't mind so much for himself, but Stork didn't need this right now. And he did hate to get his best friend in hot water with the major because of his own recklessness.

Well, there was nothing he could do about it now. The damage was done. He just hoped that Stork would find it in his heart to forgive him.

★ ★ ★

Stork shifted his pack and wiped the red dust of the Mississippi back roads out of his eyes for the hundredth time. All around them—in the gullies, over fence posts and barbed wire, up utility poles and across telephone lines—the weird climbing vine known as *kudzu* loomed, as if it were waiting for an opportunity to thrust out its tentacles and absorb them the moment they stood still. *Hirohito's Revenge,* people called it, and for good reason. From what Stork had heard, kudzu had been imported from Japan as a ground cover, the miracle answer to erosion in this land of red clay. But it wouldn't stay put. Wherever it took root, it took over, sometimes at the rate of a foot a day.

It was spooky stuff, Stork thought, creating landscapes that would look more at home on Mars than in Mississippi. He resisted the urge to look over his shoulder to see if it was following him.

Stork's feet burned, his legs ached, and his mouth and throat were filled with grit sprayed up from the jeep that Slaughter drove in front of them. He glanced over at Link, who had been uncharacteristically quiet during most of the march. At first Link had tried to explain, to apologize, to make things better. But Stork was in no mood for his friend's excuses. Because of Link, he had missed out on OCS; because of Link, he had endured the terminal boredom of gas school; and now, also because of Link, he was spending his Saturday afternoon on a sixteen-mile forced march. And whatever further punishment awaited them when they got back to camp, Stork didn't have the courage to guess. Maybe God would show mercy; maybe they'd die out here on the road.

Just bury me in the kudzu, Stork thought miserably. *That stuff will cover up anything, and they'll never find me.* It would be a fitting end to an otherwise unremarkable military career.

Ahead of them, Slaughter slammed on the brakes, revved the engine of the jeep, and added a burst of carbon monoxide to the noxious dust Stork and Link had been breathing for the last three hours.

"Four miles to go," Slaughter said jovially, turning off the engine and jumping down from the driver's side. "Take a water break—five minutes."

Stork dropped to the ground in the middle of the road, and Link sprawled down beside him.

"We're gonna make it, pal," Link said, grinning broadly.

Stork slung his rifle off his back and slanted a glance at Link. "If I don't shoot you first."

"Ah, you don't mean that." Link pulled off his helmet and ran a hand through his hair.

"Don't I?" Stork lifted his upper lip in a sneer. "Surely you don't imagine you deserve to live through this?"

A cloud passed over Link's face, and his expression turned serious. "I really am sorry, Stork," he said contritely. "I never expected to get you into this kind of trouble. I didn't think—"

"Right. You didn't think. You never think," Stork growled. "Well, think about this: What do you suppose the major is going to do to us when we get back—assuming, that is, that I don't kill you before this is over."

Link scratched his head. "I don't know." He turned to Slaughter, who had settled beside them and was using his pocketknife to pry the top off a bottle of Barq's root beer. "Where'd you get that?" Link said. "You got any more?"

Slaughter threw back his head and laughed. "I came prepared. I'm not the one on Major Minefield's blacklist, remember?"

Stork watched enviously as Slaughter took a long drink. Then Stork tipped up his own canteen and nearly choked on the tepid, stale water. It smelled—and tasted—like metal.

"I wouldn't worry about the major," Slaughter was saying. "He's not as mad as you might think. I expect this is the worst of it."

Link grinned and punched Stork on the shoulder. "See, pal, it's not so bad. Owen thinks this is the worst we'll get."

Stork stared at him. In his book, a sixteen-mile forced march behind a stinking jeep was bad enough. "But what about Mansfield's 'other assignment'?" he prodded.

Link frowned. "I forgot about that. Owen, do you know what he's got in mind?"

Slaughter chuckled. "Yep."

"Well, are you going to tell us?" Link prompted.

"Nope."

Stork leaned back against the red clay road and groaned. "Why not?"

Slaughter finished his root beer, tossed the bottle into the vine-clogged gully, and got to his feet. "Because," he said deliberately, dusting off his seat, "I wouldn't want to spoil the major's little surprise."

Link splashed water from his canteen onto his face, then replaced the cap and stood up. "Can't you just give us a hint? So we can be prepared?"

Slaughter shook his head and climbed back into the jeep. "I could," he said, "but I won't." The engine roared to life, and he yelled over his shoulder, "But believe me, boys, it'll be one you won't soon forget!" With that, he slammed the jeep into gear and spun away.

Stork scrambled to his feet and began to jog after Slaughter with Link close on his heels. *Great,* he thought, *an unforgettable surprise ending to the worst day of my entire life.*

It wasn't the worst day, and Stork knew it. But it might well have been in the top five, and it made him feel a little better just thinking that it was all Link Winsom's fault.

★ ★ ★

"Dance duty?" Link repeated stupidly. *"Dance duty?"*

The major nodded and smiled—a secretive, satisfied smile. "A busload of girls from the surrounding communities—Grenada, Eden, Childress, all over Tullahoma County—will be arriving at the USO at seven o'clock. I want you to round up twenty men and have them waiting at the door."

Link glanced down at his watch. It was 6:25. Exhausted, filthy, and discouraged, he and Stork had reported to the major's office directly from their march, while Owen Slaughter had tooled off in the jeep to get some dinner. Slaughter knew about this. He was going to pay; he wasn't going to weasel out of this one.

"But, sir," Link protested, "that's only half an hour from now, and—"

"And nothing, Sergeant," the major interrupted. "Do I need to remind you that you are in no position to object?"

Link shook his head. The major had caught him red-handed. No excuses this time. "No, sir."

"Fine. Now get cleaned up and round up your boys. I want the best this base has to offer represented at that dance tonight." Major Mansfield turned on his heel. "Dismissed."

Link turned to go, but Stork still stood at attention. "Major, sir," he ventured.

The major wheeled around. "What is it, Simpson?"

"Well, sir, I request permission to be relieved of dance duty."

"On what grounds?" The major was not happy. Link wanted to grab Stork's arm and jerk him out of there before he got into even bigger trouble, but all he could do was stand and watch.

"Uh . . . on the grounds, sir, that . . . I'm married. My wife is pregnant."

The major cocked an eyebrow. "Congratulations, Sergeant. Now, dismissed."

"Uh, sir?" Stork persisted.

"What?"

"Am I relieved of dance duty?"

Major Mansfield shook his head so fiercely that his jowls vibrated. "You are not, Sergeant."

"But, sir—"

"For heaven's sake, boy, you don't have to set up housekeeping with them! Just dance—dance! Will that compromise your precious integrity?"

The look on Stork's face told Link that he knew he was beaten. "No, sir."

"Then get out of my office. NOW!"

They ran for the door, and the major slammed it behind them.

"What was that all about?" Link asked when they were outside. "It's not like you're out looking for a girl, you know. It's just a dance. I know you're exhausted, Stork; so am I. But it's not worth getting the major even madder at us than he already—"

Stork held up a hand to silence Link, then turned and faced him with a look of utter despair on his face.

Something was wrong—really wrong. "Stork?" Link prodded. "What is it?"

His voice was quiet, his expression miserable. "I can't dance," he said. "Not a single step."

Link tried to take Stork's agony seriously, but he just couldn't manage it. He began to laugh, doubling over and pounding his thigh with his fist. Clouds of red dust stirred up around him until his laughter turned into a fit of coughing.

When he finally got control of himself, Link stood up and threw an arm around Stork's bony shoulders. "It's OK, pal," he said. "The way my feet feel, I'll be lucky if I can *walk.*"

15

★ ★ ★

The Princess and the Peons

Libba Coltrain sat across the aisle from Willie and Mabel Rae as the army bus bounced up and down the rutted gravel roads of Tullahoma County. She alternated between looking out the window, daydreaming about Freddy, and casting covert glances at her two cousins.

Libba didn't mind sitting alone. There was hardly room in the narrow seat for the yards of cream-colored organdy in her skirt, much less another body. She hoped the bus wouldn't fill up tonight; it wouldn't do to have her skirts crushed and wrinkled when she met Freddy.

She glanced down at her shoes, which matched the color of her dress. It was absolutely unheard-of to wear white shoes before Easter, but these weren't white, not really. Besides, who cared about the stupid rules people made up—when you could wear patent shoes or white ones; when you had to wear gloves and a hat?

Libba wished she could wear gloves all the time, to hide her chewed-up cuticles. But she hated hats. She was too short to wear a hat gracefully; she looked like she was walking in a ditch. And her hair, after all, was her best feature; she certainly didn't want to hide it.

In the final analysis, Libba simply did what she wanted to do. She never wore a hat except to funerals, and she wore white, or almost-white, shoes whenever she got the notion. What mattered, after all, was how you looked. And Libba was determined to make a good first impression—or second or third, for that matter.

Libba glanced across at Willie and Mabel Rae and sighed under her breath. She would never understand why those two didn't try harder, didn't do better with themselves. Why, Willie wasn't a bad-looking girl. She was big and tall and had sort of a rawboned country look, but she could have made more of what she had. If she'd just use a little rouge and powder and try to do something with that unruly mop of strawberry-blonde curls!

And Mabel . . . well, Mabel had a little further to go. She was round and plump, with a moonish face and a gap between her front teeth. But she did have striking eyes—dark brown eyes, like melted chocolate. Almost nobody else in the family had those eyes except Willie and Mabel Rae's daddy, Uncle William. Mabel could have made more of her looks by playing up her eyes, but as it was, you looked at her face and just got the impression of an enormous cookie with two big chocolate chips at the top.

Libba had tried to give them the benefit of her advice, but they didn't seem interested. Willie was always in the kitchen cooking or holed up in her favorite chair with a book. Mabel was either eating what she and Willie cooked or ruining her eyes with sewing and needlepoint and cross-stitch. Mabel Rae Coltrain would have the most beautifully stocked hope chest in the Deep South, but Libba doubted that it would do her any good. You could hope all you wanted, but if you didn't present a pretty package, nobody was going to buy.

Suddenly Willie looked up and caught her staring. With a jerk Libba turned back to the window and fiddled with the gold locket around her neck, pretending to gaze out on the familiar rolling hills. Well, it was no skin off her nose if they didn't care to listen and benefit from her superior wisdom. And it was certain the two of them would be no competition for her at the dance tonight.

★ ★ ★

Mabel Rae nudged Willie in the ribs. "Why does she have to be so snooty?" she whispered, nodding her head toward Libba.

Willie looked down at her sister and smiled. "She's not snooty, Mabel. Not really."

"Well, what do you call it?" Mabel wrinkled her nose and for a brief instant looked like a grimacing jack-o'-lantern. "She thinks she's better than us, I'm telling you. Well, she can kiss my foot."

"Mabel Rae Coltrain!" Willie reprimanded, still whispering. "Daddy would have you over his knee for saying such a thing. She is family, after all."

"Daddy was always entirely too generous about Uncle Robinson."

"Well, they are brothers, and—"

"And Uncle Robinson managed to keep his silk shirt through the Depression, while Daddy struggled to eke out a living on a dirt farm. And I ask you, did Uncle Robinson ever once offer to help? No!"

Willie patted Mabel's arm. "Daddy is too proud to accept anybody's help, you know that. And we've done all right. We're good people, honorable people—"

Mabel uttered a snort of disgust. "Honor doesn't hold much water with Miss Priss over there. She treats us like servants. And you can bet your petticoats that once we get to the dance, she won't even own that she knows us."

Willie smiled indulgently. Mabel had Daddy's eyes, but she got the rest from the Irish side of the family—especially her temper. She didn't have much patience with what she called Libba's "uppityness," but she was a good soul at heart.

And so, Willie was convinced, was Libba. Where this faith came from she wasn't quite sure, but Willie believed that someday something—or someone—in Libba's life would eventually bring out the best in her. Right now Libba seemed to be getting more and more like her father, but Willie trusted in the finer elements of the Coltrain heritage, that good-hearted spirit that had sustained her own family through the Depression and the difficult years that followed. Time would tell, she thought, what Libba Coltrain was really made of.

If she didn't go off and do something stupid, that is—like running away to marry that simpering Freddy Sturgis.

As if she had read Willie's mind, Mabel Rae leaned over and whispered, "I suppose Prince Freddy will be waiting for Her Majesty tonight."

Willie nodded. "No doubt. Otherwise she probably wouldn't risk the fury of Uncle Robinson when he finds out she's sneaked off to this dance."

Mabel shook her head sadly. "You know, Willie, I have my problems with the Princess, but given where she's come from, she could be a lot worse than she is."

Willie squeezed her sister's hand. Mabel had a tender heart despite her temper. And usually she came around to see the other side of the situation where Libba was concerned.

"I know," Willie said at last. "I wouldn't want to live with Uncle Robinson, would you? He treats her like a child and browbeats her terribly. And he doesn't treat Aunt Olivia any better."

Mabel sighed. "They may have all the money in this family," she said, "but I'll take our side of the Coltrain clan any day. In our house you might not have new shoes, but at least you know that you are loved." She paused.

"Someday," she went on in a wistful tone, "I hope somebody comes along who can bring out the better side of Libba."

Willie nodded. "That's just what I was thinking. The problem is, I don't think Freddy Sturgis is man enough for the job."

The bus jerked to a halt, and Mabel pointed out the window. "Speak of the devil."

Willie turned and looked. There, leaning against the side wall of the USO building, doing his best to look dapper and debonair, stood the little cocker spaniel, spiffed up in his dress uniform, waving to beat the band.

★ ★ ★

Libba's heart began to race as she took Freddy's outstretched hand and stepped daintily from the bus onto the gravel parking lot next to the USO. A brief flash of guilt ran through her, for it was not the sight of Freddy that caused her pulse to pound.

Standing around the door, at least twenty soldiers jostled each other to get a first look at the girls coming off the bus. Somebody let out a piercing wolf whistle, and before she could stop herself, Libba smiled.

It wasn't becoming to a lady, of course, to encourage such behavior. But it was almost her patriotic duty to show the boys in uniform a good time. That's what these USO dances were all about, after all—keeping up morale.

Libba's stomach wrenched as her father's words echoed in her mind: *I know what kind of morale those boys are interested in.* It was a nasty thing to say, and Daddy had no right to make such an assumption. There was nothing immoral about a harmless USO dance.

She closed her eyes for a moment and shook off the memory of her father's words. He would not spoil this for her. She would not give him that much power over her. She had defied him by coming here in the first place, and she would take whatever consequences came of her actions. In the meantime, she intended to have a wonderful evening.

Freddy let go of her hand and reached out to help Willie and Mabel Rae off the bus. While his back was turned, Libba gave the soldiers a quick once-over. She shouldn't even be considering anyone else—she was practically engaged to Freddy. For months now they had been talking about trying to find a way to get married without Daddy's consent. But things hadn't progressed much past the talking stage.

Freddy was only a private. He had no clout with the army whatsoever. And apparently he didn't have very much imagination either. He kept promising that he'd find a state where the legal age for marriage was eighteen—as soon as his promotion came through. Or as soon as he was accepted for Officers' Candidate School. Or as soon as he got a little more money together.

Libba suspected that the truth was, Freddy was afraid of Daddy. Afraid of what he might do if they got married behind his back. Libba was a little afraid, too—but she was more afraid that she might never get out of her father's grip. And she was becoming increasingly impatient with Freddy's delays. Why couldn't he just be a man, stand up to Daddy, tell him—?

But nobody ever told Daddy anything. Especially not Freddy.

So Libba let her glance sweep over the group of soldiers milling around the door of the USO. A sorry lot for the most part—fresh young faces with eager expressions that reminded her too much of the puppy-dog look in Freddy's eye. She began to fear that there wasn't a real man in the bunch.

Then she saw him, near the back of the crowd, standing next to a lanky, blond fellow who reminded her of Scarecrow in *The Wizard of Oz*. There was nothing particularly remarkable about him—he was medium height, with brown hair and olive skin. But he was looking directly at her, into her eyes, with a bold, almost rakish, smile on his face. She met his gaze for a moment, smiled briefly, then looked away. When she glanced up again, he was still staring at her in a most disconcerting manner—as if he knew her . . . or knew something about her.

Then he winked.

Libba's heart jumped, and she glanced around frantically. Where was Freddy—safe, loyal, adorable Freddy? Her mind reeled, and in her confusion she took a step backward—right onto Freddy's foot.

"What's the matter, Libba? Is something wrong?" Freddy's voice was sweet and solicitous, earnest.

Trembling, she took his arm. "No . . . nothing," she stammered. "I just—the bus ride was a little bumpy. Could we—could we go inside?"

"Of course." He clenched a sweaty palm over her hand and steered her through the crowd toward the entrance to the USO. Like the Red Sea parting for Moses and the Israelites, the horde of soldiers moved aside.

Just as they reached the door, the soldier with the piercing dark eyes and flirtatious expression stepped forward and smiled, giving Libba a little salute. There was no avoiding it. The sleeve of her dress brushed his arm as she went by.

16

Bewitched, Bothered, and Bewildered

"Link? What's the matter with you?"

Stork's voice snapped Link out of his reverie. He turned to his friend, standing next to Owen Slaughter, and motioned with his head toward the other side of the dance floor. "Take a look, pal," he said dreamily. "I've just met the woman of my dreams."

Stork frowned and peered down his hawk nose at Link. "We've only been here ten minutes," he said. "You haven't had time to meet anyone." Stork looked over his shoulder, addressing Slaughter. "He's lost his mind. Must have been the pressure of Mansfield's little forced march."

Slaughter nodded. "Certifiably insane. Call the medics."

Link grabbed Stork by the elbow and shook his arm. "I'm not! Didn't you see her?"

"See who?" Slaughter interjected. "There must be fifty dames out there."

Link turned and looked down at Slaughter. Poor little man; the lack of altitude must have affected his brain. Or maybe he was just too short to see over the crowd. Otherwise he wouldn't have called her a *dame*.

He turned Slaughter in the right direction and pointed. "Over there—see the three girls standing together?"

Slaughter stood on tiptoe and craned his neck. "Oh, yeah, the tall one with the blondish hair and blue dress—"

"Not her, idiot. The other one."

"The short round one?"

"Not her either," Link snapped, exasperated. "The one in the cream-colored dress; the one with green eyes."

Slaughter let out a low whistle and punched Stork on the arm. "Your pal has the eyesight of a chicken hawk," he said. "I can't even see her eyes from here. Does she have one or two?"

Stork leaned forward and squinted. "Two, I think. Maybe three. It's hard to tell from this distance."

"I saw her when she came in," Link said with deliberation, glaring at the two of them and trying to keep a lid on his temper. "It's the girl from the Paradise Garden Cafe. Thelma wouldn't give me her name, but it's her—I'm sure of it. She has green eyes. She looked right at me. And smiled."

Slaughter clutched at his heart and feigned a swoon. "She *smiled?* Well, that explains *everything!* Of course she's in love with you. How stupid can I be?"

Pretty stupid, Link thought, but he didn't say it. Instead, he turned to Stork. "What do you think?"

Stork peered across the room again and stroked his chin. "Hmm. Well, I'd like to say she's the most beautiful creature I've ever seen—"

Link nodded eagerly.

"But she's not," Stork finished. "She's OK, I guess, but she doesn't hold a candle to my Madge."

Link sighed. These two were impossible. Slaughter was completely cynical about anything that had to do with romance, and Stork was so in love with Madge that he couldn't see the nose on his face, prominent as it was.

"I'm going over to meet her," he said. "Come on."

Stork balked. "Why us? Why don't you just go by yourself?"

"Because," Link explained with exaggerated patience, "she's here with two girlfriends. I need someone to run interference for me."

Just as he was about to walk away, Slaughter grabbed Link's arm and wheeled him around. "If you want our help, pal, you'll have to pay for it."

Link stared down at him, puzzled. "Pay? Pay what?"

"This is the girl of your dreams, right?" Slaughter said.

"Uh-huh," Link replied absently. What was Slaughter getting at?

"I'll help you get to Miss Green Eyes over there on one condition."

"What? What?" Link was growing more impatient by the minute.

"On the condition that you give me your little black book."

"My what?"

Slaughter threw back his head and laughed. "Your list, Link. All the girls you've met and dated since you've been here. Names, phone numbers, addresses, personal preferences—everything."

Link stared intently at Slaughter. "Sure, Owen, you've got a deal."

Stork clapped a bony hand to his broad forehead and groaned. "He's really serious, Owen. He's gone over the edge this time."

"I'm telling you, this is the one," Link said firmly. "Now, can we get going?"

"First the book." Slaughter held out his hand.

Link fished into his back pocket and pulled out a small address book—not black, but brown, its pages rumpled and creased. He handed it over.

Slaughter took the book gingerly, with a thumb and forefinger, as if it might be covered with some lethal strain of germ. He lifted it to his nose, then sniffed. "What did you do to it, Winsom? Shower with it? It smells like a wet dog."

Link leveled a withering glare in Slaughter's direction. "It was in my pocket on this afternoon's march," he said curtly.

"Yuck," Slaughter said, wrinkling his nose. "Sixteen miles of sweat."

"Do you want it or not?"

"Yeah, yeah, I want it." Slaughter slipped the book into his breast pocket, then apparently thought better of it and transferred it to his hip.

"Now, if we're all ready," Link said sarcastically, "let's go. I'm about to meet my destiny."

★ ★ ★

Mabel Rae had been wrong about Libba, Willie thought as she stood between them at the side of the dance floor. She hadn't abandoned them as soon as they got off the bus; instead, she had stayed close, almost as if for protection. Libba seemed nervous, jumpy. She didn't act very happy to see Freddy the Wonder Boy—in fact, at the first opportunity she had sent him off into the crowd in search of a Coca-Cola.

Willie slanted a glance at Libba. She couldn't pick at her cuticles unless she wanted to chew through the fingers of those ridiculous gloves, but she already had that curl at the nape of her neck twisted into a knot. What was the girl so agitated about?

Suddenly Libba let out a gasp. "They're coming!" she whispered frantically. "They're coming this way!" She held a hand at her waist and pointed discreetly toward the dance floor.

Willie's eyes followed the direction of Libba's finger. Sure enough, three soldiers, all with sergeant's stripes, were threading their way through the crowd. The one in the lead, a dark-haired, dark-eyed man with an intense look about him, seemed to be zeroing in on Libba. Behind him came a tall, gangly fellow and a short, muscular one with curly brown hair and striking blue eyes.

The small entourage stopped in front of them, and the dark-haired soldier offered a brief, flourishing bow. "Ladies," he said grandly, "permit us to introduce ourselves."

The short one with the curly hair caught Willie's gaze and flashed a brilliant white smile, revealing deep dimples in both cheeks. His blue eyes sparkled. The gangly fellow just looked at his feet.

"I am James Lincoln Winsom," the brown-eyed sergeant was saying. "My friends call me Link. This is my buddy, Stork Simpson—" He pointed to the tall man. "And this is Sergeant Owen Slaughter." The short one gave a brief nod and grinned even wider. "Would you ladies care to dance?"

The question was obviously addressed to Libba, but she seemed incapable of answering. The look on her face reminded Willie of rabbits on a night hunt, caught in the beam of the flashlight, frozen in place, unable to run or resist. When at last Libba was able to tear her eyes away from the soldier named Winsom, she looked to Willie with an expression of undisguised and utter panic.

Willie took over. "Why, thank you, gentlemen. My name's Willie Coltrain. This is my sister Mabel Rae, and this—"

She got no further. Libba put a hand on Willie's arm and gripped hard. "Pardon me," she said, her voice half an octave higher than usual. "But southern ladies don't dance with men they haven't been properly introduced to."

Willie's jaw dropped, and she gaped at Libba. What on earth was the girl trying to do? Before she could say a word, Libba swiveled on her heel and walked away.

Willie turned back to the soldiers, who were standing there with confounded looks on their faces. "My cousin is a bit out of sorts tonight," she said smoothly. "If you'll excuse us for a few moments—"

The soldiers nodded mutely, and Willie went after Libba.

★ ★ ★

"Well, I guess you struck out on your dream girl," Slaughter said morosely. He took a drink of his Coke and leaned against the bar. "You know," he went on with a sigh, "that girl was really something—"

"Miss Green Eyes?" Stork interrupted. "You must be kidding. She was a snob. A perfect 'Southern Lady' snob."

Link seethed. He grabbed Stork by the front of his shirt and pulled him forward until they were nose to nose. "Not a word," he said. "Not a single word."

"OK, OK," Stork protested. He wrenched Link's hands from his shirt and smoothed out the wrinkles. "Sorry. I didn't know you were so touchy."

"I'm not touchy," Link snapped. "And I didn't strike out." He set his glass down with a resounding thud. "I'm not done yet."

"What do you mean, you're not done?" Stork asked. "You heard the girl—she won't dance with someone she's not been *properly introduced* to."

"Then I'll get properly introduced," Link declared. He turned to Slaughter. "Owen," he said, "you're about to earn your little brown book."

"Book?" Slaughter looked puzzled. "What book?"

"The one in your hip pocket," Link reminded him. "*My* book. The one with all the names in it."

"Oh, that," Slaughter said dreamily. "I forgot."

"What's with him?" Stork said.

"How should I know?" Link turned to Slaughter. "What is with you, Owen?"

Slaughter looked up foggily. "She's a fine woman, don't you think?"

"Who?" Link and Stork responded in unison.

"Willie," Slaughter answered.

"*Willie?* The Amazon cousin in the blue dress? *That* Willie? You've got to be kidding, Owen. She's half a foot taller than you."

"Doesn't matter," Slaughter said. "It makes her . . . noble, somehow. Regal."

"Regal? She's a farm girl, for pity's sake!"

"Yeah," Slaughter said. "A farm girl. Clean. Pure. Salt of the earth. And she has the most incredible voice."

Link peered at Slaughter intently. This was going to be easier than he had possibly imagined. "Owen," he said carefully, "why don't you go dance with Willie?"

"Dance with her?"

"Yes, dance with her. And while you're at it, find out what's eating her cousin. I need to know how to get properly introduced."

Stork stared at Link. "You've got to be kidding. The girl's a snoot."

"The *girl*," Link said, "is a *lady*. And if you think I'm giving up without a fight, you're crazy."

"You're the one who's crazy," Slaughter said, moving away from the bar. "But I'll do what I can to find out."

17

★ ★ ★

Moment of Truth

Libba, crumpled into a chair in the ladies' room, felt a hand on her shoulder and jumped as if she had been bitten by a copperhead.

"Calm down," Willie said in a quiet voice. "It's only me."

Libba squinted up at her cousin. "I must look awful," she said, straightening up and studying her reflection in the mirror. "Oh, Willie, what am I going to do?"

"About what?" Willie's voice was impatient; clearly she was unhappy about the southern-lady stunt Libba had pulled on the dance floor. But she just couldn't help it. When she saw him, standing in front of her with that intense look in his eyes, she panicked. This was no Freddy Sturgis. This was no adoring puppy she could keep on a leash.

"About my shoes, of course," Libba snapped sarcastically. "They're totally inappropriate for this time of year." She got up and stared in the mirror, twisting the strand of hair behind her right earlobe. Then she turned and faced Willie. "About *him.*"

"Who? Freddy? He's outside right now, waiting for you."

"Not *Freddy.*" How dense could Willie be? You'd think they came out of two totally different worlds instead of the same family. Silently Libba pleaded for Willie to understand, to help her . . . somehow.

"Ahhh." Willie took Libba by the shoulders and looked her straight in the eye. "Is that why you're so agitated?" she asked. "The dark-eyed sergeant?"

Libba nodded. "I saw him when I was coming in. He winked at me."

Willie sighed. "I've never known you to go on so about a fella, Libba. What could one little dance hurt?"

Libba fidgeted impatiently. She knew it. Willie couldn't possibly understand what she was feeling, and she probably wouldn't even try. "Forget it, Willie." She tried to shrug her cousin's hands off her shoulders. "It's not important."

Willie raised an eyebrow. "Libba, all men aren't like your father—or like Freddy Sturgis, for that matter. They don't all want to dominate you or treat you like a china doll on a satin pillow. It's just possible that one or two of them might be normal, ordinary guys who just want to get to know you."

Libba gulped and lowered her eyes. "You don't know, Willie Coltrain. You don't know anything."

"Hah!" Willie said. "I know enough to realize you'll never forgive yourself if you don't take a chance with this guy."

"He probably thinks I'm an idiot," Libba protested. "And I can't exactly go out there and ask *him* to dance."

"Why not?"

"Oh, Willie!" Libba began to laugh a little. "It's just not done. I have my pride, you know."

"Yeah, I know all about your pride," Willie said. "And I'm sure little Freddy will wait outside this bathroom door until doomsday, if necessary. I'll see you later."

Libba grabbed on to Willie's sleeve. "Where are you going?"

"To the dance, Cousin," Willie answered. "There are other fish in this pond besides the one you let get away."

★ ★ ★

Willie almost ran down the cocker spaniel as she exited the ladies' room. Freddy had dragged a chair over and was sitting on the edge of the seat, staring at the door as if he could convince Libba to come out by sheer force of will.

Willie sighed and looked down at him. "Freddy," she said, "Libba's likely to be in there for a while. Why don't you go find someone to dance with?"

"Dance?" Freddy uttered the word as if it were a live coal on his tongue. "Dance? Oh, no, I—I couldn't. I have to wait for Libba."

"Suit yourself," Willie said. She was about to walk away, but his imploring puppy eyes kept her riveted to the spot.

"What—what's the matter with Libba?" he pleaded. "Did I do something wrong?"

Willie debated her answer. She wanted to say, *No, poor boy, you didn't do anything wrong—you just are wrong.* But she didn't think he could stand the truth.

"Just . . . just woman troubles," she said finally. It was partly true, but not in the way he interpreted it.

A blush crept over Freddy's face from his earlobes to his hairline. "Can I do anything?" he gulped out at last.

Willie stifled a laugh. "No, Freddy, I don't think so. Maybe she'll be out soon."

He settled back into his chair. "OK," he said. "I guess I'll just wait."

Willie shook her head and walked away.

★　★　★

Owen Slaughter searched for that magnificent, statuesque Coltrain woman for nearly half an hour. At last he spotted her coming out of the ladies' room.

The army had taught him that a frontal attack was often the most effective. He set his sights on her and moved in. Then he balked. She was talking to some simpering-looking private parked on a chair outside the restroom.

Owen decided to wait, to do a little reconnaissance. Maybe she wouldn't go off dancing with him. Maybe she would come his way instead.

At last she began to walk away. She was alone. Now was the time to make his move.

He placed himself directly in her line of vision and closed in. "Pardon me, Miss Coltrain."

She gazed down at him. Just as Stork had said, she was a good six inches taller than he, and he had to tilt his head back to look into her face.

"Hello, Curly," she said in that incredible voice—deep and resonant, with enough of the South to soften the tones but without the irritating nasal twang. He was mesmerized. It took him a full minute to comprehend what she had said.

Curly? No one had ever called him Curly before. Owen thought about it for a minute and decided that he liked it. Yes, he liked it a lot.

"Miss Coltrain," he began again.

"Please, call me Willie," she said. "But I'm afraid I've forgotten your—"

"Slaughter," he offered. "Owen Slaughter." He ran a hand through his hair and laughed nervously. "But you can call me Curly if you want. I kinda like it."

What was it about this woman that made him so utterly idiotic? He was a seasoned soldier, a trained man of war, and yet when she spoke to him, he went all soft and buttery inside. He thought he could listen to that voice forever.

She was smiling down at him . . . a nice smile, warm and friendly, with a sparkle in her rich gray eyes. She liked him, he thought—or at least he hoped she did.

Owen shuffled his feet and stuck his hands in his pockets. "Willie, then. Would you . . . like to dance with me, Willie?"

Her smile broadened. "Are you sure you want to? We might make a rather odd-looking couple."

Owen frowned. What was she talking about?

"I am a little taller than you," she explained. She pointed to her feet. "And I'm not even wearing heels. People might think it strange that—"

Ah. So that was it. Her height. Well, let them stare. Let them laugh. Owen didn't care. All he cared about was hearing that honeyed voice in his ear—or in his hair, as the case might be.

He felt his confidence return, and he looked into her eyes and held out a hand. "It doesn't matter," he said quietly. "Nothing matters, as long as you'll dance with me."

In a dance he knew he would never forget as long as he lived, Owen Slaughter took Willie Coltrain in his arms and moved out onto the floor. Willie told him about herself—about her family, about her brother Charlie, wounded in Italy, about the books she read, about her hopes and dreams—as they danced through one song and into another.

Owen wished they could dance forever. Then he caught sight of Link Winsom at the bar, waving frantically at him. *Ask her—ask her!* Link mouthed the words over and over again.

Ask her what? Then it hit him: He had completely forgotten about Link's dilemma with the snooty princess, Miss Green Eyes.

He hated to break the spell of the moment, but he had promised. The music ended, and Owen took Willie's hand and led her from the dance floor to a table.

As casually as he could, he ventured the question: "So, Willie, what was the problem with your cousin earlier this evening?"

She told him. But Link Winsom wasn't going to like the answer.

★　★　★

"She's *engaged?*" Link sputtered. It was impossible—not his dream girl. She couldn't be! "Who to?"

Slaughter turned his head and pointed toward the ladies' room, where a morose young soldier was slouched on a chair, his head leaning against the wall. "That boy over there—a private, name of Freddy Sturgis."

Link groaned. The one from the cafe—of course! He knew Sturgis, all right—at least, he knew *about* Sturgis. The joke of Camp McCrane. Sturgis couldn't do anything right. The kid had exalted dreams of OCS, but everybody knew there would be snowball fights in the underworld before Private Sturgis ever got a command. He was a sissy. An embarrassment to the army. And Major Minefield hated his guts.

"Sturgis?" Link repeated. *"Sturgis?"*

Slaughter nodded. "Yep. Seems Miss Southern Belle—Libba is her name, by the way—has a problem getting along with her father. Thinks this Sturgis kid is gonna take her away from all of that."

Link raised an eyebrow at Slaughter. How did the man get this much information during one dance? Amazon Willie must be some talker.

He looked back at Sturgis, still in permanent residence outside the bathroom. "Engaged, you say?"

Slaughter hedged. "Well, yes. That is, sort of."

Link brightened. "Sort of? Is she engaged or isn't she?"

"Not officially. No ring. No date. They've been making plans, Willie says, but nothing's coming of them . . . not yet. Still, she is spoken for."

Link turned on Slaughter and smiled—a wicked, conniving grin. "Spoken for ain't married, old buddy. A fella can speak all he wants, but until he *acts*—well, nothing's final till the preacher says Amen."

Slaughter narrowed his eyes. "Just what does that mean?"

"Watch," Link said, swinging a leg off the high barstool. "Watch and learn."

18

A Dance with Destiny

Half asleep, Freddy Sturgis sat with his chair leaning against the outer wall of the women's restroom. Link stood there for a moment, watching him. The boy's eyes were closed, and his jaw sagged open; his pouty lower lip jutted out, making him look like a small child. Link expected him to put his thumb in his mouth at any moment.

With a swift movement of one foot, Link aimed a hard kick at Sturgis's chair. The kid jumped as if he had been shot.

"Soldier!" Link barked.

Sturgis scrambled to his feet, his eyes wide with terror. He made a feeble attempt at a salute, then stood trembling at attention. "Yes, sir?"

"What's your name, soldier?" Link knew, but he rather enjoyed seeing Sturgis squirm a little.

"Sturgis, sir. Frederick Sturgis, Private First Class."

Link inched forward until his face was inches from Freddy's. "I want to see you outside, Private."

"Now, sir?" Freddy stammered. "But I—I—"

"Now!" Link turned on his heel and made for the door. He could hear Sturgis's little feet pattering behind him.

Once in the parking lot, Link took a long breath of the cool night air and turned to face the young soldier.

"You're escorting a young woman here tonight?" Link asked.

Freddy's eyebrows cocked upward. "Uh, yes, sir."

"What's her name?"

"Uh, Elizabeth Coltrain, sir." Freddy's expression clearly communicated that he hadn't the faintest idea why his date should cause him trouble with the U.S. Army.

"And what are your intentions toward her?" Link prodded.

Freddy blanched. "My intentions, sir?"

"Are you deaf, Private? Your intentions! Are you engaged to this young woman?"

Freddy screwed up his face in a frown, as if trying to find the correct answer. Finally he said, "Not officially, sir. We've talked about marriage, but I'm not in a position to—"

"To make good on your promises," Link finished for him.

"Uh, no, sir. Not right now. I guess not."

"Then you have no real claim on her affections."

Freddy scratched his head. "I don't suppose I do."

Link smiled and turned his face up to the stars. After almost a minute of silence, broken only by the chirping of crickets and the sounds of music and laughter coming from inside the building, he turned again to face Freddy Sturgis.

"Then you would have no objection to introducing me to her so I can dance with her?"

Freddy opened his mouth, but nothing came out. Link could almost see the wheels turning inside his befuddled little brain, wondering if he had the right to say no to a superior. His answer would tell Link what he needed to know. If Sturgis stood up to him and refused, he would at least be acting like a man. If he gave in like the spineless weakling everybody thought he was—well then, Link would be justified in giving it his best shot. The girl could make up her own mind.

"Uh, no, sir," Freddy finally said.

"No, sir, what?" Link asked.

"I'll be happy to introduce you." Freddy didn't sound very happy about it, but at that moment Link didn't care. All he needed was an introduction. Charm and destiny would take care of the rest.

★ ★ ★

Libba was still in the ladies' room. She had spent nearly an hour thinking about what Willie had said and fussing with her makeup. She still didn't know what she should do about the conflicting feelings inside her, but she couldn't stay in the bathroom forever.

Just as she was about to screw up her courage to go back to the dance, she heard a faint, whiny voice calling her name.

"Libba? Libba, are you in there?"

It was Freddy.

Suddenly Libba was overcome with loathing for the timid little voice and the groveling little boy it was attached to. Immediately she regretted the thought. Poor Freddy had been good to her. He had treated her like . . . well, like a queen. Like royalty. He was the perfect gentleman. He was a sweet boy. He just wasn't a *man*. Maybe he would turn into one someday, but Libba wasn't sure she wanted to wait that long. And she suspected that his adoration of her might delay the process indefinitely.

Well, there was nothing to do but go out there and meet him. She had come to be with him, after all. What might happen after tonight she didn't know, but a lady—especially a southern lady—treated her escort with respect. Freddy deserved that much.

Libba took a deep breath and opened the door. There stood Freddy, waiting for her, with his eyes fixed on his shoes and his shoulders sagging.

"Elizabeth Coltrain," he said formally, without looking up, "I'd like to introduce you to Sergeant James Lincoln Winsom." Then he stood aside.

Libba found herself looking into the darkest, most intense brown eyes she had ever seen—eyes deep enough to drown in.

"Sergeant Winsom would very much like to dance with you," she heard Freddy say, as if from a great distance. "And I—I, uh, offered to make the proper introductions."

Libba couldn't speak. She couldn't move. She just stood there staring.

"The *proper introductions?*" she managed at last.

The handsome sergeant smiled, and Libba's stomach lurched. "A southern lady," he said gently, with just a faint twinkle of amusement in his eyes, "cannot be expected to dance with a stranger—not without being *properly introduced.*"

With that, he took her hand and guided her onto the dance floor.

★ ★ ★

Up close, Libba Coltrain wasn't the prettiest girl he had ever met, Link decided. But there was something about her, something he couldn't quite identify. She had wonderful thick auburn hair, worked into curls that he longed to run his fingers through. Her eyes were, as he remembered from that first glance, green. The pale fresh green of weeping willow branches.

She wore silly little gloves that matched her dress, and she gazed at him with a vulnerable, almost fearful expression—a look that made him want to protect her. She carried herself with an almost brazen fierceness, but instinctively he felt that she was fragile, somehow—like a helpless animal caught in a steel trap, fighting to get free even if it hurt.

He thought briefly about what Slaughter had said—how Willie had told him that Libba had problems with her father and was ready to marry Freddy Sturgis to get away from him. Maybe that was the source of her woundedness. Surely she had to be pretty desperate to agree to marry someone like Sturgis.

But wounded or not, she had spirit. It blazed from her eyes and filled her every movement. She might not be the prettiest girl Link had ever met, but she could well turn out to be the most interesting.

His instincts about her had been right on target. He wouldn't be bored with this one. It might turn out to be a wild and bumpy ride, but it would never be dull. She was fascinating. She had spunk.

And holy Hannah, the girl could dance!

★ ★ ★

Once they were on the dance floor, Libba relaxed a little. Here she was in her element. She had, after all, won the Tullahoma County jitterbug contest two years in a row. Maybe her mouth was too big. Maybe she did laugh like a horse. Maybe she picked at her cuticles when she was nervous. But when it came to dancing, nobody could even come close to Libba Coltrain.

And Link Winsom, the lean, handsome soldier whose intense gaze and bold wink had so intimidated her, seemed to be enjoying himself immensely.

For the first time in ages, Libba felt free—free to be herself. It occurred to her, just briefly, that this was a man Daddy might actually approve of. But the thought didn't linger. It didn't much matter at the moment what her father thought. She was having a wonderful time.

And something else was happening as she danced with the rakish Sergeant Winsom. Something that shocked her and shook her to the core.

During one dance she caught a glimpse of Freddy lingering at the edge of the dance floor like an abandoned child. And for the first time she questioned her own feelings about the kind of man she wanted. She had told Willie she wanted someone who would treat her like a queen. But did she really? Did she need a fawning puppy who would always say yes to her, somebody who would smother her with adoration? Was it remotely possible that instead she yearned for someone who would treat her like a real person?

She didn't know how he did it, but Link Winsom was treating her that way. During the jitterbugs, when she really showed her stuff, he laughed and applauded and didn't seem at all embarrassed. During the slow ballads, he held her in his arms and spoke softly in her ear, leaning back every now and then to look into her eyes.

Libba found herself talking far too much, revealing more than she wanted to. But he seemed genuinely interested in what she told him about herself—about her teaching job, about the students, about her plans for finishing college someday.

After an hour or so on the dance floor with Sergeant Link Winsom, she finally identified what was so different about him. With him, she didn't have to *prove* that she was important. He made her feel that way without her having to do a single thing.

As the band completed its set and prepared to take a break, Libba looked over Link's shoulder to see Willie and Mabel Rae standing on the far side of the dance floor. Willie's left hand was firmly captured in the grip of a short, muscular soldier with an enormous grin. Willie caught Libba's eye and with her right hand flashed an "OK" sign.

Link followed the direction of Libba's gaze. "That's my friend Owen Slaughter with your cousin," he said. "They make an interesting couple, don't they?"

And Libba threw back her head and laughed out loud, without even bothering to cover her mouth.

19

★ ★ ★

Trouble in Paradise

Thelma leaned on the counter of the Paradise Garden Cafe and listened dreamily as Ivory Brownlee played "I'll Get By" on the piano. Ivory had been there waiting, as usual, when she returned from the eleven o'clock service. She never opened until one o'clock on Sunday, but if Ivory showed up—and he usually did—she shared a makeshift dinner with him in her tiny apartment on the back side of the cafe.

She had walked to church this morning—three blocks down to the square, then another two-and-a-half blocks east. The morning had been crisp and chill, the air laden with the scents of dogwood and redbud ready to bloom. It was the kind of early spring Sunday that always reminded Thelma of an Easter sunrise service long ago—a Sunday tinged with bittersweet memories.

It was a service she would never forget. She had been dressed to the nines that morning in a white eyelet dress and straw hat as she sat on a log in the open glade. Dawn was just breaking, and the scent of Easter lilies mingled with the smell of blossoming dogwoods to create a heavenly, almost overpowering fragrance.

Everything was coming alive again—everything, that is, except Thelma Breckinridge's heart. Robert Raintree, the man who had promised to love her forever, was gone. Thelma's reputation for being fast and loose was of no consequence to him, Robert had insisted. He adored her for herself, and he would stay beside her and protect her for the rest of her life.

Thelma had believed him. And then, on a dismal Saturday just before Easter, she found a note on her door. Robert was gone for good. He had left

Tullahoma County on a northbound train, taking with him all her hopes for a respectable life.

After a miserable, sleepless night, Thelma had put on her white eyelet dress—an ironic symbol for an almost-thirty woman who could never claim to be pure—and dragged herself reluctantly to the sunrise service. She wouldn't give the good Christian people of Eden the chance to talk behind her back, to wag their heads and say, "I knew this would happen." She didn't have much left, but she had her pride; and she would hold her head up, no matter how much effort it took.

Then, at the service, something strange and wonderful had happened. The sun had risen, splitting its beams into shards behind the huge wooden cross that dominated the clearing. The golden light washed over her like a benediction, and when the pastor declared, "The Lord is risen!" she truly believed it—perhaps for the first time in her life. All the words of resurrection and hope and forgiveness of sin were spoken that day just for her, and like a half-frozen soul drawing up to a fire, she opened her heart to the truth.

When the final strains of "Christ the Lord Is Risen Today" had dissipated into the woods, leaving only the twittering of birds to echo the triumphant song, Thelma Breckinridge still sat, transfixed, on her log at the back of the clearing. God had met her in the wilderness. A divine hand had rolled away her tombstone and led her out into the resurrection morning.

Thelma had never realized her dream of husband, home, and family. But she had received something far more valuable on that Easter Sunday—the awareness that she was forgiven and loved, and a tiny measure of the resurrection power of God.

Now, as she listened to Ivory play the piano, the words of the song took on a different meaning for her: *I'll get by as long as I have you.* . . .

Thelma smiled to herself. She did more than just "get by." She had a little piece of paradise here in Eden—her own business, friends who cared about her, and the opportunity to encourage and pray for the people God sent across her path. What else did anyone need?

"As long as I have You," she murmured, and sent up a heartfelt prayer of thanksgiving—for her life, for the springtime, for redbuds and resurrection.

★ ★ ★

Link Winsom hadn't been to the Paradise Garden Cafe for three weeks. As he jumped down from the bed of the pickup truck and thanked the driver for the ride, his heart pounded with anticipation. His buddies were giving him a hard time about his infatuation with Elizabeth Coltrain, but somehow

Link felt that if anyone would understand, Thelma Breckinridge would. And he had to talk to somebody about it or he might explode.

Except for Thelma behind the counter and Ivory at the piano, the Paradise Garden was deserted on this Sunday afternoon. Link sauntered over to the counter and sat down, trying to suppress a grin.

"Hey there, hon!" Thelma greeted him with a smile, then cocked her head and gave him a puzzled expression. "What's got into you, darlin'? You look like a kitty in a catnip crock."

"Is that good?"

"It's about as happy as they come," Thelma said. "Something's happened to you, I assume."

Link closed his eyes and sighed. "The best, Thelma. I met her last night."

Thelma chuckled. "Ah. *Her.* A girl, right?"

"Not *a* girl; *the* girl. Thelma, I can hardly believe it. Auburn hair, in these long curls around her neck, green eyes, and a jitterbug that knocks your socks off. She's—"

The expression on Thelma's face stopped Link cold. "What's the matter?"

"Jitterbug queen, huh? Red hair, green eyes—"

"Yes, but—"

"Name of Libba Coltrain, by any chance?"

Link grinned. "You wouldn't tell me who she was, but I met her last night at the USO dance. She is the most amazing girl, Thelma—" He paused and frowned. "What is wrong with you, Thelma? Aren't you happy for me?"

Thelma lowered her eyes and fiddled with her collar. "I'm sorry, hon. I don't mean to burst your bubble. It's just that—" She groped for words. "I was under the impression that Libba has been . . . uh, seeing someone else."

Link laughed and slapped his hand on the counter. Freddy. Thelma was worried about Freddy Sturgis? "I know all about it," he said. "In fact, I had a little talk with the private just last night. Got it all settled. He's out of the picture."

Thelma raised an eyebrow. "And what about the father? Have you had a little talk with him, too?"

Link looked at Thelma intently. Her face was furrowed into lines of concern, and her eyes held an unspoken warning. "What's the problem, Thelma? Don't you believe in answered prayer anymore?"

"What do you mean?" Her voice faltered.

"Well, you're always saying that you pray for me. And, judging from your obvious acquaintance with the Coltrain family, I'd guess you've occasionally prayed for Libba, too."

She nodded hesitantly. "What are you getting at?"

"Don't you think it's possible that our 'coincidental' meeting just might be the answer to one of those prayers?"

The look on Thelma's face told him that he had struck a nerve. "I reckon it's possible," she said. "But—"

"No buts, Thelma." Link grinned. "You'd better be careful what you pray for," he said lightly. "You just might get an answer you didn't expect."

"Now, ain't that the gospel truth," she muttered.

★ ★ ★

Later that afternoon, as the pie-and-coffee crowd was thinning out, Thelma looked up from clearing a table to find Libba Coltrain sitting alone in the corner near the window. The girl was staring out into the gathering dusk, absently twisting the hair behind her ear.

Thelma put the dishes behind the counter, grabbed the coffeepot and two mugs, and went to stand beside Libba.

"You look like you could stand some company," Thelma said quietly. "Mind if I sit a spell?"

An expression of relief washed over Libba's face, and she motioned to the chair at her right. "I guess I could use a listening ear at that."

Thelma sat down and poured coffee for both of them. "Fire away," she said. "I'm ready."

For a moment or two Libba stirred her coffee with a vengeance, her head lowered. When she finally did look up, Thelma saw an expression of utter misery in her pale green eyes.

"Oh, Thelma!" Libba wailed. "I've met the most wonderful man!"

Thelma had to work hard to suppress a smile. She didn't want Libba thinking she was mocking her, but it was pretty humorous. How could such a "wonderful man" be the cause of so much obvious despair?

Thelma patted Libba's hand and took a drink of her coffee. "Tell me about it, hon."

"Well," Libba sniffed, trying to compose herself, "I met him last night, at a dance at the USO—"

"Link Winsom."

Libba's head shot up, and her eyes grew round. "You *know?*" She looked around frantically. "How did you find out? Does Daddy—"

"Now, now, take a deep breath and relax," Thelma said. She considered telling Libba the source of her information, and then thought better of it. Might as well let the two of them figure this out for themselves—there was no good to be done by her meddling in their business. "Don't worry, Libba,

I came by the information honestly. As far as I know, nobody's the wiser—
not your daddy, anyway."

"But who—"

"Never mind who. Just tell me what's going on."

Libba shook her head. "Thelma, I'm so confused. You know I've been
seeing Freddy—against Daddy's wishes." Thelma nodded. "Well, last night
I sneaked out to the USO dance. I usually spend weekends at home, you
know. But this time I came back to the apartment on Saturday afternoon—
Daddy thought I was grading papers."

She paused and bit her lip. "It wasn't a lie, not really. I did have papers to
grade, only I—"

"You went to the dance," Thelma prodded.

"Uh-huh." Libba gulped. "And he was there."

"Freddy?"

"No, not Freddy. I mean, yes, Freddy was there. But I meant Link
Winsom."

Thelma shook her head, trying to get Libba's ramblings to settle themselves into some logical order. The girl was right. She was confused.

"Anyway," Libba went on, "I had a wonderful time—after I came out of
the bathroom, at least. We danced—Link and I. I'm afraid I left poor Freddy
in the lurch. And now—"

"Now you're confused about whether you want to be with Freddy or with
Link?"

Libba shot Thelma an expression of disbelief. "Of course not. I know that
much. Freddy's a boy. Link's a man."

"And a very handsome man at that," Thelma supplied.

Libba brightened. "Yes, he is, isn't he? But that's not the point. The point
is, I promised Freddy—we were practically engaged, or at least engaged to
be engaged. Now I don't know what to do."

"Yes, you do."

Libba stared at Thelma. "I do?"

"You do." Thelma squeezed Libba's hand, then leaned back in the chair.
"Be honest with me, hon. Why did you agree to marry Freddy?"

Libba hesitated. "The truth? To get away from Daddy, I suppose."

"And why are you attracted to Sergeant Winsom? For the same reason?"

Libba shook her head. "I guess I like him . . . well, because I like him.
When we were together, I felt good about myself. I didn't have to prove
anything." She thought for a minute, then concluded, "I like him because I
liked myself when I was with him."

Thelma nodded and smiled. "Does that answer your question?"

"Sort of," Libba hedged. "But what about Freddy?"

Thelma was silent for a while, thinking not about Libba, but about herself. In many ways, Robert's leaving had been the best thing that ever happened to her. It hurt, but the pain drove her to God—and to herself. She was a better person without Robert Raintree than she ever could have been with him.

At last she turned to Libba again. "Tell him the truth, hon," she said. "We all have to grow up sometime."

★ ★ ★

When Libba had left and the cafe was empty except for Ivory, Thelma went back to the corner table, sipped a second cup of coffee, and thought for a while. Those kids were probably in for a rough time of it. Libba's daddy wouldn't make it easy for them; he would find something to disapprove of in Link Winsom, that was a certainty. And on top of the struggles they'd have with Robinson Coltrain, there was a war on. They were bound to be separated sooner or later. They would face heartache and encounter challenges they couldn't even imagine. And they would both need more maturity, and more spiritual strength, than they had at the moment.

The mother heart in Thelma Breckinridge wanted to spare them that pain. But she couldn't. Maybe Link was right; maybe this was an answer to her prayers for both of them. Still, it wasn't the kind of answer she would have planned.

Then, deep in her spirit, she felt a faint nudge, and her mind heard an echo of her own words to Libba: *We all have to grow up sometime.*

Thelma chuckled to herself. She'd better be more careful how she prayed from now on.

20

☆ ☆ ☆

Dread and Determination

"What do you mean you're not going to see him again?"

Libba slumped on the bed and tried to avoid Willie's eyes, which bored intently into the top of her head. She could almost feel the heat of her cousin's anger, and she wanted to avoid a confrontation. Obviously her avoidance wasn't working.

Willie was mad—angrier than Libba had ever seen her. She wasn't going to let this go . . . not without a fight or, at the very least, a serious discussion.

But Libba wasn't in the mood for a discussion. "I'm just not going to see him again, and that's that."

"No, that's not that," Willie countered. "Link Winsom is the best thing that's happened to you in ages. We both know it. And I'm not leaving this room until you tell me once and for all what's gotten into you." With a resounding creak of the springs, Willie plopped down on the end of the bed and waited.

Libba sighed. Why couldn't Willie just leave her alone? She had to figure this out for herself, and she wasn't at all sure she wanted help. Especially not Willie's help. Willie saw entirely too much, and her perception made Libba nervous.

Especially now. Libba was upset enough about the conflicting emotions inside her without having to deal with Willie's probing.

She should have felt better after talking with Thelma. Thelma had helped her realize that she didn't really love Freddy, that she was just using him—she cringed inwardly at the very idea—to get away from Daddy. She didn't like the idea of hurting Freddy, of course, but as Thelma had said, *We all have to grow up sometime.*

Thelma was right; she had to let Freddy go. Libba knew that much. But now she was having second thoughts about Link. He hadn't called since the dance, and maybe he wouldn't. Maybe he didn't feel the way she did at all.

And where would that leave her? No Freddy, no Link. Nothing but Libba herself.

It wasn't a pleasant thought.

Still, she knew she couldn't keep on with Freddy—not after admitting, both to Thelma and to herself, why she had been with him in the first place. It wouldn't be right. It would only hurt him more in the long run.

Libba shuddered. She'd had too much time to think, that was the problem. She had gone over and over that night at the dance in her mind—the way Link looked at her, the feel of his arms around her. She had replayed her own responses as well, and what stood out most in her mind was that she had made a complete and utter fool of herself.

The truth was, she was ashamed. Ashamed of the way she had opened up to a complete stranger; ashamed of the things she had told Link Winsom—her hopes, her dreams, her ambitions. He probably thought she was a brainless little dimwit who didn't have sense enough to show any discretion. He was probably back at the barracks right now, telling his buddies how the high-and-mighty southern girl, who wouldn't dance with him without a "proper introduction," showed off on the dance floor and laughed like a horse.

She felt like an idiot. And she didn't like the feeling one bit.

★   ★   ★

Stork Simpson found Link in the USO, the scene of his conquest, sitting at a table with a Coca-Cola in one hand and a pen in the other. Link was totally absorbed in what he was writing; he didn't even look up.

Overcome with curiosity, Stork glanced over his friend's shoulder. Several pages lay on the table in disarray—a letter, apparently—and the page Link was now writing included several lines of a poem Stork couldn't quite make out.

"You really like this girl, huh?" Stork said.

Link jumped, sloshing Coke onto the table. He grabbed a couple of napkins and blotted the spill off the page, then turned and snarled at Stork. "Don't sneak up on me like that! Look what you made me do!"

Stork grinned and sat down across the table. "You'll have to be more alert than that, soldier, if you don't want your throat slit in a foxhole by some Kraut."

Link frowned at him. "Well, we're not *in* a foxhole, are we? We're in a USO building on an army base in Mississippi."

"Good, good," Stork said with a wink. "The way you've been acting, I wasn't sure you knew where you were."

Link gathered up his papers and turned them facedown on the table. "What's that supposed to mean?"

"You tell me," Stork countered. "Ever since you met Miss Green Eyes, you've been moping around like some sort of moonstruck calf. You and Slaughter. I swear, you're both acting like kids on a first date."

Link smiled—a distant, faraway expression. "I guess you're right. What's Owen's problem?"

"Same as yours, I suppose. Same symptoms, anyway. He's got it bad for Miss Green Eyes' cousin, Amazon Willie."

"You better not let him hear you call her that."

"Don't worry. I've got better sense than to stick my neck in a noose. Owen's little, but he's tough as nails. And he's made it clear he won't stand for any nonsense about The Girl with the Velvet Voice."

"The what?"

"Velvet voice. He keeps talking about her voice—how wonderful her voice is."

"He'd have to," Link chuckled. "He's too short to see above her waist."

"She's tall, all right," Stork conceded. "But Owen doesn't seem to notice. And she did seem to be a nice girl." He scratched his head. "I don't think Owen's going to get much use out of your little brown book."

Link stroked his chin absently, drumming the fingers of the other hand on his papers. "Me neither. Maybe I should look for somebody else to sell it to."

Stork cocked his head and looked at his buddy intently. He wasn't sure how long this transformation was going to last, but for now, Link really did seem serious.

Link propped his elbows on the table and rested his chin in his hands. "What's it like to be married, Stork?"

Married? How would I know? Stork thought. He had gone directly into basic training after the wedding. Three days of an after-the-fact honeymoon, thanks to Link's surprise weekend at Christmas, didn't exactly qualify him as an expert.

Still, Stork figured he had a more realistic perspective on marriage than Link did. At least he knew enough to realize that even in the best of marriages, things weren't the way you expected them to be. It wasn't all candlelight and romantic dinners; in fact, candlelight and romance was only about one percent of it. The rest was electricity bills and leftovers.

And, in the case of soldiers and their wives, a lot of separation, heartache, and misery.

Stork wanted to say, *Take it slow, Buddy. We're in a war here. This is no time to be making a lifelong commitment—especially when you have no idea how long your life will be.* But he didn't. Instead, he said, "Tell me about Miss Green Eyes."

Link didn't have to be asked twice. "She's a teacher—a high school English teacher. On temporary certification. She wants to go back and finish college." That dreamy smile spread over Link's face again; obviously the girl's resume was as fascinating to him as a racy novel.

Suddenly Link sat up and blinked, as if the lights had just come on in a darkened room. "Stork, do you believe in love at first sight?"

Stork hesitated. He should say no, counsel his friend to wait and see, to find out more about this girl—and his own future—before putting a name to his feelings. But he didn't want to burst Link's bubble altogether. "Sometimes," he hedged. "It depends."

"Depends on what?"

Stork took a deep breath. Maybe he could make Link see the truth—just a little—so that he wouldn't get in over his head. "Well, I guess it depends on the circumstances. We're in the middle of a war, you see, and there's no telling—"

Link didn't even let him finish his sentence. "That's exactly what I was thinking," he said, his eyes blazing with passion. "I mean, there aren't any promises for the future, so we need to grab onto what we've got while it's there, right? Take the bull by the horns; strike while the iron is hot—"

"Any other clichés you can think of?" Stork interjected. But Link wasn't listening.

"You're right, buddy—you're absolutely right!" Link jumped up and grabbed his papers. "She needs to know how I feel as soon as possible. We don't have any time to waste when the future's so uncertain." He looked at his watch. "I gotta go, Stork. I'll see you later." He started for the door, then came back in three strides to tousle the top of Stork's hair. "Thanks, Stork," he said earnestly. "You're a real pal."

"Think nothing of it," Stork muttered to Link's retreating back. "I always love giving good advice to my friends."

★ ★ ★

"But how do you know he thinks you're an idiot?" Willie was trying to maintain a modicum of patience with her cousin, but Libba didn't make it easy. The girl could be absolutely infuriating—shallow and self-centered one moment, morose and introspective the next. Personally, of the two, Willie preferred this introspective mode; at least it demonstrated some of the inner depth that Willie believed was hidden in Libba. But it brought its own set of problems. Willie had finally provoked Libba into telling her *what* she felt; now Willie was trying to find out *why*.

Willie knew more than she could tell her cousin about Link Winsom's feelings, but she couldn't admit that she and Owen had talked about the two of them.

"As far as I could see, the man was quite taken with you," Willie said in a comforting tone. "Why, he—"

"And how far could you see?" Libba snapped. "You had your eyes glued to Owen Slaughter the whole blessed evening."

Willie chuckled. Libba had her there. She was, indeed, smitten with Owen, and he seemed to feel the same about her. In fact, the euphoria she still carried from the dance made it difficult for her to identify with Libba's present foul mood. But she was trying. For her cousin's sake and for the peace of their household, she was trying.

"I could see enough to know that Sergeant Link Winsom kept you dancing all evening just so some other fella couldn't step in and take you over."

"Nonsense," Libba said, but she smiled just a little nevertheless. She sat up a little straighter on the bed and fluffed at her hair. "Do you really think so, Willie?" she said eagerly. "Do you think he really likes me?"

"I'm certain of it," Willie said firmly. "But how do you feel about him?"

"I'm a little scared," Libba said in a whispery voice.

"Scared? What on earth—," Willie began gruffly, then tempered her tone and started again. "Libba," she said with a sigh, "why would you possibly be afraid?"

Libba looked up, and Willie saw in her eyes a look she hadn't seen in years—the expression of five-year-old Tater, trying desperately to please her overbearing father, heartbroken because she had failed. The expression had vanished over the years, replaced by a look of fierce determination, of rebellion. Now it was back.

"Tell me," Willie said quietly.

"Promise you won't tell anyone—*anyone!*" Libba pleaded.

"I promise."

"Not even Mabel Rae?"

Willie crossed her heart solemnly. "Not even Mabel. Now, give."

"I'm afraid of becoming like Mama," Libba said.

The bluntness of the confession caught Willie off guard, and her eyebrows shot up.

"Oh, I know," Libba went on. "Y'all both think I'm so much like Daddy—bullying people, taking control. Don't bother to deny it, Willie; I've seen the looks you and Mabel Rae sling at each other. You think I picked somebody like poor Freddy so I could always get my own way. But the truth is, I'd do almost anything to avoid the kind of life Mama has had."

"What kind of life is that?" Willie prodded.

"Mama has no personality, no backbone," Libba responded decisively. "If she ever had any, living with Daddy has squeezed it all out of her. Maybe she thought she loved him at the beginning. But there's nothing there now—nothing! Just Mama catering to Daddy and tiptoeing around on eggshells so she won't upset him. It's horrible, Willie. I won't live like that."

"So you thought that having someone like Freddy was preferable—someone who'd cater to you instead?" The question came out harsher than Willie had intended, and she winced inwardly. But she couldn't call the words back, no matter how much she might want to.

Libba didn't seem to notice—or if she noticed, accepted the hard truth matter-of-factly. "I don't think I knew I was doing it—not consciously, anyway. But when I met Link Winsom, he made me feel so . . . so different. He didn't bow and scrape to me like Freddy does; he just treated me like—like—"

"Like a woman?" Willie finished.

"Like a *person*," Libba corrected. "Like I was important to him just because I was me, not because—"

"Not because you were Queen of the Universe." Willie couldn't suppress the smile that crept to her lips.

To her great relief, Libba giggled. "I guess I have been acting pretty silly, haven't I? But it wasn't deliberate. I was just trying to—" She groped for words. "To keep myself safe, I guess. To keep from making the same mistake Mama did."

Willie nodded. "So how does this relate to the fascinating Sergeant Winsom?"

Libba's expression darkened. "I like him, Willie. I like him a lot. Maybe I could even love him."

"And?"

"And that scares me. I realized when I was with him that he's not a bit like Freddy. He's different. He's—"

"A man," Willie supplied.

Libba shut her eyes and frowned. "Uh-huh. And what if he turns out to be a man like Daddy?"

Willie reached across the bed and took her cousin's hands. She waited until Libba opened her eyes. "And what if he doesn't?" she asked gently.

Libba's eyes widened, and Willie could almost see the possibilities flashing through her mind.

"But how am I going to know?" Libba asked. "What if I—" A look of pure terror shot across her face. "What if I fall in love with him and then he hurts me?"

Willie squeezed Libba's hands tightly and looked deep into her pale green eyes. "Give the guy a chance, Libba," she said. "You'll never know until you try."

21

★ ★ ★

Beware the Ides of March

Libba woke to a terrible clanging sound and fumbled for her alarm clock. With a groan she pushed in the alarm button, but nothing happened. The clanging continued. Libba stared stupidly at the clock. Seven-fifteen.

Seven-fifteen! Why hadn't someone called her? She'd be late for class—for the third time this term.

She threw off the covers and jerked to a sitting position. Then she remembered: There was no school today. The Mississippi Education Association meetings were being held in Jackson, and the students had been given three days off.

So had she and her cousins. Because they were only teaching on temporary certificates, they weren't expected to attend the meetings. They had three days—three entire, glorious days—to themselves. No students. No papers to grade. No classes. No alarm clocks.

Libba sighed and crawled back under the covers, reveling in that luxurious half sleep that came with realizing she didn't have to get up after all.

The clanging continued, not her alarm, but the sound of pots and pans rattling in the kitchen. Willie and Mabel Rae, no doubt, making some kind of ungodly concoction for breakfast.

Libba growled and pressed a pillow over her head. For heaven's sake, you'd think a herd of elephants was cooking in there, for all the racket they were making.

Going back to sleep was obviously not a viable option, although it was an attractive one. With an exaggerated sigh, she rolled out of bed and groped her way to the kitchen.

Willie stood at the counter stirring something in an enormous bowl and humming to herself. Libba narrowed her eyes and shook her head. How anyone could be so infernally cheerful in the morning was beyond her comprehension. She filched a coffee cup from the neatly arranged table and stumbled toward the stove.

"Good morning, Cousin!" Willie said with a smile that could light up half of Memphis. "Beautiful day, isn't it?"

She did this deliberately to irritate people, Libba was convinced. It worked.

"Morning," Libba snarled. She reached for the coffeepot bare-handed and burned her fingers. "Ow!"

Willie leaned over and handed her a pot holder. "Careful," she said sweetly. "'Beware the Ides of March.'"

Libba looked at Willie and shook her head. "The Ides of March?"

Willie grinned. "It's March 15. You're the English teacher—*Julius Caesar,* remember?"

"Oh, yeah." Libba sat down heavily at the table. She could barely remember her own name at this hour of the morning. If old Julius had had relatives like hers, he wouldn't have been murdered; he would have committed suicide.

She took a drink of the coffee and scorched the roof of her mouth. It burned all the way down. But Libba didn't say anything; she would avoid any more Ides-of-March comments if at all possible.

"Where's Mabel Rae?" Libba looked around as if expecting her cousin to jump out of the pantry and give her heart failure right on the spot.

"She ran up to the post office to get the mail," Willie responded.

"At this hour?"

"Mrs. Grevis puts the mail up at seven," Willie said. "Mabel will be back in a few minutes. I'm fixing banana pancakes—how does that sound?"

"Nauseating." Libba got up and refilled her coffee cup.

"You could do with a bit of syrup," Willie commented, slanting a glance in Libba's direction. "Sweeten you up a little." She pointed to Libba's coffee cup. "Black coffee makes you bitter."

It isn't the coffee, Libba thought sullenly. It wasn't even being awakened by the eardrum-shattering commotion of the Pachyderm School of Breakfast Cuisine. It was the fact that she still hadn't heard a word from Link Winsom.

She had defied Daddy to go to the dance in the first place, risking life and limb—or at least a sound tongue-lashing. She would have heard by now if he had found out. Apparently she was safe on that count.

But then, after taking her life in her hands, and after determining that she would, in fact, give Link Winsom a chance, she hadn't heard so much as a peep from him. Owen Slaughter had called Willie three times on Sunday and once last evening. By the third time, Mrs. Grevis had grumbled that Willie had more emergencies than all the girls in Tullahoma County put together and that she might as well break down and have a telephone installed in the apartment. She was getting tired of the interruptions.

Libba smiled a little at the thought. The only thing Charity Grevis ever did that she might not want "interrupted" was sit at her front window—or at the counter in the post office—spying on everyone in Eden. The woman knew who went out at night, when they came in, and probably what they had been doing while they were gone. She knew that the Bakers' black mutt had jumped the fence and fathered the puppies of the Sheridans' prize-winning apricot poodle—a scandal that had all of Eden talking for weeks. She probably knew the contents of every piece of mail that passed through her hands.

It was nothing short of a miracle that Charity Grevis hadn't found out about Freddy Sturgis's coming to the apartment that night right before Christmas. Only her bout with influenza had saved all three of the Coltrain girls from being thrown out on their little behinds.

Libba sighed. Poor Freddy. She wasn't sure quite what she was going to do about him. She had already decided she couldn't keep going out with him, pretending to be interested. That wouldn't be fair to him. But now she was beginning to reconsider. Link Winsom hadn't called, and might not, no matter what Willie thought. Maybe she should keep her options open. No point in burning bridges until you were certain you wouldn't want to retrace your steps.

Willie sat down beside her at the table and gave her a curious look. "What's on your mind, Libba?"

Not another heart-to-heart talk, please. Libba wasn't sure she could take any more of her cousin's compassionate understanding. She thought she liked Willie better when they were picking on each other. All this seriousness was beginning to take its toll.

Libba shrugged her shoulders and took another sip of coffee.

"He'll call, Cousin," Willie said sympathetically. Willie could afford to be charitable; apparently Owen Slaughter was absolutely crazy about her. People had always told her love was blind, Libba thought. Maybe it was true. Or maybe the guy just hadn't gotten a good look at Willie's face yet.

Libba reprimanded herself immediately for such a thought. Willie had a lot of good qualities. She was . . . well, noble. She had a good heart. She was smart. And she *could* cook, which was more than Libba could say for herself. Willie would make some man a good wife. A loving, loyal wife. And Libba had to admit, albeit reluctantly, that Willie deserved a man who adored her. Even if he only came up to her shoulder blades.

"He'll call," Willie repeated. "Give him time."

Libba shook off her moodiness and tried to smile. "Sure he will," she said halfheartedly. "But in the meantime, why don't you show me how to make that pancake batter? And your wonderful biscuits."

Willie's eyes widened. "Seriously?"

Libba nodded. "Seriously. Jitterbugging's important—*really* important," she said with a laugh. "But a good biscuit recipe never hurts."

★　★　★

At seven forty-five, Mabel Rae swept through the back door of the apartment with a cheery, "Beware the Ides of March!" She froze in her tracks when she saw Libba in the kitchen in her bathrobe and slippers, up to her elbows in biscuit dough.

"My stars and garters!" she said breathlessly, dropping the mail onto the kitchen table. "If this isn't a sight I never thought I'd see."

Libba turned. "Get an eyeful, Cousin. This may be the last time you ever see it."

Willie laughed and patted Libba on the arm. "You're doing just fine, Libba. Never mind Mabel."

"I never listen to Mabel anyway," Libba quipped, returning her attention to the bowl of goo in front of her.

"Now that's the gospel truth," Mabel answered, settling down at the table. "But you might want to listen this morning—there's a letter from Charlie."

Willie craned her neck to look over Mabel's shoulder as she tore open the letter. "Where is he? Still in Italy?"

Mabel scanned the first page. "Apparently not. Seems he's been transferred to a hospital in England—Birmingham."

Willie sighed. "Then it'll probably be weeks before he gets our letters. I wish they'd quit moving him around so much."

"He says he's working with a new doctor," Mabel said. "And he thinks he may be going back to his unit soon."

Willie squinted at the letter. "It's in his own handwriting," she said. "His arm must be pretty nearly healed by now." She shook her head. "I guess he still feels like he has a job to do over there, but I have to admit, I wish he'd come on home. I hate to think of him going back to the front."

Mabel shuffled pages and looked up at Willie. "You've been praying for him, haven't you, Sister?"

"Of course. Every day."

"What do you pray?"

"That God will protect him and bring him home safely, that he will heal and get stronger, that the Lord will give him direction and take care of him . . . the usual stuff."

Mabel nodded. "Me, too. But have you ever known Charlie to talk openly about prayer or God's direction?"

Willie frowned. "No. It's just not his way, I guess. He believes, I'm sure, but he never talks about it."

"Well, listen to this: 'I have prayed a lot about this decision. Because of my wound, I could have come home to recuperate, but I feel that God has something else for me to do here—something real important. I've asked to be reassigned to the front. I hope you'll understand and not be upset that it will be a little longer before I get back. . . .'" Mabel slanted a glance at Willie. "What do you make of that?"

"It doesn't sound like our brother," she agreed. "Either he's changed or—"

"Or he's hiding something," Libba interjected.

"Oh, Libba, will you stop with that 'hiding something' stuff?" Mabel snapped. "What could Charlie possibly have to hide?"

Willie raised an eyebrow at her sister. "This time, Mabel, I'm afraid I agree with Libba. Something doesn't sound right about Charlie's letter. I can't put my finger on it exactly, but there's something behind his words that disturbs me." Willie frowned. "Somehow I think our brother needs a lot of prayer right now. Maybe God *is* directing him to go back to the front, I don't know. But it sounds pretty fishy that Charlie would be so sure about it."

"It sounds like he's trying to convince you, you mean?" Libba asked.

"Or maybe trying to convince himself."

"So what do we do?" Mabel prodded.

"There's not much we can do," Willie said. "Except trust God—and pray like crazy."

Mabel folded the letter and set it aside with a sigh.

"Is there anything else?" Willie asked, waving at the stack of mail.

"I don't know," Mabel answered. "I got so excited about Charlie's letter I forgot to look." Libba and Willie turned back to their biscuits, and Mabel began shuffling absently through the rest of the mail.

Libba was intently following Willie's directions when Mabel Rae's voice interrupted her train of thought.

"Libba?"

"Not now, Mabel." Libba waved a dough-covered hand in a dismissive gesture. "In a minute."

"Libba—"

"Not now, Mabel!"

"Libba—"

Libba whirled around menacingly. "What *is* it, Mabel Rae? Just what is so important?"

Mabel waved a thick envelope in front of Libba's nose. "The mailman cometh."

"What?" Libba squinted at the letter. The envelope, addressed in a neat, masculine hand, bore the return address: *Sgt. J. L. Winsom, Camp McCrane, Mississippi.*

Libba lunged for the letter but remembered just in time that her fingers were covered with a sticky mixture of flour and shortening. She snatched up a dish towel and rubbed off most of the dough, then took the envelope from Mabel Rae and turned it over and over in her hands.

"Well, aren't you going to open it?" Mabel prodded.

Libba stared at her. "Open it?"

"Yes, silly—open it!" Mabel Rae reached for the envelope as if she would open it herself, but Willie's hand clamped down on her arm.

"Maybe our cousin would rather read her letter in private," Willie said pointedly. She turned to Libba. "We can hold off breakfast for a while."

Libba turned and bolted for her room.

★ ★ ★

With her heart pounding in her chest, Libba settled on the bed and held the letter out in front of her. She traced her finger over her name—*her name,* written in his very own handwriting! *Miss Elizabeth Coltrain . . .*

Just the idea of his writing her name made her insides go fluttery. She was acting like a silly schoolgirl, she knew, but right now she didn't care. Freddy had never made her feel like this, not once. Nor had any other boy. Maybe that was the difference. Link Winsom was no boy.

Carefully she slid a hairpin under the flap and slit the envelope open to reveal a sheaf of pages—seven in all, written in that neat, angular hand. Then, her fingers trembling, she propped a pillow between her back and the headboard and began to read:

> Dear Libba,
> I've thought about you for days, ever since that first glimpse

of you outside the USO. You, with your wide wonderful smile and your soft green eyes.

Libba gasped. He thought she had a "wonderful smile"? Then maybe he didn't notice that she laughed like a horse.

I wanted to call you on Sunday but thought better of it. It occurred to me that you might need a little time to absorb what happened to us on Saturday night. Something did happen, didn't it? I felt like it did, but maybe I was just too involved in my own emotions to notice whether you were responding the same way.

And besides, I've always been told that I'm better at express-ing myself in writing than in speaking. That may serve us well when I'm shipped out, but I'll have to work on the speaking part, too, because I intend to tell you face-to-face, the first chance I get, how deeply I was affected by our meeting.

In the meantime, I wanted to take this opportunity to tell you about myself and to let you know what you're getting in for if you agree to see me again. You will agree, won't you? I'd be devastated if you said no.

Libba smiled. Somehow she couldn't see this self-assured, confident man being "devastated" by being turned down by a woman. But it was a nice thought, anyway.

I am the youngest of seven children—the "baby," if you will—and I suppose I've been treated that way, at least by my sisters. My father is a lawyer—not the well-to-do kind, I'm afraid, but the kind who takes cases for the down-and-outers. He never makes much money, but he is a good man and is well respected in St. Joe, our hometown. Our mother died when I was five, and Dad never remarried. Too busy with his practice, I guess.

My oldest sister, RuthAnn, who is fourteen years older than I am, raised me, and she spoiled me terribly, if you want to know the truth. But I don't think it's hurt me much. I truly am a nice fellow. I'm smart and industrious—I worked at a bank before I enlisted, and I have a good job and a bright future to go back to, if I want it. The point of all this, Libba, is to convince you that I am serious about developing a relationship with you. I'm a good prospect, if you want to put it that way.

The letter went on for six more pages, detailing all the positive qualities Link Winsom had to offer the lady of his choice. He told her more about his father and his upbringing under the watchful eye of sister RuthAnn, and about his oldest brother, who had gone away to Australia at the age of eighteen and hadn't been heard from since. He wrote about his mother—how heartbroken he had been when she died, and how he barely remembered her any longer.

And then he told her why she should give serious consideration to a Yankee. Libba was impressed that he had even thought of this issue, but even more amazed at his insight into the nature of relationships between men and women in the South.

Southern men, he said, didn't know how to treat a woman properly. They made a big fuss and show about putting their ladies up on pedestals, but when it came down to the business of daily life, they either abdicated all responsibility and let the woman take over or they insisted on a rigid, ironfisted kind of control. They didn't really respect and honor their women, not in the way a woman should be respected and honored.

It was a risky thing to say, coming from a Northerner. Yankees usually didn't fare well when they criticized anything about the southern way of life. They didn't understand the South, the natives would say, or they had no respect for long-standing tradition.

Ironically, this Yankee man, Sergeant Link Winsom, seemed to understand more about the South than Libba herself did. She hadn't ever thought about it in those terms before, but what he was saying about southern men dovetailed perfectly with her own experience. He had put into words what she had never been able to articulate. Freddy Sturgis was an abdicator. Daddy was an iron fist. And somewhere there had to be a balance. Responsibility without domination. Affection without submission. A man who would love her for herself without having to make her into what he wanted her to be.

Maybe Link Winsom was that balance.

Meet me at the Paradise Garden Wednesday evening at seven, Link wrote at the end of his letter.

Wednesday . . . *today was Wednesday!* Libba's heart raced. She would see him again—tonight!

Libba read the letter three times before she heard Willie calling her to come to breakfast. She brushed her hair and went to the table with the letter still in hand.

"It smells delicious." Libba inhaled the aroma of warm syrup and salty fried bacon and smiled appreciatively. Then she looked up to find Mabel Rae and Willie staring at her curiously.

"What?"

"What was in that letter? Bad news?" Mabel Rae said. "You look kind of . . . faraway." She poked Willie in the arm. "It is the Ides of March, after all," she said. "Anything can happen."

Libba made an elaborate production of putting her napkin in her lap. "Yes, anything can happen," she said at last. "Anything. For instance—" She cleared her throat. "I believe I'm going to marry Link Winsom."

22

★ ★ ★

Paradise Rendezvous

Thelma Breckinridge leaned over the side of the piano and nudged Ivory Brownlee. "Play something nice for them," she whispered. Ivory nodded and grinned. The black spaces where two of his teeth were missing made him look as if he carried a keyboard in his mouth, but the effect was charming nevertheless. Ivory liked to see people happy—even Libba Coltrain, who usually snubbed him when she came into the cafe.

Tonight, Libba had seemed a little nicer, a bit more tolerant. She had come into the Paradise Garden a little before seven, smiling like the Cheshire cat but saying very little—a definite change for Libba. She had settled herself at the table in the far corner and sat there in silence, staring out the window, fiddling with what looked to be a letter. Thelma got the impression she was waiting for someone. She hoped it wasn't Freddy Sturgis.

Then, at ten after seven, the bell over the door jingled, and Link Winsom came in. He looked around, caught sight of Libba, and made a beeline for her. Thelma couldn't hear their conversation, but it was obvious that Libba was happy—very happy. Link looked pretty satisfied with himself, too, come to think of it.

Thelma winked at Ivory as he began playing "People Will Say We're in Love" from the musical *Oklahoma*. She chuckled. Maybe it was a bit premature, but a girl couldn't help hoping.

She took her pad and pencil and two menus and went over to the table. The two of them were already deep in conversation, and it took them several moments to realize that she was there. When they finally did come down to earth, Link looked up at her with a startled expression. "Thelma! Uh . . . hello."

"Hey, handsome," she said. "Evening, Libba." Libba didn't say anything—just smiled as if she were about to explode.

"What can I get for you?"

"Get for us?" Link repeated stupidly.

Thelma suppressed a smile. Obviously the boy was already over the edge. She patted his hand and set a menu down in front of him. "Yes, darlin'. This is a cafe, remember?"

Link scanned the menu and looked across at Libba. "Do you mind if I order for both of us?" Libba smiled and shook her head.

Now, this is one for the record books, Thelma thought. *Libba Coltrain keeping her mouth shut.* Aloud, she said, "What'll it be?"

"Two of your wonderful fried-chicken dinners," Link said, handing the menus back to her. "And—" he lifted a questioning eyebrow in Libba's direction—"iced tea?"

Again Libba nodded.

"Thanks, Thelma. We'll probably have dessert later."

Thelma took their order into the kitchen and began to serve up their plates. Through the service window she watched them sitting together, their heads close, their hands touching every now and then, and a feeling of sweet sadness came over her. She could see herself in Libba, sitting with Robert Raintree, making plans for the future . . . the future that never happened.

Tears filled her eyes, and she sent up a silent, impassioned plea that Libba would never have to endure such heartache—that when Link Winsom left, as he certainly would do, he would come back to her again.

★ ★ ★

"Now tell me about *your* family. I want to know all about you." Link shifted forward in his chair and pushed aside the plates littered with leftover chicken bones, corn cobs, and the turnip greens he had left untouched. He broke off a section of the last piece of cornbread, buttered it, and put it into his mouth. "Mmm. I never had such good cornbread." He grinned. "In fact, I never had cornbread at all."

Libba looked at him with a wry smile. "Yankees," she said with a mocking laugh. "How did y'all ever win the war without cornbread?"

"We used bullets instead, I expect," Link countered.

Libba considered telling him that her cornbread was nearly as tough as bullets, but she decided to save that tidbit of information until a later date.

Maybe she could get a few more lessons from Willie before that particular moment of truth came.

But she had to find some way to divert the conversation from her family. They had spent the last hour talking about his background—his father, his oldest sister, RuthAnn, his large and apparently loving collection of sisters and brothers, aunts, uncles, and cousins. Just hearing about the Winsom clan made Libba's heart wrench. She had always longed for such a family—a warm, supportive father like Bennett Winsom, a sister like RuthAnn.

She had Willie and Mabel Rae, of course, but she had never managed to get close to Uncle William and Aunt Bess. There was too much hostility between Daddy and his brother—mostly from Daddy's side. As a child, she had begged to be allowed to spend part of her summers on the farm with the cousins, but Daddy wouldn't allow it. They were dirt farmers, he would say, and even if they were his own kin, they weren't fit company for his Tater. Who knew what kind of bad manners she might pick up from them? And a southern lady was nothing if she didn't have proper manners.

Libba forced her attention back to Link's question. "You didn't touch your turnip greens," she hedged.

He threw back his head and laughed—a vibrant, wonderful sound that made Libba's heart race. "Where I come from, we eat the turnips and give the tops to the rabbits." He laid his hand over hers and looked into her eyes. "But if it's important to you, I'll try."

With that, he forked up a mouthful of the cold greens and swallowed. Libba winced. Hot, they were delicious, at least by southern standards. But cold and congealed, turnip greens were slimy and unappetizing to even the most die-hard Rebel.

"Marvelous," Link said. "I could eat a bushel." He raised his hand and turned as if to summon more turnip greens from the kitchen. "Thel—"

"Stop it!" Laughing, she grabbed at his hand.

Their fingers touched first, then his eyes met hers. She could not look away. The laugher died on her lips, and she sat there, transfixed, as he leaned over the table toward her.

"Libba," he breathed. Then his lips met hers—softly, like the brush of a warm spring wind. She could not have resisted his kiss if she had wanted to, and resisting was the last thing on her mind. Her heart lurched, and she felt his fingers stroking the inside of her wrist—

"Tater!"

Libba jerked back.

She turned, and her heart sank to the pit of her stomach. This could not be happening . . . it *couldn't*.

Robinson Coltrain stood in the doorway of the Paradise Garden Cafe.

23

★ ★ ★

Serpent in the Garden

Thelma had seen it coming, but there was nothing she could do to stop it.

She had never seen Robinson Coltrain look so angry, and his temper was a legend in these parts. He might be a Presbyterian deacon, but when his Irish was up, people scattered like chickens in a thunderstorm. He stood there in the doorway, and she could see his rage building from all the way across the room.

Libba sat like a stone at the corner table, looking as if she might break into tears at any moment, and poor Link appeared totally confused.

Thelma approached Robinson cautiously and put a hand on his arm. His muscles flinched under her touch, but he didn't look at her. "Tater!" he repeated, his voice quiet and menacing.

Thelma squeezed Robinson's arm to get his attention. "Now, Robinson, there's no call to get upset," she said in a low voice. "The girl's not doing anything wrong."

He looked at her, finally, and Thelma almost wished he hadn't. His eyes were blazing, and a red flush was creeping up his neck into his ears. "Stay out of it, Thelma," he snarled. "This is between me and my daughter." He jerked his arm free and stalked over to the table.

Thelma followed. Libba still sat frozen, her eyes wide and bright with unshed tears. Link turned and looked up with a curious expression as Robinson approached.

"Well," he said, ignoring Link and turning his ire on Libba, "when one of the deacons came into the board meeting tonight and asked me who the soldier was that my daughter was with over at the Paradise Garden, I told him he must be mistaken. But I see that he wasn't."

Libba blinked hard and swallowed. "No, Daddy, I guess not."

Robinson cleared his throat. "Humph. At least it's not that pansy artist."

Out of the corner of her eye, Thelma saw the crooked smile that passed fleetingly over Link Winsom's face.

Link got to his feet and held out his hand. "I'm a soldier, all right, but I've never been called an artist." He paused. "Or a pansy."

The fury in Robinson Coltrain's expression dissipated, and he shot a glance at his daughter. "Where are your manners, girl? Are you going to introduce us or not?"

As if jerked out of a coma, Libba sat up. "Daddy, I . . . of course. This is Sergeant Lincoln Winsom. Link, meet my father, Robinson Coltrain."

Link shook Robinson's hand heartily. "Mr. Coltrain, I am so glad to meet you. Libba has told me so much about you." He slanted an odd look at Libba and smiled.

"Yes, well." Robinson took a seat across from Libba, and Thelma hurriedly cleared away the remains of their dinner. In the corner, Ivory began banging out a ragtime rendition of "Accentuate the Positive."

"So," Robinson said, turning to Link, "just where did you and my daughter meet?"

Thelma held her breath and watched Libba. The girl wasn't breathing either.

"At the base, actually. We met at a USO dance."

Thelma squeezed Libba's shoulder, picked up the dirty dishes, and ran for the kitchen. She didn't want her good plates broken in the explosion.

★ ★ ★

If Libba lived to be a hundred, she would never entirely believe what was happening right before her eyes. Link and her father were actually *talking*—not arguing, but talking!

Daddy didn't seem convinced about Link, but at least he hadn't taken a swing at him yet. And he had practically ignored her, except to ask her to leave them alone for a while and go talk to Thelma.

Thelma had gone by the table twice, once with the first round of coffee, and a second time with refills and two pieces of peach cobbler—on the house, she said. Now they were on their fourth cup, and Libba was sitting at the counter with Thelma, desperate to know what they were talking about.

"They're probably talking about *me*, Thelma."

"That's a pretty good bet, hon."

"But what are they saying? I mean, Daddy doesn't look mad, not any-more, but you know how he hates soldiers."

"Soldiers?" Thelma asked. "Or just that little doughboy, Freddy Sturgis?"

Libba had never heard Freddy called a *doughboy,* but it fit, and she giggled.

"It's nice to hear you laugh," Thelma said. "For a while there, I thought you were going to cry."

Libba nodded. "Me, too. I always cry when I'm mad, and I was so furious at Daddy for coming in like he did. Like he owns me!"

"Well, I don't reckon even your daddy expected to come in here and find you kissing on some soldier."

Libba felt her face grow warm. "You saw?"

"I saw. And so did your daddy." Thelma paused and gave the girl a grin. "How was it?"

Shocked, Libba stared at Thelma for a minute, then relaxed and smiled. "It was wonderful."

Thelma pushed her hair out of her eyes and smiled. "I'm sure it was, honey. It's always wonderful at the beginning. Enjoy it. But—"

"I know, Thelma. *Be careful.* Don't worry, I won't do anything I'll regret. Link's not like that, anyway." For a brief instant, Libba recalled her father's words: *Men will do anything to get what they want.* But not this man. Not Link Winsom.

Libba continued to watch the table until the two men stood up, shook hands, and came over to her and Thelma at the counter.

"I think we'll stay and have another cup of coffee," Link was saying. "Then I'll see Libba safely home."

Libba's father nodded. "All right, but don't keep her out too long." He headed for the door, then turned and pointed a finger at Link. "Two weeks from Friday, six o'clock. Don't be late."

"Tell Mrs. Coltrain I'm looking forward to meeting her."

★ ★ ★

"He invited you to *dinner?* At our house?" Libba shook her head. This was all too impossible to believe. "What else did he say to you?"

"Oh, not much." Link waved his hand. "You know, man stuff, mostly—nuts and bolts and hardware—"

Libba dug her fingers into his wrist. "Tell me what he *really* said!"

Link turned his dark eyes on her with a somber expression. "He said that if I wanted to call on you, I had his permission, but not to get my hopes up."

Libba frowned. *Not get his hopes up?* What did that mean? She knew she should be encouraged that her father had talked to Link, actually invited him to dinner. Maybe she was just being pessimistic, but something seemed wrong about this, very wrong. She couldn't shake the feeling that her father had something up his sleeve. Something that didn't bode well for either Link or her.

THREE

PS, I Love You

APRIL 1944

24

★ ★ ★

A Friend like You

April 1944

"You can't marry this girl!" Stork shouted. "You haven't even known her a month!"

Link shook his head. Stork should understand, given how he obviously felt about Madge, but somehow, now that it was Link's Great Romance, his buddy Stork had gone logical on him. And it was driving Link nuts.

"What do you know about her, anyway?"

"She's bright and funny . . . and she can dance like crazy," Link offered with a wink.

"Dance?" Stork sputtered. "You're going to gamble your whole future on a girl because she wiggles her behind to the rhythm?"

Link sighed. There was no talking to Stork. He had his mind made up, and nothing Link said was going to change it.

Stork resumed his interrogation in a slightly more civil tone. "Who is she? What's her family like? Have you even met them?"

"I've met the father, and I'm going to dinner there—tonight. Besides, what's her family got to do with anything? I'm marrying her, not them."

Stork rolled his eyes. "Don't bet on it. When you marry the girl, you marry the family."

Link furrowed his brow and scowled at his friend. "What do you know about it? Madge doesn't have any family. You've got no in-laws to contend with . . . no family except your own—"

"My point exactly," Stork interrupted. "I'm thinking about Madge, not myself. When she married me—for better or worse—she got my family, too. With me, I hope it was for better. With Mother, I have no doubt it was for worse."

"So you wish you hadn't married her, because she's having a difficult time with your mother?"

Stork shook his head. "Of course not. I'm just saying—"

"That if Madge had taken your advice, *she* wouldn't have married *you,*" Link snapped. "But in your case, of course, there were extenuating circumstances."

It was a vicious thing to say. Stork glanced at Link, and the miserable look in his eyes made Link wish he had never brought up the subject of the baby. "I'm sorry, pal," he said contritely. "I didn't mean it like that."

Stork waved a hand in the air. "It's all right. And no doubt you're absolutely right. Who am I to give advice to my best friend? Who says that my experience should apply to anyone else? I'm a jerk. A jerk whose hormones got the best of him, and now look at the mess I'm in."

Link grinned and socked Stork on the arm. "A real mess, that's for sure," he said lightly. "You've got a wife who adores you and a beautiful baby on the way, who'll be here before you know it, grabbing at your pant legs and calling you 'Daddy.' It's horrible, Stork—I don't know how you stand it."

In spite of himself, Stork smiled. Then the smile faded, and his expression grew pensive. "The doctor says it will only be a few days now—a week at the most. And I'll be stuck here."

It was too bad, Link thought, that Stork couldn't be with Madge when the baby was born. But maybe there was something he could do about it. A little gift for Stork, for Madge, and for the tiny little Simpson who was about to make his or her entrance into the world.

★ ★ ★

"You want to do what?" Major Mansfield stared at Link as if he'd lost his mind.

"I'd like you to give Sergeant Simpson my leave, sir," Link repeated. "In fact, I'll never ask you for anything again, if you'll just give him a six-day pass so he can go home and be with his wife when his baby is born."

The CO narrowed his eyes and studied Link. "Did Simpson put you up to this?" he barked.

Link shook his head. "No, sir. He doesn't even know I'm here."

The major turned his back on Link and stared out the window behind his desk. Link followed his gaze to a small bird's nest on a tree branch just beyond the window. As they both watched, a robin fluttered down to the branch, and three tiny open beaks appeared above the edge of the nest.

"That's the father," Major Mansfield said without turning around. "I watch them every day. He and the mother share the burden of feeding the young. And those little peepers eat all the time, I can tell you."

He sank heavily into his chair and swiveled back toward Link. "I had a son once," he said quietly, as if to himself. "I wasn't there when he was born. I wasn't there for his first words, or his first steps, or his first day of school. I was always . . . somewhere else. Spending time with my mistress."

Link's eyes widened. Major Mansfield's head shot up, and he glared at Link. "The *army*, Sergeant. The army. I was too much the consummate soldier to spend any of my time or attention on my family. And now they're gone."

"Gone, sir?" Link ventured. "Did they . . . did they die?"

"Not exactly." The major shook his head. "My wife divorced me and took the boy with her. Married an asphalt salesman. My son calls him Dad. . . ." He paused, then shook himself as if trying to rid his mind of the memory. "The boy is twenty-three now. He hates me. Won't talk to me. I'm not even sure where he is. The last I heard, he was living in Portland, but that's been a couple of years ago. I don't know . . . I just don't know."

Link clasped his hands behind him and looked at the floor. So there was a heart beating underneath that chest full of medals after all! He hadn't expected anything like this. He had planned to come into Mansfield's office, charm him, give him a spiel about duty to family as well as duty to the army, play on his sympathies, and do whatever else was necessary to squeeze a pass out of the old bird. For Stork's sake, he was even prepared to grovel if he had to. Now it appeared that groveling might be entirely unnecessary.

The major jerked open a desk drawer, pulled out a form, and scrawled his signature across the bottom. Then he handed it to Link and cleared his throat. "You've got your buddy's pass, soldier. Tell him to get his tail home as fast as the train will take him. And make sure he's back here in six days. If he goes AWOL again, you're the one who will pay for it!"

Link nodded solemnly. "I'll tell him. And you don't have anything to worry about, sir. I'll take full responsibility for his being back on time. I'll—"

"Yeah, yeah," Mansfield growled. "Now go. Dismissed."

Link saluted and headed for the door.

"Hold it, Winsom."

"Yes, sir?"

"If you breathe a word to anyone about our discussion here today, I'll have you cleaning latrines for the rest of your military life. Understood?"

Link exhaled sharply. "Yes, sir. Understood." Of course he understood. Mansfield couldn't have the other men under his command knowing about this soft spot, this vulnerable white underbelly of past pain. And although Link knew instinctively that the major's revelation gave him plenty of ammunition for influence in the future, he also knew he would never use the information against the CO. In that one moment, which Mansfield would undoubtedly identify as a "moment of weakness," Link's respect for his commanding officer had increased tenfold.

He turned and faced the major, Stork's pass gripped in his hand. "You're a good man, Major," he said, trying to still the quivering in his voice. "A noble man."

"Thank you, Sergeant." Mansfield's voice was gruff. "I wish I could believe it of myself." He waved his hand. "Now, get out of here. Your buddy has a train to catch."

"Yes, sir."

"And, Winsom?"

"Sir?"

Major Mansfield reached into his pocket and tossed a wad of bills in Link's direction. "Pay the guy's fare home." His eyes met Link's with a look that could only be described as longing. "I hope Simpson knows what a good friend he's got."

★ ★ ★

Link took Stork to the station at Tillatoba, a one-street town that had little to offer besides a place to catch the next train out.

"I still don't know how you managed it," Stork kept repeating on the bumpy drive into town. "I asked Major Minefield for a pass, and he wouldn't give me the time of day."

"I keep telling you, I didn't do anything," Link hedged. "I just happened to pass by his office, and he called me in. Said he had thought about it and changed his mind. Said a man should be there to see his firstborn child come into the world."

Link wouldn't tell Stork the truth—that he had bartered his own leave, that the major had paid for the train fare as well as giving Stork the pass, that Mansfield was trying, in his own way, to do penance for the sins of the past. He wouldn't breathe a word of it—not to Stork, not to anyone.

When Stork leaned off the platform of the passenger car and waved goodbye as the train pulled out of the station, Link breathed a sigh of relief. Stork would get to see his wife—and, if she delivered on time, his new baby.

"Call the major's office!" Link shouted over the rumble of the engine. "He'll get the message to us!"

Stork nodded enthusiastically and continued to wave until he was just a speck in the distance.

Stork would call. The major would be the first to get the news of the birth. It was Link Winsom's gift to the man he would never again refer to as "Major Minefield."

25

★ ★ ★

Dinner Date

Libba Coltrain stood back and admired the dining-room table. The best china—her grandmother's gilt-edged Limoges, scattered with multicolored spring flowers. The sterling flatware, monogrammed with an elaborate *C*. The long-stemmed Rosepoint goblets. A rose-colored linen tablecloth and napkins. Candles. Fresh flowers, in pastel colors that matched the china pattern. Libba had arranged them herself.

It was perfect.

"It looks beautiful, dear." Her mother came up behind her, put an arm around her shoulders, and gave her an affectionate hug.

Libba turned and kissed her mother on the cheek. "Thank you, Mama. For everything. For this dinner—"

Mama raised an eyebrow. "It was your father's idea, Libba. Don't forget that."

Libba grimaced. "I couldn't forget it if I tried. But I still can't figure it out. What do you suppose he's up to, Mama? He seemed . . . well, so *nice* the other night in the cafe. He actually talked to Link, can you imagine that? And then, inviting him to dinner like this—well, I suppose I should be grateful, but I can't help feeling—"

"Feeling as if your father has a hidden motive?"

"Something like that."

"Don't worry, honey. Everything will be fine. You'll see."

Libba's stomach churned. "I can't help being nervous. What if Daddy makes a big scene, like he did—"

"When you brought Freddy Sturgis home?" Mama patted Libba's arm.

"That was a mistake."

"But, sweetheart, you couldn't control how your father acted toward Freddy."

"I don't mean bringing him home. I mean Freddy was the mistake. A mistake from the beginning."

"I know, dear."

Libba stared at her mother. "You *knew?*"

"A mother knows these things, honey. I knew he wasn't the right man for you the moment he set foot in this house."

"But why didn't you *tell* me?"

"Would you have listened?" Mama laughed softly. "A girl has to find her own way, discover her own mind. Freddy Sturgis was a gentleman, Libba. But he wasn't a man."

Libba nodded. She had tried to pretend with Freddy—even the idea of marrying him had not been as bad as the thought of staying under Daddy's thumb. But once she had met Sergeant Link Winsom, well . . . things had changed, almost overnight.

Freddy had cried when she told him—actually cried! And although Libba felt sorry for him, she couldn't let her pity for him get the best of her. Pity was no emotion to build a life on.

"Mama, what would you have done if I had . . . well, if I had done something really stupid?"

"Like planning to elope with Freddy, you mean?"

"Wonderful. You knew about that, too?" Was there anything her mother didn't know?

"I suspected. But you're not like me, Libba." Libba watched in amazement as her mother's eyes clouded with unspoken pain. "You've got more sense—and more backbone. And yes, if you had been on the verge of making a mistake like that, I would have stepped in—at least to warn you."

Libba smiled. Maybe her mother had more fortitude and wisdom than she had given her credit for. Or maybe she was changing, even at the advanced age of forty. It was possible, she speculated, for someone her mother's age to see the light. Libba had, after all, wished for such a change. Even prayed for it, with her limited experience of addressing the Almighty. She needed an ally in her war with Daddy, and she had always hoped that Mama would come through. But she never really expected this.

Impulsively, Libba threw her arms around her mother. "Thank you, Mama. Thanks for believing in me. And—" She paused. "After this evening is over, I want to know—really know—what you think of Sergeant James Lincoln Winsom."

"More to the point," her mother said solemnly, "is what your father thinks of him."

★ ★ ★

At six o'clock, her father came home from the hardware store, swept into the dining room, and seated himself at the table opposite Link. Libba held her breath and waited. Her father watched Link with the eyes of a hawk, waiting to pounce on him for some perceived mistake, for some sign of unbridled lust or some deficiency of character.

But Link was smooth. He treated her father as an equal, discussing with him the financial possibilities of the hardware business, giving him a banker's perspective of what the war might mean for the future of nuts and bolts.

To Libba's surprise, her father smiled once or twice—a smile that didn't quite reach his eyes, but she had to give him credit for trying. Still, Libba felt strangely uneasy, as if she had stepped into a surrealistic drama where her father was playing someone else. Everything was going too well.

Over dessert, the requisite southern apple cobbler, Robinson Coltrain dropped his bomb. He laid down his dessert spoon, looked Link in the eye, and asked, "Tell me, Sergeant, just what are your intentions where my daughter is concerned?"

Libba could have crawled under the table. Instead, she bit her lip and looked frantically from Link to her mother, to Daddy, then back to Link again.

Link didn't bat an eyelash. "My intention," he said deliberately, with just the right tone of confidence in his voice, "is to marry Libba and make her the happiest woman on earth." He reached over and clasped her hand, which was clammy and trembling, and smiled into her eyes. "That is, if she'll have me."

Libba's heart raced, and her stomach churned. She was elated—and scared to death. Almost against her will, her eyes drifted to her father, who sat at the head of the table with an odd expression on his face.

"And if I don't give my blessing to this union? My daughter will not be twenty-one for another year and a half, you know."

Libba shuddered at the cold and deliberate tone in her father's voice, and her heart sank. But Link gripped her hand tighter and kept on smiling.

"I mean no disrespect, sir," he said calmly. "Libba and I have known each other only a short time, but—" he turned and gave Libba a dazzling smile—"we love each other. This is our life, not yours. And with or without your blessing—or your permission, for that matter—we *will* be married . . . if she agrees, of course."

Libba's father stared at Link as if he had suddenly grown two heads. He picked up his dessert spoon, tapped it on the table, then flung it into his empty cobbler bowl with a clatter.

"Blast!" he said. "I'll say one thing for you, boy. You've got gumption." He turned a bright eye on his daughter. "It's about time you came home with a stallion instead of these simpering geldings you've—"

"Robinson!" Mama hissed.

"All right, all right." Daddy patted Mama's arm—the first physical contact Libba had seen between them in months, maybe years. "I'll behave myself."

Link put his arm around Libba, and suddenly everything—including her fear of her father—vanished in the wonderful sensation of being protected and sheltered by the man she loved.

Her father looked at her intently. "Tater—"

"Daddy, please don't call me Tater," she said quietly, meeting his eyes without wavering.

Her father blinked. He narrowed his eyes, and the ghost of a smile flitted across his thin lips. "Libba, do you love this man?"

Libba didn't have to think twice. "Yes, Daddy. I love him." She glanced up at Link and saw his brown eyes shining at her. "I love him."

A fleeting look passed over her father's face—the beginning of a sneer. It happened so quickly that Libba nearly missed it. Something lay behind that look, something Libba couldn't quite identify. Still, her heart lurched and her blood ran cold when he fixed his eyes on her.

"It looks like my little girl is growing up." He rose abruptly. "Do what you want," he said in a low voice. "Just don't say I didn't warn you."

26

★ ★ ★

Mabel's Hope

Mabel Rae Coltrain felt naked and exposed as she stood alone in the doorway of the Paradise Garden Cafe. It had been ages since she had gone anywhere without her sister or her cousin—or both. She hadn't consciously realized, until this moment, how much she had depended upon Willie's personality and Libba's "southern lady" presence to act as a protective buffer against the unwelcome scrutiny of others. When they were around, attention was drawn away from her. Without them, anyone who encountered Mabel would inevitably focus on *her*—her pudgy figure; her plain, round face; her unruly, mouse-colored hair . . . her bland, vanilla personality.

Mabel cringed at the thought, and she almost backed out and went home. But she needed this time alone, away from Willie and Libba. She needed to think.

She peered cautiously around the room. The cafe was nearly deserted, and she offered a prayer of thanksgiving under her breath. She crept quietly to the back booth on the left and wedged herself in behind the table. Harlan Brownlee, the one they called "Crazy Ivory," was in his usual place at the piano, but he didn't pay her any mind. He just kept on playing— "Moonlight Sonata," she thought—with his eyes closed and his head thrown back. The look on his face was pure bliss.

What would it be like, Mabel wondered, to be that happy? From what she knew of Ivory, he had precious little to be happy about. He was land-poor, out on that huge run-down cotton plantation. The big house built by his great-granddaddy before the Civil War was virtually a shambles, held together only by wisteria vines and ancient history. He lived in one of the slave shanties. And yet he seemed completely content, at peace with himself and the world.

Mabel had never known that kind of peace. She loved her family, of course, and she adored Willie, but she had to admit, if pressed, that she sometimes resented living under her sister's shadow. She was "that nice, quiet Coltrain girl, Willie's big sister," rather than Mabel Rae Coltrain, a grown woman with a name and a mind and dreams of her own.

It was those dreams, in fact, that had brought her to the Paradise Garden this afternoon, alone. The dreams she had never told anyone—not even Willie. The dreams that threatened now to break her heart.

For as much as she loved her sister and wanted to see her happy, Mabel could hardly stand being around Willie now that Owen Slaughter had come on the scene. She liked Owen, of course—she had even prayed for someone like him to come along and fall in love with Willie. Willie deserved to be loved, deserved a man like her "Curly." Mabel was trying to play her part and be the dutiful sister, thrilled by Willie's good fortune. But Willie's very happiness with Owen made Mabel's loneliness all the more evident.

So, while Willie and Libba fussed over wedding plans and dresses and their hopes for the future, Mabel had sneaked out of the apartment and come down to the Paradise Garden by herself. They wouldn't miss her. And even if they did notice she was gone, it wouldn't occur to them that something was wrong, that she was hopelessly miserable. Not good old Mabel—tough, resilient, practical Mabel. Mabel Rae Coltrain would be all right. She always was.

Mabel put her head in her hands and stared down at the table. She heaved a deep, heavyhearted sigh. Yes, she would be all right, she supposed—eventually. She would get over this and go on with her life, whatever her life would hold. But for now, the pain of her loneliness threatened to overwhelm her. The table blurred as the tears welled up and spilled over, and she blindly groped for the napkin holder.

"Here you go, honey." A warm hand pressed a handkerchief to her palm.

Mabel's head snapped up, and her tears stopped instantly. Across the table from her sat Thelma Breckinridge, leaning forward intently.

"I didn't mean to startle you, hon," Thelma murmured. "And I don't mean to break in on your privacy. But—" she took Mabel's stubby little fingers in her big work-worn hand—"can I do anything to help?"

★ ★ ★

If Thelma had learned anything in her years at the Paradise Garden, it was that the Good Lord had a right time for everything. She had seen it over and over again—people who seemed to be strong and in control, yet they eventually came to their breaking point. Sometimes it happened because of personal tragedy or heartache; sometimes just because they were worn down with the dailiness of living. Whatever the cause, Thelma knew that those moments of weakness were God's best opportunity to demonstrate love, to give people strength. And she had determined long ago that she would be available in those moments if people wanted her support.

But she also knew enough not to push. God loved people—all kinds of people. Given the chance, the Lord would pick them up, put them on their feet, and set them going in a new direction. Still, even the Lord didn't bully into people's lives without an invitation. And neither would Thelma.

With Mabel Rae Coltrain, she sensed, it was best to tread very carefully. She withdrew her hand. "I'll leave you alone if you want, hon. But if you'd like to talk, I'm right here."

Mabel straightened up, swiped at her eyes, and looked intently at Thelma. "I . . . I don't know," she said.

"Just take your time, then," Thelma said. "Want a cup of coffee?"

Mabel nodded, and Thelma fetched the pot and two mugs. When Mabel's cup was half empty, Thelma refilled it and settled back into the booth.

"Do you want to talk about it?"

Mabel fixed her eyes on the tabletop and fiddled with her spoon. "I'm not sure how," she said at last. "Things are really confusing right now."

Thelma waited, took a sip of her coffee, and waited some more.

At last Mabel flung the spoon aside and blurted out, "Why do I have to be so fat and so ugly and so . . . so awful?"

Thelma blinked. "What makes you say such things about yourself, child?"

Mabel's dark eyes blazed with fire. "It's true, isn't it? Look at me! Libba is petite and cute, with that auburn hair and those green eyes. Willie's no beauty, but she's wonderful, and everybody loves her. But I—I—"

"You're alone?" Thelma ventured. "You see Libba and Willie so happy with their new beaus, and you feel left out?"

Mabel's eyes filled up with tears. "It's more than just feeling left out," she said. "It's feeling like—" she swallowed hard, trying not to cry—"like no one will ever love me . . . just for me!"

Thelma hesitated. She wanted to tell Mabel, in no uncertain terms, that she most certainly was loved—that God had created her exactly as she was and loved her more than she could imagine. That a lot of other people loved her, too. But an inner restraint kept her from voicing the words, true though they might be. That kind of love—even God's love—wasn't what Mabel felt the need for right now, and the last thing she needed to hear was a lot of platitudes about how much God cared.

"You want a man to love you," Thelma said quietly.

Mabel grimaced. "Does that sound stupid? I have a wonderful family, friends who care about me, a community where everyone knows my name. Why do I feel as if nobody really knows me . . . or loves me?"

Thelma started to reassure the girl, then stopped before the words were out. Empty assurances wouldn't help. Mabel Rae Coltrain was on a search for truth, and only the truth would do.

"Because nobody does," Thelma said at last.

A look of utter shock registered on Mabel's face, as if she had been doused with a bucket of ice water. Obviously, she hadn't expected Thelma to agree with her. "What . . . what do you mean?" she stammered.

Thelma smiled. "Let me qualify that statement. There is one Person who knows you and loves you—"

Mabel gave a resigned sigh. "God."

"Yes, God. But I suspect that's not the kind of love you're talking about."

"No, Thelma, it's not," Mabel snapped. "And right now, I'm not so sure that even God knows or loves me."

"Well, I reckon that's for you and God to work out between yourselves," Thelma said. "But let me explain what I meant when I said nobody knows you or loves you."

Mabel waved a hand for her to continue.

"You've lived around here most of your life," Thelma went on. "Everybody knows who you are—"

"I'm 'that nice, quiet Coltrain girl, Willie's big sister.'"

"Exactly. Now, *you* know that you're much more than that, but nobody else does."

"Except God." Mabel's tone was sarcastic, but Thelma ignored the jab.

"Except God. Between Willie's personality and your cousin Libba's flamboyancy, you've kinda been caught in the middle."

"And now both of them are in love, and I'm invisible. Invisible and alone. And likely to stay alone, from what I've experienced so far."

Thelma patted Mabel's hand. "I know, honey. I know what it is to be alone."

"Oh, Thelma! I'm so sorry. I didn't mean—"

"I know you didn't, hon. Besides, it doesn't hurt so much anymore." Thelma thought about her short-lived romance with Robert Raintree. Funny how an experience that caused so much pain at the time would turn out to be the one thing in her life that gave her a connection with other people who were hurting. It was just like God to take her heartbreak and forge it into a tool to help someone else.

Thelma turned her attention back to Mabel. "Let me tell you what I've discovered about being alone." Mabel nodded, and Thelma related briefly the story of her engagement to Robert—how she had hung all her hopes for a normal life on his love, and how, when he deserted her, she had thought she wouldn't survive. "But I did survive," she said. "And God met me that Easter morning and showed me that life didn't have to revolve around a husband and a family and a white picket fence." Thelma paused. "Each of us has a path to walk, Mabel. No one's path is like anybody else's. But the important thing is that we find ways to really live and to reach out and share that life with others, no matter what our situation."

Thelma looked intently into Mabel's brown eyes. "Don't you think God has a path for you, child? A life of your own, doing something meaningful, apart from Willie and Libba?"

Mabel shrugged. "Maybe. But I don't see how. Look at me, Thelma—and be honest. I'm not attractive, I don't have Willie's charming personality, and I'm stuck in a one-horse town where everybody knows me but nobody knows me, and where meeting anyone new is about as impossible as changing the outcome of the Civil War! What on earth do I have to offer to anyone else? And how do you propose that I begin to 'reach out,' as you call it?"

Thelma smiled. "One thing I've learned, hon—God's paths aren't 'out there' somewhere. They're right here, in your own backyard."

Mabel frowned, and Thelma could almost see the wheels spinning in her mind. "Can you think of any place to start, Mabel?" she prodded. "Something you could do, right here in Eden?"

"Well, there's the Red Cross unit and the USO," Mabel said. "That's meaningful work. But Willie's really involved there, and I'd just be in her shadow again."

"What else?"

Mabel cast a sidelong glance at Thelma. "What else is there? This town has five churches—three of them Baptist—one grocery store, this cafe, a post office—" She stopped suddenly, and Thelma could see an idea forming as a brightness spread across Mabel's round face.

"Maybe that's it!" Mabel said. "Willie said that one of the women at the Red Cross was trying to enlist people to write to soldiers overseas—you know, to keep their morale up, to keep them connected to life back home. I'll have lots of time on my hands once school is out. Maybe I could be a pen pal for somebody."

Thelma nodded. "Sounds like a good idea to me."

"It's more than just a good idea, Thelma—it's perfect. I'm not attractive, I can't dance, and I'm no good in social situations. But I can write . . . and whoever I write to doesn't have to know that I'm fat and ugly and—"

"Mabel Rae!"

"OK, I get the point," Mabel laughed. "But you have to admit, maybe through letters someone can get to know me without being put off by the package." She smiled ruefully. "It's worth a try."

"It sure is, honey." Thelma got up and returned to the counter with the empty coffeepot. If she lived to be a hundred, she would never stop marveling at how God could work in a hopeless situation. And she would pray every day that Mabel's hope would carry her a little further down the path.

27

✮ ✮ ✮

War Is Hell

Stork Simpson gazed out the window and watched the miles pass. A spring rain slicked the glass and distorted the view, but he barely noticed. His mind wasn't on the scenery.

With every stop in every one-horse town along the way, he grew more anxious and agitated. Eighteen hours. He should have been at Madge's side by now. Some unexplained delay in Cotton Plant, Arkansas, cost him three precious hours, and although the engineer had been putting on the speed for the last hour or two, he couldn't move the train fast enough to suit Stork. The doctor had said that the baby could be born anytime now. Stork imagined Madge in labor, calling his name. They wouldn't let him into the delivery room, of course, but he could at least be pacing outside the door. At least she would know he was there.

But not if this train didn't get moving!

Stork sighed and ran a hand through his hair. He caught a glimpse of himself in the glass, with his hair standing up on end, and crooked a wry grin at his reflection. Link would love to see him now, nervous as a wet cat and twice as irritable.

He wondered how Link was doing . . . how the Meeting of the In-Laws had gone. Link had the ability to charm anyone; Stork had seen the man in action and knew how adept he was at managing people. But rumor had it that Libba Coltrain's father was not a man easily managed. He hoped, for Link's sake, that the Prince Charming act would be effective.

Owen Slaughter, on the other hand, didn't have Link's charm, but he obviously didn't need it. Willie the Amazon Woman was wild about him, and apparently her parents concurred. Stork figured they'd be married before the month was out.

He wished he could make Link and Slaughter see the disadvantages of falling in love and getting married during such uncertain times. But love didn't wait for the right time. His certainly hadn't. Love really must be blind.

Stork's mind drifted, thinking about love. Not just his love for Madge, but love in general. People in love were certifiably insane. They made bad decisions, jumped into situations over their heads, couldn't see the truth if it hit them in the face.

He should know.

But had his decision to marry Madge really been a wrong one? His mother certainly thought so. "Marry in haste, repent at leisure," she had said—not once, but a dozen times. Still, Stork had no regrets about marrying Madge. The timing was awful, with this war looming over their heads, but he would do it again in a minute. He loved her. She loved him. Their love had created a child, a new life.

Maybe everything happened for the best in the long run. Maybe Link and Slaughter weren't so crazy after all . . . at least no crazier than he had been about Madge.

Stork breathed a silent prayer that everything would work out—that the baby would be healthy and whole, that Madge would come through the delivery all right, that Link and Slaughter would find happiness with Libba and Willie Coltrain. Then he closed his eyes, leaned his head against the window, and tried to relax.

★ ★ ★

"We're getting married, I tell you!" Owen Slaughter couldn't sit still. He danced around Link, who was seated at a table in the USO.

"When did all this happen?" Link was dying to tell Slaughter—anyone—about his successful foray into Robinson Coltrain's castle . . . how he had faced the dragon in his den. But he restrained himself. He wouldn't take away from Slaughter's moment of delirium. The man wouldn't have listened anyway.

"I met her parents last week," Owen went on, sitting down in a chair opposite Link and then getting up again to pace around the table. "They are wonderful, Winsom—really nice folks. Just like Willie. I can see where she gets it."

Link couldn't resist. "Gets what?"

"Her . . . her wonderfulness!" Slaughter stammered. "They're farmers, salt of the earth. And—" he cast a glance toward heaven, "they like me—they really like me!"

"Everybody likes you, Slaughter," Link chuckled. "Everybody except the new recruits, that is."

Slaughter wasn't listening. "We're going to have a small wedding at their little country church—Coffeeville, the town is called." He frowned. "Or maybe it's closer to Water Valley. I can't quite remember."

"Coffeeville?"

Slaughter nodded. "We went through Coffeeville, anyway, on the way to the farm. It's somewhere between Coffeeville and Water Valley—"

"Water Valley?" Link howled. "Well, I suppose if you lived in Coffeeville, you'd be watering the valley day and night."

Owen glared at Link. "Very funny." He held up a hand in warning. "Don't you dare make any wisecracks about it when you meet her parents."

"Me?" Link sat up in his chair. "I'll be the soul of propriety." Then he frowned. "What do you mean, when *I* meet them?"

Slaughter punched Link playfully on the arm. "They're going to be your relatives, too, unless I'm sadly mistaken." He winked. "Besides, you're going to be my best man. I mean—" he sobered and looked at Link intently—"will you be my best man?"

Link grinned. "Of course I will, Slaughter. I'm honored. Now, when is the blessed event?"

"April 30 . . . a Sunday afternoon." As if suddenly brought back to reality, Owen scratched his head. "Speaking of blessed events, have you heard from Stork?"

Link shook his head and looked at his watch. "He should be there by now if the train didn't break down. We probably won't hear anything until the baby arrives." He frowned. "I sure hope the kid shows up in time."

"In time for what?"

"In time for Stork to see him, that's what." Link gave an exasperated sigh. Owen could be downright dense at times—especially when he was thinking about Willie. "Stork's only got six days. He's got to be back here by next Thursday, baby or no baby."

Slaughter nodded. "Yeah. The major will have his head if he goes AWOL again."

And mine, Link thought. That baby had better be born soon, and Stork had better get his tail back to Mississippi on time. Link could only imagine what the major would do—to both of them—if Stork came in late.

"How did you do it, anyway?"

"Get him the pass, you mean?" Link smiled to himself. "Ah, it was nothing, really. Major Mansfield had second thoughts, that's all."

"That's all?" Slaughter shook his head. "Do you know how often the CO changes his mind, Winsom? Only about once in a millennium, that's all."

"I know," Link said quietly. "I guess I caught him on a good day."

★ ★ ★

After innumerable maddening delays at every whistle-stop in the Ozarks, the train finally pulled into the station in Springfield, Missouri. Stork still had a long way to go, but at least he was on home soil. At this rate, it would take him another twelve hours . . . *if* nothing else happened . . . and *if* he didn't go crazy in the meantime.

The layover in Springfield was scheduled to be an hour and fifteen minutes—enough time to get out, stretch his legs, and get a bite to eat. He hadn't slept more than fifteen minutes at a time in the last twenty hours. By the time he got to Madge's side, he would probably look so awful that she would want *him* to go to the hospital.

He reached into his pocket, pulled out a comb, and swiped at his hair. If he was going to surprise his wife by showing up in time for the delivery, he ought to at least make an effort to look better than a walking corpse. Because Link had generously paid his train fare, Stork had enough money in his wallet for a few decent meals, flowers for Madge, and a gift for the baby, besides. Link had joked that the train fare was a new-father gift from an "anonymous benefactor," but Stork knew it had come out of Link's back pay.

Link Winsom was one piece of work, Stork mused. He could be a selfish jerk sometimes, like when he pulled that stunt of turning down OCS—but only when he wasn't thinking. Most of the time he was the best friend a guy could ever have. Maybe, if the baby was a boy, they would name him Lincoln. At least as a middle name. He would talk to Madge about it as soon as he got home . . . or as soon as she was up to it.

Stork got out of his seat, stretched his legs, and walked the length of the passenger car. Maybe after dinner he could get some sleep. By morning he would be in Agency, Missouri, population 426—soon to be 427. He would be in Madge's arms or, at the very least, in her vicinity.

Whistling under his breath at the happy thought of his wonderful wife holding their wonderful newborn child, Stork grabbed the railing and swung himself to the main platform of the Springfield station.

Then he stopped whistling.

He almost stopped breathing.

Before him stood an enormous, muscular soldier with an MP armband stretched around his bulging biceps.

"Sergeant Michael Simpson?" the MP growled.

Stork gulped. *What now?*

"Yes? I'm Sergeant Simpson."

"Come with me, please." No explanation, no information. The MP turned on his heel, obviously expecting Stork to follow like a whipped puppy.

His anger flared. "What do you mean, come with you?"

The MP turned and looked down at Stork. "I have orders to return you to your company immediately."

"Orders?" Simpson spluttered. He reached into his pocket and waved his papers under the Neanderthal's nose. "I have here a six-day pass, soldier. I am on my way home to see my first child born. All legal—signed, sealed, and, if you'll pardon the pun, delivered. Now get out of my way."

Fury had made Stork bold, but not bold enough to stand up under the withering glare of the MP. "You'll have to come with me, Sergeant," the soldier said in a low rumble.

"Fat chance. I'm going home." Stork's voice shook a little, but he turned his back on the MP and headed for the train. Forget dinner. Forget everything except getting to Madge in time.

Major Minefield must have had second thoughts about the pass, Stork speculated, and decided to call him back. Well, he couldn't do it. Stork had his pass, and he had no intention of letting it be snatched away from him now. Whatever Minefield wanted, it could wait.

A viselike hand clamped down on Stork's shoulder. The MP spoke again, but this time his voice held a note of regret. "I'm sorry, Sergeant. I hate to be the one to do this. But I have my orders. You have to return now—immediately."

Stork whirled and faced the MP, for the first time looking into his eyes. He was just a kid—a big, burly linebacker of a kid, but a kid nevertheless. He couldn't be more than nineteen.

"What's your name, son?"

Obviously taken aback, the boy stammered, "Roger, sir. Roger Holmseth."

"Well, listen, Roger," Stork said, reaching out to put a hand on the boy's arm. "What do you think would happen if, say, you just happened not to be able to find me? Then I could go on home and be with my wife, see my baby, and be back before you knew it, now couldn't I?"

The young soldier stiffened and drew himself to attention, freeing his arm from Stork's grip. "I can't do that, Sergeant. I have my—"

"Yeah, I know, you have your orders. Well, tell me this—what is so all-fired important that you have to come track me down in the middle of the Ozarks and drag me back to my outfit?"

"I can't say, Sergeant."

"You can't say, or you don't know?"

"I can't say, Sergeant. All I can say is that I have orders to find you and put you on the next train to Memphis. Your division will meet you at the Memphis station tomorrow morning."

"Memphis? What in blazes are we going to Memphis for?"

"I can't say, Sergeant."

"Well, you'd better say, if you expect me to turn around and go back to—"

Suddenly, with piercing clarity, the reality of the situation closed in on Stork. His tirade ended as abruptly as it had begun. With a swift motion he grabbed the young MP by the shirtfront. "We're shipping out!" he yelled, shaking the boy. "That's what all this is about—that's why I have to go back. We're shipping out, aren't we?"

"I can't say, sir—"

"Aren't we?" Stork shouted. "Answer me!"

The MP reached down and gripped his hands around Stork's wrists. "Yes, sir." His voice was subdued, almost a whisper. "Tomorrow morning."

Stork jerked free, and the young soldier took a step backward. "I've got to get to a telephone!" He turned to bolt for the station.

A firm hand gripped his arm, restraining him. Through his fury and his fear, Stork's mind registered a sound—a sharp, hollow click, like the sound of . . . of a weapon being cocked.

He turned his head to find the young MP holding a pistol three inches from his temple.

"I'm sorry, Sergeant," the MP said, "but I have my orders. I have to take you back—with or without your cooperation."

Stork's mind raced. This couldn't be happening—not to him, not when he was this close. He wheeled and faced the soldier, ignoring the pistol. "Don't you understand?" he pleaded. "My wife is about to have a baby—tonight, tomorrow, anytime now. My first child! I have to call, to let her know—"

"You can't, sir," the MP said, remorse filling his eyes. "I do understand. But you can't tell anyone you're shipping out."

"Why on earth not? My wife—"

"Not your wife, not anyone. Regulations. Troop trains have been sabotaged, you know. Security procedures are very clear—"

"Security procedures be hanged," Stork said fiercely. "Regulations be hanged. Shoot me if you have to, kid—I'm calling my wife."

With that, Stork jerked his arm free and ran for the station.

★ ★ ★

"What do you mean, we're shipping out tomorrow?"

Owen Slaughter stood next to Link Winsom in Major Mansfield's office. The major paced back and forth behind his desk, occasionally glancing out the window. He did not look at Link or Slaughter; never once did he meet their eyes, and he didn't even seem to notice that Slaughter had not addressed him as sir.

"Get your men ready," the CO said curtly. "You pull out at 0200."

"Two o'clock in the morning?" Link shook his head. "Why?"

Mansfield turned, finally looking at Link directly. "Security, Winsom. The top brass doesn't want to take any chances of troop trains being sabotaged."

"Sabotaged!" Owen Slaughter spat out the word. "That's ridiculous, Major. You've got a train going north, hauling maybe a hundred cars—mile after mile of cars—a train that doesn't stop anywhere. You think anybody's *not* going to know it's filled with soldiers on their way to ship out from New York?"

"That's beside the point," the major snapped. "Regulations."

"And we can't tell anyone where we're going?" Link exchanged a significant glance with Owen. "Not even our girls?"

"No one. Especially not your girls."

"But we're both engaged. They'll think—"

"They'll probably think you shipped out without telling them. Which will be precisely the case."

The telephone on the major's desk jangled insistently. He ignored it for a moment, then snatched up the receiver. "Yes?"

He listened for a minute or two while Link and Slaughter shifted nervously and eyed each other. Then he replaced the receiver and turned back toward them.

"It's a boy."

It took a moment for the news to sink in. Then Link let out a whoop and grabbed Slaughter in a bear hug. "A boy! Did you hear that, Owen? A boy! Old Stork really did himself proud. He must be delirious—"

Suddenly Link let go of Slaughter and turned to the major. "What did Stork say, Major? Is the kid handsome—or does he look like his old man?"

Major Mansfield shook his head. "That wasn't Simpson," he said. "It was Simpson's mother. She called to leave the message for him."

Link couldn't believe what he was hearing. "Stork wasn't there? What happened? Do you suppose—"

"He's on his way back," the CO interrupted. "He'll be meeting you and your men at the station in Memphis tomorrow morning."

"You mean he didn't get home at all?"

"I'm afraid not," the major said. "We sent an MP to meet his train just across the Missouri line. He's on his way to Memphis right now."

"Are you saying that Stork Simpson's wife has just delivered his firstborn son and the man doesn't even know it yet?"

Major Mansfield rubbed his eyes wearily. "You'll get to be the bearer of good tidings, I guess," he said.

Great, Link thought. *I always wanted the chance to announce to my best friend that his son has been born.* Poor Stork. He had tried so hard to get home to be with Madge. Now fate—or military stupidity—had stepped in. He wouldn't get to see his baby, or hold him, or marvel over his perfect tiny fingers and toes like other daddies did, not for a long, long time. *If ever . . .*

Link glanced over at Owen Slaughter and found him staring at the floor.

"He was right, Major," Link said miserably.

A confused look crossed the CO's face. "Who was right?"

Link sighed. "The guy who said, 'War is hell.'"

The major nodded. "Sometimes it's hell even before you get there."

28

⋆ ⋆ ⋆

You Always Hurt
the One You Love

At exactly 2:06 A.M. the convoy of army trucks pulled past the front gate of Camp McCrane and headed out toward Highway 51, which would take them straight north into Memphis.

More army idiocy, Link thought as he settled back against the hard wooden slats that formed the side of the truck. They could have caught a train at Tillatoba or Grenada and at least been comfortable. But, no. The army had decided that they would leave from Memphis—a three-and-a-half hour ride, at thirty-five miles an hour, crammed into the back of tarp-covered troop trucks.

He glanced at Owen Slaughter, just across from him. Slaughter was slouched against the slats with his arm thrown over his eyes and his legs stretched out into the center of the truck bed—or as far as his legs would stretch, anyway.

Link extended a foot and kicked the bottom of Owen's boot. "Slaughter!"

Slaughter dropped his arm, opened one eye, and glared at Link. "What?"

"Did you call?"

"Call who?"

Link gritted his teeth. "You know who." He slanted a glance at young Coker, who was seated next to him with the back flap of the tarp thrown back to let in the cool night air. As the boy's eyes widened, the whites reflected the early-morning moonlight. He looked like a blackface singer in a minstrel show.

"Sergeant!" Coker hissed, loud enough to cause grumbles from the sleepy men around him. "We weren't supposed to tell anyone we were shipping out. What about sabotage? What about—"

"Shut up, Coker." Link nudged Owen's foot again. "What about it, Slaughter? Did you get through?"

With an exaggerated sigh, Owen straightened up and rubbed at his eyes. "I tried. The landlady hung up on me. Twice."

Link groaned. "Great. What are we gonna do now?"

"We're going to get on the train in Memphis, and when we get to New York we'll send a telegram . . . or something."

"Right," Link said sarcastically. "We'll just stroll off the base and flag a cab into Manhattan. See the sights, make a few calls—"

"We'll find a way."

"What way?" Link persisted. "The major was pretty explicit—no calls, no wires. We'll be watched."

Slaughter folded his arms across his chest. "Use your famous charm, Winsom. Charm will get you anything." He closed his eyes. Clearly, the discussion was over.

But Coker wasn't finished, not by a long shot. "This is exciting, isn't it, Sarge?" He fidgeted on the hard wooden seat. "I mean, here we are, in the middle of the night, shipping out. I've never seen New York. And pretty soon we'll be in Europe . . . or the Pacific . . . or somewhere. Fighting for our country, for our honor. This is great. Really great."

Link shook his head. "Shut up, Coker," he snarled. "Just shut up."

★   ★   ★

Libba trembled with anger as she sat facing her father over breakfast on Saturday morning. "But, Daddy! Willie and Owen are getting married on the 30th. Her father's already agreed, and she and Mabel are at the farm this weekend, planning the wedding—"

"My brother was always a fool when it came to those girls," her father muttered. "He never could say no to them. Spoiled them rotten."

"And you never said yes to me," Libba snapped.

"To have a double wedding with that hayseed cousin of yours? I should say not." He picked up his fork and pointed at her. "I'll admit I like this charmer of a soldier you brought home better than that Fairy Sturgis—"

"Freddy, Daddy. His name is Freddy."

"Freddy, Fairy—it's all the same to me." Her father shrugged. "But I will not be manipulated by some smooth-talking Yankee. If you marry him— and I say *if*, mind you—it will be after a proper engagement, with a white church wedding befitting your station in society. Your mother deserves that much."

"Don't bring Mama into this," Libba countered. "And I don't give a flip about a big wedding—or my 'station in society,' as you put it."

Her father leaned forward threateningly. "Watch your mouth, Tater, or I'll wash it out with lye soap. You'll do this my way, or you won't do it at all."

"Everybody always does things your way," Libba muttered under her breath.

"What did you say?" He narrowed his eyes at her.

"Nothing, Daddy." Libba rose and tossed her napkin onto the bacon platter. "Nothing at all."

★　★　★

By Sunday afternoon, Willie was beginning to worry. Owen hadn't shown up at the farm on Saturday, nor had he telephoned. Since she and Mabel had returned to the apartment after Sunday dinner, she had knocked three times on Mrs. Grevis's door, only to be told that no, there had been no calls.

Libba hadn't heard from Link either, but she had other things on her mind. After one brief evening of hope, the old Daddy had once more reared his ugly head, and apparently he was having a hissy fit about Libba's wanting to have a double wedding. Not for the first time, Willie breathed a prayer of thankfulness for having been born into the poor side of the Coltrain clan.

Willie paced the living-room floor while Libba sat on the couch and moped. Finally Willie could stand it no longer.

"Come on, Cousin," she said, grabbing Libba's hand and jerking her to her feet. "We're going to town."

Libba stared at Willie as if she had lost her mind. "To town? What for? It's Sunday afternoon—everything's closed."

"There's a phone at the cafe. Thelma will let us use it. We're calling the base."

"The base? But we can't do that."

"Sure we can. We'll tell them it's an emergency and that we have to talk to Sergeant Slaughter and Sergeant Winsom right away."

Mabel Rae stuck her head around the kitchen door. "Where are y'all going?"

"Uptown," Willie said. "We'll be back in a little bit."

Mabel nodded. "I hope you find out something." She lifted her eyebrows. "Y'all have been totally useless the past couple of days."

"I'll help with supper when we get back," Willie promised. Then she grabbed Libba's hand and pulled her out the door.

★ ★ ★

"I could have told you!" Daddy's voice was triumphant. He actually seemed to enjoy Libba's misery. She should have known better than to think she could come home and talk to her mother without her father's interference. He hadn't left them alone for a minute.

"What exactly did they say when you called the base?" Mama asked for the third time.

"Just that Sergeants Winsom and Slaughter were 'unavailable.'" Libba shook her head. "I don't understand this. Link wouldn't just drop me like that."

"Maybe they shipped out suddenly." Her mother's voice was gentle, compassionate.

Libba grabbed on to that shred of hope. Shipping out would be bad news, but not nearly as bad as being abandoned by the man she planned to marry. "That must be it! They had to ship out, and they couldn't tell us."

"If he had shipped out," Daddy snorted, "somebody at the base would have told you. He just changed his mind, and he doesn't want to face up to you."

"But why?" Libba wailed. "We were going to be married as soon as—"

"My point exactly." Daddy lifted his head as if he had just won an important argument. "You girls were so all-fired eager to get married. Marriage scares a man off, I tell you. They run like rabbits when they hear wedding bells beginning to ring."

Libba stared at her father. Was he deliberately trying to hurt her, or was inflicting pain just so ingrained in his nature that he didn't notice anymore? The night Link came to dinner she had sensed something—some kind of premonition, an intuition about the way Daddy was acting. She had been waiting for the other shoe to drop. Now she didn't have to wait any longer.

Libba turned to her mother for comfort. "You heard him, Mama. He sat right here at this table and said that he loved me, that he wanted to marry me."

"I heard, honey." Mama patted Libba's hand helplessly.

"Well, apparently he changed his mind," Daddy declared. "Any man worth his salt has enough sense to keep his leg out of an iron bear trap."

Libba watched as a series of glances passed between her parents. She didn't know what was going on between them, but there was obviously something under the surface that wasn't being talked about. Mama was shooting daggers at Daddy, and Daddy had a smug expression on his face—the expression he always got when he knew he was in control.

She didn't know what to believe. She didn't think Link would ship out without telling her he was leaving. But what if Daddy was right? What if Link got scared off by the prospect of marriage and decided it was easier just to avoid her than to face her and tell her that his feelings had changed?

How well did she really know Sergeant Link Winsom, after all?

29

★ ★ ★

Message from Macy's

The week passed slowly. Willie put her wedding plans on hold, and Libba moped around the apartment with red, swollen eyes. Mabel Rae didn't know what to do to help them. She felt selfish about it, but more than once she found herself being thankful that she was stubby and unattractive and that she didn't have an Owen or a Link to contend with.

She had always longed for someone to love—someone who could see beyond her physical shortcomings and care about her for who she was. Mabel was twenty-three, a year and a half older than Willie and almost three years older than Libba. She seldom dated. She had only been kissed twice—and those were compulsory good-night pecks at the door. Men always seemed to focus so much on the packaging that they hardly ever got down to the treasure inside. Still, she had always hoped. . . .

Now, Mabel was beginning to believe she might be the lucky one. If romance led to this sort of pain, it was highly overrated. Love shouldn't hurt this much.

In the meantime, while Willie and Libba discussed their "situation" at every opportunity, Mabel was left with most of the housework and all of the cooking. Not that anyone ate very much of what she cooked, except Mabel herself. If this didn't end soon, Mabel would end up resembling the over-inflated tubes from her daddy's tractor tires.

With a sigh, Mabel stirred the soup, pushed the pot to the back of the stove, and took off her apron. It was four-thirty, going on five. Except for the biscuits, dinner was ready. She might as well go get the mail before the post office closed. After four days of running to the box at 7:04 every morning,

Willie and Libba seemed to have given up hope of getting a letter. Like everything else these days, Mabel would have to do it or it wouldn't get done.

★ ★ ★

A little after five, Mabel wedged through the back door and slid the box onto the kitchen table. She hadn't counted on this. The box wasn't particularly heavy, but it was huge and unwieldy. She had nearly dropped it twice on the way home from town.

"Libba!" she called. "Libba, come here!"

Mabel peered at the label on the box, waiting for Libba to respond. *Macy's,* the return address read. *New York City.*

"Libba, get in here!"

Disheveled, in her bathrobe and slippers, Libba finally appeared at the kitchen door. "I was taking a nap," she muttered irritably. "What do you want?"

Mabel stepped back and pointed to the box. "This came for you."

Libba squinted. "What is it?"

"How should I know?" Mabel snapped. "It's got your name on it. But if you don't open it, I will." She reached for a paring knife and slid it under the flap of the carton.

"Wait a minute, wait a minute. I'll do it." Libba snatched the knife out of Mabel's hand and shoved her aside.

"What's going on?" Willie stuck her head around the doorway.

"Libba's got a package," Mabel answered. "From Macy's, in New York."

"Macy's?" Willie came to look over Libba's shoulder. "Who do you know in New York?"

Libba didn't answer. She jerked the box open and lifted out a stuffed elephant, two feet long and two feet high, with huge white furry tusks.

"What is that?" Mabel reached for it, but Libba snatched it back.

"It's an elephant, idiot."

"I know that. Who's it from? Is there a note?"

"Keep your shirt on, Mabel. I'm looking."

Libba groped in the box and came up with a crumpled note, a single sheet of paper folded twice. Slowly she opened it, then put her hand to her mouth and gasped. Without a word she handed the paper to Mabel, who held it out so that Willie could read it at the same time.

The top of the page, in red ink, bore an American flag above the words, *United Service Organizations.* At the bottom, in the same ink, was the address, *USO, Camp Shanks, New York.* Scrawled in black ink across the page, the brief note read: *Elephants never forget. Neither will I. I love you.*

"There's no signature," Mabel said.

Libba looked up at Mabel Rae and Willie, tears shining in her eyes. "Of course not. He probably sneaked the note in at the last minute. But he's in New York."

Willie sank into a chair and rested her elbows on the kitchen table. Her hand, still holding the note, trembled. "They shipped out," she whispered.

Libba pounded her fist on the pine tabletop, laughing and crying at the same time. "They shipped out!" she shouted. "Do you know what this means?" She grabbed Mabel Rae around the waist and did a wild little dance across the kitchen floor.

"If they shipped out from New York, it means they're on their way to Europe," Willie said. "On their way to . . . to the front."

"It means," Libba corrected, "that they'll be back. Daddy was wrong, Willie. They didn't get cold feet. They didn't abandon us. They got shipped out."

Mabel Rae turned to the stove and set the soup pot back on the burner. "Thank the Lord," she muttered. "Maybe things will get back to normal around here."

30

☆ ☆ ☆

Long-Awaited Liberty

**Army General Hospital
Birmingham, England**

When he first awoke, Charlie Coltrain didn't know quite where he was. He felt groggy and disoriented, and he vaguely recollected that his sleep had been disturbed by nightmares, but he couldn't remember the details.

With a groan he sat up and looked around at the drab warehouselike room—bare walls lined with beds just like his. A weak sun filtered through the clouded windows, washing the room in a yellow-gray light. No one else was stirring.

It must be just after dawn. Something had awakened him—but what?

He frowned and ran a hand over his face. His eyes were still puffy with sleep, and he squinted against the light.

Charlie looked out the window and saw an expanse of green lawn bordered with hedges and crisscrossed with stone paths. Then he remembered . . . he was in England, in the hospital in Birmingham.

He slammed a fist against the mattress, furious at himself for not remembering. How could he expect to convince the doctors—particularly Alexander Worthington—that he was all right, that he could go back to the front, if he couldn't even remember where he was?

He took a deep breath and tried to calm himself. The nightmares drained him; he woke up feeling as if he had never slept. And he was exhausted anyway. Nearly two months of keeping up a facade of wellness had sapped his energy. Whenever Worthington appeared on the ward, and especially during his long sessions with the doctor, Charlie steeled himself not to shake or cry. It took all his determination to make eye contact with the man, to answer his questions rationally and calmly.

This was the hardest thing Charlie had ever done. But it was working. The doctor treated him not like a nut case but like a normal, ordinary man recovering and preparing to resume his duties. And, despite the dreams and the exhaustion, Charlie had to admit that he was feeling more normal all the time.

God must be answering his prayers. In the weeks since he was transferred to Birmingham, Charlie had prayed more than he ever had in his life. Occasionally he wondered whether he was right in interpreting this transfer as a sign from God, a way to get him back to the battle so he could die with dignity and be done with it. But how could it be otherwise? Everything was going so smoothly.

When Dr. Carter had first suggested transferring Charlie to the Birmingham hospital rather than sending him home, it had been nothing short of a miracle. Charlie suspected, though, that maybe miracles sometimes included a little work on the part of the recipient. So he was working hard, if that counted for anything in God's eyes. He was doing his part, exerting all his will and self-control to keep balanced and sane.

Every now and then Charlie entertained the thought that maybe he actually was getting better—that maybe in the process of fooling Dr. Worthington, he was deceiving his own mind into healing itself. He had overheard the doctors talking about such a process, where disturbed people were taught to *act* sane, and eventually they begin to *think* rationally. But he dismissed the idea. The nightmares still bothered him, and he still got the shakes—only now he was able to control them, because he had a higher purpose. He was on a quest—a quest to die. It would just mess things up if he let himself believe he was really getting back to normal.

A soft step behind him brought him back to reality. He turned to see Dr. Worthington coming down the corridor between the rows of beds.

"You're up early today, Charlie," Worthington said quietly, casting a glance around to make sure he wasn't bothering the other patients. "Having sleep disturbances, are we?"

Charlie suppressed a smile at the doctor's British euphemism. "Nightmares? No, Doc, no nightmares," he lied. "I just woke up early, that's all. You really should get some curtains on these windows."

Worthington looked around. "Perhaps you're right, old man. The blackout shades stay rolled up unless we have an air raid. Either we have total darkness or this—" He waved a hand and squinted against the sunlight. "Not much middle ground here."

"I thought the British were noted for their moderation," Charlie jibed, grinning.

"Quite right. In most matters, anyway." He returned Charlie's smile. "But the sun rarely shines, so we don't often have to concern ourselves with such a dilemma."

"So, Doc," Charlie said, changing the subject, "what are *you* doing here at this time of the morning?"

"Why, I'm always here at this hour," the doctor said. "But usually you're still sleeping."

Charlie's stomach lurched at the thought of Alexander Worthington walking the wards at dawn. Had the doctor seen evidence of his night-mares, of his inner struggles, even as he slept? The very idea made Charlie feel exposed, vulnerable. Was it possible that he could have given himself away and ruined everything?

He searched Worthington's face for some sign of concern, some signal that he knew more than Charlie was telling. But the doctor's expression remained passive, revealing nothing.

"Are you ready to get up, Charlie?"

"I—I suppose so." Charlie faltered for a moment, then gathered his strength and held the doctor's gaze. "There's no point in staying in bed all day, now is there?"

"My thought exactly. Perhaps you'd like to get dressed, and we could have breakfast together. Then we can go to my office and get an early start on your morning session."

Charlie sighed inwardly. These were the toughest times, these "casual" moments with the doctor. It was so easy to let his resolve waver during unguarded moments at a meal or in an offhanded conversation. And Charlie couldn't afford to let his defenses down—not for a minute. His very life, at least what he had left of it, depended upon maintaining his composure and protecting himself.

"Sure, Doc," Charlie said, forcing into his voice a lightness he didn't feel. "Give me a couple of minutes. I'll meet you in the commissary."

★ ★ ★

Alexander Worthington toyed with his breakfast absently as he waited. His mind wasn't on his food but on his most puzzling patient, Charlie Coltrain.

The man was a walking dilemma for a psychiatrist. A variety of nonverbal signals, things Alexander couldn't quite put his finger on, told him that

Charlie was still struggling, that the war of nerves was not yet won. But the outward signs—his demeanor, his control, his balance, even his sense of humor—indicated that he was making real progress in the battle.

Alexander couldn't understand it—and he was a man accustomed to understanding. If he were simply trusting the data he had collected, he would say that Charlie Coltrain was well on his way to being a whole man. If he depended on his instincts, he would argue that he had not yet reached the core of Charlie's anxiety, that Charlie was hiding something.

The problem was, Alexander Worthington couldn't depend wholly upon either of those two factors. There was another variable in the mix, a variable that most of his colleagues would openly disparage.

For Alexander was a praying man, a man who trusted God to give him direction, both in his personal life and in his practice. In earlier years, he had felt called to the priesthood of the Anglican church. He had even gone to seminary for a year, but he found that studying under cynical professors took all the heart out of him. Few of his companions viewed the priesthood as a calling; for many, it was just a job with the potential for political power. After the first year, he concluded that his call from God could better be fulfilled helping people come to mental and spiritual health. For the sake of that vocation—and for the protection of his own faith—he left theological study in favor of psychiatry.

In medical school, he found much the same kind of cynicism, only it attacked both his faith *and* his practice. Many medical students viewed psychiatry as a field that didn't belong in the study of medicine. Some even made jokes about the "hocus-pocus" doctors and their "voodoo practice." Then, when they discovered that Alexander was a Christian—not just a nominal Anglican but a devout believer—they dubbed him "Father Psycho" and mocked him, demanding that he pray over the cadavers to resurrect them.

But Alexander Worthington had held on to his faith in God, growing stronger in his convictions because of the abuse he endured. Determined not to let the ignorance of others deter him from his calling, he had made a name for himself as a psychiatrist—and, he liked to believe, helped bring a measure of respectability to the field. He studied tirelessly to keep himself abreast of new insights and theories in psychiatry, and he trusted in God's guidance both for himself and for his patients. Right now, however, what he perceived as God's direction didn't square with the facts of Charlie's case.

The psychiatrist in him was certain that Charlie Coltrain was harboring secret struggles, that he was not nearly as far along in his recovery as he liked to pretend. Charlie gave all the right answers, but Alexander could see the torment in his eyes. Indeed, the man seemed to be making a monumental effort to maintain his facade of balance and control.

It just didn't make sense. Most victims of shell shock wanted to stay as far away from battle as they could possibly get. The very idea of going back to the front made them break out in a cold sweat. But not Charlie.

Charlie wanted to go back—to prove something, Alexander supposed, perhaps to prove to himself that he wasn't a coward. There was also the possibility that he wanted to die in battle, a kind of noble suicide, motivated by a distorted view of honor. Charlie hadn't shown any signs of self-destructive tendencies, but Alexander could sense something not quite right in the way the man talked about his desire to rejoin his comrades.

Alexander would never have considered releasing Charlie based solely on his psychiatric evaluation. But the anomalies of the man's case had driven him to prayer, seeking a guidance that was beyond his own understanding. The answer that he received shocked and troubled him—and no doubt would have made him a laughingstock among his professional colleagues.

Let him go, the quiet voice in Alexander's spirit had said. *Let him go.*

At first Alexander had argued. The man was not ready to be released, and certainly not released back to the front. Perhaps he could be sent to the States, to a hospital facility where he could get ongoing therapy—

Let him go.

In the end, Alexander had given up his arguments. He couldn't understand it, but he had long ago learned that when he received such a direct and clear response to prayer, he needed to pay attention. Usually God worked in concert with his reason and his education; when an answer came that seemed to defy logic and fly in the face of his psychiatric training, there had to be justification for it, even if Alexander didn't know what that justification was. Far be it from him to second-guess God.

He knew he had heard correctly; the peace in his spirit told him that God had truly spoken. And whether or not he could comprehend the reasons, he would do what he was called to do.

He would trust God and let Charlie Coltrain go.

★ ★ ★

Charlie entered the commissary apprehensively and looked around for Dr. Worthington. He spotted the doctor in a corner next to the wall. Worthington was pushing his food around on his plate, apparently deep in thought.

Charlie got his breakfast and took his tray to the doctor's table. He was halfway through his powdered eggs and toast when Worthington finally looked up and noticed he was sitting there.

"Ah—Charlie. Here you are at last."

"I'm here," Charlie said. "Have been for the past five minutes. The question is, where have *you* been?"

"Just . . . thinking," the doctor replied vaguely. He took a sip of his tea, then grimaced. "There's nothing worse than cold tea."

"Oh, yes, there is." Charlie raised his cup. "This stuff you Brits call coffee."

"Yanks are notorious for hating British coffee," Worthington said. "'If this is coffee, bring me tea,'" he mimicked in a perfect imitation of a flat Yankee accent. "If this is tea, bring me coffee."

"My sentiments exactly." Charlie finished his eggs and drained the last bit of the disgusting brew from his mug.

Worthington pointed at Charlie's cup. "Do you want another?"

"You've got to be kidding."

"I wasn't, but the point is well taken. Shall we retire to my office?"

Charlie followed Worthington down the dismal hallway to a small office opening off to the left. As many times as he had been in this room, it never failed to depress him. There was no window, only four tan walls, bare except for two framed diplomas. The floor was the same scarred linoleum used throughout the hospital, and the only furniture was a battered wooden desk, a creaky desk chair, and a ragged upholstered armchair. Charlie often wondered how even a doctor of psychiatry managed to stay sane in such an environment.

"Sit down," Worthington said, sinking heavily into the desk chair and gesturing toward the armchair on the other side of the desk.

Charlie sat, struggling to maintain his composure. He could sense something coming—some declaration or change—and he wasn't sure he was prepared for it.

The doctor retrieved Charlie's chart from the file drawer in his desk and flipped through it for a full two minutes without saying anything. At last he closed the file, placed it carefully on his desk, and folded his hands across the top of it.

"You have been with us for two months, Charlie," Worthington began. "In that time, you seem to have made great progress."

Charlie narrowed his eyes and looked at the doctor. His words should have been encouraging, but something in his tone made Charlie uneasy.

"But?"

"No buts," Dr. Worthington said. "In fact, I was hard pressed, even when you first came here, to find the signs of severe shell shock that were listed in your medical record. It seemed odd to me at the time that a man with your record showed so few signs of difficulty."

Charlie fought back his panic. Had he been found out? Was Worthington about to ship him back to a nut ward in the States, as Dr. Carter had originally planned to do?

"Maybe . . . maybe Dr. Carter was wrong."

The doctor shook his head. "I doubt it," he said. "Dr. Carter is not a specialist, but he has a great deal of experience with cases like yours. I find it difficult to believe that he could have been guilty of such a gross misdiagnosis."

Charlie shrugged. "But you do admit that I'm better?" he ventured.

Worthington sat back in his chair and held Charlie's eyes. "Externally, you show all the signs of a fully functional person."

"What does that mean?" Charlie knotted his hands into fists and forced his breathing to remain normal.

"It means that whatever internal struggles you still have, you manage to function normally. You are rational and exhibit none of the symptoms commonly associated with your condition."

"You mean I'm cured—"

Dr. Worthington held up a hand. "We do not speak of *cures* in a case like yours," he interrupted. "As I have told you before, psychiatry is not an exact science. But you seem well enough to—"

"To go back to my company?" Charlie asked, his heart pumping wildly.

"To be returned to duty," Worthington corrected.

"That's great, Doc! Just great! When did you decide this?"

A shadow passed over the doctor's face, and for a moment he seemed very faraway. "I've been considering it for a while. I must be honest with you, Charlie, I didn't want to do this. I personally don't feel you're ready for . . . for what you will have to face if you go back."

Charlie frowned, and his mind began to turn over the possibilities. If the doctor didn't think he was ready, where did this decision come from? "What made you change your mind?" he asked finally.

Worthington shook his head. "Let's just say I had a . . . consultation . . . with someone who knows more about the situation than I do."

A consultation? With whom? Worthington was the top man in his field, at least in this hospital. There was no one to consult with. Then suddenly the truth settled on Charlie like a palpable weight.

"Doctor," he began cautiously, "are you a praying man?"

Worthington's head snapped up. "I beg your pardon?"

"Are you a praying man?" Charlie repeated. "Do you believe in God and go to God with your problems?"

A suspicious expression spread across the doctor's face, as if he knew he was being led into a trap. "Yes," he said quietly. "I believe in God. I pray."

"And this 'consultation' of yours that convinced you to release me—is it possible that you consulted with God, not with some other shrink?"

Worthington winced at the word *shrink,* and Charlie immediately regretted using it. But instead of defending his profession, the doctor let out an extended sigh. "Yes, Charlie," he said at last, "I prayed about it."

"And God told you to release me?"

"That about summarizes the conversation, yes."

Charlie grinned and reached across the desk to shake Dr. Worthington's hand. "I should have known," he said.

"I want you to know, Charlie, that I'm doing this under protest. As I said before, I do not believe—"

"You can protest all you want, Doc, as long as you sign those papers. You see, I've been praying about this, too, and it's pretty obvious that God wants me out of here and back to the front."

"So it seems," the doctor murmured. "I only wish I knew why."

"You don't need to know, Doc. I know why. And God does, too."

"For your sake, Charlie," Worthington said, "I hope and pray you're right."

★ ★ ★

Charlie was practically floating when he left Alexander Worthington's office and made his way back to the ward. He had pulled it off. His plan had worked; never mind the fact that Worthington hadn't really believed his act. With or without the doctor's cooperation, God had apparently stepped in and taken over.

Charlie's prayers had been answered. Obviously, Dr. Worthington hadn't suspected his real purpose in wanting to go back to the front. Worthington had agreed to minimize the effects of his shell shock so that the commander would be willing to take him. In two weeks—"within the fortnight," as Worthington put it—Charlie would be out of this hospital and on his way to join his new company for a month of hedgerow training. In less than two months he would be back in action, where he could end his life with honor.

God was on his side. Nothing could possibly go wrong now. Nothing could stop him from fulfilling his mission. Nothing.

31

⭐ ⭐ ⭐

Audience with the Queen

Link Winsom stood on the wharf at New York harbor and gazed up at the ship anchored in the bay.

"Golly, it's big, ain't it?" Coker breathed in Link's ear.

Link glanced over his shoulder. "Very perceptive, Coke." Stork stood at his right with his mouth hanging open, and to his left, Owen Slaughter did the same. *Redneck bookends,* Link thought. *You'd think they'd never seen a big city, or a wharf, or a real ship before.*

The truth was, Link had never seen anything like it either, but he had the good sense to keep his mouth closed. The *Queen Elizabeth*—the finest, fastest, biggest ship in history. Except maybe for the *Titanic,* which nobody cared to think about right now. This was their ship—the floating hotel that would provide luxury accommodations on their very first transatlantic voyage.

Slaughter grinned. "This is going to be a real vacation, pals."

As they watched, a soldier appeared on the deck of the ship, so high above them that they had to crane their necks and squint to see him. He held a clipboard in one hand and a bullhorn in the other. He watched the milling crowd on the dock for a moment, then lifted the bullhorn to his mouth.

"FALL IN!"

Link could hardly believe a roar that loud could come from such a small man, but like everyone else, he stopped staring and scrambled into position.

"STATE YOUR DIVISION AND COMPANY!"

The first bevy of men moved forward. "Company C, 25th Division!" the men shouted.

The soldier scribbled some notes on his clipboard. "TWENTY-FIVE C, TABLE SERVERS!" he called.

Link could see Slaughter and his company now, moving up the gangplank. "Company A, 376th!"

"THREE SEVENTY-SIX A, TABLE CLEANUP!" the man yelled and ushered them onto the ship.

Link's group was next. *Not KP,* he prayed. *Any duty but KP.*

"Company B, 376th!"

"THREE SEVENTY-SIX B, KP!" The man on the deck ordered. Link's heart sank. Then a second man came forward and spoke into the soldier's ear. The man nodded, scribbled on his clipboard, and turned to the waiting soldiers.

"THREE SEVENTY-SIX B, TABLE CLEANUP!" he corrected. The group behind them was assigned to KP.

Stork grinned and slapped Link on the back as they moved up the ramp. "That was a close call."

"You're telling me," Link laughed. "There is a God, after all."

Coker came up behind them. "I plan on getting a great tan during this crossing," he said jovially. "How tough can table cleanup be?"

★ ★ ★

They found out on the first night out.

The *Queen Elizabeth* had undergone a face-lift, and the operation did not improve her. What once had been the largest, most popular luxury liner on the high seas had been transformed into the largest, most overcrowded sardine can in history.

Below decks, huge cargo holds had been taken over for sleeping space— bunks stacked six high, line after line of them, with barely enough space to walk in between. The ship held thousands of men. The upper decks were packed, day and night, with soldiers milling aimlessly about or sitting in sheltered corners playing poker. When they weren't working, that is.

How difficult could table cleanup be? poor innocent Coker had asked. And he got his answer soon enough. From the time they got up in the morning until they dropped into their bunks at night, men lined up for meals in the enormous converted ballroom and the various dining rooms of the ship. When one group finished breakfast, another group would file in. When breakfast was finally over, preparations for dinner had already begun.

Whole companies of men did nothing but clean latrines. Other companies swabbed decks. Some worked below in the machine rooms and reeked incessantly of fuel and grease. Others sweated in the galleys preparing the massive quantities of food needed to sustain fifteen thousand soldiers. Nobody needed to ask what a guy's duty was. You could tell by the smell.

Link suspected that this was the army's way of making them look forward to going into battle. If they could survive the noise and the crowding and the monotony of this week-long nightmare, facing cannon fire and bayonets would be a welcome relief.

Compared to the other duties, however, busing tables was easy work.

And Owen Slaughter had found a way to make it even easier.

One afternoon, when the midday dishes had been cleared away and the last of the tables were being scrubbed, Owen found Link and Stork in the enlisted men's mess. "Come on," he said. "I've got something to show you."

Just as they were leaving, Coker appeared. "What's up, guys?"

"Get back to work, Private," Link told him.

"Work's done, Sarge. Where are you going?"

Link and Slaughter exchanged a glance, and Link shrugged. "OK, Coker, come on with us."

"But you've got to keep this quiet," Slaughter added.

"Keep what quiet?" Coker's bright eyes shone eagerly at this prospect of adventure.

"Don't ask questions. Just come on, and keep your mouth shut."

They followed Slaughter as he led them to the main stairway on the port side of the ship. A sign next to the stairway proclaimed, *Officers Only*.

"We can't go up there!" Coker protested when Slaughter began to climb the stairs. "The sign says—"

"I can read, Coker." Slaughter gave the boy a disgusted look. "Are you coming or aren't you?"

"Yeah, I'm coming," Coker answered reluctantly. "But if we get in trouble—"

"Stop whining," Slaughter snapped. "And keep your mouth shut."

Three flights up, Slaughter opened a hatch and stepped through, holding the door open to reveal a long carpeted hallway flanked by doors on either side. The air was cool and still, and Link heard something he hadn't heard in a long time: silence.

"It's so quiet," Stork whispered, echoing Link's thoughts.

Link stared at Owen, who stood with arms across his chest, grinning broadly. "What is this?"

"This, my friends, is our ticket to Paradise." He turned to the first door on the left and flung it open. "Your suite, Sergeant. I trust the accommodations will be satisfactory."

Link looked past him. The stateroom, decorated in subtle shades of gray, blue, and green, reminded him of the inside of an aquarium. There was even a porthole, open to the sea, letting in a fresh, salt-laden breeze. Hesitantly he stepped inside. "What do you mean, my suite?"

Owen clapped him on the back. "I did a little checking. Most of the bodies on this floating tin can are dressed in enlisted men's uniforms. There are only about a hundred officers, and they all have cabins on the other side of the ship. These cabins aren't being used—and won't be, unless we use them. Terrible waste of space, wouldn't you say? It's practically our duty to make use of what the army provides for us."

"How long have you known about this?"

"I did some scouting when we first came aboard." He reached down and picked up a small piece of paper, folded in half, and waved it in front of Link's nose. "I bugged the cabins, just to see if anyone ever came up here. Not a soul has set foot on this deck since we weighed anchor."

Link shook his head. "Owen, you're a genius."

"I am," Slaughter agreed modestly. Then he turned to Stork and Coker. "Not one word of this to anyone, all right? Otherwise we'll be swamped with guys wanting to join us, and the more people tramp up here, the more likely we are to get caught."

Coker nodded. "But what if we do get caught? What if somebody sees us? What if—"

Link caught Owen's eye, then Stork's. In unison, the three of them said, "Shut up, Coker."

Then they all began to laugh.

★ ★ ★

Libba fluffed the sofa pillows into shape, then went to the front window to straighten the star banner that hung there. It was cousin Charlie's star, technically. Willie had talked her parents into letting them keep it for a while. Officially, the serviceman's star was only supposed to be displayed by the wives and parents of soldiers on active duty overseas. But they were *practically* the wives of soldiers, Libba reasoned. It seemed to her that they had the right to hang a star, too.

Besides, she liked seeing it there when she came home in the afternoons. It reminded her of Link, made her feel as if he were close. It had been three weeks since the elephant, which she had named Lin-Lin, arrived, and she had received no further word. Neither she nor Willie had any idea where

Link and Owen were. But for the time being, just knowing Link still loved her was enough for Libba.

"I just feel so sorry for them," Mabel Rae said one night at dinner. "Imagine, sleeping in a muddy foxhole and eating cold C rations, or K rations, or whatever it is they have to eat."

"I'll just be glad when we finally start to get some news from them," Willie said. "It's so frustrating, sending letters every day to a military clearing station, never knowing when they will finally be delivered—if they ever get delivered at all. Our letters to Charlie took forever to catch up with him."

"I know," Libba sighed. "I keep thinking about Link off on the front somewhere. He's probably cold . . . and hungry. Maybe I should knit him a pair of warm wool socks. Or better yet, bake him a batch of cookies."

Mabel Rae and Willie both looked up at her in amazement. "Cookies?"

"Yes, cookies. Don't you think he'd like some nice sugar tea cakes? He could share them with his buddies, and—"

Mabel quirked an eyebrow in Willie's direction. "Better stick with the socks, Libba," Willie said.

Mabel nodded. "He might get trench foot, but at least he won't die of food poisoning."

★ ★ ★

Link pushed the unfinished portion of his second porterhouse away and groaned. "I can't eat another bite." The skins of two baked potatoes lay on his plate next to the steak, along with three clean corncobs. "That was wonderful."

Stork nodded and cut off another huge bite of rare meat. "Delicious," he mumbled, and buttered another roll.

"Even Stork will beef up on a menu like this." Link reached over and patted his buddy's stomach. "Stock up, pal. We'll be back to army rations before you know it."

Owen Slaughter had done it again. Behind a curtain on the back wall of the enlisted men's mess hall, he had discovered an unlocked door that led directly into the serving area of the officers' mess. He had managed to switch their table busing assignments so that they were solely responsible for cleaning up after the officers' dinner. There was always an enormous amount of food left over—chicken, steaks, real potatoes, sometimes even shrimp cocktail. So here they were, the four of them, glutting themselves like royalty and sleeping in luxury staterooms, while the thousands of other poor schmucks aboard this huge floating barracks crowded together in the cargo hold and argued among themselves in a futile effort to define what they received in the chow line.

Link leaned back and gave a contented sigh. After a moment or two, he sat up, pushed the dishes aside, and pulled a pen and paper out of his pocket. He had time to finish his letter to Libba before they cleaned up.

He smoothed the pages against the surface of the table and looked up. Across from him, Slaughter and Stork, obviously with the same idea, had their heads down over letters to Willie and Madge. Coker, looking decidedly uncomfortable, sat fiddling with his fingers and tapping nervously on the wood.

Coker caught Link's eye. "Shouldn't we . . . shouldn't we get finished in here?" he said anxiously, glancing around at the tables that still needed to be cleared. "I mean, what if someone—"

Link shook his head. "Relax, Coker. You worry too much. I swear, you remind me of my sister."

Lowering his gaze, Coker stared at the dirty dishes around him.

"You need a girl, Coker," Owen put in, never looking up from his letter.

Coker's head spun around, and he stared incredulously at Slaughter. "A . . . a girl?"

"Yeah, a girl," Link said. "You know, a person of the opposite sex—nice figure, soft lips, curvy—" He lifted his hands and drew an hourglass shape in the air.

Coker's mouth dropped open, and he flushed all the way to the roots of his hair.

"They're just razzing you," Stork interrupted, flashing an acid glance at Link. "Don't listen to them, Coke. Don't pay them any mind."

Coker jumped to his feet, grabbed a tray, and began clearing plates and stacking dishes. "I think I'll just get started," he stammered.

Link laughed. "You do that, kid." With a chuckle he went back to his letter.

> Dear Libba,
>
> By the time you get this letter, we will be in Europe. I can't tell you where, because I don't know myself yet, but even if I told you they'd censor it out of this letter. We're not supposed to let anyone know where we are, because if the Germans got wind of our movements, it could work against the Allies. But by now, I hope, you got my little parting gift from Macy's and realize that we had to ship out before we had a chance to contact you and Willie.

> We're doing fine. Don't worry about us. Life on board the
> transport ship is difficult, but we're managing all right. We don't
> have all the comforts of home, but I guess this will help prepare
> us for battle, toughen us up for life in the trenches. . . .

Link smiled to himself. It wouldn't do for the girls to know what they were
really doing on board the *Queen Elizabeth*. He'd let them think that they
were bravely suffering for the honor of their country, like real war heroes.
Gritty, determined men preparing for battle. The real battle would come
soon enough.

> It's cold and lonely here, and I miss you so much. I wear the
> locket you gave me all the time, close to my heart, and I'll bring
> it back to you. I keep remembering the dance at the USO, that
> first night we met—you in that cream-colored dress, with those
> adorable, ridiculous little gloves. I didn't think I'd ever get a
> "proper introduction" so we could dance. It seems so long ago,
> and yet it was only a few weeks.
>
> When I get back—and I will come back—I want us to be
> married right away. If anything happens to me, if I get wounded
> or something, I will try to get posted to Memphis so I can be
> close to you. But don't worry. I'll keep my head down and get
> back in one piece. I promise. Nothing—not even this war—is
> going to interfere with our life together.

"When do you think they'll get these letters?" Link asked when he looked
up and saw Slaughter staring off into space.

Owen blinked a couple of times, then focused on Link's face. "Huh? Oh,
I don't know. We won't be able to send them until we land, and then it'll
probably take a while."

Link stretched his neck and peered across the table, trying to read
Owen's letter upside down. "What are you telling Willie?"

Frowning, Slaughter slapped his hand across the page. "None of your
business."

"I don't mean the mushy stuff," Link said. "I mean, about what we're
doing."

"Am I telling Willie that we're living high on the hog and sleeping on satin
sheets every night? Not a chance!" Owen shook his head. "And don't you
tell Libba, either. We have a reputation to protect, you know."

Link chuckled. "I know. I feel a little bad about it, but there's no point in
raising questions we can't answer."

Owen sighed and ran a hand through his hair. "Besides, by the time they get these letters, we probably will be up to our knees in a muddy foxhole, eating K rations off the hood of a jeep and dodging Kraut grenades. We're gonna need a little sympathy."

A clatter of dishes shattered the quiet of the mess hall. Across the room, Coker was down on all fours, frantically trying to retrieve the pieces of a broken plate.

"What's the matter, kid?" Link grinned at him and shook his head. "A little nervous, are we?"

"I gotta be honest, Sarge," the boy said. "The closer we get to landing, the more scared I get. I thought this would be exciting, but now . . . well, what if I—"

"If you chicken out?" The words were blunt, but the compassion in Slaughter's tone softened the blow. "We're all scared, Coke. Every man who has any sense, that is. Just stick with us, kid. You'll be OK."

Link's eyes met Slaughter's and held them for a long time. Owen was right, as usual. They weren't playing soldiers. Soon this tub would land, and they would be facing the real thing. It was scary. But if they just stuck together, they were bound to come through it . . . no matter what happened.

FOUR

You'll Never Know

JUNE 1944

32

★ ★ ★

Mail Call

June 1944

Thelma Breckinridge looked up from her newspaper to see Mabel Rae Coltrain, alone, in the back booth. The girl must have slipped in when Thelma was cleaning up the kitchen; she hadn't heard the bell over the door ring, and except for Mabel, the cafe was empty.

Thelma waited until Mabel looked up, then called out, "Coffee?"

"Iced tea, please," Mabel answered. She gave Thelma an enormous grin. "It's a beautiful evening, Thelma . . . have you seen the sunset?" Thelma shook her head. "Well, you ought to go outside and enjoy it. 'What is so rare as a day in June? Then, if ever, come perfect days. . . .'"

Thelma fixed a glass of tea and took it over to the table. "What's got into you, Mabel Rae? I declare, I've never seen you so happy. You're positively glowing!"

Mabel waved her into the opposite seat. "Can you keep a secret?"

"Of course."

Mabel grinned wryly. "Well, if you can, you're the only one in this town who has that ability." She held up two envelopes. "My pen pals."

"Two of them? My stars, Mabel, you are really getting into this, aren't you?"

"I love it. It's so interesting." She looked at the return addresses on the envelopes. "One is a lieutenant—"

"An officer?"

"Well, a very minor officer. His name is Drew—Andrew—Laporte, and he's from New Orleans. You wouldn't believe these letters, Thelma—he's such a nice fellow. College educated—he had just finished law school when he enlisted. He writes all about his fascination with the law and with helping people who can't help themselves." She lowered her voice. "He's an integrationist."

"A what?"

"He believes that Negroes should have the same rights as white people, and he wants to be a lawyer—maybe even a congressman—so he can be a part of making that happen."

"Wish him luck if he's going to try to make it happen in the South. If he thinks this war is bad, wait till he gets home."

Mabel nodded. "I know. But he makes a lot of sense, Thelma. He says he doesn't believe God intends for one group of people to oppress another group."

"I can't argue with him there," Thelma said. "It seems to me that people are people—some good, some bad. Doesn't much matter what color their skin is; it's what's in their hearts that counts."

"Thelma, are you an integrationist, too?"

Thelma smiled. "I never thought of it that way, hon. I guess I just believe that God doesn't see skin color when he looks at his children. But it's likely to be a long time before most of the rest of the folks in the South start seeing it that way. People have just got too much to protect."

"Drew says that white people try to keep Negroes in their place because they're afraid—because they need somebody to look down on. And I have to admit, I know some folks like that."

"Do you agree with him? About integration, I mean."

"I need to think about it some more," Mabel said. "What he says makes a lot of sense, and from what I know of the Bible, God is no respecter of persons and doesn't make that kind of distinction. But it's interesting to think about what this world would be like if there wasn't any prejudice against Negroes—or against anybody, for that matter."

"What do you write to this Andrew Laporte about, if you don't mind my asking?"

Mabel got a faraway look on her face. "Lots of things. His ideas, my ideas, art and literature and politics. Stuff nobody around here ever even thinks about." She smiled. "I feel as if a whole new world is opening up to me. And the wonderful thing is that he seems to think I'm a very interesting person."

Thelma chuckled. "You mean he's getting to know the real Mabel Rae."

"Maybe that's it. And maybe, in the process, I'm getting to know the real Mabel Rae, too. Only . . . he calls me Rae, not Mabel."

"You really are becoming a new woman, hon!"

Mabel blushed a little, and Thelma realized suddenly that the girl actually did look different. There wasn't any radical change on the outside, but she seemed more confident, more sure of herself.

"For a while, when we first started writing," Mabel was saying, "I felt like a phony—like he was seeing something that wasn't there. Then I began to realize that what he was seeing had always been there, only no one had ever looked far enough to find it. Not even me." Mabel reached out and gripped Thelma's hand. "Thanks, Thelma, for getting me started on this. It has really made a difference."

"It was God's direction, not mine," Thelma said quietly. "You just found your path, that's all." She winked at Mabel. "What about the other one? What's he like?"

"Not he," Mabel corrected. "She. An army nurse named Ardyce Hanson. She's from Minnesota." Mabel grinned. "Her letters are full of funny stories. She comes from a little town kind of like Eden—a place called Frost, which in the twenties was the sugar-beet capital of the world. Apparently Frost was a Norwegian settlement, and everybody there is related to each other. She tells these hilarious tales about the bachelor farmers who come into the cafe to gossip like little old ladies—"

"Sounds a little like the Paradise Garden."

"We have a lot in common," Mabel said. "And you know, Thelma, it feels really good to have a woman friend to talk to—even if our talking is only in letters. As much as I love Willie and wouldn't trade her for anything, there are some things you can't even tell your sister. Ardyce understands, and she encourages me to find my own way and follow my dreams. And I do the same for her. Do you know, she actually plans to become a doctor when she gets home? A woman doctor—imagine that."

"And what kind of dreams does she encourage you to follow?"

Mabel lowered her head and ran a finger around the rim of her iced tea glass. "If I tell you, do you promise not to breathe a word of it to anyone?"

"Cross my heart. This is just between you and me."

"I want to be a writer."

"Really? What do you want to write?"

"I'm not sure yet—so far, it's only a dream. But I've discovered something with this pen-pal thing. When I write, I find out what I think. That sounds backwards, I know, but it's true. I find myself writing about ideas I never understood before, exploring new concepts and formulating new insights. With Drew and Ardyce, I can express things I never even really thought about before. And there's something else you'll appreciate—"

"What's that?"

"I'm finding out about God, too. Especially with Drew. He makes me think more deeply than I have in the past—not just about religious stuff, about churches and worship styles and things like that—but about the really important issues, like who God is and what God wants to do in individual lives. I don't know if he's even aware of it, but Drew is helping me find a new kind of awareness of God. And I'm discovering that relationship with God is not an experience; it's an exploration."

"Meaning?" Thelma prodded. She couldn't have been more pleased at what she was hearing from Mabel Rae, and she wanted to hear more.

"Meaning that faith is not something that happens to you just once, like at baptism or confirmation or some other point in your life. It's an ongoing journey, a continual process of growing and changing and gaining new insights."

"Maybe you should be a preacher," Thelma said with a laugh. "That's the best sermon I've heard in years."

A surprised look passed over Mabel's face, then she joined in the laughter. "A woman pastor in the Presbyterian church?" she said. "I don't think so . . . not in my lifetime, at least. Besides, writing is what I want to do, not speaking."

"And Drew's letters set you onto all this?"

"Partly. His ideas about God's love for all people, that segregation is a sin—he actually said that, a sin—started me thinking a lot about God, and reading more. But mostly it has been my own writing that has made the difference. I write every day now, Thelma—letters to Drew and Ardyce . . . and Charlie, of course, but my letters to him are different. Or I write in my journal. I write about everything. And the more I write, the more I want to write. The more I discover about God and myself, the more I want to discover."

"Well, you just keep right on discovering, honey," Thelma said. "It looks real good on you."

"I'm happier than I ever thought I could be," Mabel admitted. "I feel like I have a purpose that's bigger than anything I've ever dreamed about. I may never see my name on a book, but that's not important. What's important is what's happening inside."

Thelma nodded and patted Mabel's hand. "You got that right, hon," she said. "And don't worry, your secret is safe with me—both about the letters and about your dream."

Mabel looked up and smiled—a radiant expression, full of unshed tears. "Thank you, Thelma," she said. "Thanks for everything."

★ ★ ★

From her vantage point behind the counter, Thelma watched as Mabel Rae Coltrain sat with her head down over a sheaf of papers, writing furiously. An hour and a half had passed since their conversation had ended, and Mabel was still at it.

Two months ago, when Thelma had steered Mabel toward becoming a pen pal, her only purpose had been to help the girl get out of herself a little and find a way to reach out to someone else. But evidently God had more in mind—much more—than she could ever have imagined.

Thelma had no way of knowing where all this would lead, and Mabel probably didn't, either. But the Good Lord knew. And whether Mabel ever realized her dream of becoming a writer or not, what was happening now was a gift of God's grace. The dream itself was enough . . . enough to set Mabel Rae on a path that was clearly of God's design.

No, two months ago Thelma hadn't known where this path would lead. And she couldn't take credit for it now. She had just been obedient to the quiet inner nudging of the Spirit. God had done the rest. And, as usual, God had gone far beyond any of her expectations.

Relationship with God is not an experience, Mabel had said; *it's an exploration.* With a renewed sense of awe in her heart, Thelma Breckinridge bowed her head and offered up a silent prayer of gratitude to the Christ of the Resurrection, who still pried open sealed-up tombs and led people like Mabel Rae Coltrain out into the light of a new day.

33

★ ★ ★

Freddy's Back

Libba smiled absently as her students filed out of the classroom amid a chorus of, "Good bye, Miss Coltrain—have a good summer!" When the last back had disappeared through the doorway, she put her head down on her desk and sighed.

June second. She had thought the day would never come, and now it had come and gone in a blur of final exams, grading papers, and issuing final marks. School was over.

Libba had been generous; she was too exhausted to be tough. No one failed. No one even got a D, although Ricky Reston and his little band of cutthroats had certainly deserved them. But what did it matter now? She was through with teaching, at least for a while. In a week and a half she would begin classes again at Ole Miss, and she would be on the other side of the desk. Maybe some professor would return her kindness by being generous toward her. Heaven only knew she was in no shape to go back to college, but there was nothing else to do. She had to keep herself busy, avoid thinking about Link . . . and the war . . . and what might happen.

She had received no word from him since the cryptic message from New York. Not that she had expected a letter—not yet. He had probably landed by now, but overseas mail was slow and news from the front trickled back home in fits and starts.

Libba wrote to him every day—long, impassioned letters, letters full of news and lightheartedness designed to keep his spirits up. But what about *her* spirits? Everyone was involved in the war effort—bond drives, rubber drives, scrap drives. But little was said about the people left behind . . . wives and mothers and girlfriends who went to bed every night worrying that their men might never come home again.

Willie was finding things to do to keep herself busy. She wrote letters to Owen every day—and one a week to her brother Charlie—but she didn't seem nearly as depressed as Libba felt. Instead of moping around, Willie worked at the Red Cross office making bandages or served Cokes and donuts at the USO. Activity, she told Libba repeatedly. That was the key. Keep going; contribute something.

Well, Libba thought morosely, she had contributed enough. She had contributed Link. He was gone—off to Europe, probably, since he obviously had shipped out from New York—and she was lonely. She didn't need activity. She needed diversion. And so she was going back to school.

The ten days between the end of classes at Eden and the beginning of classes at Oxford, however, stretched out before her like a yawning chasm. How would she fill the time? How could she possibly endure ten days with nothing to do, with her mind constantly on Link and what might be happening to him over there?

She had to move, of course. Their temporary certificates gave them no assurance of a teaching job in the fall, and they couldn't afford to keep the apartment over the summer. But packing her few personal belongings and vacating the apartment would take a day at the most. She would have to go home and stay with Mama and Daddy until university housing opened up on the eleventh. And she was not looking forward to being subjected to Daddy's constant haranguing about how stupid she was to think that someone like Link Winsom would still care for her when—or if—he returned.

Libba, in the words of Daddy's favorite cliché, had put all her eggs in one basket. And the basket was on very shaky ground at the moment.

★ ★ ★

Libba was jerked from her reverie by a soft knock at the classroom door. She raised her head and straightened her collar.

"Come in."

Slowly, with a prolonged creak, the door opened and a slight man in a white shirt, navy suspenders, and burgundy bow tie stood in the doorway. For a moment Libba didn't recognize him.

Then, "Freddy? Freddy Sturgis?"

Mutely, Freddy entered and stood before her with his eyes downcast and his hands clasped in front of him. Libba studied him closely. He looked so different . . . older, perhaps. She hadn't seen him since mid-March, the week after the dance where she met Link. How could a person change so much in a couple of months?

Then it struck her like a blow. His uniform was gone. He was dressed in civvies!

Libba got up and walked around the desk to stand in front of him. "Freddy," she said automatically, extending a hand. "How good to see you."

It was a superficial politeness, and Freddy winced slightly, as if he felt the sting of her coolness. He shifted nervously, then raised his eyes to hers.

"Hello, Libba."

That was all. No conversation, no word of explanation, just *Hello, Libba.*

Libba's mind raced. She had been well schooled in the lessons of southern etiquette, and she had to be cordial. As much as she wanted to know, she couldn't just come out and say, "What are you doing here?" or "Why are you out of uniform?" That would be rude. Maybe "What brings you to Eden on this lovely June day?" would be appropriate without being pushy. Mama was always so good in uncomfortable social situations. What would she do?

Freddy saved her the trouble of any further mental gymnastics. "I guess you're wondering why I'm here," he said with a wan smile. "And why I'm dressed like this."

Libba nodded, relieved that he had broken the ice. "Well, yes, to be honest."

"I've been discharged."

"Discharged?" Libba almost shouted. "Discharged? In the middle of a war?"

Freddy hung his head. "Everybody knew I wouldn't be much good for the war effort," he said humbly. "It wasn't much of a surprise. It was a medical discharge."

Libba narrowed her eyes. "Medical discharge? Freddy, is something wrong? Are you ill?"

He shook his head miserably. "Asthma. It seems I've developed asthma." He took a deep breath and coughed. "And—" He gave her a sheepish look. "Hives. Caused by stress, apparently. The asthma is worse when I'm agitated, too." He hung his head. "I couldn't cut it, Libba. The army didn't want me."

Libba reached out and laid a hand on his arm. "I'm so sorry, Freddy," she said with genuine sympathy. "It must be terrible for you."

He shrugged. "Not so bad, really, except for what people say about a guy who stays home when all the 'real men' are off fighting. But I'm getting used to it; it doesn't bother me so much anymore." He paused and swallowed, and his Adam's apple jumped against the thin skin of his neck. "I guess . . . I guess I'll never be a 'real man' anyway—not the way most people define it," he said. "You always knew that, Libba—at least at the end." Before Libba could protest, he shoved his hands in his pockets and looked at her intently. "So I've decided just to be myself."

Libba smiled gently and squeezed his arm. "And what does being yourself mean, Freddy?"

He gave her a smile of absolute delight, and his eyes danced with more animation than she had ever seen in him. "It means," he said dramatically, "that I'm going back to school. To study art."

"Really? That's wonderful, Freddy!"

"I'm glad you think so. There's a lot of talk about GIs getting financial help to go back to college after the war. The money may not come through for a while, but my brief stint with Uncle Sam should be sufficient to qualify me when it does. In the meantime, I've got enough money saved up to get me started."

Suddenly Libba realized she was still holding Freddy's arm, and she dropped her hand abruptly. To her dismay, he noticed. But when she looked up at him again, he was grinning.

"Don't worry, Libba, I'm not going to try to get you back. I know better. I would just like for us to be . . . friends."

"Friends?" Libba repeated.

"Yes, friends." Freddy chuckled. "You know, two people who do things together, enjoy each other's company, talk—"

"And nothing more?"

"Nothing more." His tone was definite, strong, as if for the first time he was very sure of himself. "Sergeant Winsom is the right man for you, Libba. I knew that even before you told me we wouldn't be seeing each other again. I know—I cried and acted like a baby. But it was only because I felt so inadequate, so . . ." He paused, groping for words. "So uncertain of who I was or what I wanted out of life." He took her hand and held it gently. "Now I know, and losing you helped me find out. I'm going to be an artist, Libba—a good one. Maybe a great one. And nothing anyone says can make any difference to me now."

Libba stared at Freddy in wonder. Thelma had said, *Tell him the truth, hon. We all have to grow up sometime.* Well, it looked as if Freddy had done some amazing growing. He did, indeed, seem sure of himself, of what he wanted out of life. Some kind of secret joy radiated out of his boyish face. She didn't understand it, but she was happy for him; and suddenly she found herself truly wanting to get to know him—as a friend. When they had dated, she had never really known him; she had only pinned her hopes on him as an escape from Daddy's domination. But he seemed different now . . . interesting, alive.

"So," he said, "I start classes a week from Monday."

A sudden thought crossed Libba's mind. "Freddy, where are you going?"

He looked puzzled. "Well, I'm going to Alabama to visit my family for a few days, and then—"

"No. I mean, what college?"

"Ole Miss, of course. It's not the best art department in the country, but it's close by. And Oxford is a perfect place for an artist. Just think of the possibilities—the square, with its Confederate statue and the courthouse; Faulkner's Rowan Oak, with the drive lined by all those wonderful trees; the beautiful antebellum homes like Fiddler's Folly. Why, I might be able to bring in extra money doing watercolors for the historical society, or sketches during the Pilgrimage—"

"Freddy," Libba interrupted, "did you know that I'm going back to finish my degree?"

"Are you?" he said innocently. "At Ole Miss? Why, that's marvelous. Where are you living?"

"For the time being, on campus. After summer school is over, I've got a chance at one of the apartments in the back of Isom Place, the big planter house on Jefferson. The apartment's only one big room, but it's nearly as cheap as campus housing. And Mama knows the landlady . . . otherwise I'd never get in."

"I've rented a small house down on the other end of Jefferson," Freddy said. "Two houses west of the cemetery." He smiled. "It'll be great, Libba."

She looked at him and narrowed her eyes. "Just friends?"

"Just friends." He nodded. "Now, come and have dinner with me. I've got a lot to tell you."

★ ★ ★

The Paradise Garden was nearly deserted by six-thirty. Thelma had flitted nervously around for twenty minutes, until Libba had confronted her and assured her that everything was all right. Now she was sitting behind the counter, reading the Memphis *Commercial Appeal*. Ivory was playing Glenn Miller songs on the piano. Libba sat across the table from Freddy, stirring at her melted ice cream, trying to take in all he had told her.

"France? They've gone to France?" She had heard about the fighting on the continent in Europe; Hitler's forces were nearly impenetrable, and the battles were fierce.

Freddy nodded solemnly. "There's something big in the wind," he said.

"No one will say just what it is, but rumor is that troops have been massing in England for weeks now. Shouldn't be too long before we hear something."

Libba sighed, and her stomach churned. Just the thought of Link facing the Germans on French soil was enough to make her violently ill. "Do you think he'll be all right?"

"There's no way to tell," Freddy said honestly. He looked at Libba with a sad expression. "It's not going to be any picnic over there. Hitler's not going to give ground easily."

Libba stared miserably at her plate. "What can we do, Freddy?"

He reached across the table and took her hand. "Nothing," he said quietly. "Nothing but hope—and pray."

34

★ ★ ★

D Day

**In the English Channel
June 7, 1944**

Charlie Coltrain stood on the deck of the ship, clinging to the rail and watching. All around him, men were playing poker and gin rummy, slapping their cards onto wooden ammo boxes and listening to the strains of Bing Crosby singing "Sweet Leilani." But Charlie couldn't take his eyes off the sea . . . the sea and the beach . . . and the fulfillment of his destiny.

If a man wanted to die, this was the place to do it. All around them mortars exploded in the water, sending geysers of salt spray high into the air. At a distance he could see the same kind of explosions on the beach. The only difference was that the spray that went up there was sand . . . and bodies.

The first wave of attack had been at dawn the previous day. The plan was to take the beach and cut a swath inland for the next units of soldiers. But the Germans had the attack troops pinned down on the beachhead, almost to the waterline, dug in and not moving at all. From concrete embankments on the bluff, the Krauts had a clear view of the beach for miles in all directions, and they were laying down artillery fire in wide sweeps. On the slopes they had machine-gun nests, connected with trenches, and across the beach they had dug an immense ditch that zigzagged for a hundred yards.

The Allies couldn't move. They couldn't make forward progress, and behind them, the Channel was filled with hundreds of ships just like Charlie's, waiting.

Charlie didn't understand how his companions could play cards and smoke and laugh as if they were back on some base in the States instead of in the middle of the biggest offensive in military history. Maybe it was their way of coping with the stress. Charlie's way was to pace the deck and watch.

But maybe their way was better. The waiting was killing him.

This was the moment he had lived for—the moment of his glory, the moment of his death. Charlie watched as a body floated by on the dark water, face down, the grenades on the soldier's belt bobbing like buoys in the waves. And he envied this dead man, who had given his life in battle. His struggles were over. All that was left for him was a posthumous glory.

With a snort of disgust and impatience, Charlie pushed away from the rail and went in search of his commanding officer.

★ ★ ★

From his vantage point outside the wardroom, Charlie could see glimpses of Colonel Norton as he paced back and forth in front of Sergeant Ordway. The colonel looked agitated, and although Charlie couldn't see Ordway's face, the sergeant kept shifting around and running his hand over his neck. Charlie paused outside the door and listened.

"We're going in," the colonel was saying. "Naval gunfire has taken out the German emplacements, and we're getting a foothold. Round up the men and get them ready to move. We beach at 1300 hours."

Charlie smiled. So. The time had come at last. He turned to go but paused when he heard his own name.

"What about Coltrain?" the sergeant asked.

"What about him?"

"Well, what do I do with him?"

Charlie peered through the hatch and saw the colonel's face light up in a sinister smile. "You know what to do with him."

Sergeant Ordway got to his feet. "I know what you said, Colonel, but he did pretty well in hedgerow training. Maybe he really has changed."

"Once a coward, always a coward," the colonel snarled. "Don't forget that, Ordway. Coltrain's yellow, and the army's got no place for the likes of him." Colonel Norton turned and fixed Sergeant Ordway with a menacing glare. "A lot of good men are going to die today, Ordway. A lot of good men have already died securing that beach. We march inland over the bodies of our own people. Coltrain's a lily-livered misfit who doesn't belong in the same outfit as the courageous men who have already given their lives. Now, do as I say. Put him up front. If he dies—and he will, mark my words—so much the better. The army will have one less coward to wet-nurse through the rest of this war. Better to have his sorry tail blown to pieces than yours."

Sergeant Ordway shifted and scratched his head. "I guess so, Colonel. But—"

"No buts, Sergeant. Just do it. I'm getting rid of this little weasel once and for all."

Charlie backed away from the door and leaned against the bulkhead, his breath coming in short, shallow gasps. He had to get away, to think.

He made his way to the forward deck and clung to the rail. "God," he moaned, "this isn't the way it's supposed to be. There's no honor in being squashed like a bug, getting your head blown off because your CO hates your guts and wants to see you dead. I wanted to do this—I wanted to die, to redeem myself. But not this way." His hands began to shake, and he gripped the rail even harder.

He flung back his head and howled into the wind. "I am not a coward! I AM NOT A COWARD!"

A stiff salt spray blew into his face, and Charlie opened his eyes. He took a deep breath of the brine-laden air and clenched his fists. "All right, God," he muttered. "This might not be the way I planned it, but it looks like there's no turning back now."

Casting a glance around to see if anyone was looking, Charlie made the sign of the cross over his chest. He had never done this before, and he felt awkward and uncertain how to do it right, but somehow it made him feel better. "Into thy hands I commit my spirit," he said under his breath.

Then he shouldered his pack, straightened his shoulders, and moved forward to debark.

★ ★ ★

Artillery fire was coming from all directions, but in shorter bursts than it had an hour ago, and with longer lapses in between. A corridor had been cleared a few hundred yards inland, past the beach and into the grasses and woods beyond. Charlie lifted his head and peered over the edge of his foxhole, a small trench dug into the sand.

As far as he could see, the beach was littered with debris—overturned tanks and jeeps, supplies and weapons, bodies, whole and in parts. Just to his right lay a carton of cigarettes, sodden with seawater. A gust of wind blew a sheet of paper into his trench, and he picked it up. Some soldier's letter to his family back home, half finished . . . now never to be completed. Charlie heaved a shuddering sigh and closed his eyes.

"Move out!"

The command jerked Charlie into action. He saw Sergeant Ordway ahead on the beach, motioning with his arm for the men to follow. Charlie readied his rifle, ducked his head, and made a run in Ordway's direction.

"Coltrain!" the sergeant bellowed.

Charlie slid to a stop beside Ordway. "I'm here, Sarge."

"Stay with me. We're going in."

With Charlie on his heels, Ordway started running, low to the ground, in a zigzag pattern. Charlie followed, diving into a foxhole next to the sergeant just as a blast of artillery fire ripped the ground at their feet. The sergeant pointed to the bluff above them. "See those concrete bunkers?"

Charlie nodded.

"Navy fire has taken out most of the German emplacements, but there are still Krauts all around here—snipers and machine gunners. We've got to get to the bluff and clear them out."

Charlie nodded again. "Right, Sarge."

Ordway narrowed his eyes and gave Charlie an odd look. "You OK, Coltrain?"

"I'm fine, Sarge. Let's get going."

"All right. Fan out to the left and take out those nests with grenades. I'll go to the right and meet you at the top."

Charlie made his way to the left and up toward the top of the bluff as if he were in a dream. None of it seemed real—the shelling went on around him, and he saw the bursts of light but heard nothing. He circled around behind a machine-gun nest and, as if in slow motion, watched himself jerk the pin with his teeth and lob the grenade into the nest. The two German soldiers turned at the last minute, their eyes wide, and Charlie saw them cover their heads just before the grenade exploded. But he kept moving, lobbing grenades left and right. Before he knew it, he was at the top of the bluff with Ordway beside him. His hands trembled a little, and he was sweating profusely; but he was alive.

Charlie paused and looked around. He saw dead German soldiers everywhere, and the artillery emplacement was a smoldering ruin of twisted metal and broken bodies. For a fleeting instant his mind flashed to the soldier he had killed at Messina, with his accusing blue eye and his death grip on Charlie's arm. Then Charlie took a deep breath, and the moment passed.

Ordway pointed behind them and gave a thumbs-up sign. Down on the beach, Allied soldiers sorted through the wreckage, salvaging equipment and ammunition. Fresh supplies were being unloaded from ships, and mine detectors were at work clearing the beachhead. For the moment, all was calm. Charlie wondered absently if he looked as bad as the sergeant did, blackened with smoke and dirt.

"What next, Sarge?"

Again the sergeant gave Charlie that same odd look, then shook his head and shrugged. "Down there."

Charlie's eyes followed the direction Ordway was indicating. Past the ridge, the bluff gave way to an apple orchard, with woods beyond. The scene was deceptively peaceful, with soldiers moving through the trees as if out for a springtime stroll.

"The woods are full of snipers," the sergeant said. "Our job is to widen the corridor."

Charlie nodded curtly, fixed his bayonet, and turned to go down the hill. But Ordway grabbed him by the arm and spun him around.

"What's with you, Coltrain?"

"What do you mean, Sarge?"

"Well, you're not . . . not yourself, exactly."

Charlie fixed him with an intent stare. "You mean I'm not acting like a coward."

Ordway lowered his head and took a deep breath. "Sorry, Coltrain. You didn't deserve that. You did real good back there."

"Thanks, Sarge." Charlie punched Ordway in the arm and grinned. "Come on. We've got a job to do."

★ ★ ★

Patrolling through the woods was an eerie and difficult assignment. Like everyone else, Charlie was aware that he could encounter a sniper at any minute, and he had to stay on guard at all times. But that wasn't the weird part. For Charlie, the odd thing was this feeling he had that something—or someone—was calling him forward, deeper into the woods. With every step he took, his sense of destiny increased, until he felt as if he were being propelled by a power beyond his control.

Then, without warning, he came to the edge of a clearing. He narrowed his eyes and stared into the trees beyond. Could it be his imagination? No, it was real all right, though hidden in the shadows of the trees—a small, tumbledown shack, overgrown with moss and lichens.

"Sarge!" he called. "Sergeant Ordway!"

Ordway appeared at his elbow. "What is it, Coltrain?"

"Look."

The sergeant looked. "A shack! Good work, Coltrain. Blow it up."

"What?"

Ordway unhooked a grenade from his belt and handed it to Charlie. "You found it, you do the honors."

"Wait a minute." Charlie took a step into the clearing.

"What are you doing, Coltrain?"

"I'm going to find out what's inside."

"Are you crazy? You want to get your gut filled with ammo from a Kraut machine gun?"

Charlie turned and faced Ordway. "It's my risk, Sarge. Besides, if you bring me back dead, the colonel will probably put you in for a medal."

The sergeant's face went pale under the dirt and grime. "How'd you know?"

Charlie shrugged. "It doesn't matter. I know—let's leave it at that. Shoot me in the back if you want to, but I'm going to see if there's anything in there."

Quietly, one step at a time, Charlie moved into the clearing. He could hear Ordway's breathing behind him. Well, if the idiot wanted to come, let him. Charlie would do what he had to do.

When he reached the shack, Charlie got a grip on his rifle and gingerly stretched his left hand toward the door. In one motion he slid back the latch, flung the door open on its creaking hinges, and braced himself. But he didn't fire.

There, in the far corner of the tiny shed, three pairs of eyes stared at him in terror. Three thin, dirty little faces shrank away from the muzzle of his weapon.

"Kids!" Ordway murmured over Charlie's shoulder. "I'll be jiggered. It's kids!"

Charlie handed his rifle to the sergeant and reached out a hand to the three children. "Don't be afraid," he crooned. "We won't hurt you. We're American GIs."

The oldest child's face brightened, and he grabbed at the arms of the two smaller ones, a boy and a girl. "GI," he repeated to them excitedly. "GI." Then he let go a sentence or two in rapid French, and the three, still huddled together, stepped out of the shed into the clearing.

By this time other soldiers had begun to gather around. "Does anyone here speak French?" Ordway asked.

A burly private with the name Lansky stenciled on his breast pocket pushed his way forward and shoved his face down toward the children. "You no be afraid-o," he shouted. "Us good guys. Us friends-o."

Ordway jerked him back. "That's not French, idiot," he snarled. "That's gibberish. And they're not deaf. They just don't speak English."

Charlie removed his helmet and poured water into it from his canteen. He offered it to the oldest boy. "Water," he said quietly, gesturing that the child should use the helmet like a drinking cup. The boy took the helmet eagerly and raised it to his mouth, gulping several times before Charlie stopped him. "Easy, boy," he said. "Not too much all at once."

The lad passed the water to the other two children, and Charlie retrieved a chocolate bar from his ration kit. He broke off a bit of the hard chocolate and placed it in the boy's hand. The child ate it in two bites and held out his hand for more. He began talking rapidly, gesturing to the two smaller children.

"He says the two little ones are his brother and sister," a soldier in the crowd said quietly.

Ordway wheeled around and glared at him.

"I'm Peter Dupree. My grandfather came to the States from France," the soldier explained. "I don't speak the language much, but I grew up hearing it, and I can understand most of what the boy's saying."

"Well, why didn't you say so?" Ordway growled.

"I didn't get the chance before French-o here stepped in," Dupree said. Lansky reddened and faded back into the crowd.

"They've been here for two days," Dupree continued as the boy spoke. "They came out to look for food—wild berries and fruit, that kind of thing—and got pinned down by the Germans when the invasion started."

The rest of the men had begun digging into their rations for chocolate, and the two older children crowded around them. But the smallest boy, an emaciated child of about six, held onto Charlie's hand and refused to let go.

"The oldest boy's name is Jean," Dupree said. "His sister is Angelique, and their little brother is Charles."

"Charles," Charlie murmured thickly, picking the little boy up. He turned to Dupree. "How do you say, 'My name is' in French?"

"Je m'appelle."

Charlie looked into the boy's enormous brown eyes. *"Je m'appelle Charles,"* he said. "Charlie."

The child's eyes filled with tears, and he gave Charlie an enormous grin. "Char-lee," he repeated, twining his spidery arms tightly around Charlie's neck. *"Merci, Char-lee. Merci."*

★ ★ ★

Charlie Coltrain had never felt better about himself. If he lived to be a hundred—an ironic thought, given his personal mission to die—he would never forget the sensation of that child's arms around his neck, the wetness of the boy's tears against his cheek. In wonder, he stroked the side of his face, grimy and stubbled, where little Charles had hugged him.

But Ordway would not leave him to his reverie. "I don't understand you, Coltrain," the sergeant kept repeating. "I thought you'd want to take those kids to the medics yourself. You did save their lives, after all."

"Because I wouldn't let you toss a potato masher into that shed?" Charlie knew his words sounded harsh and caustic, but he couldn't help himself. He had just about had enough of Sergeant Ordway. "If you had your way, both those children and I would be history by now."

"Look, Coltrain," the sergeant said, grabbing Charlie roughly by the arm and jerking him around. "I said I was sorry, OK? I don't have anything against you. It wasn't personal. I was just—"

"Just following orders," Charlie finished. "Yeah, I know. Following orders to get the yellowbelly out of the way once and for all. Well, I—"

Charlie paused. Something had happened to him back there in the clearing when little Charles had smiled through his tears and hugged him. For the first time in months he thought that his life just might be worth something. That maybe, after all, he had something more to live for than a noble death. That wasn't the plan, of course. God had worked out all the details—getting him out of Italy and into the Birmingham hospital, getting him released and back to duty—for the sole purpose of giving him a chance to die at the front, where he could redeem himself and not be labeled a coward.

Now he wasn't so certain about the plan. He wasn't so sure he wanted to die.

"You've proved yourself as far as I'm concerned," Ordway was saying. "The way you took out those machine-gun nests on the bluff. The way you found those kids and saved them. There could have just as easily been a Kraut with a machine gun in that shed. You could have—"

Suddenly a burst of machine-gun fire ripped through the quietness of the woods and echoed off the hills. Charlie hit the ground, with the sergeant right behind him, and crawled on his belly to the protection of an ancient tree.

"Krauts!" Ordway gasped.

Charlie rolled his eyes in exasperation. "I'd expect so."

Another round of gunfire split the air. "It's coming from over there." Ordway pointed with his bayonet. "They've probably got some of our guys pinned down."

Charlie got to his feet. "Let's go."

They wound through the trees in the direction of the gunfire and at last spotted a small contingent of soldiers converging from the opposite direction.

"We're almost to the end of the open corridor," a lieutenant named Baker said. "The Germans are dug in just ahead about a hundred yards, and a couple hundred yards on either side of us. Our guys have pushed them back a little, but we've got casualties, and we need to get the wounded out. Medics are on their way, but there's not much time."

Ordway nodded and turned to Charlie. "Ready?"

"Ready as I'll ever be."

"This is likely to get nasty." The sergeant looked at Charlie with an intense, searching gaze.

"Remember Cochise?" Charlie asked.

"Cochise?"

"The Indian chief. The one who said, 'It is a good day to die.'"

Ordway grinned. "I think it was Geronimo." He slapped Charlie on the shoulder. "The colonel was wrong about you. Dead wrong."

Charlie cocked an eyebrow. "Interesting choice of words, Sarge. But thanks."

★ ★ ★

When Charlie came over the crest of the hill, he lost his footing and went down. Just as he fell, a round of machine-gun fire whizzed over his head, ricocheting off the trees and making his ears ring. He stayed low, rolling onto his belly, and looked back over his shoulder.

Ordway lay on the ground, gripping his midsection. Blood poured out of a gaping wound in his stomach.

Without thinking twice, Charlie ripped a section of his shirttail off, wrapped it into a tight ball, and pushed it into the wound. Holding it there with one hand, he fumbled for his canteen and held it to the sergeant's lips.

"Sarge!" he said urgently. "Hold on, Sarge."

Ordway's eyes fluttered open. "I'm dead, Coltrain," he muttered, his voice thick with pain. "Leave me."

"Forget it, Sarge. I'm not leaving. And you're not either. You're going to make it. Hold on."

Another burst of gunfire rang out overhead. "Medic!" Charlie yelled.

★ ★ ★

Several minutes later the medics arrived. "We got him, Private. We got him." Gently the medic extracted Charlie's hand from Ordway's stomach and examined the wound. "He's bad," the medic said. "But I think he'll live—thanks to you."

Charlie looked at the man blankly.

"Where'd you learn to make a pressure bandage, Private? He would have bled to death in minutes without it."

Charlie closed his eyes. "I don't know. I just did it."

"Well, you did it right." The two medics slid Ordway carefully onto a canvas stretcher. "It's pretty clear behind us," the first one said. "We should be able to get him to the battalion aid station without any trouble. Are you coming?"

Charlie shook his head. "I'm going on. Take care of him, will you?"

"You got it, soldier." The medics lifted the stretcher and began moving back. "He's a good friend, huh?"

"Yeah," Charlie said. "A friend."

Charlie watched until the two medics disappeared over the rise with Ordway. Then he turned and looked, for the first time, into the wooded valley before him. Bodies lay everywhere—some deadly still, some moving about and groaning in pain. *It is a good day to die,* he had told Ordway. Now he wasn't sure that's what he wanted at all.

But what Charlie Coltrain wanted apparently didn't matter anymore. Just as he was struggling with the temptation to run, he heard a faint, thready voice: *"Help me!"*

Charlie looked in the direction of the sound. There, in the grass about thirty yards to his left, he saw a hand lifted in supplication.

"Help me!"

Charlie scanned the area, then made a scrambling dash toward the soldier. He slid to the ground next to the man and took his outstretched hand. "What's your name, soldier?"

"Johnny," the soldier gasped. "Johnny Silver."

"Well, just hang on, Johnny. The medics are on their way."

Charlie pulled the helmet off the man's head and looked into his face. Johnny Silver was just a boy—maybe nineteen, no older than Boz Hamilton back at the hospital in Italy. And here he was, broken and wounded, far from home—and undoubtedly scared out of his wits.

Charlie looked in vain for signs of the boy's wounds. "You'll be OK, Johnny. Where are you hit?"

"Doesn't hurt," Johnny murmured groggily. "Can't feel anything."

Then Charlie saw it—the dark ooze of blood draining into the dirt under Johnny's back. He closed his eyes for a moment and offered up a silent prayer for the boy.

"You got a girl, Johnny?" Charlie asked, forcing a tone of lightness into his voice.

Johnny's face brightened. "Alicia," he slurred.

"I'll bet she's beautiful," Charlie went on. "And she's waiting for you to come home. Just think, Johnny—the medics will be here any minute. They'll take good care of you, and before you know it, you'll be back in—" He paused. "Where are you from, Johnny?"

"Iowa . . ." The boy took a deep breath, and the effort started him coughing. Blood mixed with spittle on his lips. "Forest City, Iowa." He closed his eyes.

"You'll be back in Forest City real soon, Johnny. And Alicia will be waiting for you."

Suddenly the boy's head snapped up, and he grabbed Charlie's arm. "Harry!" he shouted, his eyes glazed with terror. "Harry's out there!"

"Take it easy, Johnny. Who's Harry?"

"Harry Painter, my buddy," Johnny gasped. "My best friend. You gotta get him."

"I'll get him, son," Charlie soothed. "As soon as the medics get here for you."

"Went through basic together," Johnny muttered. "Promised to stick together. You gotta get him."

"Don't worry, kid. Just take it easy."

The boy gripped Charlie's arm harder, and a rattle filled his throat. "Promise me . . . get Harry."

"I promise."

Johnny's grip relaxed and a peaceful expression came over his face. "Tell him . . . he was always . . . my best . . . friend. . . ."

The boy's head sagged, and the light went out of his open eyes. Charlie replaced Johnny Silver's helmet, pushed his eyelids shut, and went in search of Harry Painter.

★ ★ ★

Charlie found Harry—seventy yards or so inland, leaning against a tree trunk.

Charlie sat beside the body for a minute and talked to Harry, even though he knew Harry couldn't hear him anymore. He told Harry how his pal Johnny had died bravely in battle and how much Harry's friendship had meant to Johnny. "I guess you're together now," he murmured to the corpse, not sure why he said it. Still, it felt like the right thing to say.

After a few minutes, Charlie did a cursory examination of Harry's body.

He was dead, shot through the left temple. But something wasn't right. A bullet to the head should result in immediate death. But here was Harry, sitting upright against an apple tree, as if he had just been relaxing, enjoying the countryside. This didn't look like a war wound. It looked more like . . .

Like an execution.

Before Charlie had time to scramble to his feet, he heard the click of a weapon being cocked behind his ear. Slowly he turned his head, and his eyes scanned upward over scarred jackboots, past a black-belted uniform, to the scowling face of a blue-eyed German soldier. The Kraut extended his hand and took aim at Charlie's neck.

So, Charlie thought dispassionately, *this is the way it ends, once and for all.* He breathed a silent prayer of thankfulness to God—for getting him back to the front, for giving him a chance to help little Charles and his brother and sister, for the opportunity to keep Sergeant Ordway alive. Most of all, he was grateful that he didn't have to die a coward.

Then he closed his eyes and waited, amazed that he wasn't the least bit afraid.

35

☆ ☆ ☆

Eden on the Edge

"I declare, I never saw two such pretty girls looking quite so down in the mouth." Thelma Breckinridge plunked two pieces of black-bottom pie onto the table in front of Libba and Willie Coltrain. "The pie's on the house." She slid two glasses of iced tea from her tray. The last of her chocolate ration had gone into that pie, and she couldn't afford to be giving it away, but she had to do something to try to cheer these two up.

Thelma watched as Libba poked her fork into the rich bottom layer of dark chocolate and tasted it. "It's great, Thelma. Thanks." Libba attempted a halfhearted smile she obviously didn't feel. "But I'm not really hungry." She pushed the pie away and began twisting the curl at the nape of her neck.

Thelma shook her head. If Libba Coltrain was refusing black-bottom pie, the situation must be graver than she thought. The girl was crazy for chocolate. Up till today, in fact, that had been her biggest complaint about the war—the shortage of chocolate and stockings.

"Have you read this?" Libba pushed a newspaper across the table and pointed.

"Ernie Pyle's latest dispatch." Thelma nodded. "Everybody's read it."

"He was there," Willie interjected. "He was right there, at the invasion."

"I know, hon." Thelma patted Willie's hand. "And I'll have to admit, it sounds absolutely awful. But everybody says that this is the beginning of the end, that we've got the Germans on the run and it won't be long before this war is over and everybody's home."

"Everybody except the ones who—" Willie couldn't go on.

Thelma closed her eyes and sent up a silent prayer for help. When she opened them, Libba and Willie were both staring at her, a look of utter despair filling their faces.

"Listen to me, you two," Thelma began, trying to sound authoritative. "You have no way of knowing that those two fellows of yours were part of the D-day invasion." She pointed to the newspaper. "Why, even Ernie Pyle admitted that he couldn't reveal which troops were there. We may not know that for quite a while. So why borrow trouble when—"

Libba silenced Thelma with a look. "The last letter I got from Link was sent from England," she said flatly. "The last letter Willie got also came from England." Libba glared at her. "Where is the English Channel, Thelma?"

"Between England and France," Thelma whispered. She felt thoroughly humbled, chastised for her glib attempt to give them a false and empty hope. That wasn't usually her way, and she knew for a certainty it wasn't God's way. "I'm sorry, Libba. I didn't mean to sound flippant. I just meant that until you know something definite—"

"Until we know something definite, we'll be on pins and needles, and nothing anyone says can change that." Willie leaned back in her chair. "Charlie was there, too—I just know it."

"Charlie?" Thelma looked at Willie. "I thought Charlie was recuperating in Italy."

"We got a letter from him about a month ago." Willie sighed, and her eyes clouded over. "He had been sent to England—Birmingham—to be treated by some new doctor. He said he was going back to the front. But, Thelma, something just didn't seem right about Charlie's letter."

"Charlie seemed . . . I don't know . . . so *definite* about going back," Libba added. "Why would anyone in his right mind *want* to go back to the front if he could take a medical discharge and come home? It was like he was trying to prove something. But what does he have to prove?"

Thelma glanced over her shoulder to where Ivory Brownlee sat at the piano. He wasn't playing, just sitting, gazing off at nothing. Thelma knew Ivory better than anyone else in Eden—and from him, she knew enough about shell shock to suspect that Charlie Coltrain's wounds didn't all come from a shrapnel hole in his arm. If he did have shell shock and faced the prospect of mockery and rejection and pity, he just might have a good reason to try to get back to the front. A very good reason, indeed.

Thelma had wondered about Charlie Coltrain for a long time, but she had kept her mouth shut—except to God. And she kept it shut now. Letting Willie in on her suspicions certainly wouldn't make the situation any better. There was nothing anyone could do for any of those boys except pray. In the meantime, God had purposes beyond anything human beings could understand, and God was quite capable of seeing those purposes fulfilled.

"I guess we just have to pray . . . and trust," she said at last.

Libba and Willie heaved a deep sigh in unison. "Trusting isn't easy," Willie said.

Libba nodded. "You know, I was always raised to be a Christian. Mama and Daddy always took me to church and Sunday school, and Mama talked to me a lot about my 'duty' as a Christian. But this war has changed everything. What I learned in Sunday school doesn't seem to have much to do with what's going on in the real world. I feel like I'm having to learn to believe in God all over again—this time as an adult, with adult problems. And it's not quite as simple as 'Jesus loves me, this I know, for the Bible tells me so.'"

Thelma smiled and patted Libba on the arm. "You're absolutely right, hon—it's not that simple. But you keep on seeking God, and you'll find what you're looking for."

"Seek, and ye shall find?" Libba asked.

"Something like that. But that sounds as if it's all up to us, and it isn't. God says that he is seeking us—like the shepherd looking for the lost sheep, or the woman sweeping the house searching for her coin. Like the father of the prodigal son standing out on the road, waiting and hoping that his boy will come home."

Libba turned woeful eyes to Thelma. "But I'm not sure God is listening—or that I'm worthy for him to listen."

Thelma frowned. "Why on earth would you think that?"

"Well, I grew up in church," Libba said. "But until I met Link and fell in love with him and he shipped out to the front, I never gave God much thought. Now I need God—I pray all the time that God will keep Link safe and bring him back home to me. But that's pretty selfish, isn't it? I've heard people talk about 'foxhole religion,' how soldiers under fire will turn to God at the last minute because they're afraid. Well, I'm afraid, too. Maybe this is just a different kind of 'foxhole religion' and I don't deserve God's attention."

Thelma chuckled, then stopped suddenly when she saw Libba's expression. "Oh, honey, I'm not making fun of you," she said. "I just understand, that's all. Why, I came to God myself during the lowest time of my life—I expect most people do. And I doubt that anyone's motives are entirely pure when they first come to the Lord. We all are driven to God out of our own need. It's only later we discover that God is worth worshiping because of who he is rather than what he can do for us."

Thelma paused and waited until Libba raised her head and caught her eye. "Besides, honey," she said, "our connection with God isn't based on what we deserve, but on what Jesus did for us when we didn't deserve anything."

Libba smiled just a little. "Well," she said, "it's a good thing, because I know I don't deserve it."

"Then you're right where God wants you to be."

The bell over the door rang, and all three of them turned their heads to look. Silhouetted in the doorway stood a thin, dark-haired young woman. She shifted wearily and set a small suitcase down on the floor, then adjusted a bundle she held in the crook of her right arm. The bundle began to squirm, and the reedy cry of a hungry infant filled the room.

Thelma got to her feet. "As I live and breathe," she murmured. "What have we here?"

★ ★ ★

Madge Simpson fought back tears as she looked around the dismal cafe. The train trip had been long and exhausting, and the bus ride from Tillatoba had been even worse. The baby, who was usually good as gold, had been fitful and restless. He was hungry by now and probably needed changing.

Madge wondered, not for the first time, if she had made a mistake in leaving Missouri to come to Mississippi. It was only mid-June, and yet the heat and humidity sapped her strength and made her irritable. She had no job and no place to stay, and she wasn't sure what she was going to do. Yet she had to come—at least, she had to get away from Mother Simpson and her interminable criticism. She couldn't have stayed in that house another minute. Even if she ended up on the street, she'd be better off. At least she'd have some peace and quiet.

Three women sat at a table near the window. Two of them looked to be about her age or a little younger, and the third was a hard-looking, work-worn woman. An odd trio, to say the least.

The older woman started walking toward her, and Madge took a step backward. How could she do this—just show up in a town she had never seen before, hoping to find help and encouragement among people she had never met? Michael had told her all about Eden, about his friends Link and Owen and their fiancées—Libby and Willa, she thought their names were. But Michael wasn't here, and she felt desperately alone. Could she even find these people who were connected to the man she loved, the father of her child? And if she found them, then what?

She had prayed about this before she had done it. Had God really led her to take such a risk, to leave everything familiar behind? Had she heard him right? Or was this just some wild idea that came to her when she couldn't stand Mother Simpson's nagging any longer?

Madge took a deep breath and tried to think, but she was tired and her brain wasn't working clearly. Her mind would formulate no prayer except *Help, God.* But it made her feel a little stronger, and she raised her eyes to the woman who stood before her.

"Hello, honey," the woman said. "Welcome to Eden, and to the Paradise Garden. I'm Thelma Breckinridge."

Madge's mind raced. Michael had written a little bit about Thelma Breckinridge—in the early letters when he had first come to the base here and reconnected with Link Winsom. She had a vague sense that this was a woman who could be trusted, and she smiled.

"You look plumb tuckered out," Thelma said. "Come sit down."

Gratefully Madge sank into a chair at the nearest table and slipped her shoes off. Acutely aware of the stares of the two younger women in the corner, she ducked her head and busied herself with the baby.

"What a sweetheart!" Thelma cooed, pulling back the blanket for a closer look. "What's her name?"

"It's a he," Madge corrected. "His name is Michael James. We—I—call him Mickey."

By this time the two younger women had come over to the table and gathered around Madge and the baby, oohing and ahhing. "He's beautiful," one of them said. "How old is he?"

"Two and a half months," Madge said. "Would you like to hold him?"

The young woman's arms reached down eagerly to scoop little Mickey up, and Madge looked into her face. She had auburn hair and pale green eyes and a look of sadness about her that Madge had seen a thousand times since the war began. Some soldier's girl, no doubt, left behind to keep the home fires burning, pray, and wait for him to return.

"He's adorable," the girl said as Mickey gave her a crooked grin and grabbed her finger. "Look, Willie—he likes me. When Link gets home, I want to have a dozen just like him."

"Sure," the second girl said. "A dozen. What was it you always told me about doing housework and nursing—"

Madge jumped up and grabbed the redhead by the shoulders. "Did you say Link? Link Winsom?"

All color drained out of the girl's face and she nodded mutely. "You know him?" She looked stricken, as if she had been hit in the stomach. "Is this—is this his—"

Madge's weariness instantly drained away, and she laughed out loud. "No, of course not. I'm Madge Simpson. Michael's wife!"

The girl looked at her blankly. "Nice to meet you. I'm Libba Coltrain, and this is my cousin Willie."

"Of course!" Madge slapped her palm to her forehead. "Not Willa and Libby—Willie and Libba!"

Still the blank stare persisted.

"You're engaged to Link Winsom, right?"

Libba nodded.

"And you—" Madge turned to Willie—"you're engaged to Owen Slaughter."

Willie cocked an eyebrow in Libba's direction and smiled wanly. "Yes."

"I can't believe it! I prayed about coming, but then I thought I was crazy to do it, but here you are, like you were just waiting for me. It's a miracle. Michael's told me all about you."

Willie and Libba exchanged glances, then said in unison, "Who's Michael?"

"My husband, Michael Simpson, of course. He was—is—best friends with Link and Owen. I know Link, of course, and Michael wrote me all about Owen . . . how you met at the dance and all that."

"Stork?" Libba interrupted. "Stork Simpson?"

Willie turned to Libba and nodded. "Stork." Then she glanced back at Madge. "Sorry for the confusion. I guess we never heard Stork's real name."

Madge shook her head. "I don't understand."

"From the time we met Link and Owen, we knew your husband only as 'Stork.' It was Link's nickname for him, and it stuck. Because he's so tall and thin, I guess, and because—"

Madge felt herself begin to blush. So. They knew the whole story—how she and Michael had . . . had been forced to have a hurry-up wedding because of Mickey's imminent arrival. Maybe it *was* a mistake, coming here. She had endured months of shaming from Mother Simpson; she didn't think she could go through that again. "I—I don't know what to say," she stammered.

Thelma came up behind her and placed a gentle hand on her shoulder. "Don't worry, hon," she said quietly. "We all understand." She took the baby from Libba and tickled him, causing him to grin. "This little guy is no mistake. And neither is your coming here."

Thelma shifted little Mickey to her shoulder and placed an arm around Madge. "War makes for unusual families," she said. "Welcome home."

★ ★ ★

"And so," Madge finished as she took the last bite of her second piece of pie, "that's how I got here."

Thelma shook her head. "It's a wonder, how God leads folks," she said. She looked over to Libba and Willie, and to the child asleep in Willie's arms. "What do you plan to do now?"

Madge gave Thelma a rueful smile. "I'm not sure." She shrugged. "Since I don't have any family, I hoped I might find a job and a place to live here. When I came at Christmas to visit Michael, we stayed in Grenada, and I never got to see Eden." She hesitated. "It's a lot smaller than I thought."

"A month ago I would have said you could live with us," Libba said. "But we gave up our apartment at the end of the school year. I'm attending classes at Ole Miss and I'm only here on weekends, and Willie and Mabel Rae have gone back out to the farm."

Willie shifted, careful not to wake the baby. "I might be able to talk to some of the women I know at the Red Cross or the USO. They're always looking for help."

"But that wouldn't pay," Libba interrupted. "And who'd take care of the baby?"

"I can't believe you all care so much." Madge smiled—a warm, genuine smile that lit up her soft blue eyes. Despite the circles of fatigue under her eyes and the limpness of her brown hair, she was almost pretty, Thelma thought—or could be, if she just had a little hope.

Suddenly a feeling came over Thelma unlike any she had ever experienced. This young woman who had appeared on her doorstep, without warning, could have been Thelma's own child, if her life had taken a different turn. This baby sleeping in Willie Coltrain's arms could have been Thelma's grandson. God had not seen fit to allow Thelma the realization of her girlhood dreams. Could it be that the Lord was now giving her something back from those dreams?

Thelma sent up a silent prayer for direction and discernment. It wouldn't do to give this girl hope only for the satisfaction of Thelma's personal desires. She had to know that this was God's doing, not her own idea. Otherwise, she would be acting out of selfishness.

Still, as she had said herself, "wartime makes for unusual families." Was it possible that God would provide for the fulfillment of a long-time need in Thelma's own life as Thelma provided for a need in someone else's?

Thelma kept silent, determined not to let her own feelings run ahead of God's direction. And as she waited, a deep peace settled over her spirit.

"You're determined to stay here until Stork gets back?" Willie was saying.

"If I can," Madge said. "I wrote to him, telling him I was planning to come. I don't know if he'll get the letter—" Her eyes clouded over briefly, but she went on. "I mean, *when* he'll get it. But he'll be glad to know I'm away from his mother. I tried to make the best of it, but he knew how hard it was. I'm sure he'd much rather have me here."

"Then here's where you'll stay," Thelma said with determination. "I've got an idea."

All eyes turned to her—Willie's and Libba's with questioning looks, Madge's with a tentative expression of hopefulness.

"What kind of idea?" Willie prodded.

"I've been thinking I could use some help around here," Thelma began, looking directly at Madge. "I can't pay you much, but I've got an extra room in back that's big enough for a bed and a crib, and you could eat in the cafe. You wouldn't have to be separated from little Mickey, and—"

"Thanks for the offer, Thelma," Madge said, her eyes filling up with tears. "But we couldn't take charity."

"I'm not talking about charity, child," Thelma blustered. "I'm talking about a kind of barter system. You can help me with the cooking and the serving and the cleaning up, and you'll get room and board and a small salary, plus tips." She winked at Madge. "But don't count too much on the tips."

"And what do you get out of the exchange?" Madge asked. "It doesn't look to me as if you really need much help around here."

"God knows what I need, honey," Thelma answered. "And maybe it's possible that he answered your prayers and mine with one fell swoop." Tears filled Thelma's eyes, too, and she turned away for a moment until she had regained her composure. "Do we have a deal?"

Madge reached out and shook Thelma's hand. "Deal," she said. "Where do we start?"

"We start by getting you and that beautiful baby of yours settled in," Thelma said. "And then—" she narrowed her eyes at Madge—"how are you at making meat loaf?"

"Pretty bad," Madge laughed. "But it looks like I'm going to learn."

36

★ ★ ★

On the Beach

Omaha Beach
Mid-June 1944

Link Winsom crawled out from under the jeep and blinked into the bright morning sun. Beside him on the ground, Stork Simpson and Owen Slaughter snored loudly, shifting a little as the light hit their eyes.

Amazing how any of them could sleep at all under these conditions. When he first went to boot camp, Link had tossed and turned on the lumpy bunk and swore he would never have a good night's rest again. But now, thousands of miles from home, he had slept all night on a beach littered with battle debris, with his head stuck under the front bumper of an army jeep.

Link struggled to his feet, stretched, and walked a little way down the shore. It was just past dawn, and around him men were beginning to stir. It looked like a mass resurrection—lifeless men, strewn as far as the eye could see, suddenly coming to life and rising from the earth.

There were many, of course, who wouldn't rise this morning—or any morning, for that matter. Link hadn't been there to see the first wave of attack on the beaches of Normandy, but everywhere there were signs of the carnage, supplies and personal effects of soldiers who would no longer need their razors or their writing paper.

Or their army-issue Bibles.

Link stooped over and dug a small, black-bound New Testament out of the sand. He brushed away the dirt to reveal gilt lettering on the front and spine and gingerly opened it. On the first page some soldier's name had been scrawled in pencil, but it was so faded now that Link couldn't make it out. A small faded rosebud, pressed flat, still held the absent soldier's place among the pages.

I am the resurrection, and the life, Link read. *He that believeth in me, though he were dead, yet shall he live: And whosoever liveth and believeth in me shall never die. Believest thou this?*

The words sliced into Link's heart like a bayonet hitting its mark. *Believest thou this?*

He wanted to believe. All around him lay mute reminders that life—especially life here on the beaches of France—was fleeting and uncertain. It was easy, back home in the States, to have a flippant, devil-may-care attitude about life, even to make jokes about dying bravely in battle. But the war was real now, and the prospects were grim.

Believest thou this? Link looked at the words again. *Though he were dead, yet shall he live . . . whosoever believeth in me shall never die.* Obviously Jesus wasn't talking about physical death, but something even more final—some kind of spiritual death. Maybe that was the only choice a man had out here—to believe in eternal life or to fear it.

Thousands of men had faced that decision on this very beach in the past couple of weeks. Some of them, no doubt, cried out to God for mercy as their lifeblood ebbed away into the sand. Others were blasted into eternity without the chance to give God a second thought. Had the soldier whose name was scribbled in the front of this book been reading these same words the day, or the hour, before his life ended? Was the girl who had sent him the rosebud mourning him . . . or did she even know that he was dead? What had become of that soldier?

And what would become of him?

Link shook his head. He had to stop thinking this way. Yet he couldn't help it. A sniper's bullet or a land mine could take him out at any minute, without warning. The beach where he was walking had been salted with mines—mines cleared before Link's company landed. But what if they had missed a few? What if his next step could catapult him into the next life?

Link replaced the rosebud between the pages, shut the New Testament, and slid it into his breast pocket. Somehow just feeling it there, next to his heart, gave him a little hope.

But it wasn't enough.

★ ★ ★

When Link got back to the jeep, the engine was running, and Owen and Stork were heating K rations on the engine block.

"Where have you been, man?" Stork growled. "We woke up and you were gone."

"I just took a little walk," Link said evasively. "Nature calls, you know."

"Well, nature's calling me to eat some breakfast," Slaughter put in. "Better get yours while it's hot. We've only got about fifteen minutes before we move out."

"Smells like dog food."

"It probably is—full of vitamins and bone marrow, you know."

Stork sighed. "Doesn't it make you wish you were back on the ship? We had it good, boys—steaks and chicken and real potatoes, and—"

Link exchanged a glance with Slaughter, and they both grinned. "Shut up, Stork," they said in unison.

"Sarge! Hey, Sarge!" Coker appeared over the rise, running full tilt and panting heavily.

"Take it easy, Coker," Link said.

The boy looked at the jeep, then at the bedrolls on the ground. "Did you sleep here all night?"

"Yeah. What of it?"

Coker smiled and puffed out his chest. "Nothing, Sarge—except that I found a really good spot, back there under an apple tree." He pointed over the rise. "Everybody else was complaining about how hard the ground was, but I found me a soft place. It was just like sleeping on a feather pillow."

"Sure, sure," Owen muttered.

"I did! Come see!"

"Coker, we don't have time for this."

"It's not far. You might want to find a place like that for yourself tonight."

Protesting, Link, Stork, and Owen followed Coker over the rise. Just beyond the ridge was a small apple grove, and under one of the trees lay Coker's bedroll.

"Right there. Soft as a down comforter. See for yourself."

Link walked down to the tree to take a look, then began to laugh.

"What's so funny, Sarge?"

Link kicked at the dirt with the toe of his boot. "Right here, Coke? This is your soft place, your feather pillow?"

Coker nodded.

"I wouldn't tell anyone else about this, boy. Keep it a secret as long as you can." He turned and motioned toward the bedroll. "Pack up, Private. We're moving out in a few minutes."

Coker hurried to get his gear together, and Link rejoined Stork and Owen on the rise.

"Don't say a word," he whispered as they started down toward the jeep, "but the kid's been sleeping on cow pies."

★ ★ ★

Night was falling by the time Link's unit broke for supper. They had pushed several miles inland during the day, hearing a little sniper fire now and then but seeing no real action. Still, everyone was on edge. They were bound to be getting closer to the German lines.

Owen Slaughter found Link and Stork at the edge of a clearing in the woods. "Get some chow," he said. "Then the colonel wants to see you."

When they had wolfed down their rations, Link and Stork headed for the officers' bivouac. They found Colonel Randolph surrounded by three other officers; all were holding flashlights on a map spread out on the hood of a truck.

"Sergeant," the colonel said to Winsom, pointing at the map, "we're here. We think the Krauts are holed up here, here, and here—" He tapped his finger in three spots, indicating that the Germans surrounded them on three sides. "About a mile and a half ahead of us, and a mile to either side of us."

Link nodded and threw a glance at Stork, whose face shone pale in the darkness.

"Take Simpson here, and one other man, and make a sweep of the perimeter to our left. I'm sending a couple of other units to the forward and right lines. We need to know just how close the Germans are and how soon we're likely to engage."

"Yes, sir." Link sighed inwardly. It would take hours to fan through the woods, attempting to determine the position of the enemy lines.

Colonel Randolph looked at Link intently, then at Stork. "I know you boys are tired, but this has got to be done, and done now." He pointed at the map again. "Tomorrow morning we're heading up this road. We'll sweep it for mines first thing, and then go in behind. Our orders are to keep pushing the Germans back—clear out of France, if we can get that far. Report back to me at 2300 hours."

Link turned to go, with Stork close on his heels.

"And Sergeant—," the colonel added.

"Yes, sir?"

"Take every precaution. We need this information, but we don't want anybody getting captured."

Link's heart jumped into his throat, and he saw Stork's jaw clench. He reached into his pocket and fingered the leather binding of the dead soldier's New Testament.

"Yes, sir," he said quietly. "We'll be careful."

37

⭐ ⭐ ⭐

Reconnaissance

"I don't see why I have to be the one to do this," Coker complained. "I'm tired."

"You shouldn't be," Link muttered. "You told us you got a better night's sleep than any of us, snoozing away on your soft pillow of earth."

Stork snickered but said nothing.

"Why is he laughing?" Coker asked. "It was a great place. I wish I could sleep there again tonight."

"So do I," Link said. "Now keep quiet."

As they moved further into the woods, a heaviness settled over Link, almost like a premonition. He came up close behind Stork in the darkness.

"Do you ever think about dying, Stork?" he whispered.

Stork jumped wildly and whirled, his bayonet pointed at Link's chest. "Don't do that!"

"Don't do what?"

"Don't sneak up on me like that. You could get a bullet through your liver, scaring a guy that way."

"Good grief, Stork, calm down. I'm not the enemy."

"Thanks for informing me—a little late, but better late than never. And don't tell me to calm down!"

"OK, OK. Just take it—" Link caught himself. "Sorry. So, do you? Think about dying, I mean, out here, where it could happen at any time?"

"I try not to."

"Don't you worry about what would become of Madge and the baby if you got . . . well, if something happened to you?"

"Like I said, I try not to think about it."

"But don't you ever wonder what would happen to you—where you would go if you died, what it would be like?"

"You just have to push on this, don't you, Link?" Stork snapped. "All right, I do think about it. I think about Madge and the baby, and I think about what might happen to me. I doubt there's a guy out here who doesn't think about it—all the time. And it scares the life out of me. Satisfied?" Stork turned his back on Link and began to walk.

Link caught up with him and put a hand on his shoulder. "I apologize, buddy. I didn't mean to hit a nerve. It's just that—"

"It's just that you can never leave anything alone. I swear, Link, when you get started on an idea, you worry it like a dog with an old shoe."

Link pulled the battered New Testament out of his pocket and shoved it under his friend's nose. "Look at this," he said. "I found it on the beach yesterday, buried in the sand. It's got some soldier's name in it, and a pressed flower, probably from his girl back home. There won't be any more Bible reading for this guy, and no more flowers, except the ones on his grave—if there was enough of him left to send back for burial."

Stork pivoted on his heel and glared at Link, and Link could see fear and despair on his hawkish face. "Why are you doing this?" he hissed.

"Because I'm not sure we have much time," Link said. "I feel . . . I don't know . . . something. Some urgency." He paused. "I've always sneered at guys who get religion when the mortars are coming in," he said. "They live like the devil for years, then send up foxhole prayers at the last minute. I always thought that if I was God, I wouldn't give them the time of day."

"Then it's a good thing you're not God," Stork said.

"Yeah, I know. I've been thinking a lot about that." Link put his hand on Stork's arm. "Something happened to me when I picked up that soldier's Bible. I read some things that made me wonder if maybe a last-minute foxhole faith isn't better than none at all."

Stork's face relaxed, and a curious expression filled his eyes. "I know what you mean. Madge is a Christian—a real one, not just a Sunday-go-to-church type. Her last letter really got to me, telling me how she prayed that I would be all right and that I would believe in God for myself, rather than just depending on her faith."

"Makes sense, doesn't it?" Link said. "Especially now. There are no guarantees here, and nobody can believe for you. It's just you and God. From what I saw out there on the beach, you can't count on having time to make things right after you're hit. I don't know what happens to a fellow when he dies, but if there is an afterlife, it seems to me that it pays to be prepared for it."

Stork squinted at Link's face in the dim light. "And how do you do that?"

"My father always told me that being a Christian is not so much a matter of *what* you believe, but *who* you believe in."

"You mean Jesus."

"Yeah, I guess so." Link fingered the Bible. "That's what it says in here, too. I always thought it sounded kind of stupid, trusting in an invisible God. I figured I could do all right by myself. And most of the church people I know act the same way—like it's all up to them. They make it seem like it's more a matter of doing all the right things—or rather, not doing certain things."

"Like obeying the Ten Commandments."

"That, and a bunch of other stuff they added on—like going to church all the time, not drinking or smoking, acting holy, not sinning—"

Stork sighed. "If that's true, I'm a dead man."

Link felt his pulse begin to race. "But if my father was right, and what it says in here is true, everybody sins. The whole point is, Christ died on the cross for people like us, to bring us back to God."

"You sound like a preacher."

A warm flush ran up Link's neck. "Sorry." He wondered briefly if he would have dared to talk to Stork this way in the daylight. He might have been too embarrassed, and he was grateful that the darkness gave him a little protection. Still, he was glad he had done it.

"So what are you going to do?" Stork's tremulous voice whispered next to his ear.

"I'm going to believe. I'm going to try to trust God now, before I have to. And—" he slapped Stork on the shoulder and pointed ahead into the woods— "I'm going to get this reconnaissance done, get my tail back to camp, and try to get some sleep before this night is completely gone."

★ ★ ★

Stork watched Link's back as they fanned out and moved toward the perimeter. He had a lot to think about, but he needed to keep his mind on his job. His life just might depend upon it, and he couldn't risk getting caught or killed before he had a chance to decide just what, if anything, he believed.

Stork grimaced. He was beginning to sound like Link, and Link was beginning to sound like a fanatic. Something in him recoiled from the idea—it reminded him too much of the phony camp meetings he had attended as a child when he had visited his cousin Jeremy in the Ozarks. Jeremy's mother, his father's half sister, was a wild-eyed woman who punctuated even the most dismal declarations with an upraised hand and an exclamation of praise: *"The devil's really been after me this week, praise his holy name!"* For a long time Stork hadn't been sure if Aunt Lorene was praising God or the devil. But he found out one summer when she dragged him and Jeremy to an all-day brush-arbor meeting. Poor Jeremy was suffering from chicken pox, and Aunt Lorene was determined to get him healed. Stork suspected that the countywide epidemic that broke out two weeks later had a lot to do with little Jeremy's healing service.

Still, even with the memory of Aunt Lorene hanging in his mind, Stork couldn't deny that Madge's faith was genuine. His wife truly loved God and believed in Christ. She had been despondent over the moral lapse that had resulted in her pregnancy, but she had never blamed Stork for pressuring her, and she had accepted God's forgiveness—even though Stork's mother continued to harangue her about it at every opportunity.

Yes, Madge's faith was real. Stork respected it, although he wasn't quite sure how to go about getting the same kind of faith for himself. Maybe it had to grow on you. It could be that Link was right, after all. Maybe you just started where you were, by determining to trust God, and let God take it from there. Stork thought he could do that. He could take that first step, could—

"Sarge! Sarge!" Coker's hissing whisper cut through Stork's consciousness. The boy was running toward him, gasping and panting. When he got close enough, Stork could see that Coker's face was bloodless, white as flour and pasty with fear.

"What's wrong?"

"Over there! It's—it's one of them!"

"One of who? Get a grip, boy!"

"Kraut," he stammered. "Officer, I think."

★ ★ ★

It was an officer, all right—a stupid one, to all appearances, alone in the darkness, relieving himself. Fifty or sixty yards beyond him, Link could make out a contingent of German soldiers sitting around a small fire, laughing and drinking.

Herr Reichsfuhrer, or whatever he was, would have done better to opt for safety rather than modesty. Yet here he was, squatting behind a tree, his broad rear end clearly visible. When Randolph had sent them on reconnaissance, this wasn't exactly what Link had in mind. But this was war, after all, and you never knew quite what you'd find when you went seeking the enemy.

"Let's get him," Link whispered. "If the colonel wants information, a Kraut officer should do quite nicely." Putting a finger to his lips, Link motioned Coker in one direction and Stork in the other.

Soundlessly they crept toward the officer in a semicircle. Then, just as he finished his business and pulled up his trousers, Link stepped forward and pointed his rifle at the man's back. "Halt!" he commanded in a whisper.

The officer froze, raised his hands, and turned in Link's direction. He cast a glance over his shoulder toward his comrades, oblivious to his absence, then apparently thought better of trying to make a run for it. He stepped cautiously toward Link. *"Bitte,"* he said, obviously terrified. *"Bitte.* No shoot."

"I'm not going to shoot you," Link muttered, gesturing to Coker to take the man's pistol. "But you may wish I had when our guys get through with you."

They set out through the woods with Stork in the lead and Link and Coker guarding the prisoner. After a minute or two, Link dropped back behind Coker and the German.

"I thought I heard something behind us," he told Coker. "I'm going back to check. Keep your rifle trained on the Kraut, and whatever you do, keep up with Stork. I'll catch up in a few minutes."

★ ★ ★

Ten minutes later, Link was double-timing it back to Stork and Coker. The noise he had heard turned out to be nothing—a wild goose chase. The Krauts were still drinking and laughing around their fire; they didn't even know their officer was gone. Cursing himself for his stupidity, Link almost missed Coker, sitting a few feet off the path with his head in his hands.

"Coker!" Link shook the boy's shoulder, but he didn't respond. "Coke! What happened? Where's the Kraut? Where's Stork?" Panic swept over him. If something had happened to his best friend, he would never forgive himself.

"Stork's right here," a voice behind him said. Link turned to see his friend standing a little way down the path, panting. "It was dark, and I didn't know you had left. I suddenly realized that Coker and the German weren't behind me anymore. So I doubled back."

Link turned on Coker. "Where's the prisoner, Coker?"

Coker looked up at Link with a miserable expression. "He's—he's dead."

"Dead? What do you mean, dead?"

"I—I couldn't keep up with Stork, not and keep tabs on the Kraut, too. When we got separated, he rushed me. I—I killed him."

"How? I didn't hear a shot," Stork said.

Coker picked up his rifle from the ground. The bayonet was covered with blood. "He ran onto my bayonet," he explained.

Link narrowed his eyes at Coker. "OK," he said slowly, "you killed him with your bayonet. So where's the body?"

For a minute Coker looked confused, then his expression cleared. "There's a ravine about a half mile back," he said. "All covered with vines. I dumped him in there." The boy's face brightened. "They'll never find him."

Link jerked Coker up by the shoulders and shook him hard. "You idiot! We needed that officer—the information he could have given us might have meant—"

"Take it easy, Link," Stork interrupted. "It could have happened to anybody."

"Oh, yeah, and what are we going to tell Colonel Randolph?"

Stork thought for a minute. "We tell him where the German encampment is. That's what he sent us to find out. We don't mention the officer at all—what good would it do?"

Link frowned. "You mean just keep it to ourselves?"

"Why not? The Germans don't know how close we are. If they do find their man, he can't tell them anything. Dead men don't talk."

"I don't like it," Link said. "But I guess you're right. No point in getting our tails in a sling over something that couldn't be helped." He turned to Coker. "Not a word, you got it?"

"I got it." Coker breathed a sigh of relief. "What do I do with these?"

He held out his hand. An iron cross and several medals of the Reich glittered in the dim light.

Link gaped at him. "What are those?"

"Souvenirs, Sarge. I thought I might as well keep them."

"You will not! If anybody finds those on you, you'll be up for court-martial so fast it'll make your head swim. And so will we. Get rid of them."

Coker's face fell. "OK, Sarge, if you say so. But—"

"No buts." Link snatched the medals out of the boy's hand and flung them into the woods. "Let's go." He started out in the direction of their camp, then turned on Coker with a vengeance. "I swear," he muttered, nose to nose with the trembling private, "if you so much as utter one syllable about this, I'll bring you up on charges myself. You'll spend the rest of your tour of duty scrubbing toilets in the stockade. You got that?"

Coker nodded mutely.

Link turned to Stork. "All right, let's get our report in and get some sleep." He lifted an eyebrow at Coker. "I guess there's no permanent harm done. Like Stork said, dead men don't talk."

38

⭐ ⭐ ⭐

Chateau Disaster

At dawn the next morning, Private Randy Coker found himself as nervous as a cat. He watched Sergeant Winsom's back as they moved down the dirt road, which was rapidly changing to mud in the drizzling rain. The sergeant kept alert, but he seemed pretty relaxed. He talked in low tones to Sergeants Simpson and Slaughter and even laughed now and then.

Coker didn't feel like laughing, and he certainly felt more apprehensive than Sergeant Winsom looked. But he had good reason to worry. He had lied last night, and his lie might get them all in trouble.

The Kraut officer wasn't dead in a ravine. He was very much alive, and Coker couldn't figure out a way to tell his sergeant the truth.

If he just hadn't been so stupid, it never would have happened. But no, he had to have those medals, a souvenir to take home and show everybody how brave he was—how he had captured a German officer single-handedly in the middle of the night.

When he had seen Simpson pull ahead, he realized his chance had come, probably the only chance he would get. Sergeant Winsom had doubled back, and Simpson couldn't see him. Randy had slowed down, then stopped and demanded that the Kraut remove his medals and hand them over. He only got distracted for a second or two, but that was enough time for the German to rush him. Coker had caught the officer in the arm with his bayonet, but the man was far from dead—no doubt he had gone straight back to his men with information he never should have had.

And Randy Coker had lied.

He could only remember one other time in his life when he had deliberately told a falsehood. He was twelve, and his daddy had given him his first shotgun for his birthday. He was so proud of that gun, and he couldn't resist taking a shot at one little bird high up on a branch of the tree in their backyard. He never expected to hit it, of course, and when it fell lifeless at his feet, a sick feeling welled up in his stomach. His daddy had come out and found the dead bird, and when he confronted Randy about it, Randy lied and said he didn't do it.

Randy didn't know why he had lied—it was an idiotic thing to do, when the evidence was right there at his feet. He hadn't wanted his father to be disappointed in him, he guessed. As it turned out, the lie upset his daddy even more than the dead bird did. He confiscated Randy's shotgun and stood over him while Randy buried the bird under his bedroom window. And Randy Coker had never lied again.

Until now.

Maybe it was for the same reason—because he didn't want his sergeant to be disappointed with him. He had let a German prisoner escape, and that was serious business. He should have told the truth right off. But he couldn't bring himself to do it.

Now, the longer he went on not telling, the harder it became to face the truth. And the sick feeling in his stomach was getting stronger by the minute.

★ ★ ★

Link felt the hairs prickle on the back of his neck. He motioned to Stork and Owen to spread the men out, and he moved to the ditch at the side of the road. Cautiously he readied his rifle and crept around the bend.

He couldn't believe what he was seeing. There, surrounded by a stand of ancient trees, an old chateau sat nestled against the hillside at the end of the road. It was obviously abandoned, tilting on one side, with every window broken and part of the roof caved in. But it would have been glorious in its day—the home of a rich landowner, no doubt.

Link motioned the men forward. They surrounded the house on three sides, and Link moved toward the front entry. With one kick he sent the heavy oak door creaking inward on its hinges and stepped inside.

The house was dark and quiet. Mortar and bricks littered the floor, and rain poured in from a hole in the roof. The staircase to the upper level hung precariously, the whole center section rotted out. Link picked through the rubble to the room on the right where the roof was still intact—a large parlor with tall French doors and a marble fireplace. But it wasn't the ruined opulence of the place that took Link's breath away. It was the piles of wooden boxes—munitions crates, each marked with a black swastika.

Link surveyed the supplies, jerking lids off the boxes. Rifles, machine guns, ammunition, grenades—enough equipment to sustain the German lines for a month or more.

"Stork! Slaughter!" he called. "Get in here! You've got to see this."

Owen and Stork appeared at the door, with Coker on their heels.

"It's a gold mine!" Slaughter gasped.

Link grinned. "You bet it is."

Coker's face was pale in the dim light. "What are we going to do?"

"We're going to send for a demolition team to take out this whole place," Link answered. "Without these supplies, the Krauts don't have a chance."

★ ★ ★

"OK, kid, you understand what you need to do?"

"Yes, sir," Coker said, looking Sergeant Winsom in the eye. "I get back to Colonel Randolph as quick as I can and tell him what we've found. You and the others will stay close by in case the Krauts try to get back in here."

"Right. Now hurry, but be careful. We may not have a lot of time. And watch out for the mine markers—this rain may have taken some of them out."

"Yes, sir." Randy took off running, back down the road and around the bend. His heart pounded in his chest—whether from fear or exertion, he couldn't tell. But he would get the message through. He had to. It was his chance to make up for the lie he had told.

Rain fell into his eyes, and his boots slipped on the slick road. He had to keep going, no matter what. He had to—

Randy caught a glimpse of movement out of the corner of his eye. He whirled around, and there, at the edge of the road, just beyond a row of hedges, stood a dark figure with a rifle trained on him. He squinted into the rain and could just make out a bandage of some sort—a sling, holding the man's left arm. It couldn't be!

The German motioned for him to drop his weapon and come closer, and Randy could see a sinister, evil smile on the man's face. His heart leaped into his throat. It was the German officer, the prisoner he had let escape. They had been ambushed, and it was all his fault.

As he approached the enemy, his hands raised over his head, Randy scanned the road in front of him. He moved forward slowly—one step, then a second. At last he found what he was looking for, not three yards in front of the German officer. Taking a deep breath, he closed his eyes and lunged forward, grinding his heel directly down on a mine marker in the mud.

★ ★ ★

Link heard the blast, and his stomach lurched. "Ambush!" he yelled. "Fall back!"

All around him, men scrambled into action, moving back down the road. Owen and Stork appeared from opposite sides of the chateau, and Link motioned to them. "We can't leave this ammo dump intact," he said. "It's too valuable to the Krauts."

Owen nodded. "I'll blow it with a grenade. One good shot into that parlor will take out the whole thing."

"You won't have time to get out," Link argued.

"If I go at it from the back, I can lob one in through the window, then get over the hill and be protected before it goes up. My aim's pretty good."

"It had better be," Stork said. "If you miss—"

"I won't miss. Get going. I'll catch up with you."

At the bend of the road, Link turned and looked back in time to see Owen Slaughter running around the corner of the ruined chateau.

"Good luck, pal," he whispered. "God be with you."

Link and Stork headed off down the road. Just as they rounded a curve, they heard a blast, then a series of explosions that sounded like enormous bottle rockets going up on the Fourth of July. Slaughter had done it. The chateau, with its precious store of ammunition, was history.

Link looked back. Now where was Owen? Link could see nothing except smoke, hovering against the dark storm clouds. Stork grabbed Link's arm and dragged him forward. They could just make out the rest of the platoon in the distance.

Suddenly shots rang out, sending the men diving into the bushes at the roadside. Link and Stork plunged into the ditch on the left side of the road and crawled forward, firing as they went. There was no turning back now. Slaughter would have to catch up to them on his own.

When they came up even with the rest of the men, Link peered over the edge of the ditch into the road. A crater had been blasted into the mud, and two figures lay next to it.

"It's Coker," Stork said into Link's ear. "Looks like he stepped on a mine. But he took a Kraut out with him."

Link squeezed his eyes shut, but he couldn't block out the sight of the broken bodies on the road. "Poor kid," he choked. "He was just a boy."

"Sarge! Help me . . ."

Link's eyes snapped open. "He's alive!" He lunged up out of the ditch and started for the road, but Stork pulled him back.

"He's dead," Stork said. "Or will be in a minute. Don't get yourself killed, Link."

As if to punctuate Stork's warning, a volley of sniper fire rang out over their heads. Link ducked back into the ditch and turned to Stork. "Cover me. I'm going to get him."

"Link, don't!" Stork protested. But before the words were out of his mouth, Link vaulted out of the ditch and onto the road. Stork laid down fire over his head, and Link dived into the crater next to Coker.

"It's OK, kid—I'm here." Link surveyed Coker, then the German. Coker must have stepped directly on top of the mine. The blast had gone outward, and the Kraut had caught the worst of it. His body was torn in half, his eyes still open, his right hand clutching his rifle. Coker was alive, but not for long. His legs were completely gone, and his blood was filling the bottom of the crater.

The boy looked up at him with an expression of infinite sadness. "I'm sorry, Sarge," he muttered. "It was all my fault—"

"Don't try to talk, Coker," Link rasped. "The medics will be here in a—"

"I have to . . . have to tell you," Coker interrupted. "The German we captured—" He gestured to the body on the other side of the hole. "I . . . lied," Coker whispered. "He escaped . . . ambushed us . . . but I got him."

Link looked at Coker, then at the dead German, his left arm in a sling, the chest of his uniform blank where his medals would have been. In a flash of insight, he understood.

"You stepped on the mine deliberately?" he asked, cradling Coker's head in his arms.

The boy nodded. "Had to . . . make it right. I'm sorry, Sarge. Forgive . . ."

Coker's breath rattled in his throat, and his broken body went limp in Link's arms.

Link fought for breath. "It's all right, kid," he said, tears choking the words. "It's all right." He laid Coker's head down and wiped the mud and blood from his face, then crawled to the edge of the crater. There was nothing more he could do for the boy. It was up to God now.

"Link!" Stork's voice broke into Link's consciousness. "Behind you!"

Link turned and saw Stork come up out of the ditch, firing down the road. A machine-gun blast ripped up the mud at his back. Link ducked back into the crater, flinging himself on top of Coker's body.

But he was too late. A blaze of fire ran through his legs and back, and everything went dark.

39

✫ ✫ ✫

Trial by Fire

Thelma Breckinridge watched out of the corner of her eye as Madge Simpson cleared the back booth and returned the dishes to the kitchen. In the corner, happily perched on Ivory Brownlee's lap, little Mickey cooed and grabbed at the old man's gnarled fingers, his little feet flailing against the piano keys. Thelma thought she had never heard such beautiful music in her life.

Madge had absolutely blossomed since the day she had taken up residence at the Paradise Garden. She seemed relaxed and happy, content with herself and her life. Her existence was meager enough, living with the baby in one room behind the cafe, sharing a kitchen and a bathroom with Thelma. But to Thelma—and to Madge, apparently—their life seemed like heaven.

At least once a day the girl thanked Thelma profusely for giving her a job and taking her in. It didn't matter that they didn't have much money, Madge insisted—they had a place of peace, and that was what counted most. She didn't say it directly, but Thelma understood that Madge was grateful for the sense of family she had come to know in Eden.

Thelma was grateful, too. Grateful to God for bringing this tender-hearted, sensitive girl to her doorstep. Grateful for the gift of delightful little Mickey. Grateful that, in ways she had never imagined possible, her deep unspoken prayers for herself had been answered.

Thelma looked at the child, who was gleefully tugging at Ivory's stubbly beard, and her heart melted. She couldn't have loved this baby more if he had been her own flesh-and-blood grandchild. He was a sweet-tempered boy—never gave anyone a minute's trouble, never cried unless he was hungry or needed changing. He woke up in the morning smiling, and he was perfectly content to let Thelma take him out of his crib and feed and change him while his mother got a little extra sleep.

Thelma found herself getting up earlier than necessary just to have the privilege of holding Mickey. While Madge slept, she crept around the tiny apartment with the child in the crook of her arm, fixing his breakfast and dressing him. And all the while she talked to him in low tones, telling him how much his mama and daddy adored him, and his Aunt Thelma, too. Lately she had begun telling him about all the wonderful things he would discover as he grew up, and about the Father God who created him and loved him.

Thelma might not have said all these things had anyone else been around to hear. But she firmly believed that even tiny babies like Mickey could understand more than people gave them credit for. And if she had anything to do with it, this little one would understand, first and foremost, that he was loved—by his parents, by his Aunt Thelma . . . most of all, by God.

★ ★ ★

Madge Simpson brushed the hair out of her eyes, straightened her back, and looked around at the Paradise Garden. The morning coffee rush was nearly over. Thelma had taken Mickey out of Ivory's lap and sat rocking him.

Madge breathed a deep sigh. Despite the hard work and the lack of money, she was nearly as content as her infant son. Here she had a purpose, something significant she could do, rather than just sitting around listening to her mother-in-law's nagging. Here she had a sense of being connected to people who understood what being separated from her husband meant. Here she had friends her own age, like Libba and Willie and Mabel Rae, who knew Michael and cared about him. And here, of course, she had Thelma, who was fast becoming the mother she had never known. Madge could almost feel arms of love surrounding her, just as Thelma's embrace cradled little Mickey.

As much as she cherished all this, it scared her at times, too. She knew that this time in Eden was a stopgap—God's provision for her until Michael came home and they could begin their life together. Sometimes she fought within her own heart against becoming too dependent upon this new "family" of hers. If she let herself get too close, she might never want to leave.

Madge smiled to herself as she watched Thelma kiss the top of her son's downy head. It was far too late for keeping herself distant, she mused. This was family. This was home. And when Michael came back . . . well, they would cross that bridge when they came to it.

★　★　★

When the bell over the door sounded, Thelma looked up to see Libba and Willie Coltrain enter the cafe, chattering and laughing. It was a welcome sight. The last time Thelma had seen Libba, the girl had been struggling mightily to trust God. It looked as if she had come to some measure of peace . . . or else had just pushed her anxieties back under the surface. Thelma hoped fervently that it was the former.

The two girls greeted Madge with a hug, then gravitated immediately toward Thelma and the baby. When they saw that Mickey was asleep, they lowered their voices.

"He's so beautiful," Libba whispered. She reached out to stroke the soft round cheek, and the child stirred in his sleep. "Madge, you are one lucky woman."

Madge came up behind Libba, beaming with motherly pride. "I suppose I am," she said quietly. "I just wish his daddy could see him. He'd be so proud."

Willie put a hand on Madge's shoulder. "He'll see him," she said. "Soon. And he'll be the proudest daddy ever."

Madge turned to Willie and gave her a quick hug. "You are all so good to me," she said with tears in her eyes. "Thank you so much!"

"For what?"

"For everything. For being my friends—" she turned to Thelma—"for taking me in and giving me a home and a family. I can never repay you for all you've done."

Thelma smiled warmly into Madge's eyes. "There's nothing to repay, hon. Someday you'll understand that you've given more to all of us than you could ever imagine."

It was true, although Thelma hadn't really known how true until she said the words. Somehow Madge and little Mickey had drawn them all together, giving them a common bond, a purpose—a reason to look beyond the uncertainties of war and see God's hand in the present situation.

Maybe it was the baby—a tangible, lovable, visible sign that life goes on no matter what happens . . . that the Good Lord brings joy even in the midst of suffering and death. Whatever the circumstances of this child's conception, no one could argue that he was a gift from God, a gift of love and wonder. He was a sign and symbol of hope. Not just for Madge but for all of them. Little Michael . . . their angel in disguise.

★ ★ ★

While Madge and Willie took the baby back to the apartment to settle him for his nap, Thelma brought coffee and donuts to the table for herself and Libba.

"So," she ventured cautiously, "how are things at school?"

Libba took a bite of donut and chewed thoughtfully. "All right, I guess," she hedged. "I'm enjoying my classes, especially Shakespeare, but sometimes I find it hard to keep focused on my work."

"Thinking about Link?"

Libba nodded. "And about God." She brightened. "You know, Thelma, since our last discussion I've found it a little easier to trust God for Link. I haven't received any word from him, but I keep reminding myself that God knows where he is and what he's doing, and I keep praying for God to protect him."

"And—," Thelma prodded.

"It's funny, Thelma, but I almost feel like my prayers are doing me more good than they're doing Link. I mean, I pray for *him,* and it seems as if *my* faith gets stronger. Does that make any sense?"

Thelma patted Libba's hand. "It makes perfect sense, hon."

"And I've prayed for myself, too—I found out that isn't as selfish as I once thought it was." Libba's eyes took on a faraway expression. "I pray that God will make me stronger and that I'll be prepared to accept whatever happens. Freddy's helping with that, too."

Thelma choked on her coffee. "Did you say Freddy?"

"Uh-huh." Libba grinned. "Freddy Sturgis."

"The doughboy?" Thelma tried to keep a straight face, but apparently she wasn't very successful, because Libba began to laugh.

"Freddy's studying art at Ole Miss—you knew that?"

"Yes, I knew, but—"

"We get together pretty often . . . for coffee at the Union, stuff like that. Sometimes I sit with him in the Grove while he does his sketches. And we talk." Libba paused. "Thelma, you wouldn't recognize him, honestly you wouldn't. He's . . . well, different. It's like he's found himself, discovered what he's meant to do. He's an entirely different person now."

"He'd have to be." The words came out before Thelma realized she was saying them, and she felt herself redden.

"It's OK, Thelma," Libba said. "I know what Freddy was like, and I know why I took up with him. But he's not trying to please anyone else now—not even me."

"That must be a refreshing change."

Libba lifted one eyebrow. "To be honest, yes, it is. I like him a lot better now. He's quit trying to be what everybody else expects him to be. And he's become a good friend."

"You said he's helping you understand things about God?" Thelma had a difficult time keeping the incredulity out of her voice.

Libba nodded. "It's unbelievable, Thelma. He has a deep faith, and he understands things I'd never expect him to know. He doesn't say very much about it, but he's obviously been hurt a lot, from the time he was pretty young. Maybe it's because he's an artist . . . he was always different, more sensitive than other people. And because he felt so alone, he turned to God. His faith is very real—it's not just religious talk. He doesn't give me pat answers or simple assurances. He helps me face reality."

"Such as?"

"Such as the fact that we're in a war and people are getting hurt and killed. We may never know why some people are spared and others aren't, but we have to base our belief on God's character, not on the circumstances. It's not much good believing in a God who can be controlled by our whims or desires. We have to give God the freedom to be God, and that may mean accepting things we will never understand."

Thelma shook her head in amazement. Never in a million years would she have imagined that little puppy-faced Freddy Sturgis would turn out to be an instrument of God in Libba Coltrain's life. Obviously, he had changed. Libba respected him and listened to him. And apparently he was helping her understand some important spiritual principles—ideas a lot of people never even began to grasp. But then, throughout history God had chosen some pretty unlikely mouthpieces for the revelation of divine wisdom— fishermen and tax collectors, prostitutes and pharaohs . . . even, in one case, a donkey. She guessed that God was capable of speaking through a self-effacing little artist as well. Truth was truth, after all, no matter what kind of pipeline it came through.

Thelma smiled at Libba. "That's wonderful, honey. I'm glad you've got a friend like that."

Libba sighed wistfully. "You know, Thelma, it's ironic how this war—this terrible war—is bringing people together. It's not just with Freddy, either— why, Willie and I are closer than I ever thought we could be. And Madge! We've only known her a few weeks, but we're all like sisters . . . even Mabel

Rae. Maybe it's because we're all facing a common enemy and similar losses, but—" She paused.

"But what, Libba?"

"I just hope that when this war is over and everything's back to normal we won't lose the closeness—and the faith—that we have now. That would be a shame, wouldn't it?"

Thelma nodded somberly, thinking of Madge and the baby, and her heart twisted. With every fiber of her soul she hoped—and prayed—that life would never go "back to normal" again. "It sure would, honey. It would be an awful shame."

★ ★ ★

Libba's heart leaped when she saw Madge and Willie coming through the kitchen into the restaurant with little Mickey. There was something special about that child, something that melted Libba's heart and made her smile whenever she saw him. But it was more than just the baby—it was the sense of belonging she felt with Willie and Madge, that closeness she had talked to Thelma about. Freddy would say that God was doing something special in these friendships, and he would probably be right. Whatever it was, she was thankful to be a part of it.

Libba realized suddenly that she had never felt that sense of belonging anywhere—or with anyone—before. Except, perhaps, with Link, during the short time they'd had together. Even at home, where she should have felt it, the constant tension with Daddy made life miserable. He had gotten worse since Link had shipped out, always harping on the same subject, telling her not to expect Link to come back the same as when he'd left . . . if he came back at all. The time or two she had tried to talk to him about her newfound faith in God, he had ridiculed her into silence. She had always been a Christian, he said. He had raised her right. She didn't need some pansy artist or floozy waitress to tell her what to believe. He had always been a churchgoer, a deacon, and a Sunday school teacher. That ought to be enough for the Lord.

The worse things got with Daddy, the more Libba avoided him. Some weekends she didn't even come home at all, going instead to the farm to spend Saturday and Sunday with Willie and Mabel Rae and her aunt and uncle. Her daddy had always acted as if Uncle William's branch of the family were somehow inferior to their own—less civilized, less cultured. And for a long time Libba had believed it. But now, spending more time with them, she saw how wrong her father was, and how despicably snobbish. There was no more loving couple on the face of the earth than Uncle William and

Aunt Bess. They might not have much in the way of material possessions, but they had something money couldn't buy. And they had taken her in just like another daughter, never saying a word about her father's attitudes—or hers.

So, increasingly, Libba had become part of the family her daddy called the "White Trash Coltrains." And her only regret was that she hadn't done it sooner.

Willie and Madge sat down at the table across from her, and Madge handed the baby to her. Libba snuggled the warm, soft bundle into her arms and laughed as he opened his mouth in a huge yawn. "Are you sleepy, baby boy?" she crooned.

"He wouldn't go down for his nap," Madge said. "So we finally gave up. Now look at him."

"You just want to be with everybody out here in the cafe, don't you?" Libba smoothed his hair with one hand. "That's all right, sweetheart. You just go on and take your nap. Aunt Libba will hold you as long as you want."

Madge rolled her eyes. "Between Aunt Libba, Aunt Willie, Aunt Mabel, Aunt Thelma, and Uncle Ivory, this child is going to be spoiled rotten before he ever gets to meet his daddy."

"He will not!" Libba protested. "He'll just be well loved." She leaned close to Mickey and kissed the tiny hand that gripped her finger. "Don't listen to Mommy," she cooed. "She doesn't know anything about being spoiled."

Willie began to laugh. "That's probably true. But his Aunt Libba knows all about it, doesn't she?"

Libba slanted a glance at her cousin. "It's not the same thing, and you know it."

"Ah," Willie said, "but I don't hear you denying it—"

Any other friendly barbs Willie might have thrown in Libba's direction were interrupted as the bell over the door jangled insistently. "Aunt Olivia!"

Libba looked up, and her heart sank. Sure enough, her mother stood there in the open doorway. Wonderful. Now she'd know for sure that Libba hadn't been staying in Oxford on the weekends, and she wouldn't be a bit happy about it.

Well, it was about time her mother found out that Libba was an adult, old enough to make her own decisions. If she didn't choose to come home and subject herself to her father's haranguing, she didn't have to. She would make that clear once and for all.

Libba rose and handed the baby back to Madge. "Mama!" she said. "What are you doing here?"

"I saw Willie's daddy's truck parked outside, and I thought you might be here."

Libba threw a glance at Willie, who grimaced and shrugged her shoulders. "I'm here, Mama. And if you want to know why—"

Her mother waved one hand in a dismissive gesture. "Oh, Libba, I'm not stupid—or blind," she said bluntly. "I know you've been spending weekends at your Uncle William's, and it's just fine with me. I miss you being home, of course, but I don't blame you. Your daddy's being absolutely impossible, and if I could get away from him, I'd—"

She stopped suddenly, and a dark red flush crept up her neck. "I'm sorry," she said. "I didn't mean to go on so."

Libba ran to her mother and embraced her warmly, drawing her into the group. "I'm glad to see you, Mama. I've missed you, too. Come see the baby—and meet Madge Simpson."

"Oh, he's beautiful!" her mother said, turning to Madge. "I've heard nothing but good things about him—and about his mother. I'm glad to meet you at last."

"It's good to meet you, too, Mrs. Coltrain," Madge said. "Would you like to hold him? He doesn't mind—he loves everybody."

Libba watched as her mother's eyes lit up. She hadn't seen that much life in Mama's face in ages, and it looked good on her. It made her look younger, less worn down. "I'd love to," she said. "But first—"

She held out a small square package to Libba. "I've just been to the post office," she said. "This came for you."

Libba took the package. It was addressed to her, care of her parents' post office box in Eden, from a military clearing station in New York. "It's from Link!" she cried. "I'm sure of it."

Willie and Madge crowded around her as she set the package carefully on the table.

"Maybe there's news of Michael," Madge whispered.

"And Owen," Willie added.

Libba stared at the box. "Dear God," she murmured, "please let it be from Link."

"Open it—open it!" Willie demanded. "Thelma, get us a—" She turned to find Thelma holding out a small paring knife. "Thanks." She handed the knife to Libba.

Holding her breath, Libba cut the string and removed the brown paper, then carefully pried up the edges of the box. She peered inside.

"What is it?"

"It's a letter," Libba said, her voice sounding curiously distant in her own ears. She picked up the folded paper, and as she scanned the top of the page, her heart began to pound and her hands started to tremble. "It's a letter I wrote to Link a while back, in May. I—I don't understand."

"What else is in there?" Willie slid the box across the table and lifted out a small gold locket on a chain and a battered wristwatch, its crystal shattered.

"It's the locket I gave Link when we got engaged," Libba whispered, her throat tight. "He said he'd keep it until he came home—" She stopped suddenly as tears overwhelmed her, and with a shaking hand unfolded the letter. "No! God in heaven—no!"

She held up the sheaf of tissue-thin paper. A large, jagged hole went straight through the pages. Around it, a dark brown stain spread across the words—her words, words of love to the man of her dreams—blotting them out like . . .

Like blood.

40

★ ★ ★

Secret Love

Mabel Rae Coltrain made sure the cafe was empty before she ventured inside. It was early afternoon, the time when the lunch crowd had gone back to work and the three-o'clock coffee-and-pie set hadn't yet arrived. Madge usually took an hour or so after the lunch rush to rest and put Mickey down for a nap. This was Mabel's private time with Thelma Breckinridge.

Today, especially, Mabel didn't want anyone else around. She had to talk to Thelma alone, without the possibility of anyone overhearing. As close as she and Libba and Willie had become in the past few months, she couldn't confide in them. Libba's pain over losing Link was much too raw, and Willie was beside herself with uncertainty about Owen.

Mabel shared their hurt, of course—both about their fiancés and about her own brother. No one had heard from Charlie, either, and they were all worried about him. The shadow of war had loomed over the entire nation for years, but now the dark and foreboding cloud had forked its lightning into their private world.

In the midst of all this pain, Mabel felt guilty for being happy. Still, she had to share her happiness with someone, and the only one who might possibly understand was Thelma.

Mabel seated herself in the corner booth, and Thelma brought iced tea to the table.

"How's Libba?" Thelma asked. "And Willie? I haven't seen them in a week or so."

Mabel shook her head. "Willie tries to keep on believing that Owen is all right. But after what happened to Link, it's hard for her. Libba's quit school and is living out at the farm with us. I'm worried about her, Thelma. She's just so . . . vacant. She sits on the porch and stares at nothing for hours, and she hardly ever cries."

"People take on grief in different ways," Thelma said. "Personally, I think it's healthier to cry and get mad and let out what you're feeling. But you can't force it. Give Libba time. She'll come to grips with Link's death, and—"

"But that's the problem," Mabel interrupted. "She's not coming to grips with it. When she got the package with his watch and stuff, I think she knew. I saw the letter, and all that—" Mabel shuddered. "All that blood. How can she not know? I mean, they don't send a soldier's personal effects home if he's still alive. But the telegram hasn't come, and until it does Libba refuses to believe that he's gone."

"The telegram?"

"The official telegram from the War Department—you know, the one everyone dreads."

Thelma took in a breath. "I see."

"And so she just sits. Sometimes I think she's waiting for Western Union to deliver the final news, and other times it seems like she's expecting Link to come walking up the road."

"Give her time," Thelma repeated. "It will sink in eventually, and then she'll really begin to grieve."

Mabel looked intently at Thelma. Deep circles around her eyes reflected anxiety and lack of sleep. "How's Madge doing?"

Thelma sighed. "Pretty well, under the circumstances. The girl has a strong faith, and she is determined not to think the worst until she hears otherwise. She knows that Stork was most likely with Link when he . . . well, you know. But she's holding on. She says that God will tell her when it's time to give up hope, and until then, she's going to keep on trusting."

"At least she has the baby. If Stork doesn't make it back, she'll have part of him forever." Mabel paused. "I always thought it was a stupid idea to get married in the middle of a war, when your husband might be shipping out at any minute. Now I'm not so sure. I guess things look different when you're in—"

"In love?" Thelma peered at Mabel. "Do you have something you want to tell me, hon?"

Mabel felt her heart lurch, and against her will, she smiled. "Oh, Thelma, I had to tell somebody! And I couldn't bear the thought of adding any more hurt to the load Libba and Willie are carrying right now. They'd try to be happy for me, I know, but it would only make their situations worse."

Thelma leaned across the table. "Your Lieutenant Laporte, I assume?"

Mabel narrowed her eyes and clutched Thelma's arm. "You've got to promise me that you won't tell a soul. This has to be between you and me."

Thelma put her nose in the air as if she were deeply offended. "When did you ever know old Thelma to break a confidence?"

"Sorry, Thelma, I just—"

"It's all right, hon," Thelma laughed. "Of course I'll keep it to myself."

Mabel scrambled in her purse and came up with a dog-eared envelope. She unfolded the letter and laid a grainy photograph on the table in front of Thelma. "We've been writing for several months now," she said. "And we've gotten to know each other very well. And—listen to this!" She scanned the letter and began to read. "'I find myself thinking about you day and night, dearest Rae—'"

She stopped suddenly and looked up. "He calls me 'Rae'—did I tell you that?" When Thelma nodded, she went on. "'I can't stop looking at your picture and dreaming of the day when we will finally meet face-to-face.'"

"You sent him a picture?"

Mabel shrugged. "When he wrote that he was falling in love with me— imagine that, Thelma! With me!—I decided he'd better know the whole truth, and quick. I couldn't stand the idea of him thinking I was some Carole Lombard and then being disappointed once he saw me." She sighed deeply. "I figured as soon as he saw the picture, he'd quit writing or send me a Dear-Jane letter. And if he was going to do that, I wanted to get it over with. But he didn't. It seems he loves me for what's inside, for who I am—in his words, 'for my mind and heart and soul.'"

"That's wonderful, hon," Thelma said. "And, whether you know it or not, that kind of attitude is pretty rare in a man."

Mabel curled her lip. "Tell me about it. I've spent my life being rejected by fellows who passed me over for some brainless blonde with nice ankles and a narrow waist."

"I hear you, darlin'," Thelma murmured.

Mabel stared out the window, wondering how much of the story she should tell. But she had come this far, and she needed someone to understand, so she plunged ahead. "To tell the truth, Thelma, I was terrified when I sent the picture. It was a huge risk, and I wasn't sure I was up to handling another rejection. But I had to know the truth about Drew, even if knowing hurt."

"But it sure seems to have worked out all right."

"It's worked out more than all right, Thelma. Listen to this!" She picked up the letter and resumed reading: "'My tour of duty will be up before long, and the first thing I intend to do is come to Eden to claim my Paradise Girl. If you'll have me, my darling Rae, I want to take you to New Orleans with me, to introduce my future bride to the family. No doubt they will love you as I do—only not as much, for no one could ever match the depth of my love for you.'"

"Whew!" Thelma said. "That's some letter."

"It is, isn't it?" Mabel laughed and leaned back in the booth. "And you know what, Thelma? I'm not a bit nervous about meeting his family. I should be, I guess—Drew's from Old New Orleans society, and I'm sure I'm not at all what they would expect. But he loves me, and I love him. And apparently it doesn't matter to him what I look like or what anyone else might think of me—"

"Hold on!" Thelma interrupted. "What do you mean by that?"

Puzzled, Mabel stared at Thelma for a long time before responding. "I know what people say about me, Thelma, and I can see in a mirror as well as anyone. I'm fat and unattractive. More than once I've overheard Libba, my own cousin, calling me Hopeless Mabel—a reference, I assume, to the handwork I've done over the years, stocking my hope chest. I don't have any false notions about myself."

Thelma closed her eyes, and for a minute Mabel thought she was going to cry. Then she opened them again, and a fire blazed out at Mabel that took her by surprise.

"Don't ever say such things about yourself, child!" Thelma exclaimed. "I've watched you in the past few months, and you've blossomed into a lovely woman—a woman who would make any man proud. Any man who had a brain in his head, anyway. Why, girl, you have a glow about you, a radiance that those slim-ankled, dim-witted blondes could never reproduce with a truckload of powder and rouge. Beauty like that only comes from the inside, and you should be thankful for it."

Mabel Rae was stunned, and for a few moments she couldn't speak at all. "Why, that's exactly what Drew tells me," she whispered at last.

"Then you'd better start believing it." Thelma gave a quick jerk of her head as if to emphasize the truth she had spoken. "Your Andrew Laporte is no fool, girl. I can't wait to meet him." She looked down at the photograph on the table. "Now, which one is he?"

Mabel Rae leaned over and pointed. "These are his buddies," she said. "This picture was taken on some little island in the Pacific—see the palm trees? And over here is the ocean—"

Thelma cleared her throat. "I don't care beans about the ocean, Mabel. Which one is Drew? This one?" She indicated a tall man, shirtless, with broad shoulders, a muscular chest, and dark hair. He was smiling into the camera, and even in this grainy picture, the deep dimples in his cheeks showed up. "He's gorgeous."

Mabel uttered a contemptuous grunt. Thelma could be so exasperating at times. "Sure, Thelma, that's him. Now, honestly, can you see me with somebody like that? I'd be so intimidated I wouldn't be able to say a word." She pointed to the other side of the little group. "He said third from the left. This is him—the short fellow with the mustache."

"Hmmm," Thelma said. "He's kind of cute."

"He's perfect—perfect for me, I mean. Sure, his buddy there is handsome as all get-out, but like I said, I couldn't see me with someone like that. Drew is just—well, average. But he's got nice eyes, don't you think? And he has a wonderful heart."

Thelma looked up from the picture, her eyes shining. "And so do you, darlin'. I couldn't be happier for you."

★　★　★

Libba sat on the porch at Uncle William's farmhouse, staring out over the cotton fields and swatting at the occasional fly that buzzed around her head. The afternoon was hot, and as the sun sank lower in the west, the shade from the tall oak tree shifted, leaving her squinting into the reddening light.

She closed her eyes, but the light still streamed in through her eyelids, red as the meat of a ripe tomato, red like . . .

Like blood.

Libba caught her breath, and her eyes snapped open. Everywhere, sleeping and waking, she saw it—the blood, dried on the pages of her letter to Link. She couldn't get away from it, this image in her mind of the man she loved lying dead on the beaches of France, covered with blood that could not be washed away.

She probably should have stayed in school and finished the term. It would have given her something to do, something to take her mind off Link. But she couldn't face returning to Shakespeare class, to Lady Macbeth sleepwalking, trying to wash the blood from her hands.

Libba knew what sleepwalking was like, and she knew about images of blood that wouldn't go away no matter what she did. She was empty, drained, vacant. All that was left was the blood. But unlike Lady Macbeth, she couldn't even feel the horror.

She couldn't feel anything.

Libba had only been home once, the night her mother brought the package to her in the Paradise Garden Cafe. Her father had done just what

Libba expected—had said *I told you so* a dozen times and declared that now that it was all over, Tater could get back to her life and quit worrying about some soldier half a world away.

In the middle of the night, Libba had left her parents' house, walked three miles in a steamy summer rain to the cafe, and called Willie to come and get her. She had not left the farm once since that night. She just sat in the porch swing and stared at the cotton fields and watched the gravel road.

She didn't know what she was watching for. Everybody—Uncle William, Aunt Bess, Mabel Rae, even Willie—all thought she was waiting for the final word, for the telegram to come. She had let them believe what they wanted. It was easier that way . . . she didn't have to explain.

But she wasn't waiting for the telegram. She didn't need it. She knew Link was dead, whether she got the official notification or not. What she couldn't figure out was why she didn't feel anything. She wished she could cry. She wished she could break things. On occasion, she wished she could just go ahead and die. But her eyes were dry, and her limbs were numb, and her heart kept on pumping. Dutifully she ate the food Aunt Bess set before her, tasting nothing. When darkness fell, she went to bed and slept. And then, when the sun rose, she got up again.

Libba watched her foot push against the weathered boards of the porch floor. She felt the swing begin to rock back and forth, but her mind had difficulty making the connection between the movement of her toe and the gentle undulation of the swing.

Suddenly her eyes focused on something—a movement, far down the road. Over the cotton fields she could see a dust cloud moving in her direction, coming closer. A dark shape moved into view, and as it rounded the turn, Libba could make out the lumpy shape of Charity Grevis's ancient black Buick.

The postmistress pulled to a stop in front of the house and got out of the car. Slowly she took the three steps up to the porch and stood shifting from one foot to the other. "Afternoon, Libba," she said brusquely. "Your Uncle William at home?"

Libba nodded but didn't speak.

The screen door creaked open, and Aunt Bess stood there, looking frail and small, gripping the door frame with a thin hand. "Afternoon, Miss Charity," she said. "Won't you come in for a glass of iced tea? It's mighty warm out today."

Charity Grevis stared at the porch floor and shook her head. "Thank you, no," she said uncertainly. "I—I just came to deliver these."

In her hand were two yellow Western Union telegrams.

41

☆ ☆ ☆

Faith on the Home Front

Thelma Breckinridge stood behind the counter, watching. The Paradise Garden was officially closed for a day of mourning in honor of Charlie Coltrain, Link Winsom, and Owen Slaughter, who had sacrificed their lives for the cause of freedom. Thelma felt helpless, powerless . . . but she could do that much, at least.

In the center of the cafe, four somber women sat around one table. Willie Coltrain, who in a single day had received word that both her brother and her fiancé were missing in action, presumed dead. Mabel Rae, whose joy in her secret love had been tempered by heart-wrenching sorrow. Libba Coltrain, at last accepting the finality of Link Winsom's death. Madge Simpson, trying to be brave and strong, and yet anxious because she had heard no word from her husband. Women trying desperately to hang on to faith in God, to keep the home fires burning, to go on living when living seemed the hardest thing in the world to do.

Like thousands of other women around our nation and the world, Thelma thought. American and German, Russian and Japanese, French and Italian women. The heart of a German soldier's wife broke just like that of an American woman. The orphaned child of some Axis soldier was just as fatherless as the sons and daughters left behind by the Allies who had given their lives on the beaches of Normandy. The women and children left behind were not to blame. It didn't matter, in the dark hour of mourning, what side they were on or whether the men they loved died for a noble or an ignoble cause. There were innocents on both sides of the conflict.

Something deep in Thelma's spirit stirred, and for a brief moment, as she watched these young women who had become her family, she caught a glimpse of what God must feel, looking at them. *How the heart of the Almighty must be breaking,* she thought, tears rising to her eyes. Many tears had been shed, and undoubtedly there were many more to come. But Thelma knew in her deepest soul that God's tears had been the first to fall.

There were no answers, of course, to all the questions that were left unspoken. In a fallen world, torn by hatred and strife and bloodshed and war, such things happened. Certainly Hitler, with his grand delusions of world conquest, had to be stopped. Liberty was worth fighting for—even dying for. But all the philosophical platitudes in the world couldn't make the pain go away.

Thelma loaded a tray with a pitcher of iced tea and four dishes of blueberry cobbler, sent up a silent prayer for wisdom and strength, and made her way to the table.

★ ★ ★

"It's so unfair!" Willie felt a twinge of guilt as she said the words. She should be trying to put the best face on it, she supposed—helping the others cope with their grief and anxiety, looking for a ray of hope. But she was tired of being strong. She felt trapped and weak, as if she were strangling in a bottomless pit of kudzu vines. And she was angry.

"What does this mean—missing, presumed dead?" she went on, clutching the telegram in her fingers. It was the one about Owen, and it had come to her because he had no family. "Can't the army even keep up with its men?" She smoothed the telegram on the tabletop and ran her finger over the words. Her name and address. His name, rank, serial number. *We regret to inform you . . .*

Willie looked around at the stricken faces and immediately regretted the harshness of her tone. They felt the same pain—the same anger and numbness and hopelessness—that she did.

"We don't even have bodies to bury or mourn over," she said in a quieter voice. "Charlie, Owen, Link . . . we don't even know for sure what's happened to them."

Libba gazed up at her, her green eyes red-rimmed from crying. "I think," she said softly, "that we have to acknowledge the fact that we may never know. We have to face reality, have to—"

"I don't want to face reality!" Willie said. Tears choked her and threatened to spill over.

"Neither did I." Libba reached out and took Willie's hand. "But when I finally realized what the wristwatch and the locket and the letter meant—"

She stopped and closed her eyes, taking a deep breath. "I had to let him go, to trust him to God. With or without a final word."

"I'm sorry, Libba," Willie said, remorse rising up in her. "At least we have some official word about Charlie and Owen—even if it's not very definite. You don't know for sure about Link."

Libba shook her head. "I know," she whispered. "I knew from the minute I opened that package. I just didn't want to accept it, and I didn't know how to deal with it."

Willie leaned forward and looked intently at her cousin. "So how are you dealing with it?" This was a switch, she mused—strong, capable Willie asking her flighty, superficial cousin for advice. But Libba wasn't flighty or superficial these days. The war had changed her.

The irony, however, wasn't lost on Libba, and she quirked an eyebrow in Willie's direction. Then her expression sobered. She hesitated for a moment before answering. "I think about Link being in heaven," she said at last. "I pray that God will take care of him. I pray that God will give me strength to go on without him." She paused and blinked back tears. "And I thank God that once—just once in my life—I had the chance to know what it was like to be loved . . . really loved."

Silence descended around the table. Willie watched as Madge picked up little Mickey and held him close. A strange look passed over Mabel Rae's face, an expression of compassion and understanding. And she saw in Libba's eyes a fierce determination to trust and to be strong.

Indeed, the war had changed them all.

★ ★ ★

Thelma sat quietly beside the little group and listened. She would never, in a million years, tell them what she was thinking. Their grief and uncertainty were far too raw for them to hear her perspectives on how God was working in the midst of their heartbreak. But she could see the changes, a direct result of the trials they had endured.

Madge's timidity had disappeared; she had become a confident and capable woman, a good mother, a loving wife and friend. Willie's self-sufficiency had been tempered, and she had begun to acknowledge her need of support from those who loved her. Mabel Rae had blossomed under the influence of love and no longer lived in Willie's shadow. But the most obvious turnaround had occurred in Libba, whose shallow self-centeredness had given way to a deep and genuine faith, a growing trust in God, and the beginnings of compassion for other people.

Thelma was certain that the Lord didn't bring this kind of pain upon people deliberately. But she knew God well enough to know that he did use such experiences to change people, to strengthen them, to bring them to new awareness. You didn't just jump in and tell people that God was in the middle of their hurt, of course—sometimes that left people with the mistaken idea that God was conducting some kind of sadistic experiment to see how much pain they could take. And in the middle of the chaos, few people could see the good that might come out of their hurt. Still, Thelma knew that God could—and would—use every experience of human life to draw these young women closer to the One who loved them. It was happening here, right now, in the Paradise Garden Cafe. And for that, Thelma was thankful. Thankful for the changes, for the growth. Thankful for God's faithfulness in the midst of a terrible tragedy. Thankful, most of all, that the Lord had given them each other.

And silently, as they sat together and helped one another bear the burden of the ceaseless pain, Thelma Breckinridge prayed—that God would surround them all with love and comfort, and that the Lord would open his everlasting arms and welcome those young men into the light.

FIVE

I'll Get By

SEPTEMBER 1944

42

★ ★ ★

Noble Sacrifices

Army General Hospital
Birmingham, England
September 1944

Link Winsom opened his eyes to see Stork Simpson staring down at him.

"Cut that out, Stork!"

Stork grinned. "Cut what out?"

"You know I can't stand it when you sneak around like that. How long have you been here?"

"Long enough to be serenaded by your snoring. There's a guy over in the other ward who's been in a coma for weeks. But as soon as he heard you sawing logs, he snapped right out of it. Started yelling that no lumber company could come in and strip out his daddy's woods without his permission."

Link laid his head back on the pillow. "I don't snore."

"Sure you don't. You just sleep loud. Libba Coltrain's got a real treat coming if she's going to spend the rest of her life in a bed next to you."

Link shook his head and grimaced. "You didn't break your promise, Stork. Tell me you didn't."

Stork shrugged. "No. I wrote to Madge and told her I was all right—just a minor wound." He held up a plaster-encased left arm and waved it around. "Doc says I have a little nerve damage, but the surgery put my arm back together pretty well. He says I'll be going home before long."

"That's great, Stork. Really." Link tried to infuse his voice with enthusiasm, but even to his own ears the effort came out weak. "You'll get back before I do, that's for sure. But you've got to promise that you won't give me away."

"I really think you should reconsider this, Link. Doesn't Libba have the right to know you're alive? She's probably worried sick about you."

Link narrowed his eyes and fixed Stork with a glare. "According to your letter from Madge, Libba thinks I'm dead. She's not worried; she's grieving. And she'll get past her grief. Let's leave it that way. It's better for her in the long run."

"Better for her? It sounds pretty cruel to me. Why can't you just tell her the truth?"

"You know why not!" Link struggled to raise himself, and Stork awkwardly, with his good arm, lifted his shoulders and stuffed another pillow behind his head. Always trying to help—good old Stork. Didn't he see what it did to a guy, needing help just to sit up a little?

Once he was propped up, Link surveyed the damage for the thousandth time. From midchest down, he was trapped in a body cast, with one leg extended upward in traction. Tubes ran in and out of the cast at various strategic points, depending upon their purpose.

Link didn't remember much about the attack. One minute he was in the foxhole with poor Coker, and the next he woke up in a field hospital. He had multiple wounds, the doctors said, in his legs and back. One piece of shrapnel—from a hand grenade, apparently—was lodged near his spinal cord and could not be removed without risk of total paralysis. He was lucky to be alive.

Maybe he *was* lucky. Unlike Coker, and thousands of other soldiers, he had been given a second chance. But a second chance at what? At life without legs? At being half a man?

The doctors speculated that the shrapnel near his spine might shift, making it possible for them to remove it. Or it might go the opposite direction and leave him paralyzed for life. It was a toss-up, a roll of the dice. Nobody knew. For now, they simply had to keep him motionless and wait.

There wasn't much pain. In fact, from the waist down Link could feel nothing at all. That was his blessing—and his curse. If the feeling came back, this plaster cocoon would be unbearable. If it didn't . . .

Link didn't like to think about that possibility. He was trying to stay positive, as positive as he could under the circumstances. But until he knew one way or the other, he couldn't bring Libba into this. He could not saddle her with a cripple for the rest of her life. He wouldn't. And so he had sworn Stork to secrecy, making him promise that he wouldn't tell anyone—not even Madge—that Link was alive. If Libba thought he was dead or missing, she could go on with her life. He didn't want her waiting for him, expecting something that might never happen.

"I really think you ought to tell her," Stork repeated. "She has a right to know."

"She has a right to a life, Stork. She has a right to a whole man."

"She loves you."

"And I love her. It's because I love her that I don't want to put her through any more pain than necessary. If I don't come out of this on my feet, I will not have her staying with me out of pity or a sense of obligation. She deserves more than that."

Stork stared at Link for a long time before answering. Link could see a fire building in his friend's eyes and braced himself for some kind of explosion. But the blow-up didn't come—just a sort of slow burn, white hot and subdued.

"That all sounds very noble, Link," Stork said quietly, deliberately, "and no doubt you think you're perfectly justified in making that judgment. But I don't think you're in any position to decide for someone else what's best for her life. Especially your independent little Miss Green Eyes, who, if I recall correctly, isn't exactly the submissive, obedient type." Stork quirked a halfhearted smile at Link; then his voice took on a new intensity. "You lie there, so righteous, thinking you're making some kind of holy sacrifice for the woman you love. But did you ever once think about her? About how she feels? Maybe she wants you, with or without legs. Maybe, just maybe, she loves you—*you!* Not your ability to run a hundred-yard dash or jitterbug all night long. And maybe she would like to be respected enough to be told the truth and allowed to make up her own mind."

Stork leaned over the bed, and Link instinctively tried to pull back, but he had no place to go. "Where did you get the idea that you have the right to make such choices for someone else?" Stork whispered fiercely. "Who died and made you God?"

The last barb found its mark, and Link turned his head against the pillow and sighed. Out there, in the heat of battle, he had determined to open himself to God. Whether it was the fear of death or the reality of life, Link wasn't quite sure, but something had drawn him, kindled in him the desire to let God in. Out there, where eternity waited around every dangerous bend in the road, he had taken the first step: He had prayed, asking God to become real in his life, to lead him, to show him the way.

Now he realized, much to his chagrin, that he had not given God much opportunity to answer his prayer. He had done what he deplored in other men; he had turned to a halfhearted foxhole religion born of desperation in the heat of battle. By rights he should have been dead, killed in that mine crater next to young Coker. But he was alive. Alive, with a chance to prove to God, and to himself, that his commitment was not just a foxhole faith.

Stork was right, much as Link hated to admit it. He hadn't uttered a single prayer for guidance before making the decision to let Libba think he was dead. He had just forged ahead with his own bullheaded determination to be noble and self-sacrificing. Now, Stork made him wonder if it was nobility at all that motivated him. Maybe it was fear—fear that Libba would reject him when she found out how bad his wounds were.

Then suddenly, in a flash of insight, Link realized that this wasn't about Libba at all, about whether or not she was strong enough to deal with his condition. It was about *him*. He wasn't sure if *he* was strong enough. What if he didn't get better? What if he had to live in a wheelchair for the rest of his life? Marriage and family life—life in general, in fact—was difficult enough under the best of circumstances. If he had to deal with a life without legs, he'd rather do it alone.

He had rationalized, all right—so slickly that even he hadn't been aware of it. He had couched his logic in noble terms: He was protecting the woman he loved from a heartbreak she might not be able to handle. But he was really protecting himself; he was really shielding his own heart from the possibility of being broken.

And Stork—sensible, simple Stork—had seen right through him and poked a finger directly into the wound.

Link looked up at his friend, who was still standing beside the bed with an expression of agony and longing in his eyes. Obviously, it had cost Stork a lot to be that blunt with him. He didn't deserve such a loyal friend, but he was grateful nevertheless.

Link reached out and grasped Stork's good hand. "Thanks, buddy."

Stork shook his head as if trying to clear the cobwebs away. "For what?"

"For being honest with me. It hurt, but I needed to hear it."

Stork brightened. "Then you're not going to hold me to that stupid promise—not to tell Libba you're alive and well?"

Link held up a finger in warning. "Wait a minute. I may be alive, but it remains to be seen how well I am—or will be." He frowned and shook his head. "Give me some time on this, Stork. I will write to Libba—I will. Scout's honor. But I've got some thinking to do first."

"Thinking?" Stork lifted his eyebrows until they almost merged with his hairline.

Link grinned sheepishly. "Yes, thinking. And . . . praying."

"Ah."

"I haven't done very well in that department," Link said, looking down at his hands. "But you're right about one thing—I'm not God. And I need to get God's perspective on all this before I go off and do something I'll regret." He looked up at Stork. "I have no way of knowing what the future holds. You're right—I can't go making decisions for Libba out of some self-centered, distorted kind of nobility. God may not give a rat's whisker about my puny little problems, and he may not give me any kind of direction about this. I'm sure I don't deserve any attention from the Almighty. But I've got to try. If I don't get any answers, I'll . . . well, I'll figure something out."

Link fixed Stork with an intent look. *"But—,"* he said, emphasizing the word, "I need to do this in my way, in my own time—or God's time, whichever comes first. At any rate, Libba should hear this from me, not secondhand from you or Madge. I need your word that you'll keep quiet about it for a while longer."

"But you will get in touch with Libba?"

Link made an X over his chest and grinned. "Cross my heart. Soon. As soon as I . . . well, as soon as I know what I'm supposed to do."

Stork smiled and slapped Link on the shoulder. "All right. I'll keep my mouth shut. For now." He sobered. "I just don't want to see Libba hurt."

Link sighed. "Neither do I, pal. Neither do I."

★ ★ ★

Link's initial effort at communication with the Almighty left him more confused than ever. He had determined that he wouldn't be guilty of any more foxhole pleas for help, so he didn't pray that God would miraculously heal his legs or disintegrate the piece of shrapnel that lay perilously close to his spine. He remembered—perhaps from his reading or perhaps from his father—that somewhere the Bible encouraged people to pray for wisdom. *If anyone lacks wisdom, ask God, who gives it abundantly*—or something along those lines.

Link prayed, haltingly at first, because the exercise was unfamiliar, but gradually gaining confidence as he went on. He told God he was sorry for ignoring him and for attempting to figure things out for himself. He promised to try to do better, but he reminded God that it was hard to change old patterns of self-sufficiency. He thanked God for Libba and for Stork, and as he prayed he vaguely remembered Thelma Breckinridge's encouragements and thanked God for her, too, asking that God would use her to minister—he thought that was a spiritual-sounding word—to Libba in her time of need.

At last he decided that it was time to quit fooling around and take the plunge. "I don't know what to do, Lord," he said. "I don't know what I need, and I don't know what Libba needs. Sometimes I think it would be better for her if I simply faded away so she wouldn't have to deal with all this. But maybe that's just my own selfishness, to protect me from the possibility of being hurt or rejected. I love her, God, and I don't want to give her up. But I couldn't stand it if she looked at me with pity and felt obligated to marry me. I need wisdom and direction. I'm confused." He paused, not enjoying this feeling of helplessness, desperately wanting to regain a sense of control. "I guess," he finished lamely, "I need you."

Link didn't know quite what to expect in answer to his prayer, but instinctively he felt that if the Almighty was going to do him the honor of listening, he should at least return the favor. He lay there staring at the water stains on the tiles above his bed, and somewhere in the recesses of his mind he recalled a Bible story about handwriting on the wall. He didn't exactly envision an answer written on the ceiling, but he hoped for something almost as specific.

He waited. No answer came.

After a while his mind began turning over the possibilities. Should he tell Libba about his condition or not? Yes or no? Right or wrong? There had to be an answer. Soon he felt as if he was right back where he started, pulling the petals off a daisy: *tell her, tell her not; tell her, tell her not.* . . .

Link tried to clear his mind of the options and exercise a little patience. Maybe these things took time—especially for a novice like himself. Maybe God was busy answering other prayers, and his hadn't gotten through yet. He tried to pray again, but he felt like he was repeating himself, and his mind began to wander. He had heard of people praying for hours at a time, but he couldn't imagine how they did it. Who in the world would have that much to say to God? He had only been at it fifteen minutes, and he was already getting sleepy. . . .

★ ★ ★

Link struggled against the restraints that held him down, and his eyes snapped open. Darkness. Total and complete darkness, so thick that he could feel its weight pressing against him. He reached a hand down to his thigh and felt, not the body cast, but some sort of sticky cloth wrapped tightly around him, holding him fast. In panic he flung the other arm out and struck a wall, cold and clammy and rough, like the inside of a cave.

But a very small cave it was. When he extended both arms, he could touch the walls on either side. He lay on a hard slab, and the dampness crept into his body from below and chilled him to the bone.

The dark closeness of the place crushed him, and claustrophobia began to set in. He breathed rapidly, great lungfuls of moist, fetid air, and tried to calm himself. His heart pounded wildly, and the pulsating roar in his ears grew so loud that he thought his eardrums would burst.

Then he heard ... something else.

Breathing.

Not his own frantic gasps, but the tranquil, exhaled sigh of someone else, very close by.

"Who's there?" His voice, shrill, echoed in the darkness.

"Fear not." It was a whisper, barely audible. Was he hallucinating?

"Fear not." The words came again, and gradually, almost imperceptibly, he saw a form take shape—a translucent form, bluish in color, with a light that seemed to emanate from within.

"Who are you?"

The figure smiled, and the light grew brighter by degrees. "It's time to go."

"Go where?" he said, trying to sit up. "Am I dying?"

The figure shook its head and smiled again, then lifted an arm and pointed toward the wall at Link's feet. With a rumble that shook the cave to its bedrock, a stone twice as tall as a man began to move, rolling backward to reveal a huge opening.

Sunlight streamed in, and Link raised a hand to his eyes. Beyond the cave lay an open glade, lush and green and sheltered by tall trees, with multicolored flowers carpeting the forest floor. Somewhere a mourning dove called to its mate.

"It's time to go," the figure repeated.

Link swung his legs over the side of the rock slab and stood shakily to his feet. This all seemed familiar, somehow, and yet ...

He made his way to the mouth of the cave and stared into the morning light. The air was fresh and sweet, laden with the scent of blooming things. A small brown rabbit, completely unafraid, hopped up to him and sat at his feet, twitching its nose and staring up at him with liquid eyes.

"What is this place?" Link whispered. "Where am—" He turned back toward the cave, but the figure had disappeared. The cave was empty, the great stone door rolled to one side. Inside, on the slab, lay the cloths that had bound him.

He knew this place, all right—from his childhood, from the stories his father had told him when he was a boy. It was just as he had imagined it. And yet it was different. He was here. Always before it had been Someone Else. . . .

A movement in the woods beyond caught his eye—a woman, dressed in a robe of soft ivory, her head covered with a light brown scarf. She hurried toward the cave, then stopped suddenly, her face turned toward him.

Auburn hair escaped around the edges of the scarf, and she gazed at him in silence with eyes the color of weeping willow branches in the spring.

Then she smiled and, raising one hand, began to twist at a curl behind her right ear. . . .

★ ★ ★

"Libba!"

Link jerked awake to the sound of his own voice. He tried to sit up, then realized where he was. Still in the hospital. Still in the body cast.

He lay back against the pillow, and despite the thudding of his heart, a strange feeling of well-being washed over him. Something had happened— but what? Then he remembered . . . the dream.

He smiled and put his hands under his head, gazing at the water stains on the ceiling. His mind wrapped around the dream, recalling the details, reveling in the feelings. Instinctively he knew that the images in his dream were significant, that somehow they held answers for him.

Did it mean that God was going to heal him, that he would walk again? He had started out bound and then was free. But somehow he didn't think that was all there was to it. There was more, much more, if he could just understand.

Libba was there, as if waiting for him. He had seen the love in her eyes when she looked at him. Was that his answer—that God intended them to be together, whether he was healed or not?

"Fear not," the angel in the tomb had said. Was God trying to tell him not to be afraid of the future? He—

Wait a minute! An angel? A tomb? A stone that was rolled away? Those were the words, the images that came to Link's mind, and yet in the dream itself he had not identified the cave as a *tomb* or the figure of light as an *angel.*

All Link's childhood memories of Easter morning and the resurrection story came rushing back, but he tried to push the idea away. If this was a resurrection, why was *he* the one in the tomb?

Then, unbidden, the words crept into his mind . . . words he had read in the dead soldier's Bible that morning on Omaha beach . . . words that had started him on this quest in the first place: *I am the resurrection and the life; he that believeth in me, though he were dead, yet shall he live.* And the next verse, the one that had haunted Link from the moment he read it: *Believest thou this?*

But this time, instead of a knot in his stomach, Link felt a pounding in his veins and a swelling in his soul. "Yes," he whispered. Then, louder, "Yes!"

The dream was not a product of his imagination or a vain expression of his hopes. It wasn't about Link's legs or even about Link and the woman he loved. It was about Link and his God. It was about going into the grave with Christ and coming out again into the resurrection.

When Link had prayed, he hadn't known what he needed. But God knew. And God had answered his prayers.

Certainly, he needed guidance and direction. He needed to know what was the right thing to do where Libba was concerned. He needed healing—maybe even a miracle.

But what he needed more—what he needed first—was a firm place to stand in his relationship with God. Not a vague God-if-you're-up-there kind of faith, but a God-I-know-you're-right-here belief in the One who went into the tomb and came out again.

Fear not, a voice in his heart whispered. *Trust. You are not alone.*

Link closed his eyes and sighed. For the first time in his life he felt a presence with him, the same presence he had felt in the dream before the angel had appeared. And he remembered something else his father had taught him as a child—that Jesus, the Christ, had another name.

Immanuel.

God with us.

43

★ ★ ★

The Death of a Dream

Libba Coltrain fingered the small banner that hung in the front window of Uncle William's farmhouse. One star. Charlie's star. For the brave young son, missing in action . . . presumed dead.

There should have been three, Libba mused. But the army had its rules, and the army couldn't—or wouldn't—acknowledge that "family" sometimes meant more than ties of blood and name and heritage. No star hung here for Owen Slaughter. No star for Link.

For nearly three months now, Libba had been toying with the idea of contacting Link's family—maybe even going to Missouri to mourn with them over the loss of the one they loved. Link's stories about his close, loving family tugged at her heart. She had looked forward to becoming one of them—not just to being Link's wife, but to being embraced by the entire clan. She had dreamed about finding the father she had never known in Bennett Winsom, about sharing secrets with her new sister, RuthAnn.

But the dream was just a fantasy. What did she intend to do—just barge in on them, a total stranger, introduce herself as Link's fiancée, and assume that they would open their arms and accept her? She couldn't do it. She would be an outsider, brazenly interrupting their grief to claim a part of the son and brother they had adored for twenty-four years. They would resent her, no doubt, and she would be pushed to the fringes, more isolated than ever.

Besides, she had to get on with her life. Fall term was about to begin, and whether she felt ready or not, she was determined to try.

Libba twisted the curl at the nape of her neck. It was getting better, she thought. At least the raw pain and anger had subsided, and the gaping hole in her heart had closed a bit. People kept telling her that time healed all wounds, but she didn't believe it. Time didn't heal anything—it just pushed you further from the immediacy of the anguish.

She opened the screen door and went out to sit in the porch swing. The endless fields washed scarlet in the setting sun. Vaguely, as if the idea came to her from a great distance, Libba realized that the color red no longer conjured up images of blood. Perhaps she was healing, after all. Perhaps in a few more months—or years—she would no longer think of Link the first thing in the morning and the last thing at night. Perhaps this throbbing misery would eventually subside and she would quit probing at it the way you unwillingly prod at an aching tooth.

But the dry socket would still be there . . . the emptiness . . . the chasm in her soul.

★ ★ ★

Charity Grevis looked up over the counter as Robinson Coltrain entered the Eden post office. Such a strange family, she thought, and getting stranger all the time. She hadn't seen Olivia Coltrain in months, and according to her sources, young Libba had left the house entirely and moved out to the farm on the old Coldwater Road with William and Bess. With her own eyes Charity had seen Libba there the day she went to deliver the telegrams, but she didn't know it was permanent, and as much as she had wanted to know the inside story, she didn't dare ask.

It galled Charity to have to hear the news from somebody else—especially that meddling busybody LaNelle Howard down at the Curl Up and Dye beauty salon. Didn't LaNelle know that being chief historian of the community was Charity's position? The woman practically gloated when she delivered the news—and in front of half the women in town, right in the middle of Charity's semiannual coloring job.

Well, Charity had one up on LaNelle now. She reached for the stack of mail in the Coltrain box, handed it to Robinson, and waited. On top of the pile was an official-looking envelope from a New York military clearing station. Maybe it was the final word about that poor boy, Link Winsom. And if it was, Charity intended to be the first to get the inside scoop.

"Not bad news, I hope, Robinson?" she prodded, putting on her most sympathetic smile. She watched, holding her breath, while he slit open the envelope. He read dispassionately, his face giving away nothing. Then, without blinking, he folded the pages neatly and slid them into an inside coat pocket.

"Some word from the front?" Charity murmured solicitously.

Robinson looked up and glared at her. "Family business," he growled. "And none of yours, I might add."

Charity blinked and swallowed hard. "I beg your pardon?"

Robinson narrowed his eyes. "Perhaps I should remind you, Mrs. Grevis, that the last time I checked, mail in this country is private, protected by federal law. As postmistress of this town, you are obligated to maintain that privacy. Do we understand one another?"

She felt her stomach knot, and she placed her hands firmly on the counter to keep them from shaking. "Why, Robinson, I wouldn't dream of prying into—"

"Of course you wouldn't." One side of his mouth quirked into an eerie smile, but his eyes were as cold as a snake's. "It's merely small-town gossip that you read all the postcards before you put them up, and that on occasion certain people have received envelopes with the flaps steamed open."

The knot in her stomach twisted. "I never—" Her voice shook, and she stopped.

Robinson's half smile vanished. "Certainly not," he said in a low, deliberate tone. "After all, that might cost you your job, mightn't it?"

He snatched up the rest of his mail from the counter, saluted her with it, and disappeared out the door.

★ ★ ★

When he left the post office, Robinson Coltrain went directly to the hardware store. Threading his way through narrow aisles flanked by rows of pipe and wire and bins of nuts and bolts, he entered the small office in the back of the store, shut the door, and sat down at his desk with a sigh.

That Grevis woman was absolutely insufferable. He was pretty certain she had been the one to spread the news all over the county that Tater had moved out and was living with his white-trash brother and that scarecrow of a wife. It was embarrassing and infuriating, not being able to keep a rein on his own daughter! And even Olivia had begun to show signs of rebellion, staying away for hours with no word of explanation when she returned. Twice last month he had gotten home only to find her gone—no dinner on the stove, no note saying where she'd gone . . . nothing. He suspected that she was out at the farm spending time with Libba, but she refused to answer his questions.

No one on the deacon board had said a word, of course, but Robinson could sense their disapproval. How could he be a leader of the church if he couldn't keep his own family under control?

Robinson figured he had put a stop to Charity Grevis's gossiping with his little show of power today. It was no idle threat. He had a friend or two in state government who could get an investigation under way within a week if he gave the word, and the old bag would be out on her ear before she knew what hit her. But it probably wouldn't be necessary to call in such favors. Charity needed the job, and before long would need the government pension even more. She'd keep her mouth shut from now on.

His daughter was another matter. He had been certain that if he gave her enough rope with this Winsom, she'd hang herself. He had even pretended to like the boy, to encourage their relationship. Winsom was smart enough, certainly, not to be trapped into marriage by a girl like Tater. When he left her, as Robinson was sure he would do, the girl would see that her daddy had been right about men all along.

Robinson hadn't considered the possibility that Winsom might really be in love with Tater, of course. The whole thing could have backfired on him. And nearly did.

But now he had an ace up his sleeve where she was concerned. He knew something she didn't know, and knowledge was power. He might not be able to keep her from embarrassing him, but he could certainly keep her in her place.

Robinson pulled the letter out of his inside pocket and spread it on the desk before him. So—Link Winsom, Tater's little soldier boy, was alive and recovering in a hospital in England! He scanned the letter, paying close attention to the details. Multiple wounds. Body cast. Shrapnel near the spine. And the fool had the impudence to write to her, to assume that she would still want to marry him.

The little idiot probably would, too. She would no doubt think that love would conquer all, that nothing could stand in the way of their happiness, that God would provide what they needed to survive.

God! Robinson shook his head. The very idea! He believed in God, of course, but this new *faith* of Libba's irritated him no end. Religion wasn't some kind of mystical experience—it was an institution, an essential element of civilized society, a mechanism to ensure control and maintain moral standards.

And *his* moral standards demanded that he keep a tight leash on his wife and daughter—for their own good, of course. No child of his was going to marry a cripple in a wheelchair. She might not be under his roof any longer, but she was still his daughter.

He fingered the pages of the letter, thinking. There was only one thing for him to do.

He reached into the bottom drawer of his desk and drew out a small steel strongbox. Opening it, he placed the letter inside, locked it, and put the key into his watch pocket. Then he replaced the box in the drawer and locked it as well.

Tater thought Winsom was dead. When the box of his personal effects had arrived, Robinson had told her that it was better this way, that now she could get on with her life. He had been right about that, and he was right about this present decision. He would protect her from herself, from any fool notions of obligation or commitment she might have.

He was her father, after all. Her welfare was his responsibility.

44

⭐ ⭐ ⭐

Stalag

Prison Labor Camp
Somewhere in Germany

Shoved roughly from behind, Owen Slaughter nearly tripped over the threshold as he fell into the darkened barracks on the far perimeter of the prison camp. It was the third time he had been moved, carted about in the stinking boxcar of a German train. He had no idea where he was, and by this time he didn't care much. One stalag was pretty much like the next—lice-infested death traps controlled by swaggering Krauts who delighted in torturing their enemies. At first he had attempted to stand up to them, to maintain his dignity and his honor. But after two or three beatings and three days of solitary confinement in a sweatbox, he forgot about dignity and simply began to concentrate on staying alive. He jumped when they commanded him to jump, refrained from talking back, and kept his eyes on the ground.

The door shut behind him, and Owen gripped the nearest bunk and waited for his vision to adjust to the darkness. The room smelled strongly of mice and human excrement. He suppressed a gag reflex and tried to catch his breath.

Out of the dim recesses of the barracks, several men began to come toward him, watching him curiously, saying nothing. Their faces, shrouded in shadow, looked eerie and unnatural. Most were painfully thin, with dark circles under their eyes.

At last a tall, emaciated man with a ragged mustache stepped into the weak light of a single bulb. "Leftenant Colonel Marshall Effington," he said in a clipped accent. "RAF." The man saluted, then extended his hand. "It seems I'm the ranking officer of this little cadre, unless—" He broke off, raising his eyebrows in question.

Owen shook his head. "Master Sergeant Owen Slaughter. American Infantry." He sagged against the bunk. "OK if I sit down, Colonel?"

"By all means, my good man. And call me Marsh. We don't observe the formalities much around here."

Owen sank onto the bunk as the other men gathered around him, introducing themselves and shaking his hand. Two more Brits, one Aussie, and three Americans.

Then the questions began. Where had he been captured? What was going on at the front? How long had it been since he'd heard news from home? Any chance that the Allies were on their way?

He shook his head and held up a hand. It was the same in every camp. And his answer was always the same: "I don't know."

The fact was, Owen didn't know anything. His dog tags told him who he was, but beyond that, nothing. The past was not a blur for him, but a blank. He remembered coming to on a hillside . . . in France, he told them. Some Kraut soldier was pointing a rifle at him. He didn't know where he was, how he had gotten there, or what unit he belonged to. At that point he didn't even remember his own name. By now he was getting used to the name, but it still seemed foreign, as if it belonged to someone else and he was just borrowing it for a while.

"You don't remember *anything?*" one of the Americans persisted.

"Nothing," Owen said miserably. "Nothing except what has happened since I was captured—and I wish I could forget that."

Someone handed him a canteen, and he drank eagerly of the stale, tepid water. It seemed he was always thirsty, could never get enough. His throat hurt and his eyes itched, and he wished he could just lie down and sleep forever.

"C'mon, mate," the Aussie was saying. "You'll bunk over here." The man drew Owen to his feet and led him to a lower bunk on the opposite side of the room. With a sigh he leaned back on the filthy mattress ticking.

It was horrible, not remembering. Worse than the beatings. Worse, even, than the sweatbox. It was like being in a huge black hole with no light and no escape. His mind constantly darted about like a wounded bird, trying to find something to hang on to. A vague image flitted through his mind— something about a flood, and a bird flying, searching for a place to land. But there was no place. Only darkness, emptiness. A terrible, unutterable loneliness.

A tear seeped from the corner of his eye and tracked down his cheek. He had to stop thinking about it . . . somehow. If he didn't stop thinking, he would go mad.

★ ★ ★

Owen awoke to find one of the Americans standing over his bunk—a homey-looking fellow, salt-of-the-earth type. Probably a farmer. He looked to be about thirty, but it was hard to tell. The war—particularly in a prison camp—tended to age people beyond their years. But this guy, apparently, hadn't forgotten how to smile yet, and when he did, the expression gave him a youthful, hopeful appearance.

"I brought you something to eat," the American said, holding out a rough bowl and a chunk of brown bread. "The soup's pretty thin, but it'll keep body and soul together."

He sat down on the edge of the bunk and handed the bowl to Owen. "My name's Charlie," he said. "Charlie Coltrain."

Something triggered in Owen's brain, a brief flash. Then it was gone. What was it about this Charlie? The name? The farm-boy face? The accent? Obviously, he wasn't from Iowa. Texas, maybe, or someplace in the South.

Owen's mind raced. Maybe he was from the South, too. Maybe . . . but, no. He didn't have that accent. And there were a million Charlies in the world. He had to stop grasping at straws or he'd go nuts.

He looked up to find Charlie staring at him, a strange mixture of curiosity and compassion on his face.

"How long have you been here, Charlie?"

"About three months. I was captured right after D day, near Omaha Beach."

Omaha. Again the flash, like a camera bulb going off in his eyes. But no illumination.

"You seem to be doing pretty well. Not like some of the guys I've seen in camps."

Charlie shrugged, and a strange light came into his face. "As long as there's life, there's hope," he murmured, half to himself. Then he looked back at Owen. "It's not so bad here, really. The Krauts torment us—just like everywhere else, I guess. But we get fed regularly, and apart from the idle time on our hands, we do all right." He leaned forward. "Still, we've heard things—disturbing things. . . ."

Owen sat up and leaned against the splintered wood frame of the bunk. "Like what?"

"Marsh—Colonel Effington—speaks German. The Krauts don't know it, so they talk pretty freely around us. From conversations Marsh has overheard, it seems that the Nazis have set up a whole series of—" he paused and shook his head miserably— "death camps."

Owen felt his stomach lurch. "For prisoners?"

Charlie looked away. "No . . . for German civilians. For their own people—can you imagine that?"

"Who? *Why?*"

"Hitler hasn't exactly been keeping his plans a secret from the world," Charlie said. "Years ago, when this whole Third Reich thing first started, he apparently declared his intention to purify the Aryan race for posterity, to—"

Confused, Owen stopped him midsentence. "Hold on a minute. Who's this Hitler? I've heard that name before—some kind of greeting the Germans use with one another."

Charlie smiled. "I forgot. You don't remember any of this."

"I'm afraid not."

"Didn't any of the guys at the other camps try to fill you in?"

Owen shook his head. "They were all too busy just trying to survive. Nobody seemed particularly interested in making friends with a nut case."

"Don't I know it." Charlie leaned closer. "Hitler is a madman—certifiably insane. He has this idea that all so-called corrupting influences must be purged from the pure German bloodlines. That means Jews, particularly, but also the mentally ill, the retarded, homosexuals, the aged, the sick. And not just men. Women and children, too. Even babies."

The very idea chilled Owen to the core of his soul, and he shivered. His appetite vanished. Slowly he laid the bread and the bowl of soup on the foot of his cot. "And all of these people go to the death camps?"

"Many of them. According to what Marsh has heard, there are labor camps, too, and experimental laboratories. They're killing people by the thousands. The guards here make jokes about some of the 'corrective surgeries' being performed. Brain surgery on live people—" Charlie paused. "Without anesthetics."

"Do the Allies know about this?"

"We don't know," Charlie said softly. "Marsh doesn't think so. But they will. The whole world will know when our troops find these camps." His voice grew quiet, grave. "We didn't realize it when the war started, but this is what the fighting's all about."

"What do you mean?"

Charlie looked at Owen intently. "I'm going to tell you something almost nobody else knows—and trust you to keep it to yourself. I was wounded at Messina, in Italy. A superficial wound in my arm. But I stayed in the hospital for months." He tapped his head with a forefinger. "Shell shock." He lowered his gaze. "If I had been here, in Germany, I'd be dead by now—probably in pieces on some mad scientist's examining table." Charlie looked into Owen's eyes. "I know what it's like to be crazy, Slaughter. And I know that God still had a purpose for my life, even when I wanted to die." His eyes misted over, and for a moment he couldn't go on. "Everyone has a purpose," he continued at last. *"Everyone.* Even people the rest of society sees as useless. That's what this war is all about—guaranteeing people the freedom to live their lives without interference, protecting the weak and the powerless from authorities that would try to destroy them."

Charlie smiled wryly and shrugged. "I don't know why I'm telling you all this, Slaughter, except—" He paused. "Except that losing your memory must feel a lot like going crazy. You don't know what's real and what's not. I guess I just want you to know that you've got a friend here—someone who understands a little bit of what you're experiencing. You're not alone."

For the first time in months, Owen Slaughter felt a glimmer of light falling into his dark hole. *You're not alone.* The words played over and over in his mind, like a hymn, like a prayer . . .

Like a promise.

★ ★ ★

Charlie Coltrain wasn't quite sure why he had opened his soul to the newcomer. Maybe it was just what he had said to Slaughter—that because of his experiences, he could understand a little of what the man was going through.

But he suspected it was more.

For one thing, he *liked* Slaughter. There was something about the man—something honest and vulnerable—that a fellow didn't see every day. Maybe it was the loss of memory. Maybe having a clean slate for a mind cleared everything else up, too, set a person free from having to live up to other people's expectations. If you didn't remember what you were like in the past, how people responded to you and categorized you, you didn't have to keep up the charade. You had a fresh start, a second chance to be whoever you wanted to be.

Charlie smiled to himself. He had been given a second chance, too. He remembered his past, of course, and when he first met Slaughter, he had experienced a pang of envy or two for the man's memory loss. But if he was honest with himself, he'd have to admit that he wouldn't really *want* to forget. He wanted to remember, for the rest of his life, where he was when God reached down into his pit of despair and rescued him. Now that he was out of his own black hole, he dared not disregard the fact that God's grace had brought him to where he was today.

The irony of the thought made Charlie laugh. Who on earth would believe it was God's grace that had landed him in a German prisoner-of-war camp? To someone on the outside, this would seem more like God's judgment, divine retribution—the Almighty's punishment for his sins.

But Charlie knew better. In the months of his captivity, he'd had a lot of time to think about his life. And looking back, he could see the hand of God guiding him, answering his prayers—not in the way Charlie had expected, but answering nevertheless.

Back in Italy, and in the hospital in Birmingham, Charlie had wanted to die—had prayed to die. He got his chance, of course, on the beach after D day. But he survived. And not only did he live, he was given a *reason* to live.

All the events that led up to his capture formed a collage in Charlie's mind. Rescuing the three little French children . . . keeping Sergeant Ordway alive until the medics got to him . . . comforting Johnny Silver in his last agonizing moments of life . . . fulfilling Johnny's last request to look for his friend Harry. Any one of those incidents would have been sufficient reason to live. Any one of them could have represented God's purpose in getting him back to the front. Not to die but to keep living, and to have a positive impact on someone else's life.

When Charlie looked back on his past, he saw how every experience fit like a puzzle piece into the next, forming the larger picture of God's work in his life. Maybe God did use him to rescue those children, to keep Ordway alive, to help Johnny Silver make a graceful exit from this life. But more important, God used those people, those experiences, to change Charlie Coltrain.

When he considered it that way, Charlie couldn't help believing that God had a purpose for him in this camp as well—a purpose that might influence someone but that certainly would draw Charlie closer to the God he was learning to trust. Even in this place of darkness, a light shone in Charlie Coltrain's soul. He had hope.

Yes, God's grace had brought him here. God's grace would take him out again—if not through liberation, through death—and then Charlie's original prayer would have been answered. But it would be on God's terms, not

Charlie's. And Charlie would go into eternity a different man from the one he had been when he began his quest to die.

In the meantime, he was here, he was alive, and he suspected that God had brought someone into his path for a purpose. Owen Slaughter.

45

☆ ☆ ☆

Eliminate the Negative

Freddy Sturgis sat alone at a table in the Ole Miss grill with his back to the early morning light. On the art pad in front of him were sketches of faces—a sorority coed with long blonde hair; a soldier in uniform, surrounded by three adoring girls; the old black woman behind the counter, her countenance mapped with deep lines, her wide grin showing a gap where her left incisor should have been.

The old woman was decidedly the most interesting. Her face, as Freddy had drawn it, revealed decades of hardship, but her eyes bore the unmistakable gleam of joy in living. It was good, he mused, studying the sketch with an objective eye. The nose wasn't quite right yet, but he had caught the expression perfectly.

Freddy took a rubber eraser from his pocket, eradicated the offending nose, and sketched in a new one—more rounded on the sides, and a little broader and flatter. As he worked, his eyes flicked from the pad in front of him to the woman's face, then back again.

It was too bad, Freddy thought absently, that you couldn't do the same with living, breathing people—rub out the offending spots, erase their pain, keep working until you made everything perfect and flawless. He was thinking of Libba Coltrain, of course.

Freddy would have given anything—even his art—to relieve Libba of the suffering she had endured. In the past few months they had become close friends, and Freddy agonized with her over Link's death. He no longer harbored any jealousy about Libba's obvious love for Link Winsom. When Libba had abandoned him for the other man, God had done something

280

miraculous in Freddy, setting him free to discover himself and find his place in the world. It was all part of the plan. And now God had given Libba back to Freddy—on honest terms, this time—as a friend with whom he could share his heart.

He had missed her when she went back to Eden to her cousin Willie's farm. He was glad, certainly, that she was out from under the thumb of that dominating father of hers, and he understood her need to be with family, particularly Willie and Mabel, and with Madge, who could understand her loss better than he could. But her sudden departure had left an emptiness in his life, a gap that he had filled with work—paintings and sketches, and even a little sculpture. It took up time, and it was emotionally satisfying in its own way, but it could not take her place.

And he had to admit, both to himself and to God, that he had been a little envious at first—jealous of the fact that others, like Thelma Breckinridge, were the ones helping Libba to heal and grow spiritually. He had confessed his jealousy, a little sheepishly, and in the end God had given him peace. It didn't matter, after all, what channel God used to draw Libba closer to him and comfort her, as long as it was happening.

He had seen Libba several times since she went back to Eden—once very soon after she received the news about Link, when she came back to campus to drop her summer term classes. She hadn't tried to hide her pain from him, and for that he was grateful. They had cried together and prayed together. And at least once a week during the summer he had gone down to Eden or met her in Grenada for dinner, and each time she seemed stronger—still grieving, but more in control.

Now, at last, she was coming back. He was picking her up in Eden this evening. She would have to make up the first couple of weeks of the term, but she intended, she said in her letter, to get back into life, to finish her degree. Out of respect for her "situation," Libba's landlady had held her apartment for her over the summer, so Libba would be within walking distance of Freddy's little house on East Jefferson.

Freddy's heart soared at the idea of having Libba back in Oxford. He loved her deeply—not in a romantic sense, but as a friend . . . his best friend. God had changed him, had changed her, and had forged between them a very special—and unusual—bond. Freddy fully intended to nurture that friendship and to be there for her . . . always. Maybe even help erase some of her pain.

Freddy peered down at the sketch pad in front of him. Without realizing what he was doing, he had altered the old black woman's face—taken out the crevices, smoothed the skin, made her young again. Young and beautiful.

As if she had gone back in time, the years had disappeared. The craggy lines that spoke of hardship and suffering had vanished. But something else had happened, too. The character was gone . . . the creases of her smile . . . the laugh lines about her temples. And the eyes, once full of life and joy, stared back at him, black and vacant and desolate.

★ ★ ★

Early afternoon sun slanted through the smoke-hazed glass door of the Paradise Garden Cafe. Mabel Rae Coltrain—or Rae, as she now liked to be called—drummed her hands impatiently on the table in the back booth as she waited for Thelma to come over with the coffeepot. Her dark eyes danced with excitement, but Thelma knew it wasn't coffee she wanted. It was conversation. And Thelma would have bet her title to the Paradise Garden that she also knew the subject—Andrew Laporte.

"Come sit down!" Rae demanded, biting her lip with anticipation. "Forget the coffee. I've got something wonderful to tell you."

"Let me guess. The war is over? Who won?"

Rae frowned. "Stop kidding around, Thelma. This is serious."

Thelma worked hard at suppressing a smile. "Sorry, hon. I couldn't help myself."

"Well, try, will you?" Rae accepted the cup of coffee Thelma pushed across the table toward her, and then sat quiet for a minute, fiddling nervously with the handle of the cup.

"All right, darlin'," Thelma said, wedging herself into the other side of the booth. "You have my undivided attention. What gives?"

"It's Drew."

Thelma rolled her eyes in mock surprise. "Really? I never would have guessed."

"Stop that!" Rae poked Thelma's arm, then fixed her with an intent look. "He's coming home!"

Thelma threw back her head and laughed. "That's wonderful, Mabel—I mean, Rae. When's the big day?"

"We're not sure. Two or three weeks, maybe a month. And—get this. He's coming *here,* to Mississippi, to meet Mama and Daddy. Then he wants me to go to New Orleans with him to meet his family." Suddenly Rae's joy-filled countenance crumpled into despair. "Oh, Thelma, what am I going to do?"

Thelma shook her head. This emotional ride was a bit too much for her brain to take in—rather like the rickety old roller coaster at the state fair in Memphis. "I'm not sure I follow," she said after a minute or two. "This wonderful man has been corresponding with you for months. He's declared his love for you and wants to marry you. What is the problem exactly?"

A dark cloud settled over Rae's face. "It's—it's . . . well, you know."

"I'm afraid I don't."

"It's . . . Mama and Daddy. The farm. Everything!"

What on earth was the girl talking about? Then it hit her. "You're *ashamed* of them?"

Rae's cheeks flamed. "Well, don't put it like that, Thelma."

"And just how would you put it?" Thelma asked.

"You don't understand."

"I understand perfectly well, thank you. Your lieutenant, Andrew Laporte, is from a fine, well-heeled old New Orleans family—name, money, prestige, probably a fountain in the courtyard. In comparison, your family—your wonderful, loving family—is a clan of dirt-poor, undereducated, unsophisticated cotton-choppers."

Rae lifted her eyebrows. "Maybe you should be the writer, Thelma Breckinridge. You do have a way with words."

"And you're ashamed of your kin."

"Yes," she whispered. "I guess I am."

"Answer me one question," Thelma said, leaning forward. "You've told your lieutenant about your family, I assume, and about yourself. You've written to him all these months. You've sent him a picture. Does he or does he not love you for yourself, for who you are on the inside?"

"He does," Rae admitted. "He says he does."

"Do you believe him?"

"Yes."

"Then what does it matter if the house needs paint or the rugs are a little shabby or your daddy's truck is in need of a new carburetor? You are from fine stock, Mabel Rae Coltrain—good Christian, down-to-earth stock. You've got nothing to be ashamed of."

"I guess not."

Thelma narrowed her eyes. "Would you be less embarrassed if Robinson Coltrain, with his fine house and his nice little hardware business, was your father?"

Rae's eyes widened in horror, and she began to giggle. "Well, when you put it that way—"

"I thought so."

"Wouldn't that be just awful, Thelma? If Uncle Robinson was my daddy? I can't think of anything worse."

Rae began to laugh, and Thelma leaned back in the booth and watched her. She had become a remarkable young woman, Miss Rae Coltrain—even if she did have occasional lapses of foolishness now and then. She would make Andrew Laporte a splendid wife. And no doubt she would give his high-and-mighty family a run for their money.

★ ★ ★

Madge Simpson, scrubbing down the counter with six-month-old Mickey on her hip, looked up as the bell over the door of the cafe jingled. She squinted at the clock. It was a little after five—an odd time for Libba Coltrain to be entering, especially pushing a huge suitcase in ahead of her. Libba gave the case a final shove across the linoleum with her foot, left it by the door, and came over to the counter.

"Ibba!" Mickey squealed, reaching out for her. Madge handed him to her friend, grateful to be relieved of the weight for a few minutes. He had started to crawl early, and if she put him down, he could disappear in a matter of seconds—under the customers' feet, behind the piano . . . wherever she would have a hard time getting to him. Already he was picking up a few words—garbled, perhaps, but words nevertheless. It was a little hard to tell the difference between *Ella* and *Illy* and *Ibba* and *Ivy,* but Thelma, Willie, Libba, and Ivory all seemed quite sure that Mickey understood their names and distinguished between them.

His favorite word by far was "Uh-oh." When he had gotten into something or made a mess, he would look up at her, flash his enormous hazel eyes, and say, "Uh-oh." It usually worked, too, the little conniver. Madge could hardly help laughing when he was so cute. Michael had better get home soon, before this child was spoiled beyond all hope.

As if Libba had read Madge's mind, she turned from playing with Mickey and said, "Have you heard any more from Stork?"

"Just the two letters," she answered after a moment's hesitation. Even after all these months, she still had trouble thinking of her husband as *Stork.* For that matter, she had a little trouble thinking of him as her *husband.* They loved each other, but they had been together so little. And as eager as Madge was to have him back again, she couldn't help being a little apprehensive. What if he had changed? What if she had? Well, that second question wasn't even up for debate. She *knew* she had changed. Life on her own, here in Eden with Mickey and Thelma, had challenged her, brought her out of her shell. Motherhood had matured her. She wasn't a girl any longer. She was a woman—and a strong one at that. She hoped the changes wouldn't be too much for them to adjust to.

"Madge? Are you all right?" Libba's voice brought her out of her reverie.

"Sure, I'm fine. I was just thinking." She smiled and patted Libba's hand. "The last letter I got, Michael said he should be coming home soon, but he didn't know what *soon* would be. Apparently he hasn't gotten my letters—it went to his parents' address."

Libba raised an eyebrow. "I'm surprised his mother forwarded it to you."

"It was probably Dad Simpson who sent it. He has my address, and he has been known to stand up to her on occasion."

"Well, I'm glad you got it, anyway. You must have been relieved to find out that he was all right."

"His arm was pretty mangled, it seems, but he says it's healing well. All things considered, he was pretty lucky. Not like—" Madge stopped, wincing inwardly. How could she be so stupid?

Libba sighed. "You can say his name, Madge. Not like Link."

"I'm sorry, Libba. I never intended—"

"Of course you didn't. It's all right. I'm getting used to it. And, frankly, I'm tired of everybody walking on eggshells around me. Link is gone. He *died.* See? Saying it isn't so bad. Besides, sometimes I wish somebody would talk about him. People are so careful about avoiding his name, it's like he never existed." She paused and tickled Mickey under the chin. He rewarded her with a grin and a giggle, and she smiled in return. "Did Stork's letter say anything about Link . . . about what happened?"

Madge shook her head. "Not a word. Maybe it's too painful for him to talk about."

"I suppose," Libba murmured.

"How's Willie doing?"

"Willie," Libba said deliberately, "is doing just fine, if you ask her. If you ask me, she's just closed up like a steel safe."

"Closed up?"

Libba avoided Madge's eyes. "This may have something to do with your news that Stork is all right and on his way home," she said hesitantly. "And I think it has a lot to do with Mabel Rae's news about her New Orleans lieutenant. Poor Mabel. Do you know that she didn't want to tell Willie about Drew at all? She was afraid it might hurt her. She's been sitting on this for months, not saying a word. I think the only reason she finally told us was because he's coming here, and she couldn't exactly get married without anyone knowing about it."

Libba turned and looked at Madge. "Don't get me wrong. Willie is very happy for you—for both of you. But she says that marriage is out of the question for her. Her Owen is the only man she could ever love. Once she got past her anger and pain a little bit, she went back to being Willie—strong, in-control Willie. Now she has decided that she'll just be an old maid schoolteacher for the rest of her life."

"She'll change her mind."

"Maybe. Maybe not. You know how stubborn Willie can be."

Willie's not the only Coltrain woman with that particular characteristic, Madge thought. But she didn't say so. Instead, she asked, "What about you, Libba?"

"What about me?"

"What are you going to do?"

Libba slid Mickey back over the counter to Madge and stood up. She pointed to the suitcase by the door. "I," she said dramatically, "am going on with my life."

"You're leaving?"

Libba nodded. "I'm already two weeks behind, but Ole Miss has agreed to let me start the semester. Willie dropped me off, and Freddy Sturgis should be here any minute to take me back to Oxford. I just came to say good-bye."

Madge's heart wrenched. Libba had become like a sister to her, like an adoring aunt to little Mickey. She had shared Libba's grief, prayed for her, and watched her grow. They had, truly, become a family, and now one by one the family was moving apart.

She came out from behind the counter and awkwardly hugged Libba, with Mickey between them. "I hate to see you go. I'll miss you so much."

Libba took a deep breath. "I'll miss you, too, Madge. And Thelma, and Willie, and—everybody." She stroked Mickey's cheek. "And especially you, you little charmer. But I need to get back to school, to do something with myself. I can't sit around on Uncle William's porch forever. And Oxford's not that far away. I'll be back—soon. I promise."

A car pulled up outside, and Libba went to the door and picked up her suitcase. "Pray for me," she said, her eyes resting longingly on the baby. "Give Thelma my love, and tell her I'm sorry I missed her." Libba opened the door. "I'll be in touch."

The door closed behind her, and the jingling bell echoed into silence. Madge looked around. Suddenly the Paradise Garden Cafe seemed very empty indeed.

46

★ ★ ★

Link to the Almighty

A dark cloud of misery had hovered over Link all day, and he knew why. Stork was leaving—walking out of this hospital, boarding the next ship back to the States, hopping the fastest train from New York City to Eden, Mississippi. Actually, he couldn't get to Eden from New York, Link mused. He'd have to get off at Tillatoba and hitch a ride.

In spite of his black mood, Link smiled. He remembered the last time he and Stork had been to the station at Tillatoba . . . that fateful day Stork began his cross-country trip to see his baby born . . . and crusty, tender old Major Mansfield paid the guy's train fare.

That trip hadn't turned out so well for Stork—interrupted by their orders to ship out—but undoubtedly this one would be better. Madge's letters had finally caught up with him. She was in Eden with the baby, on her own, working with Thelma Breckinridge in the cafe. A gutsy girl, Stork's Madge. He was lucky to have her.

Link closed his eyes and leaned back on the pillow, his mind conjuring up images of Stork's reunion with his wife and son. He could imagine Madge standing on the station platform in the autumn mist, with the baby in her arms . . . a character right out of a William Powell movie. She would search the train windows with eager eyes, watching for a glimpse of him. Stork would step off the train with his bag over his shoulder, catch sight of them, and run, in slow motion, toward the woman he loved, toward his destiny, toward his future. . . .

Link sighed. Madge and Mickey wouldn't be at the platform, of course, unless they wanted to wait for days for the right train to come. The reunion would probably take place in the Paradise Garden Cafe, with Stork straggling in, disheveled and dirty, lugging his duffel bag behind him. He would probably catch Madge off guard, with her hair sticking up and meat loaf sauce on her apron, and Mickey fussy in dirty diapers.

That was a more likely scenario, but Link preferred the romantic one. He closed his eyes again. This time Libba Coltrain stood on the platform, in a plum-colored suit, clutching his letters to her bosom, waiting . . . for him. The train screeched to a halt in a cloud of steam, and he leaned out the doorway to see her emerge from the mist, running toward him, crying. . . .

Suddenly Link realized that *he* was the one who was crying. A tear slid down his cheek and lodged in his ear, and he shook his head angrily. He might as well drop the romance and be realistic. This was a scene he would never play. If and when he did get home, it would be flat on his back, hauled around by orderlies and transported in an army ambulance. And Libba, apparently, would *not* be waiting for him—not at the station at Tillatoba, not at the Paradise Garden Cafe, not anywhere.

Link simply couldn't understand it. He had written to her, explaining in specific detail what had happened to him and why it had taken him so long to get in touch with her—although he had hedged a little on that issue. Letter after letter—sometimes three or four a day—declaring his love for her and asking her to wait for him. He had written pages about his new relationship with God, about how the Lord had comforted and sustained him during his convalescence. He had told her about his dreams of her and how he wanted them to share their lives together, trusting God to help them through any difficult times they might have to face.

He had written. He had been honest. He had risked everything.

And there was no answer.

Nothing. Not a single word from Libba Coltrain.

There were only two possibilities he could see, two explanations for her silence. Either she couldn't stand the thought of living with a cripple, or all his talk about God made her think he had become some kind of wild-eyed fanatic. Well, he supposed it couldn't be helped, in either case. Like it or not, his body had been wounded—severely—and he might never recover the use of his legs. On the other hand, his soul had been restored—radically—and he could not deny the importance of his relationship with God.

Link rapped his knuckles on the body cast and stared absently at the water-stained ceiling tiles. *Lord,* he prayed silently, *I don't understand this, and you know it hurts like crazy. But this is reality. I can't do anything about my legs, and I won't deny you or demean the gift you've given me by trying to minimize your importance in my life. Besides, I can't build a life on pretense,*

*trying to be what somebody else wants me to be. Help me accept things the way
they are and trust you. And if you could give me some little clue about where
I'm supposed to go from here, I'd sure appreciate it.*

Link exhaled loudly. He felt a little better, more at peace. He had discovered, much to his surprise, that even when prayer didn't improve the
situation, it seemed to make a difference in him. Just the act of telling God
what was on his mind relieved the pressure. Maybe that's what prayer was
all about—expressing your heart, your concerns, to the Lord so that you
could focus on God's character rather than on the circumstances. People
said that "prayer changes things," as if the act of praying were some kind
of magical incantation to get what you wanted. Link was pretty new to all
this faith stuff, but he was more inclined to believe that prayer changed
people—from the inside out. Maybe that's what God had in mind all along.

He leaned back and closed his eyes, listening. God didn't always answer
immediately or specifically, and Link no longer expected it, but he did
intend to respect the Lord enough to give him a chance to speak.

A few scenes drifted through his mind like clouded images in a movie
dream-sequence. In the first, he was with Libba, but he quickly thrust that
one aside. His imagination wandered on to other options, and he envisioned
himself at home, in Missouri, with his father and his sister RuthAnn.

Link smiled. No matter what happened next, he was determined to spend
time with his dad, to get to know him better. Now that he had come to God
for himself, Link saw his father's faith—and his career—in a whole new
light. Bennett Winsom was not just a softhearted do-gooder of a lawyer who
didn't have the guts for litigation and couldn't cut it in the real world. He
was a man who had his priorities in order—a man who loved God and his
family and who poured himself out for people who couldn't help themselves. For the first time in his life, Link understood his father's legal career
for what it was—a ministry to those who needed help.

Bennett Winsom could have been a wealthy man. He was incisively
intelligent, charming and popular, and he carried himself with style and
dignity. If he had chosen, he could have been a partner in a big Kansas City
firm . . . maybe even governor of the state, or a senator. Instead, he had
spent his life in a crowded two-room office and in dismal county court-
rooms, defending the rights of the poor and the underprivileged.

Link's father didn't flaunt his faith or set himself up as some legal messiah
to the poor and downtrodden. He just did what was right and went about
quietly living out his faith. Sometimes he got paid real money; more often
he came home with chickens and bushels of beans. But the family never

went hungry—either physically or emotionally. Bennett Winsom was, for all of them, a walking, breathing example of the love of Christ.

Suddenly Link opened his eyes. Perhaps this was where God was leading him! He couldn't see himself settling down with anyone besides Libba, but he certainly could imagine going back to Missouri, attending law school, and working in his father's practice. You didn't need legs to be a lawyer—you needed heart and soul and mind. And, in his father's case, a deep and unwavering commitment to God.

That might just be Link's answer. When he was released, he would go back to St. Joe, recover, and begin his law school studies. It all made so much sense, now that he thought about it. RuthAnn would be delighted. His father would be proud, and grateful to God for his son's commitment. There, Link would be surrounded by people who loved him. Family. All except . . .

He pushed the thought of Libba to the back of his mind. Her silence had told him what he needed to know. It was time to stop dreaming about something that was never going to happen and get on with his life.

★ ★ ★

Stork Simpson stood at the foot of Link's bed for a minute, watching him sleep. Gently he lowered his duffel bag to the floor. Link looked so peaceful, lying there with his mouth open, snoring softly. From the chest up you'd think there was nothing wrong with him . . . just another weary soldier getting some much needed shut-eye.

Stork reached into his pocket and fingered his transfer papers. He was going back to Eden, back to Camp McCrane to serve out his term as assistant to Major Roland Mansfield. He had been promoted to second lieutenant—as had Link—and the bars weighed down his collar. On his chest he wore the most coveted award among GIs, a silver Master Marksmanship Rifle, for exemplary duty in combat. His Purple Heart was in his bag, nestled in a box amid his neatly folded underwear.

Well, this was it. At 1400 hours he would leave for Scotland. Tomorrow morning he would board a transport ship for the States. In ten days he would be back in Mississippi, holding his wife and kissing his baby for the first time. The war would still be going on—for how long, only God knew—but Michael Simpson would be home. He had made it. He had survived.

Admittedly, Stork had a little apprehension about seeing Madge and little Mickey. His heart yearned for them, but he wasn't quite sure what it would be like, being a family man with responsibilities, a husband, a father. He had changed, certainly, and no doubt Madge had, too. A lot of adjustments lay ahead for them.

He took a deep breath, and his eyes traveled down the length of his friend's body cast. *Everything* had changed. Owen and Coker were dead. Link might be in a wheelchair for the rest of his days. And even if he recovered, they would undoubtedly go their separate ways, creating individual lives with different friends and experiences they could no longer share. It was sad, this parting. It marked the end of an era.

The war had made different men out of all of them, thrusting them out of their safe little cocoons of innocence into a tumult of bloodshed and death. He would never forget seeing Coker die in that mine crater, watching as Link went down amid a volley of machine-gun fire and hand grenades. He would always recall that last moment when Owen Slaughter disappeared behind the chateau, calling that he would catch up with them as soon as he could. He knew the memories would never go away. He would live with the ravages of that ordeal for the rest of his life.

But he remembered the good times, too—the laughter, the bending of the rules, the feeling of safety when he knew his buddies were behind him on patrol. God willing, he could cling to those positive images. Friendships forged in wartime last forever, people said, and he knew it was true. He would not forget. He would carry these friends in his heart as long as he lived.

Stork moved closer to the bed and tweaked at the toes sticking out from Link's cast. His spirits sank when he remembered . . . no feeling. No response.

"Link?" he said quietly.

Link's eyes fluttered open. "Hey, Stork."

"You doing OK, pal?"

"Sure, I'm doing fine. Just a little tired, that's all." He blinked. "What time is it?"

Stork glanced at his watch. "Around 1350."

Link adjusted the pillow behind his neck and surveyed Stork. "I hardly recognized you in that dress uniform. You look like a real human being. Nice, very nice."

Stork did an awkward pirouette and bowed from the waist. "Thank you, m'lord. I did it just for you."

"Sure you did. Well, you're gorgeous. If you weren't already married, I'd propose to you myself." Link grinned and gave an exaggerated wink.

"Gee, thanks. I'll keep that in mind." Stork lowered his head to avoid Link's gaze. "I ship out this afternoon."

"I know."

Stork heaved a ragged sigh. Saying good-bye was going to be harder than he'd imagined. "You'll be right behind me, Link. You'll see."

Link looked at the ceiling. "Uh-huh. Look, Stork, when you get back to Eden—"

"I know." Stork held up a hand. "If I see Libba, don't talk to her about you."

"You may not see her. She may be gone back to college or . . . or something." Link's eyes flitted about the room, coming at last to rest on Stork's face. "She always wanted to finish her degree," he said, half to himself. "She's very intelligent, you know."

"I know." Stork shifted from one foot to the other and twisted his wedding ring.

Link looked up, a pleading expression on his face. "Don't let on about how I responded to her not writing, OK? If you do see her, just tell her . . . tell her that I wish her all the best."

"I'll tell her."

"And call my father, will you? I've written to him, but he'd appreciate hearing from you. Once I get released from here, you can reach me in St. Joe."

"You're not coming to Mississippi?" A wide, empty hole opened up inside Stork. "I'll be at Camp McCrane for a few months yet. Madge would hate it if you didn't come see us and the baby."

Link squeezed his eyes shut. "I can't, Stork. Not at first. Maybe someday." He sighed, then brightened a bit. "But you'll be moving back to Missouri when you get discharged, won't you?"

"I don't know." Stork shrugged. "Madge and I haven't discussed that part of it. She's gotten pretty settled in Eden, and I gather Thelma Breckinridge has become sort of a grandmother to Mickey."

Link chuckled. "Now there's a thought that would put your mother right through the roof!"

"Mother," Stork said through gritted teeth, "can go *live* on the roof, for all I care. The way she's treated Madge, she doesn't deserve to be called a grandmother." He paused. "If we decide to stay in Eden, well, she can just deal with it."

He looked at his watch again. "It's time for me to go, Link."

Link shifted his eyes. "All right." He held out a hand. "Take care of yourself, buddy. I'm going to miss you."

Tears filled Stork's eyes, and he blinked them back. "I'll miss you, too, Link—more than you know." He reached for Link's hand and felt himself pulled forward into an awkward hug around the body cast and his own immobile arm. The warmth and sincerity of the embrace embarrassed Stork a little, but he didn't push away. Instead he held on, letting his tears fall on Link's bare shoulder. This was his best friend, and although he couldn't say the words out loud, he was determined to let Link know that he loved him.

At last Stork withdrew, wiping his cheeks with the heel of his hand. "I promised myself I wouldn't do this."

Link cleared his throat. "It's OK," he said shakily. "Don't forget me."

Stork put his hand on Link's shoulder and gripped hard. "I could never forget you," he said, then crooked a grin at his friend. "You're the guy who kept me out of OCS and got me assigned to—"

Link began to shake with laughter. "Gas school!"

"Believe me," Stork said, "I could *never* forget that!"

"But you got your bars anyway, Lieutenant." Link reached up and fingered Stork's collar.

"No thanks to you."

"We had some good times, didn't we?" Link said quietly.

"The best. And some not-so-good times, too."

"But we got through them. We survived." Link smiled up at Stork. "Have a safe trip. Give Madge and the baby a hug for me."

"I'll do that." Stork hefted his duffel bag and turned to go.

"Pray for me," Link called out behind him.

Stork glanced over his shoulder. "I'll do that, too." He walked to the doorway of the ward, turned for one last look, and waved good-bye.

"I love you, Link Winsom," he muttered under his breath. Then he stepped into the hallway and began his long journey home.

47

★ ★ ★

The Freddy Factor

Libba Coltrain smiled at Freddy Sturgis as they walked slowly along the sidewalk on Jefferson Street toward the ridge that sloped off into the cemetery. A warm autumn sun shone on her face, and just a hint of chill in the air teased her with the promise of fall. The cool nights and mild days of the past week had invigorated her spirits. For the first time in months she felt at peace. It was a perfect Saturday morning. Perfect.

Freddy walked beside her, a bulky sketchbook under one arm. She preferred this leisurely stroll—it allowed her to savor the day—but she stepped up the pace a bit. Freddy seemed eager to get to the graveyard, to begin his sketch of the huge circle of cedar trees in the center.

The cedar circle, with its ancient tombstones surrounded by a waist-high iron fence, was a landmark in Oxford—one of those community icons which defines the ambiance of a town. The historical society, planning an updated brochure for the annual Pilgrimage, had decided to use original pen-and-ink drawings rather than photographs for their representations of the great homes, tombstones, and monuments of the War Between the States. They had chosen Freddy for the job, and Libba had promised to keep him company.

Libba could hardly believe the change in Freddy Sturgis since he had, in his words, "discovered himself." All the old puppy-dog insecurity was gone. There was a fire in his eyes and a confidence in his step, a firmness in his voice when he spoke his mind.

And speak it he did. Straightforwardly, honestly, without apology, he talked to Libba about what God had done in his life to bring him to his senses.

He spoke of pain and isolation, and the incredible freedom that came with giving in to God and becoming who he was meant to be. He told her of his dreams, of what he wanted to accomplish, of the motivations within his heart to be an artist of excellence—and of spiritual depth. When he spoke of his art, his countenance changed, and a tender yet powerful vulnerability came over his face. For a long time Libba couldn't quite identify this look. Then one day she caught the expression out of the corner of her eye, and the truth struck her like a blow. It was the look of a man in love.

Freddy was in love with his art—and, by extension, in love with his God. The two were inseparable for him, connected by an invisible cord that bound his creativity to his spirituality. When he had found himself in God, he had uncovered the creative springs within his own soul, and his love for Christ was expressed in countless ways in his work. An ethereal, heavenly light radiated from the eyes of his subjects, even in the rough preliminary drawings. When he sculpted, he caressed the clay like a lover stroking his beloved's cheek. When he sketched, his fingers moved lightly over the lines the way a blind man's hands explore the contours of a cherished face.

Freddy was in love with art. He was not in love with Libba.

He loved her, of course—as a dear friend. He looked at her with sensitivity and compassion; he drew her out of herself, encouraging her to talk about her feelings; he listened. When she needed a shoulder to cry on or an attentive ear, he was there. Without question, without demands. Usually without unsolicited advice. Always with prayer and hope and understanding.

He loved her, but he wasn't in love with her. And that was just fine with Libba.

The gaping wound in her heart that came with the acceptance of Link's death had gradually closed, leaving a dull ache and a vague emptiness. She wasn't sure she could ever turn to another man for romantic love, but she could turn to Freddy for friendship and companionship. Sometimes, when she and Freddy were deep in conversation or prayer, she had to pinch herself to remember that this was the adoring doughboy who had once catered to her every whim. Now he took the lead, both spiritually and emotionally. He had become a man—a man she cared for deeply. And, by some incredible miracle of God's grace, he was helping her come to grips with her grief and go on with her life.

★ ★ ★

Freddy walked in silence beside Libba, absorbed in his own thoughts. It was a perfect Saturday. Perfect. Libba beside him, a morning of sketching before him, the birds singing around him, the presence within him. A line from Browning flitted through his mind—something Libba had read to him last week: *God's in his Heaven—all's right with the world.*

Freddy fingered his sketchbook and thought about his assignment for the Pilgrimage brochure. This job was a godsend in the truest sense. The pay was good—some anonymous donor had apparently given a gift to the historical society with strings attached, strings that demanded the cultivation of promising young southern artists. But even more important than the money was the possibility of fringe benefits. His name would be on the brochure: *Frederick Gardner Sturgis.* The original pen-and-ink drawings would be exhibited in the museum, prominently displayed among the "regional artists" collection. There would be prints and note cards and other Pilgrimage paraphernalia, sold during next year's annual trek back in time, with Freddy receiving a portion of the profits. He would be known—locally, at least—in a town noted for its writers and artists. His talent would be recognized. Other assignments would follow.

It was the open door Freddy had dreamed of and prayed for. The opportunity of a lifetime, the first step toward a profitable career. And, Freddy suspected, God's way of confirming a change of direction for his life.

Recently the Lord had begun to open up a new window for Freddy, something he wouldn't have dreamed up in a hundred years. At first it seemed unthinkable . . . outrageous . . . totally out of character for God. Freddy must be hearing wrong. Panicked, he prayed, seeking guidance. He got the same answer. He prayed again. No change. Then he seized on the practicalities of the situation. He was still a student, with little money and an uncertain future. He couldn't do what God was asking without some kind of stable financial base. He breathed a sigh of relief; he was off the hook.

Then the Pilgrimage job dropped in his lap, with its respectable retainer and its potential for launching his career. Still he argued with God. It wouldn't work. It was just impossible—completely, absolutely impossible.

But God often asked people to do the impossible, didn't he? The biblical woods were full of people who said yes when God asked the unthinkable of them. Noah, who built a floating barn on dry land and invited the animals to join him on his little cruise. Abraham, who went out in faith to seek a land he had never seen and did not know. Esther, who laid down her national pride and her Jewish heritage to become consort to a foreign king. Even Mary, who offered her reputation—even her life—upon the altar of obedience and accepted the unborn Son of God into her virgin womb.

Freddy was honest—brutally honest—with God about his reservations. But he had learned the hard way that obedience was the best course. He would just have to trust God to make sense out of all this in the long run. For his part, he knew what he had to do and, despite his better judgment, was determined to do it.

On this bright and beautiful fall morning, Freddy Sturgis intended to take a leap of faith and ask Libba Coltrain to marry him.

★ ★ ★

Libba watched Freddy closely as he sat cross-legged on the ground, sketching the circle of trees that surrounded the oldest section of the Oxford cemetery. He seemed unusually agitated this morning, nervous about something. Not like the old Freddy, who was nervous about everything, but simply distracted, preoccupied. Several times she caught him muttering at his sketch pad, and once he ripped a page out and stuffed it in his pocket.

Sitting on a gravestone outside the ring of cedars, Libba pulled up a few late wildflowers and strung them together. After a few minutes she stood, walked up behind Freddy, and dropped the daisy chain around his neck.

He looked up, startled. "What do you want?"

Libba smiled. He hadn't meant to be harsh . . . he was just extremely focused when he was working, and Libba had learned that he couldn't do two things at once. If they were talking, he would give her his undivided attention. If he was sketching or painting or planning, any attempts at conversation were futile. Being with Freddy was a good exercise for Libba. She was learning self-control.

She placed a hand on his shoulder. "Is something wrong, Freddy? You seem . . . I don't know. Agitated. Upset."

He closed his sketchbook, stood up, and stretched his back. "You know me too well," he muttered. He cleared his throat. "You're right, Libba. I am preoccupied—and not just with my work. I need to talk to you."

"This sounds serious. So talk. I'm listening."

Freddy shook his head. "Not here." He thought for a minute. "Are you up for a walk?"

"Sure. It's a beautiful day."

"Let's swing back by the house. I'll drop off my sketch pad and we can pick up a couple of Cokes."

"Where are we headed?" Libba was intrigued.

"I thought we might walk through Bailey's Woods up to the back of Rowan Oak."

Libba narrowed her eyes. "Is Faulkner at home?"

"I don't know. Why?"

"Because I've heard he's a crazy man, that's why. He may be a great writer, but he's not all there, if you know what I mean. He's an absolute maniac about privacy—takes a shotgun to people who trespass on his precious property." Libba put her hands on her hips. "I've heard that he wrote the outline for one of his books around his study—right on the walls!"

Freddy gave her a wide-eyed, innocent look. "What's so crazy about that? Michelangelo painted on walls all the time."

"I'm serious, Freddy. He scares me."

Freddy shrugged. "He gets a little wild when he drinks too much—which is a lot of the time, from what I understand. But otherwise he's all right. Takes good care of his horses. He was nice to me."

"You know him?" Libba couldn't comprehend this tidbit of information. Why hadn't Freddy told her? "You've met William Faulkner—in the flesh?"

"So to speak." Freddy started walking, and Libba raced to catch up with him. "Rowan Oak is on my list for the Pilgrimage sketches," he said. "I was out there last week to ask permission to come on the property. There's a really good angle I want to catch, from the big magnolia tree at the end of the walkway. I thought I'd have magnolia blossoms hanging across the foreground, and—"

"Freddy, plan your sketch on your own time!" Libba protested. "Tell me about him—what's he like?"

They had reached Freddy's neat little house, and Libba followed him inside as he put away his sketch pad and retrieved two Coca-Colas from the tiny electric refrigerator.

"We didn't exactly have tea and conversation, Libba. I told him what my assignment was, asked permission to stand in his front yard for half a day, and said thank you and good afternoon."

"Yes, but—how did he *seem?*"

"He seemed like a man with a lot of work to do who didn't have time to waste jawing with a wet-behind-the-ears art student."

Libba reached over and rubbed the back of his ear playfully. "Seems dry enough to me."

Freddy brushed her hand away. "Stop it. That tickles."

Coke bottles in hand, they made a loop around the Square and cut across in front of the Episcopal church toward College Street. Freddy kept up a running commentary about the drawings he planned—like the Episcopal church, an ancient brick structure that, except for the sign out front, had changed little since antebellum days.

On College, close to the west grove of the campus, they made the mistake of walking on the left side of the street. Old Miss Ramey-Falkner's peacocks, perched high on the catwalk, made a swooping lunge to the ground and came after them, screaming and raising a terrible ruckus. Libba jumped into the street. Freddy stood his ground and stared them down.

"They are beautiful birds," he commented as one strutting male spread his plumage and stalked about the yard. "Miss Ramey-Falkner's house is on my list, too. I think I should include the peacocks, don't you?"

Libba slanted her eyes at the cock, who was advancing toward her again. Beautiful they might be, but she didn't trust them. "They're pretty much a fixture in this town, I'll grant you that," she said. "Last week they came all the way down to the Grove and ran off three students who were trying to study on the grass."

Freddy stood eyeing the house. "Miss Ramey-Falkner is kin to the great Mr. William, isn't she?"

"Yes, but I'm not quite sure what the connection is. The county is full of Falkners—most of them dirt poor, who resent William Faulkner's success . . . not to mention his changing the spelling of the family name." Libba got a little bolder and shooed the peacock back onto the old woman's property. "Some New York critic came down here for a story. Faulkner wouldn't give him the time of day, so he interviewed one of Faulkner's relatives—a cousin, I think. The cousin said, 'We always tried to keep Bill from writing like that, but he never would listen.'" Libba chuckled. "I don't think they understand Faulkner's writing."

"Neither do I," Freddy snorted. "I tried to read one of his books—*The Sound and the Fury,* I think it was. Strange, very strange. I gave up."

"'Life is a tale told by an idiot, full of sound and fury, signifying nothing,'" Libba quoted.

"It sure seems that way sometimes."

★ ★ ★

By the time they got into Bailey's Woods, Freddy was getting anxious. He jerked at the foliage along the path, praying for all he was worth. He even thought about turning back a time or two or making up some story so he wouldn't have to tell Libba the truth. What if she laughed in his face? She would probably think he was out of his mind, at the very least. And she might be right at that.

Halfway to Rowan Oak, Freddy stopped and sat down heavily on a fallen tree. It was very quiet in the woods. Birds twittered overhead, and a gentle breeze rustled the leaves. He sighed morosely, digging a twig into the dirt at his feet.

Libba sat down beside him. "OK, Freddy, you've stalled long enough. What's on your mind?"

Freddy took a deep breath and held it for a moment, trying to calm himself. His stomach churned, and he clenched his fists to keep his hands from shaking.

"Is something wrong, Freddy?" Libba prodded, an expression of concern in her eyes. "You're not sick, are you?"

"No, Libba, I'm not sick—although I feel a little queasy at the moment. It's just that . . . well, I feel as if God is asking me to do something—something radical. Something that will change my whole life. And maybe yours, too."

All the color drained out of Libba's face, and her hand went instinctively for the curl behind her right ear. "Are you moving away, Freddy? Please tell me you're not moving. You're my best friend, and—"

Freddy reached for her hands and held them gently in his. There was no easy way to do this, no way to save face, no way to get out of it. He might as well get it over with before Libba's imagination ran away with her. "I'm not going anywhere, Libba."

Libba's blood began circulating again, and some of her color returned. "Then what?"

"Libba," he said cautiously, "I believe God has instructed me to ask you to marry me."

Her eyes widened, and she jerked her hands away as if she had been scalded. *"What?"*

"I believe God has instructed me—"

"I heard you the first time, Freddy. I just didn't believe what I heard."

"I don't mean right now, today, Libba. In a few months—maybe next June, after you've turned twenty-one."

"Well, that makes all the difference in the world."

Freddy exhaled loudly—a long, shuddering sigh. "I know this sounds insane, Libba. Believe me, it sounded pretty bizarre to me at first, too."

"That's an understatement." She looked at him. "Freddy, you don't love me."

"No, I don't," he said. "I mean, yes, I do. But not in a . . . in a romantic way."

"You're not . . . attracted to me?" Libba's voice sounded very small, like a child pleading for attention.

"Of course I am!" Freddy protested, realizing even as he said it that it wasn't true—not in the way she meant it. He was telling her what she wanted to hear, trying to protect her. But it wouldn't work. In the long run, it would just hurt her more. And he wouldn't go back to those patterns again. He couldn't. "But not that way," he corrected quickly. "I just don't think of you like that anymore." He sighed, running a hand through his tousled hair. "Look, Libba, we're getting off the track here. Let's get back to the subject."

"The subject being—"

"Marriage, of course."

"Of course. How stupid of me."

Freddy recaptured her hands and looked directly into her eyes. "I'm always honest with you, right?" She nodded. "Even when it hurts?" Another nod. "All right, let's think about this logically."

"Logically?" Libba smiled—just a little. "Sure. Logically."

"You're not attracted to me, either—not romantically, anyway. But we have a lot in common. We can talk. We pray together. We've grown very close. You like me."

Libba squeezed his hands and forced him to look up at her. "I *love* you, Freddy," she corrected. "You're my dearest friend. I can talk to you about anything—even things I can't tell Willie."

So far so good, Freddy thought. Then suddenly it occurred to him that he didn't have to convince Libba of anything. If this was God's idea, God could do the convincing.

"Libba," he said, "I believe God has some purpose in all of this. To be perfectly honest, I haven't the faintest idea what it is. But we know each other well. We're friends—good friends. We enjoy being together. We complement each other. We share the same spiritual values, and we help each other grow. That's not a bad basis for a marriage."

Libba nodded but said nothing.

"In addition," he went on after a moment of silence, "God has opened some doors for me in my career—this Pilgrimage assignment is only the beginning. I have a nice little house and some money set aside. We could live comfortably, and you could finish your degree—go to graduate school, if you like. What do you think?"

"I have no idea," Libba responded candidly.

"Fair enough." He stood up and extended his hand to her. "The offer stands. All I ask is that you think about it—pray about it."

"I'll pray," she said. "Believe me, Freddy, I'll pray like I've never prayed before."

They walked back through the woods toward College Street, not looking at each other, not saying a word. Freddy felt a surge of elation. He had done it. He had responded to the Spirit's nudging—or, more appropriately, *shov-*

ing—with obedience, and his soul was at peace. But he was also scared out of his wits.

What if she said yes? What would he do then? The idea terrified him. Obedience was one thing. Committing your life to another human being's welfare was quite another. *Forever* was a pretty serious promise.

On the other hand, what if she said no?

Freddy watched Libba out of the corner of his eye, and a warmth spread through him—not passion, but tenderness. She had been hurt so much. He wanted to take her in his arms, to hold her and comfort her, to give her a safe place to heal and grow. Maybe that's what this was all about. Maybe God could use him to fill some of the emptiness inside.

He reached for her hand, grasped it firmly, and held on.

★ ★ ★

Libba didn't pull her hand away. It felt good, being touched again. She could never respond to Freddy the way she had to Link, of course, but she didn't expect that. And neither did Freddy.

Other men apparently had different expectations where she was concerned. Ever since she had returned to classes at the university, she found men—mostly soldiers back home from the war—coming around her, asking her for dates, looking at her with expressions that made her uncomfortable.

Especially Gordon. Tall, handsome, muscular Gordon Conway lived in the apartment next door to her—the first cousin of her landlady's oldest grandson, she thought. Gordon had been a flyer, a fighter pilot who had parachuted out of his plane over some remote Pacific Island. He was captured, escaped, lived in hiding in the jungle for a while, and then swam out to be rescued when an Allied PT boat came by. A genuine hero, decorated for bravery.

Gordon obviously expected her to fall at his feet in worship, and when she didn't, he took it as a personal challenge. He would come by in the evenings, lean against the screen door, and regale her with stories of his exploits. He talked to her incessantly about letting the past go and living for the moment.

The problem was, Gordon Conway was beginning to make sense. Libba couldn't help being attracted to him. He exuded a subtle kind of sensuality that both frightened and enticed her. Here was a man who might even be able to make her forget Link Winsom. And Libba didn't want to forget.

Under the seductive scrutiny of Gordon's deep blue eyes, Libba felt the full impact of her emptiness, her need for love. And the feeling scared her.

Maybe Freddy was right. Maybe his proposal, unromantic as it was, held the answer for both of them. Life with Freddy would be comfortable, if not exciting; intellectually interesting, if not passionate. And safe. Secure. Undemanding.

The prospect of security appealed to Libba more than she was willing to admit. With Freddy, she would be protected from feelings she didn't know how to handle. She wouldn't have to give up her love for Link. It wouldn't be the kind of marriage she had always dreamed about, of course, but now that Link was dead, she had abandoned that idea anyway. At least with Freddy she could be herself, and she wouldn't have to confront the unsettling feelings that arose every time she looked into the eyes of a man like Gordon Conway.

Besides, other obstacles were developing that Freddy didn't know about yet. Her father was becoming a problem. Last week he had written a brief, to-the-point letter informing her that if she didn't come home and give up "this college nonsense" immediately, he would cut off her school funds and leave her high and dry. This term's classes were paid for, and her mother had been sending her a money order every month to pay for food and the rent on her apartment. She could last until December, but after that . . .

Libba sighed. There was a lot to be said for Freddy's idea of marriage, even thought it had seemed pretty crazy at first. Maybe this was an answer—a way out—for her. At least with him she would be safe, protected, and cared for. Not a bad bargain.

She had told Freddy she would pray about it, and she would. But she was fairly sure, now that she thought about it, that her answer would be yes.

48

⭐ ⭐ ⭐

Reluctant Prophet

October 1944

Link held the papers up to the light and read them for the hundredth time. Transfer orders. For him. To the States. He was going home.

Well, not home, exactly. The army had messed up—again.

He had made his decision, had concluded that the best thing for him to do was to go back to Missouri, to his father and family, and try to put Libba Coltrain as far out of his mind as possible.

Now this.

He read the orders for the hundred-and-first time, hoping he had made a mistake. But there was no mistake. It was right here in black and white: Kennedy General Hospital, Memphis, Tennessee.

A few months ago, he would have been ecstatic. This was what he had planned for, hoped for. In one of his earliest letters to Libba, he had told her that if he got wounded, he would try to get assigned to Kennedy, the closest VA hospital to Eden. She could come to him. They would be together.

Now fate—or something—had stepped in, and he was on his way to Kennedy after all. The idea seemed like a mockery. To be that close and not see her . . . to be within spitting distance, practically, of the Mississippi state line . . .

Stork, of course, would be delighted. But for Link it would be pure torture.

The Birmingham doctors said that he was recovered enough to travel—still in a cast, of course, but minus most of the irritating tubes that made him look and feel like an eight-cylinder Packard engine. The surgeons at Kennedy General apparently felt they could do something for him—remove the shrapnel, perhaps. He might even walk again, although they gave him no guarantees. What he was assured of, however, was that for better or worse, Second Lieutenant Lincoln Winsom would go under the knife, and when it was all over there would be a medical discharge waiting for him.

It had been three weeks since Stork had left—three interminably lonely weeks. Link had had more time than he wanted, to ponder . . . and to pray. And despite all his prayers to the contrary, he couldn't seem to get Libba Coltrain out of his mind. She haunted his dreams and invaded his waking thoughts. And despite his firm intention to let her go, Link had to admit to himself that he still loved her.

Now, staring at the orders that would take him painfully close to her, Link's anger flared. Not at Libba—he was past being angry at her. At God.

How could God do this to him? It seemed like a cruel joke, some kind of cosmic taunt, ridiculing the bleakness in his soul. He had been obedient, hadn't he? He had responded to God, had surrendered his life, had opened himself fully to the Lord and to the woman he loved. But the woman he loved had rejected him, and the God he served seemed bent on destroying him—or at the very least, making his life as difficult as possible. . . .

A faint whisper within his spirit silenced him. *If you ask for bread, will I give you a stone?*

Link frowned. The last thing he needed right now was biblical double-talk. But the whisper persisted: *If you ask for a fish, will I give you a serpent?*

Bread and stones? Fish and serpents? What on earth did that mean? Link wasn't in the mood for word puzzles. Still, his anger subsided, and he waited.

Silence.

By now Link's curiosity had been aroused, and he reached for the black leather Bible that sat on the table at his bedside. The dead soldier's New Testament, the one that had helped bring him to God in the first place. The words had a vaguely familiar ring. Link thumbed through the Gospels until he found what he was looking for—the Sermon on the Mount. He leaned back against the pillows and began to read.

> Ask, and it shall be given you; seek, and ye shall find; knock, and it shall be opened unto you: For every one that asketh receiveth; and he that seeketh findeth; and to him that knocketh it shall be opened.

Or what man is there of you, whom if his son ask bread, will he give him a stone? Or if he ask a fish, will he give him a serpent?

If ye then, being evil, know how to give good gifts unto your children, how much more shall your Father which is in heaven give good things to them that ask him?

Link propped the Bible on his cast and considered what he had read. He had experienced the "good gifts" which his heavenly Father had promised to him. Life itself, for one thing. Answers to his prayers. Friends like Stork Simpson and Owen Slaughter, God rest his soul. No stones or serpents there.

He cleared his throat. "But what about Libba Coltrain?" he muttered under his breath. "I can't seem to get away from her—you won't *let* me get away from her. Why?"

Link's eyes drifted to the preceding page, two chapters back: *If thou bring thy gift to the altar, and there rememberest that thy brother hath ought against thee; leave there thy gift before the altar, and go thy way; first be reconciled to thy brother, and then come and offer thy gift.*

He snapped the book shut angrily. *Be reconciled?* God had to be kidding. He was supposed to take the first step, to reconcile with Libba? She was the one who had abandoned him, for heaven's sake!

Be reconciled. . . .

No. He would not do this. He couldn't. He had suffered enough humiliation just by her silence, her failure to communicate with him. God couldn't really expect him to face her directly, to actually talk with her. If there was going to be any "reconciling" going on here, she was the one who should take the initiative. She was the one who should ask for forgiveness!

Be reconciled . . . as I have reconciled you to myself. Forgive, as I have forgiven you. . . .

Suddenly Link understood. Libba didn't deserve forgiveness. She hadn't asked for it. She had made no overtures toward him, no effort at communication. And yet, hadn't God forgiven him in the same way—before he realized his need to be forgiven, before he asked?

Christ had gone to the cross for him while he was still separated from God, in need of grace. That was what grace meant, after all. If you deserved it, it wasn't grace.

He could at least go to Libba and extend the same grace. Difficult as it might be, he could talk to her, try to set things right between them. He had no hope that the outcome would be any different. But the results, after all, were God's department.

Link raised an eyebrow and grimaced in the direction of the ceiling. God had set him up, that was for sure. He was on his way to Kennedy General, less than two hours from Eden, Mississippi. Army inefficiency was the great fish that would deposit him like Jonah on the shores of Nineveh.

49

☆ ☆ ☆

Keep the
Home Fires Burning

Rae Coltrain paced up and down in front of the counter, nervous as a cat under a full moon. "It's almost five, Thelma. He said he'd be here by five. Do I look all right?"

Thelma sighed. "You look lovely, hon."

"Is my hair in place? I've got that flat spot on the back of my head, you know, and I don't want it showing. What about my stockings—are my seams straight?" Rae turned her back to Thelma and displayed her calves.

"Straight as a Baptist preacher on Sunday morning," Thelma said. "Now relax, will you?" Thelma rolled her eyes behind Rae's back. The girl was driving her crazy—absolutely crazy. She hoped Andrew Laporte wasn't late. If she had to spend another half hour with Rae in such a state, she might toss the poor girl right through the front window.

It was understandable, of course. Meeting your fiancé after an extended separation must be pretty nerve-wracking—especially when you've never seen him before. Thelma reached across the counter to give Rae a comforting pat on the shoulder. Rae nearly jumped out of her skin.

"Have some coffee, honey, and try to calm down."

"Coffee?" Rae looked at her blankly. "I just brushed my teeth."

For the tenth time, Thelma thought. *He'd better get here soon, or you won't have any enamel left.*

Rae fingered the dog-eared picture of Andrew Laporte and his buddies. Drew's face—third from the left—was circled in red. Thelma thought the red circle made him look a little bit like a target, but she didn't say so.

She had to admit, Rae looked marvelous for her first in-person meeting with the man she intended to marry. Her round face had been softened somewhat by the judicious application of cosmetics, and her dark eyes were emphasized by a gray brown eye shadow—very subtle, but very effective. Her hair curled softly around her face, and she was wearing a linen suit of soft heather blue.

"Sit down, Rae," Thelma repeated for the umpteenth time. "He'll be here."

"I can't sit down," she protested. "Linen wrinkles horribly."

"Well, you're going to have to sit down eventually, wrinkles or no wrinkles."

"Eventually. But not until he gets here. I'd prefer to get wrinkled later." Rae continued pacing.

Thelma picked up the photograph from the counter and studied the face in the bull's-eye. Not too tall, sandy-looking hair, a furry mustache. Average. That was probably for the best. He loved Rae for who she was, not for what she looked like. By Rae's own admission, she would have been intimidated if he had been handsome. And he was pretty ordinary looking. But from Rae's descriptions of their correspondence, there was nothing ordinary at all about the heart and mind and soul of Andrew Laporte.

The bell over the door sounded, and Thelma looked up.

A soldier in a lieutenant's uniform strode into the room, looked around, and then made a beeline for Mabel Rae Coltrain. He stood in front of her, took her hands, and looked into her eyes. "Hello, sweetheart," he said. "I can't believe I'm finally here."

Thelma gasped and glanced back at the photograph. Not third from the left, but third from the *right*. The gorgeous movie star with the dimples and the chest a mile wide. Handsomest man in the group. Handsomest man Thelma Breckinridge had ever laid eyes on, for that matter.

Thelma looked at Rae. Her eyes had gone wide, and her mouth hung open a little. All the color had drained out of her cheeks. There she stood, like a little round statue, her hands still clasped in his grip.

Finally Rae found her voice. "Who . . . who *are* you?" she squeaked, a full octave above her normal range.

He frowned, then grinned broadly, the dimples in his cheeks only slightly less deep than pictures Thelma had seen of the Grand Canyon. "Rae, you have such a sense of humor! It's one of the things I love most about you—"

He bent down and kissed her—a long, lingering kiss. Thelma thought she saw Rae's knees buckle, and she, in fact, had to hold onto the counter to maintain her equilibrium.

When he let her go, Rae snatched the picture from the counter and thrust it under his nose. "You can't be!" she stammered. "This—this is Andrew Laporte. Third from the left."

The soldier squinted at the photograph, then began to laugh, a low bass, rolling like distant thunder. If that voice were any deeper, Thelma thought, he'd set off shock waves along the New Madrid fault line.

"No," he said, the laugh fading into a chuckle. "This is me—third from the *right.*" He cocked an eyebrow at Rae. "My mistake, I guess. That fellow is Harvey Ringwald, clerk of the company. Harvey always told me I'd get myself in trouble, not knowing left from right. Nearly got us killed a time or two." He fixed his deep blue eyes on Rae. "I hope you're not disappointed."

"Disappointed?" Rae gulped. "No, of—of course not. Just . . . surprised, that's all. It's just that you're so—so handsome, not like I pictured you at all. And I'm so—"

He silenced her with another kiss, then straightened up and put his arm around her. "Beautiful," he finished for her. "Just like I pictured you."

★ ★ ★

With his hand on the door of the Paradise Garden Cafe, Stork Simpson paused and took a deep breath. The ride from Tillatoba had been interminable, and he had a pounding headache and a knot the size of St. Louis in his gut.

Too impatient to wait for the next bus, Stork had accepted a ride with a garrulous farmer in a broken-down Ford pickup. Between the grinding of the gears, the jolting of his rear on every pothole in Tullahoma County, and the old man's incessant yammering, Stork had been certain that instead of going home to his wife and son, he had somehow died and was headed for the nether regions. Hell wouldn't be fire and brimstone—it would be an eternity with Booter Johnson.

He had thanked Booter profusely, of course, and tried to pay him for his trouble, but the old man waved away his money. "Naw, son, it's my pleasure. Not often I get the chance to talk to one of our fine brave boys in uniform. Why, if we'd had fellas like you, we'da won the war for sure!"

The old guy meant the Civil War, Stork finally concluded. He didn't have the heart to tell Booter he was a Yankee and that his ancestors had fought on the "wrong side" of the Mason-Dixon line. He just thanked him politely, for the seventh time, and shut the door.

Stork took another deep breath and leaned against the glass. This was it—the moment of truth. He peered at his reflection in the glass, swiped at his hair, and entered the Paradise Garden Cafe.

The cafe was just as he remembered it—the cracked yellow linoleum, the tables teetering precariously on uneven legs, the faint scent of old grease and stale cigarette smoke. In the corner, Ivory Brownlee was playing softly on the piano. One couple—a soldier and his girl—sat with their heads together in the back booth. An odd pair, Stork thought briefly. He was tall and handsome, she was short and round and looked a little bit like—

He looked closer. Why, he believed it *was* Mabel Rae Coltrain. He hadn't seen her in a long time, of course, and she did look a bit different . . . more *finished,* somehow. It seemed a strange match, but who was he to judge? People might think he and Madge were mismatched, too. You just couldn't tell from appearances.

Thelma Breckinridge sat behind the counter, reading a newspaper. As he started toward her, she looked up.

"Evenin', soldier," she said amiably, putting her paper under the counter. "Just have a seat anywhere, and I'll be with you in a minute. Coffee?"

"Thelma," he said, easing his duffel bag to the floor.

She looked up, really focusing on his face for the first time. Her hands flew up to her cheeks, and her mouth dropped open. "Merciful Lord in heaven," she breathed. "It's you!"

Stork smiled. "It's me, Thelma."

She steered him toward a table, then sat down across from him. "How are you, Stork? Are you all right? How was your trip? How's your arm? When did you get to the States?"

Stork held up his good hand. "I don't mean to be rude, Thelma, but we can do all this later. Where's Madge? And my son?"

Thelma jumped to her feet. "Of course—how stupid of me. Madge is in back, feeding Mickey. I'll get her."

Stork got up. "If you don't mind, Thelma, I'd rather go myself. Just point the way."

★　★　★

Quietly, Stork opened the door to the tiny apartment and slipped inside. The last rays of the setting sun came through the window, illuminating the faces of his wife and child as she sat rocking him, the empty bottle on his chest. Mickey lay with his little mouth open, just on the verge of sleep. Madge was humming softly, a lullaby. The waning light touched her hair and flamed it to life like a halo. It could have been a Renaissance painting: "Madonna and Child." He had never seen anything so beautiful.

Tears sprang to Stork's eyes, and he swallowed hard. This was his wife. His son. His family.

"Madge?" he whispered.

She stopped rocking. Stopped humming. For a moment she froze, then turned her face toward him. She closed her eyes and opened them again, and the tears began to flow.

Madge jumped up from the chair, clutching little Mickey, and covered the space between them in three strides. "Oh, Michael," she murmured, burying her face in his chest. "Oh, Michael."

Little Mickey, startled from his sleep, began to cry—softly at first, then louder, a genuine wail. Madge withdrew a little and held him out. "Sweetheart, I'd like you to meet your son, Michael James Simpson. Mickey, honey, this is your daddy."

Daddy. The word struck Stork like a physical blow, and he reeled inwardly. It was real, all of it. He was a husband, a father. This was his family.

He held Mickey in the crook of his good arm and jiggled him up and down. "Is that horrible noise coming from my son?" he cooed. "Now, now, it's all right. Daddy's here."

"Michael, be careful," Madge cautioned. "He's just had his—"

The warning came too late. In one swift motion Stork handed Mickey back to Madge and looked down at his dress uniform, smeared with sour milk. Something that looked like mashed carrots splattered across the sling that held his cast in place.

He began to laugh. "Baptized into fatherhood," he chuckled. "I guess I'm officially Daddy now."

Madge grabbed a washrag and wiped Mickey's face. "The bathroom's through there," she said, pointing. "In case you want to clean up a little." She wrinkled her nose at him. "I'll get a fresh shirt on Mickey and put him down. He'll go to sleep pretty quickly—he's very good."

Stork took off the sling and rinsed it out, hanging it over the shower curtain rod. He sponged his uniform clean the best he could, then removed the jacket and hung it on the back of the bathroom door. When he came out again, Mickey was in his crib, and Madge was bustling around in the tiny kitchen alcove with a coffeepot.

He came and stood behind her. "I—I thought you might want some coffee," she said.

"No coffee." He kissed the back of her neck.

"Are you hungry? You must have had a long trip. I could probably fix something here, or we could go out to the cafe—"

He kissed her again, this time behind the left ear. "No dinner. No cafe. But I am hungry."

He turned her around, looked into her face, and saw there the same apprehensions that he had experienced, the same uncertainties. "Madge," he whispered. "We have a lot of adjustments to make, I realize that. This will be very new for both of us."

He smoothed the hair at her temples and smiled into her eyes. "But God has given us a great gift. When I came in just now and saw you and Mickey sitting there, I thought I had died and gone to heaven. This is where I want to be—with my wife. With my son."

"Oh, Michael, I've missed you so much. I've been so worried about you. And now you're here—it just seems like too much to believe, like it's too good to be true."

He put his arm around her and drew her as close as he could around the cast. "It's true. I'm here. Forever. Always."

50

⭐ ⭐ ⭐

A Light in the Darkness

Bright October sunlight streamed into the tiny bedroom. Stork, propped against the headboard with Mickey on his stomach, took a long sip of coffee and replaced the cup on the nightstand.

"Alive?" Madge sat straight up in bed and stared at him. "Are you telling me that Link Winsom is *alive?"*

"Of course he's alive. He was shot up pretty bad, and he may never walk again, but he's definitely alive." He tickled Mickey in the ribs. "Say *Daddy,* Mickey. *Daddy."*

Mickey grinned broadly and blew spit bubbles. "Da-da." He giggled. "Da-da."

"Did you hear that?" Stork demanded, bouncing his boy up and down. "He said Da-da."

"Michael Simpson, look at me."

He looked. She was wearing the rose-colored satin nightgown he had bought for her at a little shop on Fifth Avenue in New York, right before he had boarded the *Queen Elizabeth.* It was nothing short of a miracle that he had gotten home with it. Downright amazing, considering all the detours he had taken getting back to the States. And even more amazing, the way she looked in it.

Stork gazed at his wife with open admiration. "You are beautiful, do you know that?" He leaned across Mickey in an attempt to kiss her. "Absolutely beautiful."

"Stop that, Michael. Pay attention."

He winked at her. "I thought that's what I was doing."

"Be serious."

"If Link weren't alive, *that* would be serious. But he is alive. He'll be coming home soon—back to the States, to Missouri." He turned his attention back to his son. "We won't be able to see him very often, but—"

Madge put a hand under his chin and forced him to look into her eyes. "Michael, listen to me. Libba doesn't know."

"What are you talking about? She knows he's alive—he wrote to her."

"No, he didn't."

Stork stopped playing with Mickey's toes and gave her his full attention. "Are you saying that Libba never received any letters from Link, that she still believes he's dead?"

Madge nodded. "The last communication she received—months ago, back in June—was that package from the War Department." She closed her eyes and took a deep breath. "I wrote you about it. His wristwatch. A locket she had given him when they got engaged. A letter—" she paused, "with a hole through it. Drenched in blood."

"You told me. And it sounds horrible, I'll admit. It's no wonder she thought he was dead. But the letters—"

Madge shook her head. "There were no letters, Michael. We all became very close during that awful time—Libba, Willie, and me. Even Mabel Rae, although apparently she was keeping one little secret from us." She smiled, then became serious again. "If Libba had gotten any letters, we would have heard about it. The whole town would have heard—if not directly from Libba, at least from that nosy postmistress, Charity Grevis."

A jolt ran through Stork like lightning. Was it possible that Link had lied to him, that he hadn't really written the letters after all? Stork thought about it for a minute. No, Link was pretty devastated when Libba didn't write back to him. And Link was a changed man, a man who believed in God and tried to do what was right. He wouldn't be deceptive about something like this.

"Link wrote letters—dozens of them. At first he didn't want to, of course. Had this crazy idea that Libba would be better off without him. But then he changed his mind—or maybe I should say, God changed his mind."

"God?" Madge interrupted. "You mean Link's become—"

"A Christian?" Stork grinned. "Oh, yes, he has. And quite a Christian, believe me."

Madge edged closer. "That's wonderful."

"Link didn't think so. I mean, he was excited about all the changes in his life, and grateful for God's work in him. But he was also convinced that part of the reason Libba didn't answer him was that maybe she didn't like the idea of this new faith of his."

"That's because he had no idea what was happening to Libba."

"Her, too?"

Madge nodded. "The war changed all of us, Michael. Made us all realize what was really important. Libba's not the same girl you knew. She's settled, matured. A woman. And not just a woman—a woman with a pretty strong faith."

"How on earth did that happen?" Stork was intrigued. "Miss Green Eyes was pretty much of a snob when we first met her, although Link couldn't ever admit it. She was self-centered, shallow, and—"

"Not anymore." Madge shrugged. "I guess she found out that her Sunday-school religion wasn't strong enough to carry her through all this. She had some help, too."

"From you?" He shifted Mickey to one side and snuggled up next to her. "You've always had a strong faith. That was one of the things that kept me going out there, that made me think about my own relationship to God. I knew you were praying for me."

Madge kissed him on his cheek, then rubbed at the stubble. "I did pray for you, too. We all did. And I suppose I helped Libba a little, gave her a bit of support. It was mostly Thelma, though, and Freddy Sturgis."

"Freddy?" Stork frowned. "Surely you're not talking about that little toad of a private who was squiring Libba around before Link came into the picture."

"The very same." Madge laughed lightly. "But you wouldn't recognize him, either. He's certainly not a toad. I didn't know him before, of course, but he's a very nice fellow. And he's really helped Libba come to terms with her grief."

"I'll bet he has," Stork growled.

She patted his arm. "It's not like that. They're just friends. You'd like him."

"I doubt it. Especially not if he's trying to horn in on Link's territory."

Madge sat up a little straighter and glared at him. "Libba Coltrain," she said deliberately, "is nobody's *territory*. And don't forget that she thought Link was dead."

"You've got a point. But I don't get it. Link wrote all those letters—I'm sure of it. When he didn't get a response, not a single word, he concluded that either Libba couldn't live with a cripple or didn't want to deal with a fanatic. Either way, not responding was a cowardly way out."

"From Link's perspective, I guess it was," Madge said. "But Libba didn't get the letters. And believe me, if she had, she would have answered. She loved him. She wouldn't care that he was in a wheelchair, and she would have been delighted about his faith." She sat straight up, her eyes flashing. "Oh, no, Michael! We've got to tell her—fast!"

Stork frowned. "I don't know, honey. Link's not coming back here when he gets released. He's going to Missouri. Maybe it's just better to let things run their course naturally—"

"No! Don't you understand? Libba didn't hear from him, and she thinks he's dead. Link thinks Libba doesn't care about him. We've got to do something!"

"All right. We'll write to Link at his father's house—or call, if you prefer. When Link gets home, his dad can give him the message, and then Link can decide what he wants to do about it, if anything. But—"

"Libba's coming here, tonight," Madge interrupted. "She sent word to Thelma that she has a big announcement for us and that everybody's supposed to be at the cafe at seven."

"So?"

"So, the last time I saw Libba she was talking about getting on with her life, about how she'd like to have a baby just like Mickey someday."

"Surely you don't think she's planning to marry Sturgis."

"I don't know what she's planning. I can't imagine her marrying Freddy, but I do know that some handsome hero of a fighter pilot has been coming on pretty strong to her. Thelma told me about it—in confidence, of course. Asked me to pray with her about it. Thelma said Libba was pretty uncomfortable with his attentions, but he did seem rather persistent. Thelma suspected that Libba was attracted to him in spite of herself."

"And you think this is Libba's big announcement?"

"What else could it be? Michael, we can't let her do it—not until she and Link have had the chance to sort things out."

"You really do care about this, don't you?"

"Don't you?" Madge tugged at his arm.

"Yes." He hesitated. "Of course I do. I just don't think we should go meddling in other people's lives."

"But this is important. They're made for each other. You know that as well as I do." She paused. "If we were in this mess, you'd want somebody to help us, wouldn't you?"

Stork pulled Mickey back onto his stomach and hugged him tenderly. The baby reached out and gripped his father's finger. "I can't imagine living without the two of you," he said quietly. "All right. We'll tell her—tonight. But you have to promise to let me handle this. It's going to be a shock."

"Not nearly as much of a shock as marrying somebody else and finding out later."

★ ★ ★

The morning sun cast a dim light through the drawn shades of Robinson Coltrain's office behind the hardware store. He shut the door and drew two keys from his vest pocket. With one he unlocked the bottom drawer of his desk. He pulled out a small steel strongbox and inserted the second key into the strongbox lock and flipped the lid open.

Robinson wasn't quite sure what brought him back, again and again, to read his daughter's letters. He got a perverse sort of pleasure in rifling through the stack, almost as if they were gold or stock certificates. Thirty-seven letters. Thirty-seven. And she had never seen a one of them.

Tater had done her best to get out from under his control, he would give her that. Going out to his trashy brother's farm to live. Returning to college without so much as a by-your-leave or a kiss-my-foot. No doubt Olivia had been slipping money to her, but that was all about to end. Libba hadn't responded to his threat to cut off her tuition, but it didn't matter. She'd be home soon enough. Home, under his roof, where she belonged. No more gallivanting all over the countryside. No more talk of graduate school. The girl would play his game and play it by his rules.

He removed the letters from the box and slipped off the rubber band that held them together. Link Winsom was a fool. All these absurd words of love—not just from a cripple, but from a cripple with a religious mission. Robinson didn't know what disgusted him more—the idea of his daughter marrying a gimp or the possibility that she could love a fanatic. Either way, it was of no concern to him. It was over, and he would have her back. Soon.

The letters had stopped coming almost a month ago. Link Winsom had given up. Robinson Coltrain had won.

Tater would get down on her knees and thank him someday—thank him for keeping her from making the greatest mistake of her life. If he ever told her the truth, that is. He hadn't decided about that yet.

Robinson replaced the letters and reached with the strongbox down to the bottom drawer. As he leaned over, a pain shot through his shoulder and left arm. *Got to get that checked,* he thought absently. *Must have pulled a muscle unloading that last delivery of copper pipe.*

He sat up and gripped the edge of the desk. The room had begun to spin, and he felt light-headed. It was stuffy in here, very stuffy. He stood up and reached for the window, but his legs wouldn't hold him. As if an iron clamp were tightening around his chest, the pain in his shoulder spread downward like a fire.

He dropped into his chair and reached for the telephone.

"Number, please?" the operator's whiny voice said, as if from a great distance. "Number, please? Is anyone there?"

He couldn't hold on. The receiver slipped from his grip and fell back onto its cradle, and Robinson Coltrain slumped over his desk, two small keys clutched in his other fist.

★ ★ ★

Libba Coltrain boarded the bus from Oxford to Eden at 4:25. It would have been a lot quicker if she had let Freddy drive her in his car, but she needed the time to think.

Everyone would be there, she was sure of it—all of her friends, waiting at the Paradise Garden Cafe for her big announcement. The announcement, known only to her, that she was engaged to be married to Frederick Gardner Sturgis.

It was a logical decision, and yet saying the words, "my fiancé, Freddy," gave her no joy. In fact, her heart grew heavier every time she thought of it. She envisioned a big church wedding with Willie and Mabel Rae and Madge as attendants, the Presbyterian sanctuary decked with white flowers. And Libba walking down the aisle to meet . . . Freddy.

Libba closed her eyes. Behind her eyelids she could still see the scene, but in her mind she pictured someone else at the altar, waiting for her. Link. Always Link.

God, why did you have to let him die? Libba thought. *I needed him.*

It was the first sincere prayer she had uttered in a long time, she realized with a flash of remorse. Oh, she had prayed about the decision to marry Freddy, but her requests for wisdom and insight were merely perfunctory. If she was honest with herself, she'd have to admit that the decision had been made long before she ever got to the first *Amen*.

But it was such a reasonable course of action. Freddy was safe. He would be good to her. He wouldn't demand some kind of romantic passion that she couldn't deliver. She would be able to continue with her studies, to go on to graduate school, perhaps.

Why, then, did she feel increasingly rotten about the decision? Why did she dread facing her friends and loved ones to give them the news? She could imagine their horrified responses. They would pretend to be happy for her, and she would pretend to be happy for herself. It would be awful, simply awful.

But she had no choice. She needed Freddy, needed the security he offered. Needed the way out.

Didn't she?

Libba sat up straight in the bouncing bus. It was the first time this thought had ever occurred to her. Did she need someone else, someone to take care of her and protect her from feelings she couldn't quite cope with? Or was it possible—even imaginable—that she was strong enough to face life on her own? Life without . . . without Link.

Libba gazed out the window. The sky had clouded over, it had begun to rain, and drops of water gathered on the glass. She could see her own reflection staring back. Raindrops flowed across the image like tears.

It had been a long time since Libba had cried—really cried. She had thought it was a sign that she was getting better, healing. Now she wasn't so sure. Maybe she had just pushed everything down, refused to confront the pain inside. Once she was away from Eden, away from the constant reminders of Link, Freddy had always been there for her. She hadn't really faced herself, looked deep into the mirror of her soul to see what was there.

Libba thought about the months—it seemed like years—since she had first met Link Winsom and fallen in love with him. She wondered if he would even know her now, she had changed so much. When he left, she had been a girl—a shallow, self-centered child only beginning to discover herself. Link's love for her had helped her accept herself, helped her realize that she didn't always have to be in control.

When he had shipped out, she had begun to reevaluate her life . . . and her belief in God. She had weighed her faith in the balance and found it wanting. And gradually, through prayer and the encouragement of people like Freddy and Thelma Breckinridge, she had exercised what little faith she had and felt it grow. God had prepared her for the shock of that day when she opened the box and found Link's personal effects, even if she hadn't felt prepared. And through the long nights of grief and pain, she had become stronger—strong enough, even, to encourage Willie and Madge, to get out of her own suffering and help someone else.

Libba fingered the locket around her neck—the small gold locket she had given to Link a few days before he shipped out. It had come back to her, even though he hadn't. Now she wore it all the time, a reminder that once—just once in her life—she had been truly loved.

She could never have that kind of love with Freddy Sturgis. Dear as he was, she could never even come close to loving him the way she loved Link. She knew it, and he knew it, too. Why, then, had she agreed to marry him? And why had he asked in the first place?

Libba wasn't in love with Freddy, but she trusted him. Particularly, she trusted his ability to listen to God, and she knew that he invariably responded to God with obedience, even if it was difficult. He had said as much the day he asked her to marry him: *God has instructed me to ask you.* . . .

Freddy hardly ever talked that way. He didn't go around saying "God told me" the way some people did, as if they had a direct line to heaven and weren't to be contradicted. If Freddy said, "God told me," you could take it to the bank. It was true.

So, if God really *had* told Freddy to ask Libba to marry him, why? Even though Libba had said yes, she wasn't at all sure she was supposed to marry Freddy—and she was becoming less sure by the minute. What purpose could being engaged to Freddy possibly serve, if God didn't want her to go through with it?

The answer jolted Libba so hard that at first she thought the bus had suffered a blowout. She peered out the window. No, they were rolling along just fine, the tires making whispering sounds on the wet pavement: *Gor-don, Gor-don, Gor-don.* . . .

Gordon Conway.

Could it be? Was it possible that God had allowed her to become engaged to Freddy to keep her out of the clutches of the handsome fighter pilot—or someone else like him? Libba had been attracted to him, she had to admit. And he was extremely persistent. She might have given in to him eventually, except that . . .

Except that Freddy had asked her to marry him.

As soon as Libba had said the word *engaged,* Gordon Conway had vanished from the picture like mist under a summer sun. For some reason, God didn't want her involved with Gordon. And apparently the Lord had used Freddy's proposal to take care of the situation. To protect her from the Gordon Conways of this world who might prey on her vulnerability, her need to be loved.

Libba leaned back in the seat and began to pray. "All right, Lord," she murmured, "some of this is beginning to fall into place. I'm beginning to feel that I'm not really supposed to marry Freddy at all, but that I *was* supposed to be engaged to him. It doesn't really make sense, but right now that doesn't matter so much. What does matter is where you want me to go from here."

Trust me.

"I mean, I want to trust you, but I don't understand. I need to know what to do."

Trust me. Not Freddy. Not your own wisdom. Me.

Suddenly a light went on in Libba's mind. She hadn't thought she was strong enough to deal with Link's death, but when the time came, she got through it, with God's help. She wasn't sure she was strong enough to face life alone, but maybe she was. She believed—most of the time, anyway—that God had a purpose for her, a plan. Maybe, just maybe, she was strong enough to do whatever God asked her to do.

A warmth flowed into Libba's veins, and she sat up and looked out the window. The rain had stopped, and in the distance she could see one bright ray of sunshine coming down through a rift in the clouds. A snatch of a song played through her mind: *"Though there be rain, and darkness too, . . . I'll get by as long as I have you."*

Libba smiled. At the next stop she would get off the bus and call Freddy. He would understand.

And she would have a very different announcement to make to her friends at the Paradise Garden tonight.

51

★ ★ ★

Evening in Paradise

By the time the bus from Oxford had lumbered to a stop in front of the Paradise Garden Cafe, Libba Coltrain felt stronger than she had ever felt before. A ten-minute stopover in Water Valley had given her time to call Freddy, and as she had predicted, he understood completely. So completely, in fact, that Libba had felt a twinge of rejection. He had sounded downright *relieved*.

When she got back on the bus for the last leg of the trip, Libba had stewed and pouted about Freddy's reaction, but only for a few minutes. Then she had begun to laugh—at herself, at her incredibly irrational response, at the unbelievable sense of liberty and peace she was experiencing.

She was, indeed, strong enough to do this . . . with God's help. Without Freddy taking care of her, without Daddy's financial support. She would keep her apartment, get a job—maybe a part-time secretarial position on campus. She could type pretty well, and she was extremely organized. She would finish her degree. It might take her a little longer, but she could do it. She would make it—on her own.

Willie would be proud of her, Libba thought. More important, she was proud of herself. And in a strange way she didn't quite understand, Libba suspected that the Lord, too, took pride in this daughter who was finally standing up under her own power . . . and his.

★ ★ ★

Thelma Breckinridge glanced at the clock behind the counter—6:25. Everyone was there, drinking coffee and eating the last of her buttermilk pound cake. Waiting. Waiting for Libba Coltrain.

Madge and Stork, with Mickey on Stork's lap, sat at a table near the window, talking in low tones and keeping an eye on the parking lot. Rae and her handsome lieutenant sat in their customary back booth, side by side, their fingers entwined and their heads together, laughing. Willie, on a stool at the counter, swiveled aimlessly, watching Mabel Rae and Drew. They waved at her to come join them, but she declined, smiling weakly in their direction and then returning her full attention to the half-empty coffee cup before her. In the corner Ivory Brownlee, in a starched white shirt and red bow tie, was playing "As Time Goes By" on the battered old piano.

Tears misted Thelma's eyes as she watched them—her family. A lot of pain was represented here. And a lot of joy. The grief of loss, the death of dreams . . . and the rebirth of new life and new love. None of them were the same as they had been a year ago. The soldier boys, facing the horrors of the battlefront, had become men. The girls, dealing with the anxieties of the home front, had grown into women. They had all been changed—a little less romantic and optimistic, a little more jaded, perhaps. Certainly more realistic. But for the most part, stronger in their faith, too.

Some people seemed to think that trust in God had to be founded on some kind of brainless, heartless acceptance of the unbelievable. But Thelma knew that real faith was based on real truth. God never demanded that people suspend their doubt and questions; in fact, faith stood up best under the harsh light of realism. And these young men and women who filled the Paradise Garden tonight proved it.

The bus rumbled to a stop in front of the door. All conversation ceased. Heads turned toward the glass. Ivory stopped playing. As one, they held their breath.

The bell over the door jingled, and Libba Coltrain entered, smiling.

★ ★ ★

Madge had told Stork about the changes in Miss Green Eyes, but still he wasn't prepared for the new and improved Libba Coltrain. She didn't stand in the doorway, preening and waiting to be admired, as he had seen her do in the past. She headed straight for him and Madge, scooping little Mickey up and delighting him with nonsensical baby talk. Then she turned to Stork, kissed him on the cheek, and welcomed him home, asking about his arm, his trip to the States, his plans for the future. She told him what a remarkable woman and what a good friend his wife was, how supportive Madge had been, and how lucky he was to have such a wonderful little family. She seemed genuinely glad to see him, genuinely happy for him.

This was a different Libba, all right.

Stork shifted nervously and watched as Libba went over to greet Willie and Thelma with a hug and a peck on the cheek, then gravitated toward Mabel Rae to meet her handsome lieutenant. She listened with interest as Drew told her a little about his family and his plans to take Rae to New Orleans, and commented sincerely that they made a beautiful couple and she was delighted that God had managed to get them together. She even made a point of going over to the piano to speak to Ivory, whispering something in his ear that made him laugh, playfully tweaking his red bow tie.

Not once did she try to steer the conversation toward herself or ask leading questions designed to garner approval or affirmation. All the old snobbery was gone, and she treated every person in the room—even Ivory Brownlee—like a cherished friend.

Stork followed all this with a growing sense of apprehension. He had promised Madge that he would tell her about Link tonight. But she seemed so composed, so . . . so *whole*. What would the news do to her?

★ ★ ★

Libba stood next to Willie and leaned her elbows on the counter. A hushed murmur ran through the room, and then everybody quieted and looked at her.

"I suppose you wonder why I've called you all here tonight," she began, and a brief wave of laughter rippled over the little group assembled before her. "I told you I have big news. Well, I do."

Libba took a deep breath and looked into the eyes of her friends. Willie, somber and a little sad, who had become so much more than a cousin to her. Mabel Rae, whose happiness radiated from a face now beautiful, lit from within by joy and love. Madge, clinging to Stork's good arm, a strange expression of apprehension filling her features. Thelma—wonderful, big-hearted Thelma—who had helped her discover God's care during a dark and fearful time. Even Ivory, whose music flowed from hidden springs deep within him. They had become her family, the ones she turned to for help and comfort and support. And suddenly Libba realized that, although she had determined to go on with her life alone, she wouldn't be alone. Not really. Not as long as she had such friends.

"Things have been pretty confusing for me over the past few months," she admitted, looking down at the cracked linoleum under her feet. "And you've all been there for me. I want you to know I appreciate you all, that no matter what happens in the future, I'll always thank God for giving me friends like you . . . family like you."

She paused and took a deep breath. "I came here tonight to share with you what should be the happiest moment of a woman's life." She looked intently at Mabel Rae, then at Madge. "To tell you that I'm planning to be married—to Freddy Sturgis."

"No!" Madge interrupted. "Libba, you can't. You—"

Stork reached out and took his wife's arm. "Let her finish, honey."

Libba looked down at Madge. "You're right. I can't. I thought I could, at first. I thought it was God's way of getting me out of a difficult and frustrating situation. I thought I needed someone, someone to take care of me and protect me. Daddy has cut off my tuition money, and I don't know how I'm going to manage school expenses and living on my own. But tonight, on the way here to make the announcement of my engagement, God spoke to me. I know I don't say that very often—in fact, I usually hate it when other people say it. But there's no other way to explain it. God helped me see that I am strong enough to make it on my own."

Silence reigned in the Paradise Garden. Even little Mickey gazed up at her with wondering eyes.

"Marrying Freddy would have made things a lot easier," she admitted. "But I'm not sure that just because something is easier, it's the right decision." She turned toward Stork and Madge. "Marriage," she said quietly, "should be based on love, not on need. Marriage should give you the strength to endure difficult times, not protect you from having to face them. That's the kind of love the two of you have."

Tears sprang to her eyes, and she blinked them back. "I had that kind of love once. Maybe, God willing, I will have that kind of love again. But in the meantime, until God sees fit to put that kind of relationship in my life—if ever—I know now that I'm strong enough to go on with my life, to do what God has called me to do."

Libba cleared her throat. This would be the hardest part, and she didn't want to cry. "Link loved me for myself," she went on. "His love taught me something important about myself—that I'm acceptable, to God and to others, just as I am. Without pretending to be something I'm not. It's Link's love that has given me the ability to say no to the easy way out."

She looked around the room, and nearly everyone was wiping tears away. "Link's love," she continued, "and God's grace. No, I'm not going to marry Freddy. I'm not going to marry anyone. I'm going to trust God to help me discover myself a little more, to become the person God has created me to be." Libba smiled. "It won't be easy, I'm sure, and I'll need a lot of help and support from all of you. But with friends like you and the grace of the Lord, I'll make it just fine."

Libba shrugged. "That's it, I guess. Except to ask all of you to pray for me. I'll need a job, and I'll certainly need a level of faith that seems pretty far beyond me right now. But I know this is the right thing to do—not just to honor Link's memory, but to be available for whatever God may want to do in my life."

Everyone crowded around, hugging Libba and promising to pray for her. All except Stork and Madge. Libba looked over Thelma's shoulder and saw them hanging back, whispering between themselves and glancing at her with furtive expressions.

Finally she broke away from the group and went toward them. "Is something wrong?" she asked hesitantly.

Stork stared at his feet. "We need to talk to you, Libba. Don't misunderstand—we were both touched by what you had to say, and we're proud of your decision. But there's something you need to know."

Puzzled, Libba led them to a table in the corner and stood opposite them. Stork looked so serious, so—

"Sit down, Libba," Stork said, motioning to a chair. "This may be difficult for you to understand—"

He never got any further.

The bell over the cafe door rang loudly, and Stork jerked around to see a woman standing in the doorway.

"It's Olivia Coltrain," Madge whispered. "Libba's mother."

The woman looked awful. Her hair was a mess, her eyes were red rimmed and bloodshot, and the tail of her white blouse protruded from the waistband of her skirt. Had she been drinking?

Then Stork saw that she was waving something in her hand, something that looked vaguely familiar to him. Envelopes, he thought, bound up with a rubber band. A sheaf of . . .

Letters.

Stork's heart sank. Before Olivia Coltrain said a single word, he knew where those letters had come from and why they had never been delivered.

52

Death and Life Are in the
Hands of the Lord

"Daddy's dead?"

Libba couldn't believe what she was hearing. Her father, dead of a heart attack in his office behind the hardware store. Apparently he had died early that morning. He had been there for hours, her mother said, slumped over his desk. His assistant, that nice young Richard Taylor, was quite capable of running the store. Richard thought it was odd that he hadn't seen Robinson all day, but he hadn't been concerned. Nobody thought to look for him until he didn't come home for dinner. And then, when they unlocked the office, they found him with his hand on the telephone. He had tried to call for help, the sheriff surmised, but it was too late.

Libba walked around the cafe in a daze. She didn't feel much of anything—not grief, not anger, not remorse. Certainly not sorrow. Her main concern was for her mother, who was acting very strange.

"Mama, sit down before you fall down. I'll get Thelma to get you some coffee."

"I don't want any coffee. I want you to pay attention to me."

Libba sat across from her and looked her mother in the eye. "All right, Mother, I'm listening."

"When they found your father, they found something else." She paused. "A key. Two keys, in fact. They had to pry them out of his hand." Another pause. "One went to his bottom desk drawer."

Libba was getting exasperated. She wished her mother would just get to the point. "So what? He had a dozen keys."

"The other," her mother continued as if Libba had never interrupted, "fit a small strongbox that was inside the drawer. In the strongbox were these." She placed a stack of letters on the table between them. "I'm sorry, Libba. I had no idea."

Libba slid the letters toward her, and her heart stood still. V-mail. The return address was a military clearing station in New York. She yanked the first one out, ripping the envelope, and stared at it. "It's from Link." She fought for breath. "All of them are from Link."

"Thirty-seven," her mother sighed. "All written from a hospital somewhere in England."

Libba began to weep—great racking sobs that shook her entire frame. "He's alive? And Daddy kept this from me?"

Her mother nodded. "After you got the package with Link's wristwatch and . . . other things . . . you were certain he had died. We all were." She looked blankly around at the faces that encircled the table. "Robinson began picking up the mail—insisted on it, in fact. He said that he didn't want me anywhere near that gossipy Charity Grevis, that this family had suffered enough humiliation because . . . because his only daughter had defied him and moved out to his white-trash brother's house." She glanced up apologetically at Willie and Mabel Rae. "Sorry, girls. You know I don't feel that way, but Robinson—"

"It's all right, Aunt Olivia," Willie said softly, patting her on the shoulder. "We all knew what Uncle Robinson was like." She gazed sorrowfully at Libba. "At least we thought we did. I guess we didn't know how cruel he could be."

Libba scanned the letters while her mother spoke. "Robinson kept telling me that all this 'nonsense,' as he called it, would soon come to an end. That he had a way to bring you back home where you belonged. I had no idea what he meant, and he wouldn't explain himself. Just said that he had a responsibility as a father, and he intended to fulfill it."

"Responsibility?" Libba gasped. "The responsibility to control and manipulate me, to keep me from knowing—" she shook one of the letters in her mother's face—"that the man I loved was alive!"

Libba closed her eyes and fought for control. Her father was dead. Her mother needed her love and support. But all she could think about was Link. Not dead in a mass grave on foreign soil—alive!

"That's what I was about to tell you," Stork said softly, stroking her arm. "When Link didn't get any response to his letters, he figured that you didn't want him and didn't have the courage to tell him."

Libba's tears flowed again. "It must have been horrible for him," she said, "believing I could just abandon him like that. If only he could have known how much I loved him, how much I wanted him to come back!"

"He is coming back—eventually," Stork said cautiously. "Only he's not coming back here. He's going to Missouri when he's released, to his father and his family." He paused. "Libba, do you still love Link?"

She stared at him. What a stupid question—just like a man! "Of course I love him. I could never love anyone the way I love him."

"Even if he doesn't walk again? He was pretty badly wounded, you know."

Suddenly it struck Libba that all the time she was making plans, trying to "go on with her life," God knew that Link was alive. God had kept her from making a terrible mistake—even used Freddy's proposal to keep her safe . . . for Link.

"I don't care if he's in an iron lung. I love him for who he is, for his heart and mind and soul . . . not whether he can walk—" she slanted a glance at Willie—"or jitterbug."

She grabbed Stork's sleeve and shook it. "I have to go to him. To Missouri, or wherever. I have to—"

The bell over the door jangled again, and Charity Grevis came in. She said hesitantly, "I thought somebody might be able to tell me where I could reach—" Her eyes scanned the room and lighted on Libba. "Oh, you're here. Well, I have something for you." She glanced at Libba's mother nervously, not meeting her eyes. "Sorry to hear about Robinson."

She didn't look sorry, Libba thought briefly. She looked . . . relieved. "You said you have something for me?" she prodded.

"Oh, yes." She held out a wrinkled Western Union telegram, turned on her heel, and disappeared into the night.

Libba frowned at the envelope. Her heart sank, and her mind began to spin. Only bad news came in telegrams. Maybe Link hadn't made it after all. Maybe . . .

The cafe grew deadly quiet.

"Open it," Willie whispered, squeezing Libba's shoulder. "Whatever it is, we'll face it together."

Libba attempted a smile in response to Willie's encouragement and, with shaking hands, pulled open the flap and removed the telegram. She spread it on the table and read it out loud:

"'Hospitalized soon, as hoped. Stop. Praying you'll come. Stop. Love, Link.'"

Libba read the message over and over again. It couldn't be true. Link, coming to convalesce right at her front door, practically, at Kennedy General in Memphis? But it was. He was on his way, probably at this very moment. He hadn't gone to Missouri. He hadn't given up on her. And he had signed the telegram "Love, Link."

Love, Link. She ran her fingers over the words, caressing them. He still cared for her, and he would know soon enough that she cared for him, too. *Love, Link.* It was a miracle . . . as if God had reached into the grave and brought him back, like Lazarus, from the dead.

For a long time she gazed at the telegram, barely aware of the friends and loved ones gathered around her. At last a voice brought her back to the present.

"What does it mean—*hospitalized soon, as hoped?*" Thelma asked.

Libba fingered the gold locket she wore around her neck. "It means," she said, her heart leaping, "that God is bringing Link Winsom home. Home to me. Home to all of us."

Epilogue

Link Winsom sat with a blanket around his shoulders and looked past the ship's rail at the waters of New York Harbor. His new traveling cast—lighter and slightly less cumbersome than the original—still held his lower back immobile, but allowed him a little more flexibility. With some clever maneuvering and two or three burly soldiers helping him, he had managed to wedge himself into a wheelchair and be pushed up onto the deck. His legs still stuck straight out in front of him, and he reclined at an awkward angle with the chair's back extended as far as it would go, but it was better than being confined to a gurney belowdecks.

His second view of the Statue of Liberty was no less awe inspiring than the first. The one other time he had seen the great lady, he had been on his way to France, with his jovial buddies at his side. They had been determined to go overseas, get the war over with, and return in glory.

Things hadn't worked out exactly as they had planned. But some of them—like Stork, and like Link himself—had managed to survive and come home to . . .

To what? Link wondered. He had taken an enormous risk, sending the telegram to Libba Coltrain. She might not even respond.

But he couldn't deny that he still loved her. He had to take one more chance, even if it only meant greater heartbreak in the end. If he didn't try, he'd never know.

One thing he did know: God was with him, and God would never leave him or forsake him. In his deepest heart, of course, he prayed that Libba would come, that he would have one last chance to work things out with her. But he didn't place his hopes for his future on that.

No, his hope lay far deeper than what did or didn't happen with Libba. His hope was in his God, who had led him this far and wouldn't let him down now.

The lady in the harbor lifted her arm high, beckoning, and he recalled the words on the base: *I lift my lamp beside the golden door.*

The golden door. Link had no idea what was on the other side of that door, whether it would bring him joy or heartache, sorrow or fulfillment. But he knew that God had opened the way for him. On his feet or in a wheelchair, alone or with the one he loved, he would go through that door into the future prepared for him.

Link looked out over the waves, glittering in the sunlight, and smiled. Where there was life, there was hope. A hope as deep and as wide as the ocean he had just crossed. A hope as sure as the One to whom he had surrendered.

Come, Liberty seemed to whisper. *The door is open. Come home.*

Link raised a hand in salute. "I'm coming," he answered, his words flung to the winds. "Whatever it means, wherever God leads, I'm coming. Coming home."